THE PASSION OF DELLIE O'BARR

Also by Cindy Bonner

Lily

Looking After Lily

THE PASSION OF
DELLIE O'BARR

a novel by

CINDY BONNER

Algonquin Books of Chapel Hill ❈ 1996

Special thanks to Wesley Saunders of the Rapides Parish Library for his help with the Cheneyville section, and to Paula Rudolph of the Huntsville Public Library and Mary MacLean of the Huntsville Prison Museum for their help in determining how and where female prisoners were housed during the time of this book. Also, thanks to Jay Brandon and to Tom Garner for advice on legal procedures, and to Luellen Smiley at the Yorktown Library for digging up so many helpful books. I'm also grateful to Nat Sobel for having faith in me, to Shannon Ravenel for her encouragement and on-target editorial advice, and to Bettye Dew for sorting out the details. And finally, thanks to a great friend and confidante, Janis Arnold, for listening to me complain ad nauseam.

Published by
ALGONQUIN BOOKS OF CHAPEL HILL
Post Office Box 2225
Chapel Hill, North Carolina 27515-2225

a division of
Workman Publishing
708 Broadway
New York, New York 10003

Library of Congress Cataloging-in-Publication Data
Bonner, Cindy, 1953–
    The passion of Dellie O'Barr / by Cindy Bonner.
       p.   cm.
    ISBN 1-56512-103-1
    1. Man-woman relationships—Texas—Fiction.   2. Married women—Texas—
Fiction.   3. Adultery—Texas—Fiction.   I. Title.
   PS3552.06362S57   1996
   813'.54—dc20
                                                                      95-25537
                                                                          CIP

10   9   8   7   6   5   4   3   2   1
First Edition

For Mother, in memory

THE PASSION OF DELLIE O'BARR

PART ONE

It would be easiest to blame everything that happened afterwards, the change in me and everything else, on the death of Papa. People in town did. Daniel did. But I believe a woman has an obligation to herself to accept responsibility for the part she plays in shaping her own life—to take the blame for it and not look for excuses elsewhere. To stand tall and say, "I did this to myself, it's all my fault and mine alone," is the first big step toward total independence in this world. That is assuming she wants independence. So many women don't appear to. It's much easier for them to place the blame on others.

All fall and winter Papa had been ill, although with spring, he seemed to feel much better. Dr. Rutherford said it was not unusual for Papa's kind of cancer to ease for a little while. "The calm before the storm," the doctor explained. "He could get worse, though, when this passes." So naturally I was surprised when Nathan came by to tell me that Papa would accept our invitation to the Confederate Veterans' Reunion in Elgin.

"The doctor's got him on some new kind of medicine," Nathan said. "He thinks Papa can get through the day all right."

We supplied a beef and four hogs to the reunion committee. Daniel sent the beef and the hams on ahead in the company of Andy Ashland, who ran a teamster's wagon in addition to farming the land he rented from Papa. In fact, Mr. Ashland was available for almost any odd job. These were hard times for a poor rent farmer.

The railway companies offered special excursion rates from points of departure all over Texas, and a large turnout was expected at the reunion. On the given day, the eighteenth of April, our little crowd, consisting of myself, Daniel, Nathan, Papa, and Mother, and two couples, the Craddocks and the Slaters, all departed the McDade station bound for Elgin some twelve miles away.

J.T. Craddock was a Masonic friend of Daniel's, and Belvin Slater was another old vet, like Papa. The Slaters' daughter, Priscilla, had come along to help them celebrate the day. Priscilla Slater and I had grown up together. She'd been my first bridesmaid at my wedding two years before, and was still my good friend, though lately I'd begun to feel I'd outgrown her just a little bit. She was mad for Nathan, and had gotten plain silly about it, struggling past me when we boarded the train so she could grab the place next to where he sat in his ball uniform, across the aisle and two seats forward.

Flowers—yellow baby suns and blazing firewheels—mingled together like a colorful carpet down along the tracks. A banner advertising the special sixty-five-cent round-trip fare was strung from the roof of the station and popped in the breeze. Papa wore his army hat, a thing I'd never seen him do, though I'd known he still had it. Nathan had found it years ago, when we were children, tucked away inside an old leather-bound steamer trunk. Before that April morning, the only person I'd ever seen wear that hat was Nathan, and always in the secret shadows of the attic. In broad daylight, and on Papa's gray head, it looked a little moth-eaten and stiff, the rope band and tassels coming unraveled.

Thirty-one years had gone by since General Lee surrendered to Grant at Appomattox Court House, yet this was the first reunion Papa had ever attended. It wasn't the sort of thing he liked to do normally. He wasn't one to celebrate—much of anything, but especially not the war. "Best done with and forgotten," he always said when anyone brought it up. Every day but that day. That day he felt like talking. That day he might have been a stranger to me.

"I ever tell you about how I lied on my age so they'd take me into the regiment?" Papa said out loud, to which of us I don't think anyone knew, but he got the attention of our whole crowd speaking out like that so uncharacteristically. "Was afraid they'd get done with the fighting before I could get in some myself." He sat there smiling, and just that alone was enough to flabbergast me. Papa wasn't a man generally given to easy smiles.

Mother—who wasn't our real mother at all but had married Papa when I was eight and Nathan was ten—sat beside Papa giving him a rapt look. I don't believe she'd ever heard him speak so frankly on this subject either, though she knew far more than I did about Papa's life before he came to Texas. She'd been our real mama's friend years ago, and I imagine that was how she came to know the stories she told us of Papa's family, of them dying out in a flu epidemic that swept through northern Mississippi right after the Yankee occupation. "Brought all their dreadful diseases with them, is what they did," she had said the first time she told us the story. "Damned Yankees," she said in a whisper, and it was the only time I recalled ever hearing her swear.

She sat there holding the cake she had baked in her lap and watching Papa. She could bake a deliciously pretty cake with flower petals and fruit shapes, and even fancy handwriting if the occasion called for it. In fact, Mother was almost famous for her cake baking, and got asked all the time to make cakes for parties and weddings. No one had asked her this time, but to her it was next to a sin not to take something to a gathering.

"Brother Morg had done been and gone," Papa said out loud, again to our friends there on the train with us. The whistle sounded and drowned out whatever it was he said next. We all saw his lips still moving. Daniel strained forward to hear, his ear canted slightly Papa's way.

The cars began to move, jolting us. Mother balanced the cake plate, holding tight to the tin dome. The conductor started down the aisle, collecting tickets. Priscilla whispered something in Nathan's ear. He bobbed away from her as if she had startled him, then wrinkled his nose and gave her a smile. It was a polite smile, I knew, but I don't think Priscilla saw the difference. Her face was lit with adoration. Even with his back to me, I could tell by the square of his shoulders that he felt trapped sitting there between the window and Priscilla.

Papa's voice became audible again, midsentence, as the train settled into its chugging rhythm. ". . . come home after Iuka on a discharge with one less foot and a box with the minié ball that had took it wrapped up in a corn husk. By then we had Grant right out our back door." He held on to his knees and shook his head with remembering. I shook mine, too, purely floored to hear Papa talking so openly.

"What year was that, Josh?" Daniel said from his place at my side.

"Winter of '62 and '3," Papa said, still rocking backward. "Right in the thick of it."

"Indeed," J.T. Craddock said. His wife, Daphne, reached up to dust something off his cheek and he brushed her hand aside.

"Mustered in at Holly Springs," Papa said. "Was the nearest to our home place—"

"You came in the year after I did," Belvin Slater said, but the tone of his voice was less strident than Papa's, almost bored sounding.

"Walked five miles in a cold driving rain," Papa said, as if he hadn't heard Mr. Slater's interruption. "Was December. The nineteenth, I believe. No, maybe it was the twentieth. Van Dorn's raiders had already took the town back from the Yankees, and word had got out to us on the farm. My mama begged for me not to go. And then she threatened me. Said she'd tell them I was underage." He stopped for a moment, grinned around at us all. I swear, he positively glistened with self-pride. I was pleased to see him feeling so well. "Threw me right in there with them other fellas, battle-hardened boys from East Texas most of them. You could've been one of them, Belv."

Mr. Slater shook his head. "I was with Green's Brigade. You know that plainly, Josh."

Papa braced himself against his knees. "I don't recall I do, Belv."

"We sorted it all out once before. Back years ago. I was in artillery," Mr. Slater said. "I've told you that before." Mrs. Slater wound her arm through her husband's and gave him a little, almost undetectable, yank.

Papa squinched his eyes at Mr. Slater, and then he squinched them at me. I couldn't help but squirm. Out of habit. I'd never been fond of attracting Papa's attention, and I didn't know what I'd done to get it now.

"I pitched in to helping torch the Yankees' stores," he said, talking right at me, yet I saw that he wasn't actually speaking to me, or to any of the rest of us either. It was more like he needed to recount these memories for his own sake, as if they'd been weighing on him to get told. Later I came to see that Papa was afraid to die; afraid he'd take something unwelcome to the grave with him, and all the talking he did that day was a purging of sorts.

"Stole me a Yankee horse." He gleamed around at all of us. "And I was in the cavalry. That was sure something for a back-woods plowboy like me. Got some seasoning on me right quick. They give me a uniform had belonged to some other fella before me. Two sizes too big. Just my galluses kept the britches from falling down around my knees. They never did ask me for my age." He shook his head and got a far-off look on his face. "Reckon it didn't matter much by then."

I tore my eyes off Papa and glanced around for Nathan. He'd gotten up from his seat and left Priscilla sitting there alone. I wished he was hearing all this. I glanced toward the front of the car where he'd moved to sit with the rest of the McDade nine. They were into their own conversation, laughing at each other, plying imaginary bats. Priscilla looked ready to cry, sitting sideways in her seat. She flashed a pitiful glance back at me.

Papa went on talking, strangely leaving off horrors he must have seen, horrors I'd always assumed had kept him silent all these years. He told about marching north into Tennessee, raiding railroad lines across the border, and about his tentmate from the Delta country, who carried a blunderbuss so ancient it singed the hair off his wrist when he fired it. "Licked flames back plumb to his elbow," Papa said, laughing; and he told us of the captain who had led the battle at Thompson's Station, riding a high-stepping, hot-blooded carriage horse, because by then, most other mounts had been used up. The cavalry had even been set afoot. And I could picture it all, the dashing officer, Papa and the other men charging out of the trees, surprising the Yankees.

Our party, and some strangers from Giddings in the seats nearby, all sat quiet and listened while Papa talked, Mississippi crawling in his voice, more pronounced than usual, a lightsome smile upon his lips. There was a rosiness underneath all that old-fashioned face hair neither Mother nor I could convince him to shave away. A healthy rosiness that had been missing for months.

"He's been like that all week," Nathan said after we arrived at the Elgin depot. We stood together watching Papa and Mother and Daniel and the rest head for the line of hacks from the local livery. "Mother says it's the new medicine he's taking. Got him feeling spry again."

"Well, maybe so," I said. "But after today, I don't feel as if I've ever even known him."

Priscilla waved for me to catch up to the others. I waved at her to go on. Her face was still gloomy. She gave a glance in Nathan's direction. He turned his back to her.

"Please, will you keep her occupied today," he said to me. "I don't want to have to keep fending her off like some pesky gnat."

"I'll try," I said. "But you don't have to be rude. She admires you is all."

"I'm trying not to be."

"You don't find her attractive? Not the least bit?"

"She's too forward."

I shrugged. I wasn't through wondering over Papa. I watched him give a hand to Priscilla, helping her climb up into one of the hacks. I said, "Do you think it's the cancer causing him to act so odd?"

Nathan joined me in staring after our crowd. It was safe for him to look their way now with Priscilla otherwise occupied. "He's been speaking of Dane and Sister lately." I couldn't hide my shock, and Nathan nodded. "Not that he's buried the hatchet, or even said he wants to, but he did speak their names a time or two. First one, and then the other. Not two days apart. Me and Mother both noticed it. Something about when they were babies."

"Well, maybe he *does* want to make peace. Maybe that's what all of this is about."

Papa was helping Mother and Mrs. Slater now to get up into the wagon. He looked to still be pontificating, his head thrown back. I heard Daniel's laughter and Mrs. Slater's fluttering. It was all too strange. And I had a hateful thought, standing there watching them, that it was too bad Papa hadn't gotten sick sooner if it was the cancer making this difference in him.

Members of the Elgin nine came up then and took Nathan's attention from me. The other ballplayers had gathered on the platform and all eighteen of them were raising a ruckus. The Elgin club had come to escort our boys to the playing field at the picnic grounds for the contest that would be held after the barbecue and festivities had ended. A lot of backslapping and sizing up of each other went on amongst the ballplayers for several moments, and then they filed away jabbering like a flock of jackdaws, while I continued to ponder Papa.

Suddenly, it struck me hard and certain that his death was coming, and near. For a moment I couldn't breathe. I found a bench to sit on while my heart raced. My thoughts, too, were racing, back to Dr. Rutherford's words, *the calm before the storm*, to Papa's parched complexion all last winter during Sunday dinners that didn't rest easy on his stomach, to the hot-water bottle Mother fixed for him to lay against the pain in his side. I'd chosen not to look at his sickness, but the cancer would kill him. Dr. Rutherford had said so. It was killing him even now, this instant, despite how well he might seem. The noise of the train letting off steam, the people bustling by me, the clutch of pigeons roosting in the gable of the station roof, everything blurred together in my mind and before my eyes.

I could not imagine a world without Papa. Not that we were close. We weren't, particularly. We had gotten into a pattern early and stuck to it through the years: Papa told me what to do and I did it. Simple as that. From going off to Miss Langburn's School for Young Ladies in Hearn, to marrying Daniel O'Barr because he was good for me, because he had land and a college education and could take proper care of me. Papa mapped out my life. "For your own good," he told me, and I believed him. I wasn't a rebel like Sister and Dane, who had balked at Papa's iron rules and run away. I could never have borne the years of silence like they had, or the exile—the cold. I knew. Papa's silences could outlast the sun.

Of all of us, only Nathan had found the way to get on with Papa, the knack of arguing with him yet making him feel it was all in good sport. Only Nathan could stand up eye to eye with Papa and not back down. Mother said it was because they were just alike but I didn't agree. There was something inside Nathan that made it so, some kind of faith in himself, a confidence, something as elusive yet steady as rainfall. Something I did not have.

I caught my reflection in the window of the depot, and I stared at it until I lost all feeling, until I seemed only a shell of a person wavering there in the glass, with eyes and a nose and a mouth, but no soul. I stared until I frightened myself.

"Dellie?"

I looked up and saw Daniel coming for me. He was tall, thin, with hair as black as night, silvering a bit at the temples. He was thirty-two, twelve years older than me. Not handsome, but then neither was I. He was a tidy man. I was tidy, also. Our marriage was satisfactory.

"Are you coming?" he said, holding out his hand for me. He wore a worsted suit, pale blue cravat knotted smartly at his neck.

I stood up, tugged at the ribbons under my chin. My hat was heavy with too many flowers and feathers piled on top. I could hardly swallow.

"Are you all right? You seem pale." He wrapped my hand around his arm, then laid the back of his fingers against my cheek, as if checking for a fever.

"I'm fine. Just overcome for a moment." I smiled up at him.

His expression was too serious. I waved my hand in front of my nose. "The fumes."

He raised his chin as if to say "ahh," and his features relaxed.

We started for the hacks where everyone else waited. Everyone except Nathan. He'd gone off laughing with his teammates in the back of a hay wagon.

❀   ❀   ❀   **2**   ❀   ❀   ❀

Professor Alf Jung and his Silver Coronet Band led the parade onto the picnic grounds. Then came the veterans. Some marched in amid the cheers from the onlookers. Others straggled along out of rank. A few were crippled, either from the war or from life lived after. Some had empty sleeves. Most carried little Confederate flags, handmade and donated to the reunion committee by the ladies of the Bastrop Eastern Star.

"Where is he?" Mother said, gripping my hand. "I don't see him."

I strained to look over the people directly in front of us. I saw several cavalry hats among the old soldiers, the tops of their heads being mostly all I could make out with my view blocked by the crowd.

"There." Nathan pointed. "He's coming now."

"Where?" Mother craned her neck. "I don't see him."

Nathan took her hand, and I half expected him to lift her onto his shoulders the way he used to do with me, until I grew to be almost as tall as he was. "There. See?" He pointed, his arm extending so far into the crowd that the man directly in front of us turned to glower.

Mother broke into a grin. "Look! There he is." She rose on her toes, holding my arm for balance. "Would you just look at your papa."

I spotted him then, marching in beside Mr. Slater, who didn't look nearly as youthful and radiant as Papa did. To someone who didn't know different, you would think it was Mr. Slater who had the cancer. Papa's mustache was moving, and I thought at first he was talking to himself still, like he had been on the train over. Then I realized it was "Dixie" he was singing, right along with the Silver Coronet Band.

When the parade went past, the entire crowd of spectators moved in one great surge for the food tables lined up underneath the picnic pavilion. In the rush, I lost sight of Papa and Mr. Slater, and of Mother and Nathan. In fact, I got lost from everyone I knew, and just sort of drifted with the throng of people close around me. I saw Daphne Craddock, but she was too far from me and I couldn't get her attention. She appeared to be lost, too, and in a bit of a panic about it, flailing her arms above her head, at who or what I couldn't tell.

Someone bumped into me from behind. I turned and it was Mr. Ashland. Andy Ashland, Papa's rent farmer. He had his little girl and boy with him; the girl on his hip, the boy by the hand. He looked surprised, and somewhat embarrassed, to see it was me he'd hit against.

"Miz O'Barr." He reached for his hat, but I stopped him.

"Never mind." I shook my head. "Too many people." I was having to hold on to my own hat to keep from having it jostled off by the crowd.

Mr. Ashland's cheeks colored up, but he didn't bother with his hat. He was wearing suit pants and a white shirt with a stiff collar. I didn't think I'd ever seen him out of overalls. His suspenders were bright red and yellow stripes. He guided his son by the hand around to walk in front of him. In the crush of people, all anyone could take was the tiniest of forward steps.

"Tell your husband," Mr. Ashland said, "that I got the meat delivered on time yesterday. They started in cooking it last evening and haven't quit yet." He lifted his nose as if to sniff the air, and as he did, I suddenly smelled the odor of the meat and mesquite coals, too.

"You stayed in town all night?" I said, for conversation's sake.

We were having to talk loud. The band had stopped playing but the din of a thousand voices filled the air.

He nodded. "We camped out. There were lots of folks doing it."

I reached to stroke the curls on his little girl's forehead. She was about three, with beautiful big blue eyes and golden hair—coloring like her papa's. She turned her face inward to his shoulder.

"She looks tired," I said.

"She's shy with people at first." He shifted her weight and she fussed, clung to him like a little monkey, with both her arms and legs. He said to her, but also to me, "Hannah, don't tell me you don't remember Miz O'Barr."

I had seen the Ashland children briefly at Mother's house once, and a few times from a distance in town. Mrs. Ashland, the children's mama, lived at the insane asylum in Austin. No one knew anything more than that. At least Mother didn't know and she was the one who would if anyone did. Mother kept track of everyone and thing within a forty-mile distance of home.

"It's all right," I said, giving Hannah Ashland a pat on her shoulder. "I used to be shy like that, too. When I was little like you are."

"My daddy's going to give a speaking today," the Ashland boy announced, and I looked down at him. He was as dark as his papa and his sister were light. His eyes took up half his face. I guessed him to be around seven.

"He is?" I said, and glanced at Mr. Ashland.

"This is Quintus. He isn't shy. As you can see." Mr. Ashland broke into a proud, sunny grin that even the straw hat on his head didn't shade.

He wasn't as old a man as I had recalled him being, and I tried to think of anything else about him I'd heard Mother say. He'd come from East Texas somewhere, Liberty or San Jacinto County if I remembered right. He had six mules, these two small children, and last year he hadn't made enough on his cotton crop to pay all his rent. His face was well worn, with a nose that bumped out at the bridge like it had been broken. Weather lines creased his forehead. Underneath his hat, he wore his hair slicked down and darkened with a rose pomade, the cheapest brand from Mr. Bassist's store. I recognized the smell. He wasn't a lovely man, but his smile was contagious. And he had pleasant eyes, like twinkling chunks of blue sky poked into his sockets.

"There you are." Priscilla's arm linked through mine and I jumped. "We've been searching all over for you," she said.

The crowd was thinning. I hadn't noticed. She jerked me along and I went, glancing back once at the Ashlands. They had already started off in another direction, but Quintus turned as if he sensed me looking. He gave me a little two-fingered wave goodbye. I waved at him, too.

The food tables overflowed with the hams and beef, with barbecued chicken, cakes in all flavors and shapes, including one iced in red, white, and blue that made Mother green with envy. There were pies and custards, and coffee served in tin cups to finish with. A breeze blew, so flies were kept to a minimum. There weren't enough picnic tables for the whole crowd in attendance, which numbered, someone from the reunion committee said, around two thousand. But Mother had fought for a table and won, so she made one of us stay to guard it at all times. I took my turn while Major Sayers addressed the crowd.

Major Sayers got his rank in the war and had been wounded at the battle of Valverde. He had thrice been elected to Congress from our district, and was considered next to a saint in Bastrop County, where he even had a town named after him. So when he spoke of the bravery of the Confederate soldiers who had fought so gallantly against such fearful odds for the love of their homes and country; when he said we should never forget, nor allow our children to forget, the chivalry, the daring, the self-sacrifice of the men who had fought for our land, he brought the crowd almost to tears. The Silver Coronet Band struck into "Dixie" once again, and this time the flag-waving and singing grew to a frenzied pitch.

Then Miss Mamie Kirkland of Austin took the platform and recited a poem her father, who had also fought at the battle of Valverde, had written shortly before his death a year ago. The verses of the poem sounded suspiciously like "The Charge of the Light Brigade" in meter and rhyme, but no matter. By the time she was done, there was hardly a dry eye among the ladies. A few of the men were also sniffling.

When our group came back to the table, with more coffee and cake, Major Sayers's speech was all Papa wanted to talk about. He didn't think I had been able to hear properly, and he began to retell everything Major Sayers had said. Daniel and the Craddocks wandered off to join a croquet game that had begun on the greens. Nathan went off with his ball team to begin loosening up for the game. Mother and Mrs. Slater found some ladies from the Baptist church in McDade to gossip and stroll with. Only Priscilla and Mr. Slater, bless them both, stayed with me at the table listening to Papa. His chatter had begun to wear me out.

Once, while Papa and Mr. Slater argued about some little detail of something in Major Sayers's speech, Priscilla leaned near to my ear. "Let's go over by the ball diamond and watch Nathan."

"When Mother comes back," I said in a whisper.

"But she might be gone for hours. I want to go watch him now."

I looked close into Priscilla's face. She had smooth skin, a graceful arch to her eyebrows, long, drooping lashes, and a down-turned nose. There wasn't a thing for Nathan not to like. "Maybe you should try not being so forward," I said.

"Dellie?" I jumped when Papa spoke. It was my normal reaction to him whenever he said my name outright that way, even though there was nothing normal about Papa on this day.

"Yessir?"

"Did the major say we should teach our children to call us rebels? Or not to call us rebels?" He glanced at Mr. Slater like he knew I was about to prove some point.

I tried to remember. I was standing back quite a way from the platform while the address was given. Papa looked at me again, this time frowning because I was taking so long to give him the answer he was looking for. I wished I knew what that answer was.

Priscilla saved me. "He said that the children of the South should be taught that while their fathers fought against the national flag they were in no sense rebels. He said they were animated by as lofty a sense of patriotism as ever stirred the heart of a Patrick Henry or a George Washington."

"See," Papa said, smacking his hand against the tabletop. His eyes glowed bright, maybe too bright. "I told you. He said we ain't rebels."

"Did you memorize all that?" I whispered in wonder.

"Prissy is mistaken," Mr. Slater said calmly, a little smugly. His commanding officer during the war had been Major Sayers, so Mr. Slater naturally enough considered himself an authority on all the major would think or say.

"No, I am not, Daddy. That is just exactly what he said."

"It surely is. Just exactly. Dellie"—Papa's hand slapped at the table again—"it's high time—past time—you and Daniel gave me some grandbabies. Two years of marriage is plenty long enough to get to know each other. I want a grandbaby before I die."

I felt my cheeks burn hot. It wasn't the sort of thing a person spoke of out in public that way, and I glanced around, grateful that Daniel was busy playing croquet across the lawn. I wished Mother would come take watching this table off my hands. Watching Papa, too. There was something terribly the matter with him today, and I didn't know what to do about it. Or how to respond to him.

Under the table, Priscilla gripped my knee. "Dellie and me want to go over and watch the team practice." She stood, pulling me up with her. She leaned over and gave Mr. Slater a kiss on his head. I kept my eyes off Papa. Yet, as we walked away from the table, I thought I felt him watching me.

"Forget it," Priscilla said when we were far enough away. "Have you heard the word *senility?* It's a new term they're using for old people when they get like children."

"I don't think that's it. He's just odd today. I think the cancer might've gone to his brain." We walked. Past the croquet game. Past some children playing leapfrog. "Besides. He's already got grandbabies. Four of them." I thought about the photograph of Sister and her family hanging on the wall in my room, sent last year at Christmas. "A girl and three boys up in the Panhandle."

"They don't count with him."

"Well, they ought to."

"I know." She took hold of my hand and squeezed it. She knew I wanted children, and that I feared I was unable. It wasn't something I liked to talk about. "Come on," she said. She wanted me to run, or at the least to hurry. We could already hear the crack of the bats out at the ball field.

Away from the reunion grounds, but close enough that the older children could venture over, a regular amusements circus had set up. There were some vendors selling candy-dipped doughnuts, apple flitters, peppermint, and lemonade. There was a juggler, a fire-eater, a marksman's booth, and a curtained ambulance wagon with a red sign that said BILL JOHNSON, THE PETRIFIED MAN. A gaggle of young boys, some with their mamas but most without, had gathered to hear Dr. Wood's Medicine Show. Priscilla veered us away from all of this confusion, and I let her, even though I was a little curious to see what a petrified man might look like. She didn't give me the chance to find out what it would cost to step behind the curtain.

We got to the ball diamond and found a place to sit on the hill just off the first-base line. The few wooden benches behind home plate had already been taken, one by some McDade girls, Lottie Matson and Jinsy McCarty. Lottie's brother was on the team, too, but I knew, and Priscilla knew, the girls were here to watch Nathan the same as she was. She touched the nape of her neck where some of her hair had fallen out of its knot. I helped her with the hairpins.

"Don't worry. He doesn't like them—" *Either,* I almost added, but stopped just short of it. She gave me a look as if she knew what I'd been about to say. We sat in silence.

Nathan played second base, and he was fairly good at it. At least he seemed so to me, although I was no expert on the game. Once, when he made a difficult catch, I heard Lottie call out to him and his face turned a little redder than it was already with the sun and the exertion of the practice. Priscilla kept her eyes straight ahead, and I was proud of her. She reached inside her handbag for a stick of chewing gum, unwrapped it, broke it in two, and gave one half to me. It was spruce. My favorite flavor.

Once the game started, the reunion crowd slowly filled the area around the diamond. Mother and Mrs. Slater found us on our knoll, and Mother started in yelling for Nathan just as loudly as Lottie Matson and Jinsy McCarty. Daniel came, and the Craddocks. Daphne spread herself on the other side of Priscilla.

Daniel knelt beside me and watched the game for a while, before he leaned in closer to me.

"J.T. and I are going into town for a little while. He has something he wants to show me. I'll be back before the game's finished."

"What does he want to show you? In Elgin?"

A little line appeared, and then disappeared, between his brows. I wasn't supposed to ask questions. "It's to do with business. A new strain of cattle. We won't be gone long."

I tried to focus on the game. I pretended interest, applauded with everyone whenever our side did something worth applauding, but my legs fell asleep from sitting on them. And someone nearby had foul breath, garlic or raw onions from the barbecue. And Daphne was keeping Priscilla company. And the crowd had grown so big we couldn't hear Lottie and Jinsy cheering anymore.

I stood up, dusted off my skirt. Mother raised her face my way, questioning. I acted as though I hadn't seen her. I threaded my way through the crowd, and as quickly as I moved through, the people closed around my path, just as if I'd never been there. I strolled down toward the amusements. The line for the petrified man had grown long, and anyway, I'd lost my desire. I stood and listened to Dr. Wood talk about pulling tapeworms, and when it looked like he might try the procedure on a boy of about seventeen who complained of stomach ailments, I decided to leave there, too.

It was a beautiful day. The sky so clear. A bluebird day. And I didn't blame Daniel for not wanting to stay cramped in the middle of such a crowd as this. He never had been much for crowds. He had his friends from the lodge and from church, the hands on the ranch. Those were about as big as he liked his crowds to get. He was a quiet man, a smart man.

He had graduated from the university in Austin with his baccalaureate, then read for the bar and, for a year and a half, practiced law in Austin, before his father left the O'Barr ranch to him. Daniel was the next youngest of four children but the only one to make it into adulthood. The two oldest had died in infancy, and his younger sister, Charlotte, had died in the fire that destroyed the old O'Barr homeplace in '89. That same fire forever damaged the lungs of his father, and three years later Jonathan O'Barr died of pneumonia at the lying-in hospital at Bastrop because there was nowhere else with nurses to tend to his every breath. He died while all around him others were giving birth.

And so with his father gone, Daniel had dedicated himself to making the ranch a success and to the scientific farming he had learned at the university. I knew all of this, and yet I resented the time it took him. He was always, it seemed, either working at his desk or out on the range with the hands. And when he wasn't doing either of these then he was gone to Bastrop or Austin or Galveston arranging business, seeing new developments, learning from other, bigger cattlemen, or visiting his mother who had gone to live with a widowed sister in Navasota. When we were first married, I had gone with him on some of these trips, but I was left on my own in cities I was unfamiliar with, and with ladies much older than me. So now I usually just stayed home.

Daniel was a temperate man. I had nothing to complain about on that score. On rare occasions he would drink a glass or two of wine, and then usually to give himself the courage he needed to step to my room after the house was quiet and dark. I always made a place for him in my bed, though truly, the whole business caused us both great embarrassment. It seemed so out of character for a fastidious man like Daniel to have such base needs. And yet, I couldn't help but wonder: Was there really a new strain of cattle he'd gone into town with J.T. to see? J.T. had the reputation of being somewhat of a rounder. I didn't know if such things as that were catching.

I saw Papa and Mr. Slater still sitting at our table. Mr. Slater smoked his pipe, and though it wasn't where I wanted to go, I strolled that way. I thought maybe Papa didn't realize the ball-game was going on, and that I should tell him since he enjoyed watching Nathan play.

Before I got to the table my attention was drawn away by a group of people gathered around the platform where Major Sayers had given his speech. Even from this distance, I recognized Mr. Ashland's red-and-yellow striped suspenders. I couldn't make out more than the general sound of his voice, but whatever he was saying, the crowd around him responded in agreement, shouting and applauding.

"Anarchist." Papa's voice came at me loud, and I turned. He had his gaze straight on me. He nodded toward the platform where Andy Ashland stood. "You tell your brother I want that Socialist off my land." I stepped in closer to the table so Papa wouldn't have to speak so loud, but it didn't matter. He kept on, nearly yelling. Mr. Slater looked uncomfortable. "Income tax is what he's preaching. I pay enough damned taxes already. On my land. On the land that Socialist lives on."

"Papa—"

"Don't try to shut me up. I can say what I want to." He put his hands on the table and sort of lifted himself. "It's a free country!" he hollered in the direction of the platform. No one up there seemed to hear him.

"I came to tell you that the game's started already," I said. I went around behind him and laid my hand on his shoulder. It wasn't something I would've done in normal circumstances. We weren't demonstrative like Priscilla and her father were. I would have never dreamed, for example, of giving Papa a kiss on the top of his head. Or even a hug, for that matter. We just didn't do such things in our family, but Mr. Slater seemed relieved that I was there.

Papa rose to his feet. "I want that Socialist off my property, you hear?"

"Come on, Papa." I took him by the arm. We started off, headed toward the baseball diamond.

"Your brother is going to pay attention to me on this," Papa said. "I want that man moved off my land."

"Fine, Papa. Let's get over there and watch the game."

He slung my hand off his arm. "I don't need you hanging on to me. And take that gum out of your mouth. You look like a floozy popping your lips thataway."

I stopped, and they went on, him and Mr. Slater. I watched them go and I felt like I could cry but I didn't. My whole life, it seemed, had been spent fighting back tears over some unkind remark Papa said to me. This was nothing new. It just seemed worse after his earlier good humor. I opened the face on my pendant watch. It was two-thirty already, but I had a feeling that the rest of the time, until the train left at six, would go by much slower. I watched Papa and Mr. Slater walk away and I didn't take the gum out of my mouth. The sweet wasn't all gone from it yet.

I glanced again toward the platform where Mr. Ashland stood, gesturing with both his hands outstretched. His voice was just a rumble on the wind, so I moved closer.

It was Populism Mr. Ashland was preaching, not Socialism. I realized this after I joined the party standing around the platform. He spoke against the "swiggers from the pots of privilege." Those were the words he used, but I found out later he didn't make them up himself. They were the same words other Populists used. They had their own vocabulary. He said the farmer, the common man, was drowning in a sea of poverty, beholden to the merchant, to the ginner, to the Wall Street man with his swagger stick and his patent-leather spats. "And that ain't the way it ought to be, my friends. Without us they ain't got those pots of privilege they've been swigging from."

He went on and on, about women's suffrage, about free silver, about term limitations for elected politicians until his throat got hoarse. Then he went on and on some more. I can't say what it was that made me feel so interested to hear what he said. I had never known a person who could get up in front of a crowd that way, and tell them things that made them shout out their agreement.

"Every day another farmer loses his land. Good, hard-working farmers, plain folk like you and me. And why? Not because he's lazy. Not because he spent too much and produced too little like the eastern money-grabbers say. Not when the same bale of cotton that sold for fifty cents a pound last year sells for forty-three cents today." He stopped, let his eyes roam the crowd. "We're here today to remember the great war that was fought on American soil, and to honor all the fine men who participated in that war. Major Sayers already spoke much better on that subject than I ever could. But there's a war to be fought right now, on this soil, on this day, among these fine men and women." His hand swept over the crowd. "And I say this is a war we can win. This is a war we have to win. There's no other choice for us. Not if we want to keep the money sharks from owning our land. Not if we want our children and our grandchildren to live in a world better than the one we're living in right now today."

I glanced and saw little Hannah asleep in the lap of a lady I didn't know. Quintus sat on the ground beside them, watching his papa. Mr. Ashland was the perspiring kind, and though it was a cool spring day, his white shirt had turned gray. I lost track of how long he was up there. Over an hour. My feet ached from my high-button shoes.

When Mr. Ashland came down from the platform, all the people were clapping for him, slapping him on the back as he passed through. He went over and lifted Hannah out of the woman's arms, then gave an overhand wave as if to say to the crowd that they'd given him enough applause. Some other man took the platform and began to speak, but I was watching Mr. Ashland.

Quintus shook a handkerchief out of his pocket and, with adoring eyes, offered it up to his papa. Mr. Ashland wiped his forehead with it, then put his arm around his son and hiked him up on the opposite hip from his sister. The load was too much, though. Mr. Ashland wasn't a particularly big man. He let both children down onto their feet. Then he looked up and saw me staring. It was too late for me to look away. I'd been caught. He came my direction. He held both his children by their hands.

"Miz O'Barr," he said. "I didn't know you were interested in politics."

"No, I didn't . . . I didn't know you were either. Are you running for something?"

"Some public office, you mean?"

"Yes. It sounded that way."

"Someday maybe. We haven't thought that far ahead."

"We?"

"Me. And Hannah and Quint." He pressed their hands together and smiled down at them. Quintus smiled back at his papa. Hannah was staring at me. "You know Willie, don't you? Willie Betts?" Mr. Ashland nodded at the man who had taken the platform. "He's the one who influenced me to become a lecturer. He thought I had some things to share with all these folks."

"Do you really believe in all that? Those things you were just saying?" I asked him. "You think women should have the vote?"

"You don't?"

"I don't know. The Constitution doesn't say anything about women, does it? It says that all *men* are created equal." I thought I sounded lighthearted but he made a wincing sound.

"Appears to me you've been listening to too much of the Democrats' hogwash. They don't want anybody voting except the white man who owns his land. Things might get out of hand if all those undesirables were to vote. Could cause some changing to happen, and they sure don't want that. No sir. No changing for the Democrats. They want things status quo. Want to keep everybody else quiet, and things like they are."

"My husband's a Democrat, you know. And so's my papa."

"I figured it." He gave me a grin. "Mr. DeLony . . . your papa, he's done all right for himself. But he had to marry it, didn't he?"

My spine stiffened. I felt my face flame. He saw it.

"I don't mean to seem impolite. But you-all were living out where I do before, weren't you?"

"And Papa owns that land outright."

"Oh, I know he does. I'm not meaning to speak against you or your papa. I'm sure he did what he felt he had to. I know what that's like. I've done what I had to do just about all my life."

I didn't know what to say to that. I felt I should defend Papa some more but I couldn't think of a good argument. Mother *was* ten years older than Papa. She'd been a widow-lady with 501 acres. Our old place only had 64. More folks than just Mr. Ashland had suggested Papa married Mother for convenience sake. It had been pretty well bandied about for the past twelve years. Nathan and I had long ago suspected there was some truth to it.

Hannah found a rock at her feet and bent to pick it up. Mr.

Ashland let her hand go. He let go of Quintus, too, but the boy didn't move from his papa's side. "Would *you* vote for me?" Mr. Ashland said, cocking his head. "If I was to run for, say, the state legislature? That is, assuming I could change your mind and half the country's about a woman's right to vote?"

I looked at him, not saying anything. After hearing him speak before the crowd, I thought he seemed rather more extraordinary than he had before, and an awful lot of what he had said made perfect sense to me. I answered, "I really don't know anything at all about politics, Mr. Ashland."

"Well, maybe we can fix that." He smiled at me, and there was something about when he did that, something uplifting. I returned the smile.

"Dellie!" I heard Priscilla, then Daphne, calling me.

"There's your friends again." The smile still flickered on his face. I flushed. "I *do* need to go."

"Are you acquainted with Willie Betts? You didn't say."

I looked at the man up on the platform and it came to me who he was. "He's an editor, isn't he? For a newspaper."

Mr. Ashland nodded. "The *Plaindealer*. I work for him on Wednesdays and Saturdays. Do you know where he keeps his office in town?"

"Beside Flaxman's clothes store, isn't it?"

"Above. Come by, if you've a mind to. We can talk some more. Get to the bottom of those beliefs of yours." He let out a good-natured chuckle.

I laughed, too, but mine was only pretend. Get to the bottom of my beliefs? I wasn't at all sure that was possible. I didn't know myself what I believed in. I'd never had to decide before. No one, that I could recall, had ever asked me.

I made my goodbyes, turned, and practically ran to meet up with Priscilla and Daphne.

"Seventh-inning stretch," Daphne said.

Priscilla grabbed my arm. "Oh, you should have seen it. He hit a homerun. It was fabulous. Wasn't it fabulous, Daphne?"

I had to consciously keep myself from turning to look back at Mr. Ashland and the speaker's platform. I matched my steps to the two of theirs.

Four days after the reunion, Papa took his old .44 pistol out of the lowboy where he kept it, cleaned and oiled the barrel and all six chambers. The soft rags he used were still on the kitchen table later, stained a brownish orange from the rust. Out in the barn, he cranked the handle on the feed bin for the milch cows, then milked them one by one while they ate. When he finished with that chore, he turned the cows out, even carried the brimming, foamy pails to the back stoop, and left them covered with a fresh cheesecloth, before he returned to the barn. There, he sat back down on the milking stool, put the loaded .44 in his mouth, and pressed the trigger.

It was just past dawn. Patches of dew still lay on the ground. Nathan was already up and out with the herd of scrub stock Papa called his cattle, bringing them to an oat field nearer the house. Two of the hired hands rode at the rear of the herd. When the report of the pistol shot broke the quiet of that pale morning, Nathan stopped in his tracks, rose in the stirrups to give a quick, startled look around, then spurred his golden bay in the direction of the barn. Papa had always been one to make his own choices. It seemed to me that this was just one more.

We buried him on Friday—a foggy Friday—in the city cemetery right next to our mama's grave. Emmaline Louise DeLony was the name on her monument. Mr. Townsend, the stonecutter, said we had to leave Papa's spot unmarked for a while, until the ground around settled. And Papa's casket didn't have the glass piece set inside the lid like normal. Even after the mortician, Mr. Hardaway, cleaned Papa up, his body still wasn't fit for public viewing.

A big crowd attended the services. Practically the entire town. Not because Papa had been such a popular man, but suicide was a novelty. An unnatural act. Mother was so ashamed, she never once raised the black veil from her face, not even to dab at the tears that dripped out and stained the front of her dress.

Andy Ashland was there, wearing a black suit that had either shrunk in the wash or come down secondhand from someone with shorter arms than his. He'd brought along Quintus and little Hannah, all done up in blue ribbons. He spoke to Mother, something that made her nod her head. He shook Nathan's hand, and then he shook Daniel's. To me, he said, "I'm sorry for your misfortune. Your daddy was a fine man."

It surprised me how I took it, watching Papa go underground. I stayed well after everyone else had gone. Daniel tried to get me to leave, too, but I waited until the grave diggers had pitched every shovelful of black dirt back into the hole they had dug, before I could turn away. For the next two weeks, I came back each day just after dinner, driving the one-horse gig Daniel gave me on my last birthday, and dodging the stumps and holes left untended down the center of the road. I came to tamp the fresh-turned earth on the grave, and to watch grass runners take root, then sprout. I don't know why it occupied me so, visiting Papa more dead than I had alive. I just couldn't believe he was gone. Truly. Completely. Gone. I felt at loose ends.

Our brother, Dane, came all the way from Parker County, answering the letter we sent. Nathan and I went to the train depot to meet him. Eleven years had passed since I'd seen Dane, but he hadn't changed much in looks. He was twenty-seven, had put on weight, though he was still a slight man, as serious and unsmiling as I remembered him.

He shook Nathan's hand, and didn't seem to notice me at all

for the longest time. Not until we were in the buggy did he speak directly at me, and then what he said was, "You married Dan O'Barr, I hear."

"Two years ago," I answered.

He wore a pair of eyeglasses that he had to keep pushing up on the bridge of his nose. He looked at me over the tops of them. "Time will get by you, won't it?" Then he turned back to the front where he sat beside Nathan. He spoke low, but I heard him say, "Take me to the graveyard first."

When we got there, Nathan pulled the buggy off the road and tied the team to the stake-and-rider fence that surrounded the cemetery. Dane didn't wait for Nathan to finish with the team. He didn't offer me a hand either, but started off across the grounds, barely dodging gravestones as he went. I followed after him, watching him. I couldn't stop watching him. It seemed so odd to have him here. I wanted to know what kind of man he was.

I had only been nine when he left home, running off to join Sister up in North Texas. I never knew exactly what happened to cause him to go. A fight with Papa. Accusations. Something about a Durham bull Mother had paid to ship over from England.

The bull had come on a train, up from New Orleans where the ship landed. Once he got to McDade, the bull caused a commotion, snuffing and bellowing, banging into the side of the train car before the rail workers could get him unloaded. For a while, every man with a cow in season was begging Papa for the use of that bull. But he was meant for the upgrading of *our* stock, or Mother's stock. And Papa had never leaned toward generosity.

I remember a lot of hollering out by the barn the day Dane left, taking our workhorse, old Joe, with him. Not too long after they were gone—a few days, a week maybe—that Durham bull keeled over dead in his pen. Tick fever. For some reason Papa blamed Dane for it. He mourned the loss of that prize bull far longer than he did the loss of his own flesh-and-blood son. Dane's name, like Sister's, became one more we couldn't say out loud in Papa's presence.

When we had walked halfway across the cemetery grounds, Dane stopped. He stood close to where our mama lay across from the Billingsleys' family plot, and he looked down on Papa's grave, still harsh and new despite my tending. Then he glanced back up at me, nodded at the bare mound before us. "This him?"

"Yes. The stone is at Mr. Townsend's if you'd like to see it later." I watched Dane walk all around the plot of ground. I heard Nathan coming up behind us.

"We kept the inscription simple. Just his name and dates."

"No poetry," Nathan said, halting next to me. He gave me a pitying smile and put his hand on my shoulder. I think he knew I had been coming here every day. I'm sure Daniel had told him. Nathan patted my shoulder like he believed me to be half-crazed with grief, and that just being here might cause my mind to crack.

"Poetry," Dane said, with a little grunt of laughter, as he moved back to the foot of Papa's grave. He stared down. "Poetry."

All of us stared down for a moment, at the clods and clumps of dirt mounded there. And then Dane let out his fly buttons, making just enough of a movement that my gaze was caught. I couldn't help it, I shrieked when I saw him reach inside the gap. I turned my back to him, clasping my hands to my cheeks. My neck prickled.

"Great God!" Nathan said. "Jesus Christ Almighty! What do you think you're doing?"

I heard the stream of water hit the ground with a thud and a dull splash that kept coming, on and on until I laughed. From embarrassment. From disbelief. I *had* to laugh. I couldn't stop myself. I balanced myself on Nathan's arm and I laughed till I thought I might choke to death.

Dane would not stay at our house, or at Mother's either. He didn't want to see her. He said, "I hadn't got nothing to say to that old woman."

I sat with him in his room at the Station Hotel. Since there was no dining room, we ate supper on the writing table in the corner—a roast joint of beef, peas, and new potatoes I'd brought from home, along with plates, napkins, and utensils. Daniel had escorted me to the hotel, but then he left shortly after paying quick respects to Dane. They had been friends once, or at least fairly well acquainted, but neither of them seemed to know what to say to one another anymore. I didn't have that trouble. I was eager to know about Dane's life, and he seemed pleased to tell me.

He was living up near Weatherford, farming land owned by Sister's brother-in-law. It suited him, he said. "We got a hundred and sixty-two acres under plow already, and we're breaking out more every season. He's got a total of three hundred and ninety, and we'll have it all broke in three years. You got to plant ever speck of land you got these days just to break even, with money so short and all. And with the drouthy weather we've been having. It's good ground, but our profits ain't nothing to holler about."

"What about Sister?" I asked. "Do you hear much from her?" I knew they kept in touch, though she'd long since moved off with her husband. They lived up on the Canadian River, her last letter had said. But that was nearly a year ago now. Our letter-writing had become more and more infrequent of late.

"What you want to know?" Dane scratched at his head. White flakes fell out of his hair onto his suit coat. I resisted the urge to reach over and sweep them off. He needed someone taking care of him—some woman. I wanted to ask why he had never married.

"What is she doing? How is she getting along?" I said.

"Well, she's going to have another baby come fall. I told her she keeps squirting them out like she does, and pretty soon she's going to settle up the whole Panhandle by herself."

He was such a plain talker. It was shocking and wicked, but I liked it somehow. As if this were a part of myself I'd never known before. I knew my face was as red as wine. I sat up straighter in the easy chair. "We sent her a letter about Papa, but I don't know whether she got it. They move around so much."

He nodded. "That's her husband's fault. He's always scheming up something supposed to make him a rich man."

All I'd ever heard Sister's husband, Marion Beatty, called was a no-account, jailbird, outlaw scoundrel. In the photograph Sister had sent last Christmas, he stood holding the youngest of their four children, smiling bright into the camera. He was a hand-some man. Almost as handsome as Nathan. They were all of them, Sister's family, out in front of a tumbledown house of clap-board and cedar shake. The yard fence needed mending. Roof had been patched. Sister looked worn out.

"Is she contented, do you think?" I said.

Dane thought about that for a few seconds, considering it like it had never occurred to him before to wonder. "I reckon so. They hadn't got a pot to pee in, but I reckon so. Hadn't either of us got much of a pot." He laughed out at himself, then he leaned toward me, across the writing desk. "Lily ain't changed any, Dellie. Just got a little older. And got all them young'uns swarm-ing around her like a sow pig. But she's just the same. Still as hardheaded. I think that husband of hers could do better by her, but she won't let you talk against him. Not one word."

I was glad to hear it. I had always admired Sister's spunk, and envied her for it, how she'd run off with the man she loved despite the wrath of Papa, despite what gossips in town might say. Sister didn't need any of them. It gave me hope somehow, and then I wondered, hope for what?

"How about you?" Dane said. "How come you to marry a man so much older than you?" His eyes, magnified by his spectacles, narrowed at me.

The question stalled me for a moment. No one had ever asked me such a thing before. They might have thought it, but no one had ever dared to ask.

"Well . . ." I considered each word. "For one thing, he asked me. No one else ever did that much." I laughed; Dane didn't. He moved his mouth around in a way that made his nose twitch, as if he had an itch in there or was about to sneeze. "He's a good and honest man," I said, serious now.

"Always was."

"He treats me well."

"Good for you." Dane's smile had grown wider, but also un-kind. Bitter almost. And I wondered why. Had Papa done this to him? My brother, this stranger sitting here with me? He sneezed, blew his nose into his handkerchief. When he looked at me again his eyes were red and watery behind his eyeglasses. "Spring fever," he said. "I get it ever year something terrible." He wiped his eyes with his handkerchief, his nose again, then tucked the handkerchief back into his pocket.

"Papa shot himself," I said. "I don't think Nathan told you that. There was a cancer. It would've killed him eventually, but he didn't give it a chance to. Papa was in considerable pain all last winter."

Hearing this didn't seem to surprise Dane. Neither did it soften his hard smile. "So—he turned out to be a coward, too."

He said it matter-of-fact. "A bastard *and* a coward. Well, what do you know. Thank God he's dead. Thank God."

There was venom in his voice like I had never heard from anyone speaking of a person so recently passed away. I wanted to ask why he hated Papa so much, and after so long a time. Didn't he feel something besides contempt? Anything at all? A little bit of caring, or at least respect?

"He'd been in pain all winter," I said again, in case he hadn't heard me the first time, though I was sure he had.

We sat silent for a spell. The curtains over the window billowed into the room and then fell back, as if the walls were breathing. A dreamlike picture of Jesus Christ hung above the bed, put there, I was sure, by Hoy Lusby, who owned the hotel and was a deacon at the Baptist church. I stared at the picture, at the halo and the rays of sunlight fanning out from Christ's head.

When, finally, I looked back at Dane again, the ugliness on his face had cleared away. It seemed to leave him weary. He gave me a listless smile. The room was well lit with gas lighting, but even in the brightness, his cheeks held shadows. He leaned one elbow on the table. "Tell me something: Do the O'Barrs still have all that land?"

"Most of it." I brightened, relieved to be on a different subject. "Some was sold after the winter of '87. We had a big die-up down here. And then Daniel had to sell more of it right after his papa died to pay off some debts. But there's still somewhere around six thousand or so acres. About a third of it fenced." I laughed. "It's the fence that keeps Daniel busy."

There were around thirty-five hundred head of cattle with the O-BAR-J brand, or needing it, and that was twice as many head as the land could support on pasture. Daniel had three goals. The first one was to sell off the surplus cattle, bringing the herd down to a manageable size. The second was to get all six thousand acres under fence with water from the West Yegua, which cut through the land, or with a system of cisterns and windmills. Daniel's last goal—and the one that excited him the most since it required scientific knowledge he'd learned at the university— was to upgrade the quality of the herd by crossbreeding for more meat and weather hardiness.

All of this I told to Dane, glad to be sounding as if I knew something of the ranching business. Most of it I had overheard Daniel tell to Nathan and Papa at Sunday dinners. Dane watched me talk and appeared to listen, but after a while, he seemed bored, taking off his eyeglasses, wiping them out with his dinner napkin, putting them back on his face, then taking them off once more. Without them, his eyes seemed shrunken and deep-set on his face. There was a long gouge across the bridge of his nose from where the spectacles rested, and he rubbed at this place. When finally he pulled out his watch and flipped open the spring face, I stopped talking. He looked up at me as if noticing my sudden silence.

"Well then," he said. "I reckon you did all right for yourself." He put his watch back in its pocket. "Papa tried to get Lily to marry old Daniel O'Barr once, too, but she wouldn't have none of it." He shook his head. "I never knew a man more land-hungry than that old bastard was."

Slowly it dawned on me what Dane was saying—that he thought Papa had arranged my marriage, and that he'd done it for his own gain. I felt suddenly sick to my stomach, sinful some way, insulted, too. All I could do was stammer.

"That isn't what he—*no*! He wanted what was best for me—"

Dane saw that I was frantic, realized that maybe he'd gone too far with me, and with his condemnation of Papa. His face got straight and solemn. "Oh, that's right," he said quickly, and then he switched the subject onto a will if there was one, which there was, giving everything Papa owned to Mother. Daniel had been named the executor of Papa's estate. But I didn't say any of this. I let Dane speak.

"I don't want nothing he's got, and Lily won't either, so don't worry about us. You and Nathan take it all. You two deserve it more than we do. Y'all are the ones who stuck it out down here. Heaven only knows how you did it."

Not too long later, Sinclair came saying Daniel had sent him to fetch me home. Sinclair was the quiet sort and I was glad of it. I didn't feel like talking. As we rode to the ranch, everything Dane had said ran through my mind.

It was true that after Jonathan O'Barr died, and after Daniel came back to McDade, he had become the most sought-after bachelor around. On account of the land and his family's standing in the community, and because he was educated. And it was true that he had courted Sister back when I was still a girl in pigtails. But Sister was pretty and sweet and everybody loved her, so I couldn't fault Daniel if he had, at one time, had his eye on her. Sister had done what she wanted to, and so had I. Papa hadn't forced me. And if he had encouraged me to make the marriage, it was only because he'd been thinking of my welfare. Not his own. Surely Papa wasn't that self-serving.

Yet, it was also true that Daniel allowed Papa the use of O'Barr land and of the O'Barr hands. That much could not be denied. Papa's cattle benefited from the increased grazing that six thousand acres gave. And at round-up time, Daniel's hands separated out Papa's brand from O-Bar-J stock, or drove them to market all together and settled up later, whichever way Papa preferred. For quite some time, Daniel and Papa had been as good as business partners.

Sinclair took the team right up to the carriage shed, and then he helped me down from the seat. Our two heelers came running and barking to greet us. The younger one, Britches, tried to jump up on me but Sinclair cropped him on the snout with the butt end of his coach whip.

"It's all right," I said. "It's all right," and I leaned down to give both dogs a hearty rub behind their necks.

"Mister Daniel say don't let the dogs jump up," Sinclair said, but then he leaned down with me to rub Old Boy.

Sinclair was simpleminded, childlike though he was well into his thirties. He was good with animals, horses most especially, though Daniel had another man who tended them out on the range. Sinclair was with us because he was Tante Lena's nephew. They were Bohemians with a last name pronounced nothing like it was spelled. They had worked for the O'Barrs since Daniel was small, and lived in the cottage across the road. Some folks in town thought it unseemly the way they lived together over there, man and woman, even if they were aunt and nephew. But then people will have unclean thoughts, even when they know better.

Our house, the house Jonathan O'Barr had been building when he died, was large, much too large for just Daniel and me. Lightning rods pointed skyward from every gable. Two galleries bellied out around the front and over to the eastern side—one upstairs, its twin below. There were five bedrooms, a parlor and drawing room, dining room, and study. Enough space for all the ranch hands and Daniel's mother to have lived with us, but they didn't.

The hands, the six Daniel kept on steady through the year, all had their own places in town. Four kept rooms at Weede Millage's boardinghouse near the fire station. The other two were married men with a few acres they farmed on the side. Big ranches in western Texas and in the cedarbrake hills north of Austin had special bunkhouses for their hands to live in. It was something I knew Daniel dreamed of for the O-Bar-J some day.

In the kitchen, Tante Lena had already set the tea kettle on for me, and she fixed me a cup. She told me I looked plumb ragged and tried to get me to sit with her awhile. She had been fussing over me and treating me like a sick child ever since Papa's funeral.

"The supper was just fine," I told her, and she took the basket with the dirty dishes from my hand. She set it on the sink.

"Won't you sit down here with Lena. Tell me 'bout your brother Dane. I ain't seen him in so long I don't reckon he'd know me."

The big double-weighted clock in the front hall struck eight o'clock, well past the usual time Tante Lena and Sinclair walked across the road. I told her to go on and leave the dishes on the sink for tomorrow.

"I'm tired. I think I'll go up to bed and read awhile." I patted her hand and took my tea to Daniel's study.

He sat at his desk marking entries into his journal by the light of a brass-shaded lamp. Everything in the room, the padded leather chairs, the dark wooden shutters folded back from the windows, the books lining the cases, all smelled of pipe tobacco. When I stepped through the door, he looked up at me, his eyebrows raised. He smiled, the kind of smile you'd give an indulged child.

"Did you enjoy your visit?" The lamp flame made the gray in his hair look like strands of corn silk. His father had grayed prematurely. It was in his family to do so. I wondered what he would say if I were to touch him there, at his temples, or rub his neck as I just had the dogs outside?

"Yes," I said. "He's leaving tomorrow on the eight o'clock."

He nodded and reached for the pipe burning in its crystal stand. He held it cupped in front of his face, both elbows propped on the desktop, but he didn't smoke it. He kept his eyes on me, watching me as if I were an intrusion he could barely tolerate. I knew he was busy. There had been letters back and forth between him and a Mr. O. C. Canaday in Chicago regarding eight hundred steer Daniel had ready to ship. I could sense his impatience as I browsed through the bookcase, searching for something I hadn't read. He seemed relieved when I finally chose one. I told him good night, and took the tea and the book upstairs to my room.

The book was a love story, a tragedy about a woman whose beloved is lost at sea and never found, another book bought at the urging of Daphne Craddock. She belonged to the Wednesday Club, a group of ladies in town who read books and got together to talk about them. It was Daphne who kept us up to date on all the popular novels. I had a hard time concentrating on this one, though, and had to keep rereading paragraphs and scenes. My mind was stuck on Daniel, remembering the way he had asked me to marry him all those months ago, starting off bold, "If you'd be so inclined," and ending just above a whisper, "I'd like you to become my wife." He had seemed like a different man then. Not so somber. More lighthearted.

We met at a swing-and-turn party at the Matsons' house. The Matsons were Baptists, like so many others in McDade, and didn't hold with dancing. But we could clap our hands and chant words and walk together to the tempo, swing and turn. There was hardly any difference, but since no fiddles played, the Matsons found it acceptable. So did Mother.

Daniel came to the Matsons' party. Heaven knows why he came; he was a grown man compared to the rest of us. Nearing thirty. I'd known him my whole life but we renewed our acquaintance there at the Matsons', and afterward, I saw him regularly. We went for drives in the country, berry picking by the creek. Sometimes we took a picnic with us. He read to me, almost the whole of *Silas Marner*. He was a good reader. A much better reader than he was a talker. Strange to say about a man who fancied himself an attorney-at-law.

His proposal of marriage was not a surprise. Papa had already told me of Daniel's intentions, and as I now recalled it, Papa could barely contain his eagerness. He had always said Daniel O'Barr wasn't afraid to get his hands dirty. Papa admired the work in a person above all other traits.

"Why?" was my answer to Daniel. I wanted to know what it was about me he wanted to marry. We had never even kissed.

His head jerked back as if I'd struck him with my question. He studied me until his eyes glazed over. "Because you're bright," he had finally said. "And you have good manners."

Bright. And good manners. At the time it had felt like enough. . . .

I had managed to struggle into the second chapter of the book when Daniel tapped on my door. He had a way he did that— four taps spaced out and light, reminding me of a cat scratching.

"I'm sorry to disturb you," he said, coming into my room. "I saw the light." He had taken off his coat and vest. His tie was gone, and his suspenders hung down around his hips.

I laid the book facedown on the bedside table, and rearranged myself on the bed. He perched himself at the edge of the mattress. He smelled of his pipe, and faintly of some liquor. Brandy, I thought. Since it was unlike him to drink spiritous liquor, my interest was instantly awake.

"I wanted to talk to you about Dane," he said, then took his time about it, pulling off his collar and folding it against his knee. Both his cuffs came next, one at a time, and I began to suspect he had come for more than just talking. If so, I wanted the lamp out.

He smiled, then let the smile go. He reached for my hand, then only let one finger touch me, light and quick, along the back of my knuckles. "He relieved himself on Josh's grave," he said at last, uneasy, clearing his throat. "Is that so?"

I sat up straighter against the pillows. "Nathan told you that?" They talked. Too much and too often they talked.

Daniel nodded. "Said, as a matter of fact, that it seemed to be all he came for."

"Maybe." I looked toward the long windows that faced out onto the upper gallery. The night had become silent and calm. "Maybe it was."

"You seem awfully nonchalant about it, Dellie."

"I'm not going to condemn him. You know they had their troubles, him and Papa." I reached for my cup of tea. It was bone cold, but I drank it anyway, determined not to feel foolish.

"You don't care that he desecrated your father's resting place?"

"He was Dane's father, too."

"Nathan said when he—when Dane . . ." Daniel tapped the folded collar and cuffs against his thigh. I could feel his eyes on me. "Nathan said you laughed about it."

The back of my neck got hot. I glanced again at the window, wishing for a breath of air from outside, just a breath. "It struck me as funny," I said, sounding more defiant than I intended.

His head cocked just a little, almost imperceptibly, to the left. Then he looked away from me, at the floor and his feet, at the book on the bed table, anywhere but at my wicked face. I knew what he was thinking, perched there, absently rattling the collar and cuff buttons inside his fist, as if he held a handful of dice he was about to fling. He wanted to reprimand me.

"He's leaving on the eight o'clock. I'm planning to see him off," I said, deciding it in that instant.

My declaration had the desired effect. Daniel stood up. "Well, then . . ." He studied me again for just the briefest second before he leaned toward the lamp. "Do you want me to get this?"

"I'll do it. I think I'll read awhile yet."

"All right. Well—" He looked toward the door, back at me; smiled. "Good night."

When he was gone, I pulled the covers up around me. I didn't reach again for the book or the lamp. For the longest time I stared at the wall opposite the bed, and at the chromolithograph that hung there of Cupid and a cluster of fairies in a forest of dark trees. Daniel had bought the picture when we were on our honeymoon in Galveston. He liked it, he said, the colors and the Cupid. He had had the picture crated back ahead of us on the train.

In our honeymoon room there in Galveston, we had slept in the same bed, uncomfortably, awkwardly, both of us attempting to stay politely to our own side. We had different habits. Daniel couldn't stand the covers except on the coldest nights of winter. Even then he used only a lightly batted quilt. And he had to have a pile of pillows stacked beneath his head, so that while he slept, he sat practically upright. He didn't snore. Everything he did he did quietly. But he had been affectionate in his sleep, reaching now and then to touch my shoulder or my back. And he mumbled, putting muted, nonsense words to dreams he was having. Sometimes, even now, I could hear him through the wall that separated us. It made me feel curious, and alone, these mumblings in the night.

For the first two months of our marriage, his mother had lived with us. Then she'd said that two mistresses in one household only begged for trouble; besides which, she had a sister in Navasota that needed her, a sister in frail health with a serious malady of the heart. With his mother gone, I had thought Daniel would move into my room, or that I would move into his. It had been my mistaken belief that it was having his mother in the house with us that inhibited him. He had made a muttered, half-apologetic excuse for it, our continued bedroom arrangement. He was an early riser, he said, and he would hate to disturb me of a morning. I had accepted that as the truth. Yet now, with all these new thoughts rambling in my head, I began to feel it must be me that repulsed him in some way. If he didn't love me, if he had only married me because Papa had willed it, and because I had good manners, no wonder we slept apart. No wonder.

The next morning, I went to the Station Hotel but Dane had already checked out. He was not at the depot, though the eight o'clock to Belton and Waco, and eventually to Fort Worth, was less than an hour to departure. The only businesses open were the barber and the feed store, and he wasn't at either place. I couldn't think where else he could be, and I was just about to give up and go home when the rattle of Andy Ashland's teamster wagon caught my attention, flying up the street to the depot, well beyond the six-miles-per-hour speed limit required within town limits. Dane was on the high seat beside Mr. Ashland. He leapt down when he saw me.

"I wanted to look at the old place again," he said, reaching back in the wagon for his battered Gladstone.

Mr. Ashland touched the brim of his hat. "Morning, Miz O'Barr."

"Morning," I said back to him.

"Thanks, Andy." Dane spoke as if they were old chums.

We both stood there while Mr. Ashland drove his team away from the station. He stopped in front of the feed store and stood up, whistling through his teeth. Elias Franklow and a colored worker came out and began loading feed bags into Mr. Ashland's wagon.

"A lot's changed," Dane said. And I agreed that it had in eleven years. He said, "I wasn't expecting you to come this morning. I thought I might've hacked you off good with things I said last night. I realize I don't know you so well anymore. I ain't used to you being a grown-up woman, I know that much for sure." He gave me an uneasy smile, and I saw that it didn't come natural to him to apologize.

"I wanted to see you off."

I studied his face for a moment, the sturdy jaw, the cleft chin. He had the looks of Papa all over him, but I didn't dare say so. Yet, it made me wonder again, as I had so often before, who it was that I took after. Not Papa. Not Mama either, for Mother had always said it was Sister and Nathan who favored that side of the family. No, I had gotten the blood of someone from further back, some forgotten someone with blond hair and long bones and a high forehead. I was the different one.

"Why did you come all this way?" I said. "I wanted to ask you that."

He laughed and looked off toward where they were coaling the train, then his mouth straightened into a line. "To make sure he was really dead. It's a load off. Isn't it?" He tipped his head at me. Those magnified eyes bored into me, asking me, forcing me to tell the truth.

"In a way. I guess so, in a way." It took all my breath just to say it out loud.

We hugged. It made me feel good all over, that hug. I wished Nathan had come to say goodbye. I wished Sister were here and we could be a family again, though I suppose it was too late for all that. Papa had seen to it. I stood on the platform and nearly wept when Dane leaned out the window a final time.

❀ ❀ ❀ **4** ❀ ❀ ❀

The next time I saw Andy Ashland it was the twentieth of
May. I had gone into town for a new hat to wear with the
dress I'd made for the Masonic Celebration coming up on Saturday. Olivia Nash, our town marshal's wife, kept a millinery
table in Bassist's store. I was standing there at her table, looking
over her array of silk flowers, bobbinet, and ribbon when Mr.
Ashland came into the store.

He wore his overalls, his shirt rolled to his elbows, and plow-
boots covered with dirt, so I knew he was not in town trading.
From the way he strode in, so forthright and without bothering
to take off his hat though he'd come indoors, it was clear he was
angry about something.

Olivia Nash was saying, "I just got these spring poppies in
yesterday," but my attention had turned to the front of the store.

Mr. Ashland said to Sam Alexander, the counter clerk, "I want
to speak with Louis Bassist. Right now if you don't mind."

"Did you say your dress is blue?" Olivia asked. I turned to
look at her. She had unwrapped some more flowers. A cluster of
bluets. Some lily-of-the-valley. Absently, I picked up a bunch
and pretended to inspect them until I heard Mr. Bassist speak.

"What is it, Andrew?" He came from his office at the rear of
the store, a big-shouldered, formal man, with a German burr in
his voice, though he had lived in this country for forty years.

Mr. Ashland said, "I sent my boy up here a little while ago for
some expectorant for my mule, and he said Sam here wouldn't
give it to him."

"Those were my instructions, yes."

There weren't but a few other people in the store, its being the middle of the week, but all of us had turned to listen. Mr. Ashland stood four feet from Mr. Bassist, both of them frowning as if fisticuffs could break out between them any second.

"I have a sick mule," Mr. Ashland said. "One of my plow mules. What am I supposed to do? I need that medicine, Louis."

"You know the situation here." Mr. Bassist's voice got lower, then turned to a mumbling I couldn't hear. I took an unintentional step forward.

"Dellie? Did you want to take the bluets?" Olivia said.

I looked at her and then at the flowers in my hand. I laid them down on her table.

"Say it louder, Louis." Mr. Ashland was nearly shouting now. "Let's make sure everybody in here knows I'm a debtor. And while we're at it, let's make sure they know what kind of business you're running. You've already got my crop. What else do you want from me? My blood, too?" He held out his wrist and made a slashing motion across his pulse.

Mr. Bassist's chin stiffened. "You can try Walt Kaiser's store in Paige. You have reached your limit here." He turned and marched back to his office. Mr. Ashland's face got so red it was almost blue before he, too, spun on his heel and stormed out, slamming his hand against the door sill as he stepped through.

"Dellie, dear?" Olivia said. She was trying to pretend nothing out of the ordinary had just happened.

"Wait." I snatched up my pocketbook and hurried to the front of the store. The other customers, few though they were, had gone back to browsing, whispering amongst themselves. By noon, this little incident would be all over town.

"What was it he needed?" I said to Sam Alexander. I glanced out the door where Mr. Ashland was unhitching a gray saddle mule, its hide mottled with barbwire scars. All the animals here-abouts had similar scars. Fences were going up faster than we could get our animals trained.

"Horse expectorant," Sam said, speaking softly, clearly shaken by the confrontation just past.

I watched Andy Ashland mount his mule. "Wrap it up."

"Mrs. O'Barr. We can't credit him any—"

"How much is it?" I started digging through my pocketbook. Daniel allowed me fifteen dollars a month for odds and ends. Of course, we had an account here, too, but I didn't want to answer any questions when the bill came due. I wasn't sure whose side Daniel would be on.

"Let's see . . ." Sam rummaged through the shelves behind the counter. He grabbed a price book and began to run his finger down the list. "We don't sell so much at a cash price . . ."

"Please, hurry." I glanced outside. Mr. Ashland was leaving, headed at a trot down Main to Church Street.

"Here it is," Sam Alexander said, raising his face. "One dollar ninety cents."

I threw the money down on the counter, and I almost went out on Bassist's gallery to shout for Mr. Ashland to wait, before Sam gave me the package. It was small—no bigger than a sack of tea—to be so expensive. I raced to my buggy.

I thought I could overtake him before he reached the tracks, but Mr. Westbrook's freighter delivering milled lumber to the lumberyard slowed me up. When my little gig clattered over the railroad crossing, Mr. Ashland and his gray mule were already out of sight.

My horse, named Cintha, was spirited, and when I cracked the whip in the air above her, she nearly flew. Just past the bend in the road at Petersons' farm, we caught up with the gray mule.

"Mr. Ashland!" I slowed Cintha. She was winded. I was, too. I called again, and he pulled back on his mule. "I was in Bassist's store just now," I said, struggling for my breath. "I heard your predicament. I . . . well . . ." I reached down on the floorboard for the little brown package of medicine. "Here."

"What's this?" He took it from me, tore back the brown wrapper. He looked surprised, then his mouth went straight. "No, ma'am. Thank you, but I can't take this."

"Isn't it what you need?"

"Yes, ma'am, it is. Here. Take it back." He held the bottle toward me at arm's length, as if it had a foul stink.

"You can pay me for it later," I said.

"No, ma'am. Take it."

I did, grudgingly, and only because he gave me no other choice. His jaw was firmly set. A vein showed at his temple as if he were gritting his teeth together. I took the medicine and he rode quickly on. I watched him, and then I stared at the brown bottle in my hand.

I had no use for the tonic. It meant nothing to me, but it might have meant a plow mule to Mr. Ashland. I didn't know how sick the animal was or if it was a life-and-death circumstance, but it could have been. I could have held this year's success or failure for the Ashland family right here in this bottle. I didn't know. Only Mr. Ashland did, but he was too prideful to say. I rewrapped the bottle as best I could and placed it on the floor again, between my feet.

This time I didn't run Cintha, but kept her at a gentle pace a respectable distance behind Mr. Ashland's mule. I'm sure he knew I was back there. He turned his head once, partway and slightly to the side, as if to listen to the sound of Cintha's hoofs. But he didn't acknowledge me until after he had turned inside the gate to the farm. There he dismounted and, with his hand, popped the saddle mule on its rump. It started slowly toward the farmhouse.

Hannah was out on the porch, dressed in a pinafore, down on her knees playing with some toys. Mr. Ashland leaned on the gatepost and waited for me to catch up to him. By then, he was smiling—a wearisome smile, but it was better than his earlier dark gloom.

"Well, I guess you *would* know the way," he said.

I stopped Cintha. "Please, Mr. Ashland. I wish you'd take this medicine. I just want to help."

He reached to adjust the hat on his head. It was not the straw hat he'd worn at the reunion. This hat brim had a crack in two places so that it dipped down over his forehead in the center. He scuffed the heel of his boot against the ground and dust rose up. We hadn't had a rain in three weeks. Then he raised his face. The sun was bright and he squinted at me.

"All right," he said. "If you want to help me, I need you to pour that stuff down my mule's throat while I hold her mouth open."

My heart skipped. I had never done any such thing as that before, and I certainly wasn't dressed for farm work. I had on my good scalloped-hem orange poplin, but I gathered my skirts and got down from the buggy seat. He led Cintha over to the yard fence and hitched her in front of the house.

Hannah stood up to stare at me. She held a ragdoll loose in her hand. Its cloth feet dragged the porch floor. I could remember playing there myself, almost just the same way, with dolls I'd had, and paper dishes I'd cut out. I waved at her, but she just kept on staring. I went with her papa to the barn.

Quintus was with the ailing animal, a piebald jennet that seemed to be struggling for each breath she took. The boy sat beside her on a mound of hay in the ancient stall, stroking her rump. When we walked in the barn, a little spotted feist came from the hay pile, growling at me. Quintus scrambled to his feet, surprised, no doubt, to see me there.

"Get Patch out of here," Mr. Ashland said, hanging his hat on a nail by the door.

The barn was exactly the same as it had been when I lived here as a child. No improvements that I could see. The roof had gaping holes. The walls looked ready to fall down around us. It smelled of manure and old hay, of dried cobs and wood rot.

Quintus picked up the feist. The mule tried to rise, too, but Mr. Ashland knelt on her spine with one knee. "Crack that bottle open," he said, and it took me a second to realize he meant me.

I dropped my pocketbook. I don't even know why I'd brought it in here with me. I stepped into the stall and fumbled with the bottle of medicine. I got the paper peeled off, but then couldn't break the seal. Mr. Ashland took it from my hands and somehow managed to twist off the wire seal and keep the mule from standing. "Take your time," he said, and I didn't know if he was being fresh with me or serious. He gave me a smile so full of brooding, it told me nothing. "She's blind in her left eye, so come up on her right. Let her see you."

I nodded. I finally worked out the cork. "How much do I pour in?"

"The whole bottle."

With main force, he held the mule in a necklock and pried open her mouth. She fought against us both. Her eyes rolled back, the bright one and the milky, sightless one. Her tongue kept lolling out, getting in the way, and my hands trembled, but I got the contents of the bottle poured down her throat.

"Rub her gullet," he said, still hugging her close. "Make sure she swallows it."

I did what I could. Some of the tonic dribbled out of her

mouth. Most, I thought, went down. He let her up, and she came to her feet fighting, braying hoarsely, and choking. I jumped out of the way. It was hot in the close confines of the barn stall. I found my pocketbook on the ground outside the gate and fanned my face with it. I held the empty tonic bottle between my thumb and forefinger. It had a string of mule slobber on the lip.

Mr. Ashland stood, his hands in his pockets, and watched the mule. She walked in a circle, then seemed to huddle in next to the wall. Her breathing was still loud and rattling. "That should do her," he said, mostly to himself. He seemed to have forgotten about me for the moment.

He hadn't shaved that morning. The whiskers sprouted golden on his chin and cheeks. Sunlight coming in the barn caught them in reflection. He wiped his arm across his forehead and then he looked at me. I felt the heat of the day again and fanned harder.

"I could offer you water," he said. "I've got some fresh-drawn right inside the house."

"Oh no, I've got to get on back."

"Quint! Go get Miz O'Barr a glass of water," he said, letting himself out of the stall. He went right past me, taking the empty medicine bottle from my hand. He set it on a wall ledge beside other similar bottles. There was a tin can of turpentine, a link of chain, some baling twine.

"No, really," I said, following after him.

The boy was already up on the back porch, the little feist barking and jumping at his heels. Both of them went inside the house together. I knew what they stepped into—the jelly cupboard, and then the kitchen, the front room opening off that, and a bedroom on either side. I looked at the windows, found the one I used to sleep next to with Sister in the bed with me.

Sometimes she'd whisper stories to make me go to sleep, or she'd scratch my back, singing soft songs.

"Mr. Ashland." I turned to him. "I can't stay."

He took his hat off the nail inside the barn door and put it on his head, first smoothing back the hair from his forehead. "I wish you'd call me Andy," he said to me, and I felt the blood creep into my cheeks. He noticed it. He stopped and a baffled smile dusted his lips. "Was that wrong of me? Asking you to use my Christian name?"

"Oh. No." I could feel the dampness rolling down inside my dress. "I should go—"

"Your mother calls you Delfina."

"Oh! Heavens no." I started walking toward the front of the house. "She's not my mother. Not really. She raised me, well, in a way . . ." I thought of Sister again. "She took over when I was eight. But my real mother died when I was a baby."

He walked along with me. "I knew that. I believe she told me. Or did you?"

"Oh, she *does* like to talk."

"And you don't."

I let out a nervous laugh. I didn't know why I was acting so ridiculous all of a sudden, bashful and stammering. I couldn't seem to stop it. "No, I didn't say that. But goodness me, all you have to have are ears to find out things around here."

The slap of the back door came, and the dog's yelping, and Quintus appeared carrying two brimming glasses shakily in his hands. They were good glasses, with little flower shapes etched into the sides. The dog came right at his heel and caused an inch of the water in one glass to slosh out onto the ground.

"Here, ma'am," he said, and he sounded proud of himself. He offered me the fuller of the two glasses. There was a chip in it, right up at the rim. I thanked him and took the water from his hand.

"I brought one for you, too, Dad," he said, and Andy gave him a ruffle on his head.

We went around to the front porch and Andy pointed at some chairs there, straight-back, hard chairs, and not in particularly good repair. "Cool yourself down," he said, then waited for me to sit before he took the creaking glider for himself. Hannah crawled up to snuggle in under his arm, her doll clutched in close to her ribs.

It felt homey and familiar to me, sitting there on that porch, looking out at the road like we used to do of an evening when I was a child, listening to the mockingbird chatter in the magnolia tree full of sweet-smelling blooms. I sipped at the water. He'd had to dig a new well recently, and I'd heard he had salt in his water. I couldn't taste it if he did. This water was clear and full of mineral. I drank down every drop, then felt like a glutton and patted at my mouth. No one was watching me anyway.

Quintus was singing his alphabets while he swung round and round the porch post. Then he recited his numbers to twenty and would've gone on higher except Andy jumped in, saying, "That's enough now, Quint."

I said, "He's so smart, you must be proud of him."

"He'll make you dizzy."

The boy jumped down to wrestle with his dog on the ground just inside the yardway fence. Hannah kept playing with her ragdoll, as if the rest of us weren't there. She was a beautiful child, her hair tied back with a ribbon at her crown. Her face had been washed that morning. The pinafore could've used a laundering, but considering she had been outside playing all morning, she wasn't in too bad of shape.

"Do you find it hard? Having these children alone?"

"Sure. Sometimes. But we get by." He sounded a little bit defensive.

"Oh, I know you do, I didn't mean to imply that you didn't. It's just—" I stopped. He was staring straight at me. The maddening heat came back on me. "My papa was a widower, too, but he had my sister to do for us."

"I'm not a widower."

"Yes, I know that." I looked down at the glass between my hands, thinking of his wife at the asylum. I hated that I had steered the conversation this direction. I was never any good at small talk. "Forgive me. I didn't mean to pry into your business."

"No harm. I reckon you're just curious about Cova." He pushed the hat backward on his head. "Most folks are. It's a natural thing to be."

I shook my head, mortified to have been caught wondering about her. I stole a glance out at where Quintus rolled with the little feist. The dog growled and darted in to grab the boy's shirttail.

"Quint knows everything. We don't keep secrets around here."

I shifted. "I don't want to pry."

"She's in Austin, you know." He nodded along with his words, and I realized he was trying to make me feel comfortable. "Cova. My wife."

"Yes, I believe I did know."

He let out a gruff laugh. "Like you said, there is gossip about."

"Yes, well . . ." I gathered my pocketbook to leave, and started to stand up from the chair. There was no place to set my glass except on the porch floor and I didn't want to do that.

"We lived at Westcott before," he said, and I looked at him. He looked back at me, then down at Hannah. She bounced her doll along on its feet, pretending it was walking over her papa's knee. "You know where that is? Westcott? San Jacinto County? It's the piney woods." I nodded and stopped fidgeting. He watched me settle back in the chair, and he seemed satisfied by it, like he wanted me to stay and listen, wanted to tell me for some reason. "Cova, she'd come from the blacklands. Up close to Waco and there. Not too many trees, you understand. She wasn't used to them. It was the fall of the year. I'd been clearing some new land, grubbing stumps, back-busting work I don't ever care to do again. And one day I come up to the house for a bite, and there was Cova out in the yard with a rake in her hand." He let out a little laugh. "She had her a pile. Oak leaves and sweet gum and pine straw. She never even looked up. She just kept saying, 'All these leaves.' Kind of like a chant, over and over. 'All these leaves.' I could see right then something had gone wrong with her. She had always been kind of frail."

He glanced out at Quintus, tumbling and wrestling with the little dog, outside the yard fence now. "Watch you don't get into that ant bed," he said, louder, and Quintus rose up to get his bearings. The dog didn't stop, though, and charged the boy. Quintus laughed out and fell over backwards.

Andy turned his attention again to me. I didn't know what I should say so I sat still. Hannah walked her doll along the edge of the glider now. His hand came down to stroke her hair. "She kept after them leaves. No matter what I did, I couldn't get her to stop it. She went on and on for days. Morning, noon, and night. She had her a pile." He grunted another light laugh and shook his head. "And then she got to talking nonsense nobody could understand anymore. Hannah wasn't but a baby in the cradle. The doctor said having her might've been the thing that put Cova over the edge. He said childbearing gives some women the hysteria."

"I've never heard of that."

"Well, neither had I." He pushed the glider and it creaked into motion, soughing on rusty springs. Absently, he fingered Hannah's soft curls, and watched Quintus play with his dog. He seemed through with his story now, but I could find no polite way to get up and leave.

I said, "So you took her to Austin?"

"No. I took her to her folks. They didn't know what to do with her either. And then her mother got sick and passed away real sudden. By then, I'd lost my farm."

"I'm sorry."

My words startled a look from him, like he wasn't accustomed to hearing pity, or didn't want it. I couldn't tell which. "It had been coming. It wasn't Cova's fault. Wasn't anybody's fault. But I didn't have a place for her after that, and so I took her to Austin. To the expert insanity doctors they got there. They don't know about a cure. Say sometimes a mind will just snap back in gear without warning. They don't know if that'll be the way with Cova or not. They say we just got to wait and see." He gave a smile and bunched up his chin as if to say that's the way things go. "And so I had that freighter, and I heard about Mr. Williams's pottery factory in McDade, so I came here. Your daddy had this place for rent. And now I'm about to lose it, too."

"No, you're not." I felt I had to offer him some words of reassurance. "We won't let that happen."

He snorted, and his shoulders shook like he was laughing but no sound came out. He kept pushing the glider with his foot. A smile played bitter on his face like it had before, back on the road. "You can't stop it. There's got to be some fundamental changes in the way we run our government. That's the only hope for a man like me. It's why I speak out. I want folks to know things have got to change from the ground up. The farmers know it already. They know it takes more work and more land every year to earn the same as they had ten years ago. Or even last year. And they know it's men like Louis Bassist putting the squeeze on us all." He made his hand into a fist as if he was mashing something in his palm. "You know how much I owe that man?"

I shifted, uncomfortable. I wasn't used to people being so frank. Especially about money matters.

"Four hundred and eighty-seven dollars," he said. "Four hundred and eighty-seven dollars for two hundred ninety-three dollars worth of goods. Do you know how much interest that is?"

I shook my head. "I'm no good at arithmetic . . ."

"Over sixty percent. And what if that had been medicine I needed for little Hannah here, or Quint, instead of my mule?" Hannah, hearing her name, looked up at her papa.

"Oh, surely then he'd have given it to you," I said.

"Don't be so sure. Do you know how long it's been since I had a dollar to put in my pocket? A dollar that wasn't already promised to somebody before it was ever earned? Just one puny little dollar for my pocket. To let it sit in there and jingle around and feel good for a little bit. I've had my fill of empty pockets." He stopped speaking, realizing he'd moved clear out to the edge of the glider. He settled back, laughed, let out a breath like steam.

"Pardon me, Miz O'Barr." He chuckled again, opened his hands wide. They'd been balled into fists. I could see the half-moon crevices his fingernails had made in his flesh. "I tend to get worked up."

"I've noticed that." I smiled. "It's Dellie. Dellie's the name I use. You can call me that if you'd like."

He took in another breath, and gave me a genuine smile this time, one like he smiled that day at the Confederates' Reunion, full of sunshine and the earth, and heartfelt. "Well then, Dellie," he said, and the way my name came so easy to him, I knew he'd known it already. "I apologize for sitting here complaining to you when you've just lost your daddy. There's no trouble so grieving as a loss in the family."

"Oh . . . well . . ." I wanted suddenly to tell him I didn't know how I felt with Papa gone. That there was just this emptiness inside me about it, as empty as the water glass in my hand. "You met my brother Dane."

"The one from Parker County." He said it like he was just remembering. "He's an Alliance member, and now he votes the People's Party."

"He does?"

Andy nodded. "We talked about it a great deal. He wouldn't mind farming this land I've got. He didn't say so but he feels it's his due."

"He told me he didn't want anything that was Papa's."

"He told me that, too, but I don't think he means it. He said they had a falling out, your daddy and him. He loaned a friend a bull without asking?"

"He did?" I thought about that big Durham bull and the tick fever that killed him. "To who?"

"He didn't tell me. I figured you knew."

"If I'd have thought about it." I looked at Andy Ashland and felt funny with him knowing these private matters about my family. And yet, it seemed all right, too. His face was wide and open, eyes as clear as a crystal rain. I trusted him somehow, and I was tempted to tell him other, more intimate secrets: about Sister and how she'd run off with the man she loved. About how Papa had arranged my marriage to Daniel without me even realizing it until Dane pointed it all out to me. About Dr. Rutherford's suspicions that I had a barren womb. For a second, I felt a little crazy and out of control.

I reined myself in and stood. "I suppose I really *should* go. I know you must have work to do and the day's getting away." I set the glass on the chair, and tucked my pocketbook under my arm.

He walked me to the buggy, and helped me up to the seat. "I'm obliged to you for that medicine," he said, when I was settled. "You're a real fine lady to've done that."

I smiled and clicked at Cintha to go. Quintus and his dog came to race me to the gate, and then they stood on the road waving me goodbye. I looked back and even Hannah waved from the porch. Mr. Ashland—Andy—had already vanished from sight.

5

The Masonic Celebration was held on what the ladies of town liked to call the plaza, but it wasn't as fancy as that. It wasn't even really a park, but just an open piece of ground beneath the old hanging tree in the center of town. Whenever the weeds there got too high, one farmer or another would come with his draft mule and his mower, or else old man Dempsey would stake out a couple of his goats. Mr. Westbrook had built the barbecue pit out of brick from the Elgin kiln. And the Sons of Hermann had made some picnic tables and a few benches. There were even some lantern poles, but hardly anyone ever had a nighttime gathering. Even though McDade now had a population of two thousand, the town still closed down at dusk—except for the saloons, of course, and we had five of them now, counting the one out Paint Creek Road for colored folks. Five despite the Temperance Society's efforts to vote McDade dry.

I went without a new hat to the Celebration. It seemed a frivolous thing to me after my visit with Andy Ashland. I refreshed the flowers on one of my old ones, and no one seemed to notice the difference. Daniel surely didn't.

Priscilla had waited until the last possible moment for Nathan to ask to escort her, before she accepted the invitation of Clarence Bright, the harness maker in town. She hoped it would cause Nathan a pang of jealousy to see her with another man. She did not, or would not, understand that a person had to care for someone first in order to get jealous. She had taken special pains with her appearance, winding her hair up and over her hat so that you could hardly tell where the hairdo left off and the hat began. Her dress was pale ivory organza, with lace trimmings and leg-o'-mutton sleeves, made by Eleanora Heartson, the best dressmaker we had in town. Priscilla was easily the most handsome girl there, yet Nathan, in his indifference, played baseball all afternoon and showed no sign that he even noticed her at all.

Clarence Bright, on the other hand, was an attentive escort, more attentive than she wanted, fetching her cold drinks and plates of refreshments, finding her a comfortable place to sit out of the sun. He had spruced himself up in a stylish suit of white linen with a heavy gold watch chain falling across his vest. His tie pin had the Freemasonry insignia—the square and compass— set off with a tiny diamond that winked in the sun. But still, underneath all his finery, he smelled like harness leather, mineral oil, and wood shavings. It was not unpleasant, but Priscilla seemed embarrassed by him just the same.

"I will die, I will just die if he brings me another glass of lemonade," she whispered to me behind her fan when he had gone off again to the refreshment table.

I said, smiling, "But he's so thrilled to have you on his arm."

"Oh," she groaned. "I don't want him to think I'm enjoying all this attention."

"I should think you'd be flattered," I said, and I nodded toward where Daniel stood huddled in conversation with J.T. Craddock. J.T. was a second-degree Mason and wore his apron. Daniel had on his dove gray Sunday suit with the double-breast, satin-back vest, polite and refined. Tasteful. Mother claimed he'd learned a lot about spit-and-polish hobnobbing in Austin through those years. "Just look at me," I said. "I could be alone for all a stranger could tell."

Priscilla fanned her face. "Dellie? Are the two of you all right? You just don't seem normal lately. You'd tell me if something were wrong, wouldn't you?"

How could I explain the pall that had sunk around Daniel and me since Dane's visit when we didn't even speak of it ourselves? But her question made me wonder exactly what she meant by normal. What had been normal for us before? I couldn't seem to even remember.

"You know I would," I answered hurriedly, and I let another quick look skim Daniel's way. "J.T.'s having some sort of legal trouble and he's after Daniel for some advice, that's all. And you know Daniel, advice is what he loves to give." I tried to make it sound light, but Priscilla didn't look convinced. She started to speak again but then she spied Clarence on his way back with another glass of lemonade for her.

"Oh, for heaven's sake. I'm going to float away before he's finished." Then she smiled and reached out her hand toward him as he approached. "Why, thank you, Clarence."

"I saw you were getting hot," he said, but he was the one who looked hot. Sweat had beaded up on his chin and forehead, and dripped down behind his sideburns.

"Hold still," a voice said, and of course we all looked around. Daphne stood with her Kodak camera aimed our way. I'd seen her taking pictures earlier, of the fire brigade in their snappy new uniforms with the bibbed-front shirts and flat band hats; of John Meyers, the Worshipful Master of the McDade lodge, sopping sauce on chicken halves over at the barbecue fire, all done up in his Mason regalia. Clarence, Priscilla, and I stayed stock-still for an instant while Daphne got her shot.

"There," she said and smiled. "I'm making an album for Jeremy." She meant J.T. She was the only one who called him by his given name. Half the time people didn't know who she was talking about.

Clarence stepped over for a closer look at the photographic camera in her hand. It was the newest model, as small as a loaf of bread. She let him hold it and turned to me. "I need your help, Dellie."

"Not me, too?" Priscilla said. She would have done anything just then to get away from poor, doting Clarence.

For a moment, Daphne was flustered. Then she laughed, uncertainly, and pulled me away from the others. This would annoy Priscilla, I knew, but Clarence took my place on the bench beside her. He still had the camera and pointed it right at her face.

Daphne handed me a sheet of paper and a pencil. "Will you help us find lodging for Professor Mauney's teachers? Go around and ask the people here if anyone can spare a room or a bed for six weeks. Stress that it's only for six weeks. Most folks won't mind the inconvenience for such a little while," she said, and left me, but I was glad she'd given me something to do other than stand beside Priscilla and Clarence or watch Daniel ignore me.

For the rest of the afternoon, I wrote down names on the sheet of paper. Names and numbers. I put me and Daniel down for two of the teachers. Mother one. Mrs. Slater agreed to take one, and so on. Professor Mauney was putting on a summer normal school at the McDade Academy, and all thirty teachers enrolled would need lodging since most could not afford a hotel room for six weeks, even if we had that much hotel space in McDade, which we didn't. The *Mentor* had run an announcement asking for volunteers, but apparently not many people had come forth on their own.

Besides being an educator, Professor Mauney was the local organ and piano tuner. He had done evangelical work until his singing voice failed him. Now he taught classes at the academy and was said to be one of the finest teachers in the state. He had come from New Jersey in '89, the year the academy was finished, and the rumor was, he'd come by bicycle. I didn't believe that to be true but I understood how such gossip flourished. Professor

Mauney rode his bicycle everywhere, even to visit his lady friend in Paige, a round-trip of some twenty-eight miles.

Professor Mauney did not involve himself in soliciting lodgings for his thirty teachers. He kept to a large group of men talking politics out under the big oak tree that dominated the public square. Several men who were running for office in the next election were using this day for a bit of campaigning. For instance, since our sheriff, George Davis, was up for a second term, he'd come over from Bastrop to pay us a visit, something he rarely did under normal circumstances. We could always count on seeing a lot of him, though, in an election year. Also, we had Duvane Seawell and Cecil Strong both running for mayor on the Democratic ticket, Mr. Seawell being the incumbent. Several times the arguing between these two, and some of the others around, reached such a fevered pitch that the ears of the ladies standing nearby perked up. Then one or two would walk over quietly and take hold of her bellowing man's arm, exchanging smiles and pleasantries with the men in the crowd, until order and civility were once more restored.

After I had filled up the sheet of paper Daphne had given me, I grew bored with the whole gathering, even with all the activity going on around me. Daniel was still deep in his conversation with J.T. They both gave me a dismissing smile when I walked up to them, so I wandered over to sit with Mother. She didn't need my company either.

At first, she had protested a little overly much about the impropriety of a woman in her situation being seen at such a social gathering so soon. But it hadn't taken much convincing to change her mind. She'd worn her blackest watered silk, a hat in the latest style, tilted so far forward it looked as if it might fall over onto the bridge of her nose, and with a new type of veiling of big, fancy dots so close together they seemed injurious to her eyesight. I noticed she strained to recognize whoever spoke to her. Practically the whole entire choir from the Baptist church had gathered around her, all of them in deep sympathy for her mourning.

Mrs. Browder, the choir director, grabbed me before I could get away, and said, "We all miss your papa so much, God rest his soul." I thanked her and wandered on, and tried to remember a single time I had ever seen Papa and Mrs. Browder speak.

Nathan and a handful of his teammates, including Jack Nash, our town marshal, and the official umpire when we played games at home, were pitching a baseball around out in the street. Not a real contest, but they had removed their jackets and had a crowd around them watching. Jinsy McCarty and Lottie Matson were amongst them. Jinsy hollered at me and said, "I just love your dress, Dellie," but I knew she was only being nice to me since I was Nathan's sister. That was something I had gotten wise to after so many years. Priscilla Slater was only one in a legion of girls who did not interest Nathan.

It was worrisome to Mother—Nathan's lack of interest in females. When he was a boy she had teased him about his fair features, saying he should have been born a girl with that face of his. Now I think she feared she had spoken too loud and too often. Yet there was nothing at all womanish about Nathan. He didn't tend to himself in the mirror or even appear to know how handsome he'd turned out. There was just this single-mindedness about him when it came to work. He was like Daniel in that way—purely loving to work. It pleased Mother, but was of some concern to me. Baseball was the only leisure he participated in, and even plying the bat was like work to him. He pushed himself to hit longer and farther balls. When he wasn't out working with the cattle, he was back behind the barn swinging his heavy, black-painted bat at stones or dirt clods.

Just at that moment, Nathan hit a high fly ball that sailed

across two streets and into Weede Millage's chicken yard. Everyone started laughing and catcalling, beckoning for Nathan to go fetch his own ball since Weede Millage's rooster was known for his sharp talons and for his mean disposition. He would attack anyone that set foot inside his yard. One time he'd gotten loose and, for a few minutes, had put the whole town in terror, until the Widow Millage came with a black blinding cloth she threw over his head to catch him.

Priscilla and Clarence had moved across to sit on the steps outside Sapling's Grocery with the rest of the crowd watching the baseball players. She waved at me to come over, but for some reason, I pretended not to see her. I didn't mean to be rude, but I had tired of the whole day and was ready to go home. It had me feeling moody, thinking of Nathan and how sure he seemed of himself, of the new distance between me and Daniel, of the low-toned, pitying pitch of Mrs. Browder's voice when she spoke of Papa.

And then I spotted Andy Ashland, clear across on the other side of town. He wasn't taking part in the Masonic Celebration at all, but was coming out of Bassist's store, walking down the gallery. He held something in his hands, and I saw it was newspapers. He had on cotton-sacking farm britches but with a bright white shirt and the straw hat on his head. He walked quickly and with purpose to the end of Bassist's gallery. He stepped down and crossed Main, and I recognized his destination—the printing office of the *Plaindealer* above Flaxman's store. I recalled him saying he worked there on Wednesdays and Saturdays, and today was Saturday.

The idea struck me that if the *Mentor* could carry an item about Professor Mauney's teachers needing room and board, perhaps the *Plaindealer* would, too. I started across the street, watching Andy walk toward the door to the newspaper office.

While I was there, I could ask him how his sick mule was doing. I could also ask after his children; I didn't see them anywhere about. There were all manner of subjects I could find to talk to him about if I tried hard enough. I might even mention some of the campaigning I'd overheard, and have a laugh about the arguments, tell him that women already had the vote, they just didn't fill out a ballot.

Main Street was dusty, and the wind blew a little. Enough I felt some grit swirl up under my skirts and cling to my stockings. Andy didn't see me coming. He went in the door to the office, which was situated between Mr. Flaxman's Clothiers and Van Burkleo's Notions.

The space between the two businesses wasn't large enough for anything but the flight of stairs going straight up. At the top, I came to another door, and I could hear Andy and some other man talking. I paused, uncertain, then I let my knuckles connect with the frosted-glass piece. It rattled in its frame.

Willie Betts opened the door. He looked at me as if I were a ghost. I was surely a stranger to him. I doubted he would remember me from the Veterans' Reunion. We hadn't spoken. He wore an ink-stained printer's apron. Even the shirt underneath was smudged with black, though he wore sleeve protectors to his elbows.

"Yes?" he said.

"Is this the office of the *Plaindealer*?" I asked. My voice sounded tinny and childish.

"It is."

Suddenly, the door opened up wider and Andy was standing there, to the rear and left of Mr. Betts. When Andy saw me, he let out a friendly laugh. "Well. Look who's here. I thought that sounded like you." He took my arm and pulled me inside. Mr. Betts shut the door behind me.

It startled me to have Andy's hand on my arm. I may have jumped slightly. At any rate, he let go. I stood there, foolishly shifting, glancing around at the layout tables, the press, the stack of clean newspapers on top of a battered desk. The air smelled close, and sharply of ink, even with the three open windows.

"I came to place an advertisement," I said.

"A what?" Mr. Betts said.

I looked at Andy. He was smiling. "You want to contribute something to the paper?"

"Yes. A social item. We need to—or rather, Professor Mauney at the academy is trying to find lodging for the thirty teachers coming for the Summer Normal School that begins the twenty-fourth of June." I was relieved to have the whole thing out. Andy kept smiling at me as if I hadn't spoken.

"What?" Mr. Betts said, seeming confused.

I looked at both of them in turn. "Can't I put that in your paper?"

"A social item?" Mr. Betts didn't act as though he believed me.

"Why, sure," Andy said. "Why not. If we can print the stud fees for Early Horner's bull, we can print this."

Andy moved to the desk, picked up a pen, and dipped it into an open ink jar. He wrote down everything I said, and I couldn't help but notice that he spelled all the words correctly. His penmanship was bold and flourishing, almost feminine. His straw hat lay in front of me beside the stack of newspapers on the desk. I had the nearly irresistible urge to reach with my finger and touch the tiny feather stuck down in the tan hatband that encircled the crown.

"Who should they contact?" he said and I jumped again, startled. He gave me another grin, this one quieter.

"The academy." I thought about the questions I had planned to ask him, about the mule and his children. I thought about his poor mad wife raking fallen leaves. He wrote down "contact school" and sharply underlined the words. Then he raised up and seemed about to say something else. His eyes were gentle, smiling, interested, if only in the oddity of my being there.

Just at that moment, the door burst open. It flew against the wall so hard, the knob chipped off some plaster. And Mr. Bassist stood there on the landing, red in the face and clutching a wad of newsprint in his large hand. I could hear his breath.

"Ashland! You trying to start a war with me?" He was so angry he couldn't even say the first word of his sentences. His German accent had flooded into his pronunciations. He shook his thick first finger. "Will never win. Hear me? Never! Never!"

He threw the wad of newsprint down at his feet and stepped on it, grinding the sole of his black, square-toed walking shoes into the paper. He glared, huffed loudly, then went back downstairs. The door at the bottom slammed hard.

The office was silent, so silent the sounds from the Masonic Celebration outside on the square came ringing in through the open windows. Then both of them laughed out at the same time. And they kept at it for some little while, until Andy flopped down in the rolling desk chair and wiped at his eyes.

Mr. Betts got hold of himself then, too, and said, "I thought for a minute there, he might spontaneously combust right before our eyes."

"Or pull out a pistol," Andy said.

"Don't joke about that. Next time he might do it." Mr. Betts took out a handkerchief and blew his nose.

"What did you do to him?" I said and both of them looked at me as if they just remembered my presence.

Mr. Betts stuffed his handkerchief down in his vest pocket and jerked up a paper from the stack on the desk. He stuck it in my hands. "Bottom of the page."

I had never before seen a copy of the *Plaindealer*. It was one of those newspapers where most of the articles are written and printed elsewhere, leaving just a few spaces here and there for local news. Boilerplate, it was called. And it was easy enough to tell which were articles locally done and which were not. The typestyles didn't match. Just underneath the masthead was the slogan "Equal Rights to All, Special Privilege to None."

Down at the bottom of the page was the article about Mr. Bassist and how he had refused to sell Andy a bottle of horse expectorant. It was also in there about the gross difference in Bassist's cash and credit prices, and that the interest he charged amounted to over 60 percent. The headline read A WARNING TO HONEST FARMERS and there was some Scripture quoted from the Book of Nehemiah: "Restore, I pray you, to them, even this day, their lands, their vineyards, their oliveyards, and their houses, also the hundredth *part* of the money, and of the corn, wine, and the oil, that ye exact of them."

I lifted my face from the paper and saw Andy watching me read. I was suddenly, inexplicably afraid for him. "Why did you write this? Didn't you know it would make him angry?"

"Of course he knew it," Mr. Betts said.

"What if he makes you pay your debt to him right now? In full." I was still speaking to Andy. "He could do that if he wanted."

"Can't squeeze blood from a turnip," Andy said.

"Are you *trying* to stir up trouble?"

Mr. Betts laughed at my question. "Yeah. He is. You bet he is."

"When it needs stirring up," Andy answered. "Don't you think folks oughta know the way Louis Bassist conducts his business? Right from the outset, so maybe they won't start trading with him?"

"They're all already trading with him," Willie Betts said.

"There's other merchants around," Andy said.

Betts shrugged as if they'd had this argument before. He stepped around me and went over to one of the tables where he had some work laid out. "You know I'm behind you, Andy." He bent closer over the table. I couldn't see what he was doing. Nor did I care. Andy was staring at me with an expression I couldn't read.

To look at him, no one would ever suspect he had a rebellious spirit, that he could write a fine hand and compose articles for a newspaper complete with Bible verse. Or that he could get up before a crowd of people and hold them just by what he had to say. He looked like such a plain man, an everyday man, the kind of man you'd hardly notice walking on the street.

"You took this paper down to him yourself, didn't you?" I said. "I saw you coming out of his store."

He raised his eyebrows. "I try not to talk behind a man's back."

Across the room, Willie Betts chuckled.

I took a deep breath. I still couldn't believe it that someone would deliberately pick a fight with Mr. Bassist. He owned most of the downtown district, and he furnished about three hundred families in the area. And I had never—until Andy Ashland— heard an unkind word spoken against him.

I reached for the slip of paper where Andy had written my advertisement. "Perhaps you shouldn't print this," I said.

He grabbed my hand. "We want to."

I drew away from his grasp, and held my hand to my chest, thinking I should have never come up here. It was foolish of me and impulsive; brash. I felt I had stepped into something that had nothing whatever to do with me. I moved backward toward the door.

He picked up the slip of paper and held it out at me. "All right. Take it."

"I just don't think I understand all this, Mr. Ashland." I took the slip of paper, turned around and walked out of the office, closing the door behind me. I was halfway down the stairs before he came bounding out the door.

"Wait there," he said, coming down on me fast, his knees bobbing out to either side. He got almost level with me and stopped on the step just above where I stood. He seemed out of breath, more than he should have been from just that short flight of stairs. "I thought we said we were past all that mister and missus stuff." He moved around so that he was below me, and also barring my way to the door. "I don't know your situation or how free you are to—well—to roam about. But I wondered if it would be possible for me to—" He stopped abruptly, seemed uncertain suddenly, and flustered.

"For you to what?"

He shook his head as if to erase what he had already said and start over. "You said you didn't understand, so I thought . . . there's a meeting at Fletcher's Hall Thursday night. You know where that is?"

"The old Grange hall, yes. What meeting?"

"The Populists. We have meetings there every Thursday. I thought you might like to come to one. There's always lots of women. Some you probably already know."

"What happens at these meetings?"

"We talk, and sing." He smiled. "Some people bring chickens to sell, and sometimes butter. Or maybe they want to complain about something, or just visit with their neighbors. It's different every time."

"My papa was a member of the Grange years ago."

"I told you once, your papa was a good man."

"He called you a Socialist."

He laughed. "We never talked politics that I can recall."

"He wanted Nathan to evict you because of it."

The lines on his forehead deepened for an instant but his smile never went away. "Come if you can. Next Thursday. About sundown."

"I'll think about it," I mumbled and continued down the stairs.

When I got to the bottom, he said, "And bring your husband."

I glanced quickly up at him and pushed out the door. I was glad the collar of my dress was still stiff and new. Otherwise he might've seen how red my neck had turned.

6

As it happened, on Tuesday Daniel left for Rockport down on the coast. He had business with the packing house there, but he would be back by Friday. "Saturday at the latest," he said as he told me goodbye. He left a kiss on my forehead. I felt it there for some time after, like Tante Lena and Sinclair's cross of ash on the first day of Lent.

I didn't tell him about the Thursday meeting, although by the time he left I had decided I would attend. I didn't want him to talk me out of it, or worse, forbid me to go. I wasn't sure if he would go so far as that. He had never forbidden me anything, but this felt different somehow. Politics had never been of interest or concern to me, so what reason could I possibly give for wanting to hear the Populists at the old Grange hall out Fletcher Road? I wasn't even sure myself.

I considered asking Priscilla to go, but she would also be suspicious of my sudden political interest. There wasn't anyone I knew, or who knew me, that wouldn't be. So I made the decision to go alone. And right from the moment I made such a bold choice, I worried over it. There were so many things to consider.

Fletcher Road was rough, and since I would be coming home after dark, the four-wheel spring-seat buggy would be more practical than my little two-wheel gig, which tended to hit every bump and crater that Cintha missed. But with the buggy, I would need Scamp and Hasty, and I didn't know what excuse I would give to Sinclair about why I needed the team. I wondered if I should have Tante Lena make a special dish for me to take. I had forgotten to ask Andy about food. And I wondered, Whatever in the world did a lady wear to a political meeting?

The day Daniel left, I spent all afternoon inspecting my wardrobe. I was afraid a suit might be too dressy, and yet a street dress or a wrapper seemed much too casual for evening. I pulled out a simple shirtwaist of peach dotted Swiss with white buttons and a white sash. I couldn't make up my mind about a bustle. In the end I decided on a lightweight one of woven wire mesh, the latest style from Paris that I'd bought at Miss Minerva's the last time I shopped in Bastrop. My hair, I knotted up inside a flat rim hat, after I'd removed all the ribbons and frills. I didn't know exactly who these Populists were, but from what all I'd heard Andy say, I doubted I'd see many wearing fancy flowered hats.

Who the Populists were I found out as soon as I came in sight of the old Grange hall. As it turned out, I knew nearly all of them: The Birdwells from over across the Middle Yegua. Joe Grossner, who'd been our neighbor long ago, and was Andy's neighbor now. Wes Peterson, a farmer older than Papa, and his whole large family, sons and daughters and grandchildren. The Peelers, the Tackaberrys, the Specks, the Dillons. All were driving their farm wagons, their buggies, or on horseback. There was a regular traffic snarl at the hitch-rails on the road and along the side of the hall. And everyone carried their own buckets of water and cups or canteens. I had come empty-handed.

I started not to stop—I had lost my nerve at the last minute—but Quintus spied me. He was outside playing with some of the other children, and he jumped up as if he'd been waiting for me to appear. He left his playmates and raced inside the hall.

I pulled back on the horses. I had told Sinclair I was going to take Mother to visit some friends of hers up near Knobs Springs and needed the larger buggy. He believed the lie, but I'd had a time convincing him I didn't need him to drive us. He knew I wasn't much of a driver when it came to managing a span of horses. Scamp and Hasty knew, too, and didn't seem to even feel the yank of the lines on their harnesses. It was Andy who finally got them stopped, running up, saying, "Whoa there! Whoa!" He took firm hold of Scamp's collar. Quintus came running, too.

"You couldn't convince your husband to come?" Andy was wearing his overalls, a white shirt, no collar. Even in my plainest clothes, I felt overdressed.

"He's out of town," I said before I realized that was probably the most inappropriate answer I could have given. Proper ladies did not let it be commonly known when their husbands left town. But then proper ladies did not go about unescorted either. Especially not at night.

"Well, I'm glad you could make it," he said and helped me to the ground. "Quint, show Miz O'Barr inside." Andy got up in the buggy seat and drove the team off easily. I watched him head for the end of the line of tied-down farm wagons.

"You look mighty pretty, ma'am," Quintus said to me as he hooked his arm through mine. I almost laughed except he seemed so sincere. I let him lead me inside, just as if he were a full-grown man instead of a seven-year-old boy that barely reached above my elbow.

Just beside the door was a small table with a box marked DONATIONS. It had a slot carved in the top so I dropped in a dollar. My dollar made a lonely thump as it hit the bottom of the box. Inside the room, chairs and benches sat in a haphazard way, not neatly arranged like in a schoolroom or in a regular lecture hall. Folks were already in groups, chattering and milling around. Merle Grossner spoke to me, asked after Mother. So did Mattie Peterson. Both of them looked curious at me being there, and at Quintus holding on to my arm.

I began to wish I hadn't come, and wondered how I could leave without calling any more attention to myself. I knew I'd already caused a stir coming unescorted, though no one let on that they had noticed. I began to plan what I would say to Daniel—*I went to a meeting of the Populists while you were gone. Just took the notion.* What had I been thinking of, believing I could keep my coming here a secret? As if I expected these people to be foreigners from another country instead of friends and neighbors I'd known my whole life.

Quintus tugged me along through the crowd. He led me to a cluster of chairs near the front of the hall where Hannah sat in the lap of the same woman I'd seen her with at the Veterans' Reunion. Hannah was sprawled, almost asleep. The woman looked up at me and smiled.

"I'm Gretta Betts," she said. "Willie's wife. You're Andy's friend, aren't you?"

I stiffened for a moment, until I realized she meant nothing lewd by the word *friend*. Only kindness shone on Gretta Betts's round face. It was a relief, a balm almost, to look into her gentle eyes.

I told her my name and sat down next to her in the chair Quintus pulled around for me. We visited for a brief moment. She complimented my dress. I noticed how she patted Hannah's arm, and bounced her a little, soothing her off to sleep. They seemed so familiar, and Hannah so at ease in Gretta's arms. Watching them gave me the tiniest pang of envy.

The meeting started when Rose Barbee took a seat behind the upright piano at the front of the hall. She began chording hymns and the people began to find places to sit. The front floor was for the children and Quintus left us to get up there with his playmates.

The Reverend Barbee, the preacher at the new Methodist church, got up before the crowd to start the singing, "Nearer My God to Thee," and then an old slave spiritual, "There's No Hiding

Place Down Here." The words were all different than in church, though, and I was instantly lost. I couldn't keep up, not even with the chorus. Nor could I make out what anyone was saying until Andy swung a chair up beside me and sat down. He smiled and leaned in close so I could hear the words as he sang. I saw he was clean shaven. He smelled of bay rum.

The songs were all about the same things: unfair taxing, un-equal money, hard times, and voting the People's Party ticket. Only the tunes were familiar to me. My mind wandered. My eyes, too. Down to the scuffed toe of his oil grain boots, to the tattered hem of Hannah's little dress, to the cottonseed falling out from under the skirt of the lady three seats over from us, leaking silent and steady from her homemade bustle onto the floor behind her.

Willie Betts came from somewhere at the back of the hall and threaded his way up front to stand beside Reverend Barbee. When the current song, a version of "When the Roll Is Called Up Yonder," ended, Mr. Betts raised up his hands. I glanced at Gretta. He had her attention. Hannah was sound asleep.

"Welcome, folks," Willie Betts said, and several in the back called out a greeting as if he were talking to them specifically. He scanned the crowd. I thought his eyes stopped on me for a second before they moved on. "I'm proud to see some new faces here this evening," he said, a little more of the country creeping into his voice than I remembered from the day at the newspaper office. He said, "We asked for you all to bring a friend and I can see you did that."

I flushed and let a glance go at Andy. He wasn't paying the least attention to me. He had his full concentration on Willie Betts, but I thought I understood now Gretta's choice of words earlier when she called me Andy's friend. They were recruiting. Her husband kept on talking:

"Next time we ask that you bring *two* friends to meet us. Let them see who we are, that we're Populists straight and plain, without any trimmings or exceptions. And that we intend to continue to fire hot shot into the two old parties." This got some applause and horse whistles. He reached down deep in the pocket of his pants and kind of smiled. His hand came out with a few wadded-up slips of paper. "Speaking of business—" Everyone laughed, and he smoothed out one of the slips, held it in front of him as far as his arm would reach. Looking down his nose, he read, "Brother Murphy has a milk-cow that needs freshening if anybody has a bull in season." This brought another titter of laughter, from the ladies mostly. "Says here he can't pay in money but he'll change work with you at cotton-pulling time." He glanced out into the crowd, searching for the man who had written the note. "You'd do that anyway, wouldn't you, Brother Murphy?"

Someone in the back called, "Sure thing, but I'll have more energy if my cow's giving milk."

More people laughed. I did, too. I was beginning to relax. I looked at Andy. He was not even smiling. He reminded me of a runner in a footrace, all knotted muscle and nerve, waiting for the starter's gun.

Willie Betts smoothed out another paper. "We got somebody wanting to know what we're going to do about helping Brother Browning chop his cotton. Since he's been laid up with a busted leg, the weeds have taken his farm over." He wadded up the note. "I don't know who wrote this, but consider it done. A bunch of us'll be over at the Browning place Saturday morning, bright and early. Won't we?"

Shouts of agreement came from all over the room, and Willie Betts smoothed out the third sheet of paper. He read it to himself, slowly, deliberately, then he raised his shoulders, his eyes roaming the crowd.

"This person," he said, holding up the paper, "wants us to talk about a certain store merchant in town. A merchant guilty of usury, of inflated interest rates, of downright thievery. A merchant who holds the product of our sweat and labor on his ledger book and in his cash drawer."

Beside me, I felt Andy tense even tighter. I looked at him and he glanced back at me, and I knew in that split-second look that he was the one who had written the note in Willie Betts's hand, that this whole act was staged to get the subject of the meeting onto business the two of them wanted to discuss. I also understood that Andy Ashland was a man who held a grudge, and held it hard. I could barely peel my eyes off of him.

He was already perspiring, sending out bay rum as loud as wild honeysuckle in bloom. I didn't even hear the next thing Willie Betts said, but it caused Andy to bound to his feet. He stayed right where he was at first, standing in front of the chair, but he turned around to face the crowd.

He said, "How many families here tonight are being furnished by Louis Bassist? Can we get a show of hands on that? We're not counting, we just want a general idea."

I didn't look around to see the response. Since he was standing right beside me, I kept my head bowed, studying my hands in my lap, and tried to remain as inconspicuous as possible. When he stepped through the chairs and people to join Willie Betts up front, I felt my shoulders loosen. I raised my face.

"It's been suggested by some that we boycott Bassist's store—"

Someone in the back said, "That won't do, Andy. Kaiser's ain't got what all we need, and everybody else in town demands cash money."

Andy nodded and held up his hand. "That's right, Seamus. We know that. Believe me, we do know. But supposing we could find a merchant that did have all the things we needed and would give us credit, too, at reasonable rates of interest?"

"You're talking co-op," somebody else said. "And that's already been tried in this county."

"And failed," another called out.

The arguments went on, with this one and that one standing up to say his piece. Some of the women spoke out, too. Mrs. Speck hollered that she was sorry Andy had been having troubles with Bassist but that it didn't concern her family's business with the store. Others said the group had to stick together, that they were all brothers and sisters with a common cause. And in the middle of all this, Tory Peeler stood up and said they were selling cotton boll fertilizer at Waker's Mills in Elgin.

Andy paced around at the front of the hall, replying to one and then the other without ever once having to stop and think over his words. He was so sure of his convictions, so frank in his manner and facial expression, that it was hard not to be won over by him, or for me, mesmerized by him. He had a strength and a cleverness about him, also a stubbornness but in a good-humored way. It was like watching a good player in Nathan's ballgames field one fly ball after another, or like Daniel's cowhands at round-up time, throwing calf after calf for ear notches and brands. After a while I hardly listened to what he said, but simply sat there admiring the lilt of his voice, the cut of his jaw, the breadth of his hands.

The truth of the matter was—though I hardly would have admitted it to myself—there was little about him that didn't please me. I didn't know why he'd caught my interest, but sitting there listening to him, watching him, I came to regard him as the almost perfect ideal of a man: gentle yet strong, simple yet deep-thinking. And if he wasn't exactly handsome, he had only to smile to make you think otherwise. His face suddenly glowed. His cheeks rounded up and dimpled in. His eyes glittered. You had either to look away from that smile, or accept wherever it might lead you.

Suddenly, squeals from Rose Barbee swelled above Andy's voice. She scrambled away from the piano, overturning the stool, pointing with one hand, pressing her cheek with the other, and all the while, squealing high-pitched and sharp.

Andy turned. The crowd in the hall began to stand. The children at the front hollered, "Snake!" and a regular stampede started for the door. I caught a flash of something slithering on the floor before Gretta and Willie Betts herded me along with the rest of the crowd. Gretta had Hannah in her arms. Hannah was crying. I searched about for Quintus. Andy was still at the front of the room, swinging a chair up and clubbing at the thing on the floor. He dodged and jumped about, like he was on top of a bed of coals.

I found Quintus and snatched hold of his hand. I dragged him through the maze of people. He looked pale and excited. We made it to the front door just as gunfire began to sing out. Some of the men had evidently been carrying pistols inside their coats, and now they were shooting up the inside of the hall.

The rush and panic died ten feet outside the door. People said, "How'd a snake get inside there?" and "It must've been curled up under Rose's feet all along." Rose herself was the only one still in tears.

In another minute, Andy came out holding the dead snake in one hand and Stan Tackaberry's forearm in the other. Both men were smiling. Stan Tackaberry held a large six-shooter down at his side. Andy said, "The Populists won another round," and he raised Mr. Tackaberry's arm like he was the victor in a prize fight.

Everyone had to see the snake then, everyone except Rose Barbee. The boys, and some of the braver girls, touched the hide. It was a rattler with a long row of buttons on its tail. Stretched from length to length, the snake reached from Andy's shoulder to the ground. Stan Tackaberry said he was going to make a belt of its hide. Andy seemed relieved to finally hand over the reptile.

"Our meetings don't usually end with such excitement," he said, coming up to me. People had begun to head toward their wagons, still chattering, most of them, about the snake. "Just stick here a minute," he said. "We're going to hit it with a lick and a promise inside and then we'll see you home."

"Oh, that isn't necessary," I said.

"Well, I say it is. It's too late and too dark for a lady to be driving home by herself."

I started to protest further but Hannah came running up, saying, "Daddy, Daddy!" like she'd just seen him after a long absence. He swung her up high and she laughed, but she was sleepy and wiped at her eyes.

"Would you go to Miz O'Barr?" he asked her and she nodded. She held out her arms to me. I was surprised by it, but I reached for her. "Maybe you wouldn't mind looking after her for a minute?" he said.

"Of course not." She had already laid her head on my shoulder.

Andy glanced around as he went toward the door. "I'll come back and holler up Quint when we're done in here."

"I'll find him," I said, but Andy was already back inside and I don't think he heard me.

"He's over there." Hannah pointed behind us. It was the first time she'd ever spoken directly to me and I felt privileged, somehow elated by her trust.

"Where?" I turned the direction she pointed.

"Over there with Jordan Betts." She pointed again to some trees out behind the hall. I saw a couple of boys running in circles over there.

"Let's go get them," I said, giving her a little heft in my arms. She was heavy. When we got closer to the boys, she began to squirm to get down. I let her and she ran immediately over to the two boys wrestling in the grass.

"Quint, you're going to rip a hole in your britches," she said and laughed and fell into the middle of them, hanging on to her brother's neck. He came up laughing, too, and tossed her off. She hit the ground hard and I gave a start, but she got back to her feet and took out after the boys.

They were having great fun, playing tag, and the night was cool and clear. The sounds of crickets and frogs singing mingled in with those of the people leaving, the whinny of a horse, the clatter of trace chains. A mule brayed.

It felt strangely familiar to me, gladsome and serene—the children's laughter, the night air, the light from inside the hall gushing out to fall on the ground. As if I were a child again myself, with all the world and long days ahead of me. As if I'd been brought back to myself by that light, that laughter, the rattle of the wagons and the voices in the night wishing one another well. And there was a longing attached to it that I didn't understand, as if whatever I needed, whatever it would take to replenish me, was right there on those grounds, in that hall, in those children and that light.

They went out one at a time, all except for a single glow that I saw came from a bull's-eye lantern which Willie Betts stepped out holding aloft. "Jordan!" he called.

Gretta walked over to me. She took hold of both my hands. "I'm so glad I got to meet you," she said, and she had a sweet smile. "I hope you'll come again."

"Don't start saying your goodbyes yet," Andy said, coming up to us. "We're going to see her home."

The Bettses and the Ashlands had come together in Andy's large teamster wagon. They got all the children settled in the back, and then Andy insisted he would drive my team. I protested but he said, with a laugh, "I think you'd better let me. I saw how well you handled them before."

My protest was only for appearance's sake anyway, so I gave in fairly easily. I was glad to have him with me in the buggy. It was wicked of me, but I very much wanted his company right then. I couldn't tell what he thought of me. On the one hand, he was attentive; but on the other, he was the perfect gentleman and gave no sign that he saw me as anything other than the wife of another man. I suspected his interest in me was merely as a possible convert to his cause of Populism, and yet, not knowing for sure was part of the pleasure.

We were the last ones on the road, and he dropped the buggy back a good ways to keep the dust, from the big wagon ahead, out of our throats. Before we were out of sight of the hall, he wanted to know what I had thought of the meeting, and "It was interesting" wasn't answer enough for him.

"What was interesting? What part particularly?" He kept his face toward the road, which was treacherous with potholes and washouts, especially by night. He had lit the lamp before we started off, but its light was paltry and dull.

"The songs," I said, answering him. I wanted to talk about something else. I wanted to know of the school he'd gone to, what his parents were like, if he had brothers or sisters. I wanted to know his favorite color. "I've decided I think women should have the vote," I said.

He laughed. "That's the one thing we didn't talk about tonight."

"No, but I've been thinking about it, and I should get to vote when I'm twenty-one just like a man can. It's ridiculous to exclude one half of the adult population just on the basis of their sex. And those women—Mrs. Peeler and some of the others—they are every bit as intelligent as their husbands. As any man, for that matter."

He gave me a quick glance and I thought I must have impressed him with my strong opinion on the matter. Or maybe I'd gone too far, I couldn't tell. Most of the men in my experience didn't like for a woman to speak her mind quite so forthrightly.

"When is that?" he said.

"When is what?"

"Your twenty-first birthday?"

"Next year. In February."

He nodded and guided the team around a particularly large crater in the road. Our shoulders jostled together. "I don't think we'll get the laws changed by then." He gave a little chuckle.

"Well, no." I laughed, too, and felt giddy, and a little foolish, talking of things that had never before crossed my mind.

"You're young," he said.

"Does it make a difference?"

"A difference?" He looked across at me, and lingered a little longer than before. "We're happy to have anybody join us, no matter what their age, or their sex, or religious beliefs or anything else. All you have to be is human, and see the need for change. That's why we call ourselves the People's Party. We're for everybody. I hope you won't judge us by this one night. We didn't even get off into the candidates and the issues. That business with Louis Bassist came up and sidetracked us. And then the snake—"

"But you wrote that note, didn't you? The one Mr. Betts read to the people. Didn't the two of you set that up to get the subject around to Mr. Bassist?"

He whacked the driving lines. We'd come onto a smooth stretch of road, but still he didn't look away from his task. "What makes you think that?"

I didn't want to say I had only guessed it. "I was near enough I could see the handwriting. I thought I recognized it, from when you wrote down that advertisement."

He nodded, flicked a glance at me. "Nothing gets by you, does it?"

I smiled, pleased that he thought me clever. "I noticed because you write well, and I thought you'd gone to a good school, or that maybe you'd taught school somewhere yourself." He didn't commit to anything, so I kept on, more pointedly. "Did you come from an educated family? Lawyers or doctors? Some such something as that?"

"I've always been a farmer." He sounded gruff, and it seemed for a minute that this was all he would tell me. But then he added, almost with disgust, "My father was a circuit-riding Methodist preacher."

"Oh." I sat back, satisfied.

"What do you mean, 'oh'?" We hit a rough spot and the buggy swayed. His knee touched mine.

"That explains some things," I said.

"Explains what? And don't say you hear the hellfire and brimstone when I give a talk."

"Well . . ." It nearly was what I'd been about to say. He did sound a bit preacherish sometimes, but since he seemed touchy about it, I said nothing more. We rode on a ways in silence. We had fallen far behind the big wagon, though it was still up there, in sight.

"I have an idea to haul things in from some merchants in Austin," he said. "I've started taking pottery goods there for Mr. Williams from his factory. And I thought if I could take orders from folks around here and bring them back with me. . . . My wagon's coming back empty half the time anyway."

"To put Mr. Bassist out of business," I said.

"I doubt it'd do that, but maybe he'd feel it some."

"And how much would you make out of it?"

"Make?" He frowned at me. "Nothing. I'd do it for free."

That shut me up. He went on a little more about his plan, merchants he'd already talked to in Austin. They all charged interest but none as high as Mr. Bassist.

"Do you see your wife when you're there?" I said out of the blue, and embarrassed myself by asking. He didn't seem to notice. He nodded, but that was all.

The Bettses were waiting outside the gate at the house. All three of the children were asleep in the back of the big wagon. Andy wanted to drive Scamp and Hasty on into the carriage house, but I said I could manage from there. Lights were on downstairs, so I knew Tante Lena had waited up for me, which meant Sinclair would also be waiting. The dogs had begun to bark.

"Thank you," I said, feeling ill at ease now, with the Bettses there.

Andy said, "Come again next Thursday if you want to. We'll be there."

Willie Betts said, "Maybe you can talk Daniel into coming with you."

I didn't realize Willie Betts knew Daniel at all, let alone well enough for first names. And him mentioning Daniel with Andy right there, and with all the rest of it I'd been feeling that evening, caused me to drive the horses too quickly in through the gate and toward the house. Luckily, Sinclair came out, just as I expected, to greet me and to get the animals stopped for me.

"I didn't expect y'all to be so long," he said, offering me his hand to come down from the seat. "Tante Lena has done started to fret herself silly."

"I know. I'm sorry."

As soon as I stepped up on the back porch, with Daniel full in my mind, reality began to settle in. And Tante Lena scolding me for coming in so late, even in her good-natured way, didn't help my mood any at all.

7

A telegram came from Daniel on Friday morning, saying his trip to Rockport hadn't been fruitful and that he would head on down the coast a bit to Corpus Christi, where he hoped to have better success. He also said that he hoped I was not too lonely and he would see me soon.

A year ago, even six months, a wire like that one would have put me in a gloom. Now I felt relieved. It gave me more time to decide how I would approach him with my newfound interest in politics. I even thought, foolishly, that I might not even have to tell him about the meeting at all. Foolishly, because on that same Friday afternoon I had three visitors, all of them wanting to know what had possessed me and why I had been at Fletcher's Hall last night. Mother and Nathan came before Priscilla did.

Mother swished in through the front door in her stark black silk as if it were her own house she had stepped into. She marched around telling me that it was all over town that I'd been out alone the night before, that I'd been seen plainly sitting with Gretta Betts, the Populist newspaper editor's wife, that I could not deny it because Mattie Peterson and Merle Grossner had both spoken to me themselves. "They were so delighted, they said, to see that little Dellie DeLony had not forgotten her common roots. That's the very words they used, too. *Common* roots."

"I don't think they meant any insult by it," I said. Neither woman seemed the sort to start malicious gossip.

"And they used your maiden name. Just like you weren't a married lady now. And no wonder with you traipsing out after dark without an escort or a chaperone. What in the world has got into you, Dellie?"

"A chaperone?" I glanced at Nathan, who was keeping to the background, an awkward smile on his face, as if he felt this was none of his business. Knowing him, he didn't think it was Mother's either, though he would never say as much to her. For all he would stand up to Papa, he had never been as bold with Mother. Partly because at heart he was a gentleman, but also because, though she had tried her best, she had never really become our own true mother. I felt like an orphan now. I believe Nathan did, too.

Mother had always loved to talk, loved to rant and rave about one thing or another. Only without Papa to temper her with one of his searing looks, she tended to go on a little longer about things, fume a little hotter, criticize a little more, as if it had soured her in some way, getting called once again into widowhood.

I tried to follow Nathan's lead, to remain calm, though some of her words made my hair stand on end. Like when she said it was not in my girlish nature to want to involve myself in politics. That I hadn't been raised that way. Politics was a dirty business. Men's business, and that I needed to concern myself with making a good home for my husband, and with doing God's work at the church. I was truly relieved, however, that no mention was ever made of Andy. We had been the last on the road, so I realized we must not have been seen together. And I realized what a chance I had taken letting him drive me home, even with the Bettses and the children ahead of us. And even knowing how reckless I had been, just thinking of last night at all, and the buggy ride home, caused my mind to wander back to him beside me, to the smell of bay rum, to the feel of his knee warm against mine.

To keep from arguing with her, I went to the kitchen after some of the prune-filled kolaches Tante Lena had made on Tuesday.

Tante Lena was never shy about eavesdropping, and I could tell by the look she gave me she had overheard the conversation in the front room. She knew now I had lied about taking Mother visiting friends last night. And I felt the guilt of that as we laid out the pastries on a platter.

The sweets almost calmed Mother. At least they got her mind onto other matters. Slowly, almost reluctantly, she began to talk about the Summer Normal School and Professor Mauney's teachers who would be in town shortly. I hadn't thought much about them since the Masonic Celebration, and so I let Mother tell me in which rooms she thought I should put my two. She said she wanted to give a party for our two and her one so that we could all get to know each other. "Since we'll be sharing our homes with them. Maybe Lena could make up some of her kolaches. These today are especially good ones." She bit down on another one of the prune cakes, her third.

By then, Nathan had begun to pace around, looking out the windows. He had a restless nature, and was clearly ready to be off and on to something more productive, and would have been had Mother not needed him to carry her here. She had never learned to drive a team, and refused to even since Papa's death. I had already told Nathan he should hire someone for her, but he had only laughed at me and I knew why. Mother was particular when it came to whom she would let drive her buggy. Her first husband, Ross Kennedy, had been killed by a runaway team that had pitched him into the path of his own iron wagon-tires. He was dragged seventy yards before the horses lost steam and settled down.

Since Nathan was the one haunting the windows, he was the one to announce Priscilla's arrival with the little groan he let out. I heard the clatter of her buggy then, and joined him at the window. "Oh, it's Priscilla," I said and ignored his look of disgust with me, like he thought I had planned for her to arrive just now.

Mother said, "Probably to hear for herself what you were doing at the Grange hall last night. I swear, Dellie, you just don't know how unhappy your papa would be over this."

"Yes, I do," I said, unable to keep from defending myself any longer. Sinclair had come from the barn to hold Priscilla's horses. I nudged Nathan. "Go out and help her. Be kind."

He gave me another of his scolding looks and I almost laughed. Then he surprised me by doing just as I said, almost as if I were actually in charge in my own house. I smiled when he went out the door, and watched through the window as Priscilla's face lit at the sight of him.

I turned back to Mother. She was frowning, and I could see her mind was back on my going to the meeting. "Papa told me the Populists were anarchists," I said. "I *know* how he would disapprove."

"Then I don't understand this at all," Mother said. "Did you just want to disgrace him? Is that why you went?"

"How can I disgrace him, Mother? He's in his grave."

"His memory . . ." she said, then didn't finish, as if remembering he'd already disgraced himself well enough. She got a distant look on her face and pulled her shawl tighter around her shoulders. She wouldn't go without a shawl, even in the dead of summer. I watched her as she absently licked the sugar from her fingers, and I thought of Papa and how like him she was, so old-timey, so unforgiving.

I turned back to the window. "I just wanted to hear what they were all about. That's all. I was curious."

Outside, Nathan had taken Priscilla's hand and helped her down from the buggy. She was so obviously surprised and delighted, she was almost giddy with it, her voice coming through the window, high-pitched and gay, hands fluttering as Nathan released his hold on her, smiling like she'd just heard the jubilation song of a host of angels. I swear just the merest glimpse of him could make her happy for days. Or miserable. Or both. Though it had begun to seem to me that one defined the other.

She looked pretty in a white dress with gold cording and nautical designs, her hair loose without the rats and switches she normally tucked in front and behind. The sun caught the auburn highlights in each strand. I didn't see how Nathan could resist her, and he was, in fact, talking to her a little more than seemed usual. I wished I could hear about what, but it didn't really matter. He was bored, she was a diversion, and his going out there had done what I wanted. If Priscilla had come to question me about last night, Nathan's presence would addle her so much she wouldn't remember what she had come for. And with her here, Mother would stop her fussing, too. For how would it look if we were seen, Mother and me, to be bickering, even in front of Priscilla, and about poor, dead Papa just barely cold in his grave.

My luck held for the rest of the afternoon. Mother continued planning her supper party, including the Slaters now, since Priscilla had arrived. The location of the party had moved from Mother's house to mine, since I had more room. And Priscilla, flushed and glowing, began to help Mother plan the menu and the preparations, leaving me completely free to daydream. Only Nathan noticed my absence. I caught him staring at me once, and when I went to the kitchen for more kolaches and coffee, he followed. He stopped me in the hall.

"Where's Daniel?" he asked. "Wasn't he supposed to be home today?" I told him about the telegram. He nodded soberly and I realized I should've told him sooner. When Daniel was away, Nathan was in charge of everything: The ranch. Me. It was the way things worked. "If you need anything . . ." he said, letting his words trail off. He knew I didn't, and he always seemed a little uncomfortable as my caretaker. We knew each other too well for it.

He moved back his coat and put his hands on his hips, the way he did when he was about to say something and was testing his words first. He wore a brown vest over a blue-and-white striped shirt with a close row of buttons. He looked nice and fit, smelled clean, and I couldn't help but think of Priscilla batting her eyes at him in my front parlor.

He said, "I would've gone with you last night if you'd asked."

I couldn't hide my surprise. "You would have?"

"I might've. If I'd had some advance notice."

I almost smiled. "I didn't know you had Populist leanings, Nathan."

We were out in the hall in front of the kitchen door. I saw Tante Lena listening to us, so I moved a little deeper into the hall. Nathan understood and came with me, lowering his voice.

"Why did you go?" he said.

"Because I was curious. Is that a crime?"

"No, I just never thought of you as having a reformer's temperament."

"Because I'm a woman?"

"Is that what you are, Dellie?" He started to laugh then saw I wasn't joking.

"In case you've missed it."

He dipped his head as if to get rid of his smile. Then he said, "Well, maybe I'm a little curious, too. And don't forget, it's me who'll be voting in the next election." He tapped his forefinger into my shoulder, teasing me.

"Imagine . . . if we both of us turn out to be barefoot Populists and anarchists. Papa would just die," I said, forgetting myself and who I was talking to. Nathan could be cheerful about almost anything but Papa's death, since he'd been the one to find the bloody mess in the barn. I reached for his hand and gave it a squeeze. "I didn't mean anything."

He straightened his shoulders, but his face had gone bland. "When do they meet again?"

"Next Thursday."

"You think Daniel'll want to come?"

"You'd probably know that better than I would." It might have seemed an odd thing for a wife to say about her husband but lately it was true. Nathan talked to Daniel more than I did.

"I'd be willing to bet he does."

"You would?"

Nathan nodded and smiled again, and then Priscilla's voice came from the front room, calling, "Nathan? Come in here. Your mother has a perfectly grand idea she wants you to hear."

He rolled his eyes, then frowned at me. "Don't invite her."

I grinned. "I thought you two were getting along right well."

"Stop trying to pair me with her, Dellie. I'm serious, now. Nothing good'll come of it."

"I did *not* invite her here today, I swear. How could I have known you'd be here?"

"Nathan?" And Priscilla appeared at the end of the hallway. "What are the two of you in here whispering about?" she said, smiling and in high color. "Come along in here. Your mother has something to ask you." She held out her hand to him and wiggled her fingers as if he were a child. And I thought I understood right then in that gesture why he could not care for her. He gave me a parting look, the chill of which I felt to my toes, before he started down the hallway toward Priscilla.

Until Nathan said he would attend the next meeting with me, I hadn't even considered that I would go again. But now I got excited, with something to look forward to. There was nothing in my social life or in the drudgery of keeping house that enthralled me, and so I convinced myself, or tried to, that it was the cause of Populism that intrigued my mind, which had grown lazy since I'd finished my higher schooling and gotten married. I disregarded Andy Ashland's part in it all completely, telling myself my interest in him was nothing more than that of pupil to master. He could teach me things I had never known, but that was it. He was only my teacher.

And so, that night after everyone had gone home, I assigned myself an essay, titled it "The Call of Populism." I forced myself to sit at Daniel's desk and write down why I felt pulled toward this movement, me, a decidedly nonpolitical thinker. I hadn't done much essay-writing since Miss Langburn's school in Hearn, and not so much of it even there. We had studied diction, posture, etiquette, and just to polish things off, a little Latin, most all of which I had forgotten almost immediately. We had learned how to turn out a table, how to arrange flowers in a vase, the correct steps to a proper toilette, and to paint with oils on a gridded canvas. We hadn't spent but a week or two at most on essay-writing, and not one second on politics, a thing we would never, as proper young ladies, have a need to know anything about.

I recalled the speech Andy gave at the Veterans' Reunion, things he had said that day on his porch and at last night's meeting, and I put down everything I could recollect. I felt inspired. I wrote so quickly and for so long, I dazzled myself with my brilliance. And then I moved to the window seat, and in the light of the vanishing sun, I read it all back, every word, even those I had scratched through and written above. And none of it, not one syllable, rang with any true persuasion. I was a fraud.

Because the truth was, deny it though I might, it *was* Andy

Ashland who had caught my fancy, him and his children and his poor wife in the madhouse. Not the movement, not the cause of Populism, but Andy himself. And I could not for the life of me answer my own question why. All I knew was when I thought of him it was with longing and with hope, and also with crippling guilt once Daniel crept to mind. I had been happy with Daniel and my life for two years. Hadn't I been happy? I wasn't even sure anymore that I knew the answer to something as simple as that, or even what the word *happiness* meant. Only that I had changed, and in a hurry, and nothing that had seemed important before felt that way to me any longer.

8

On Saturday, I drove Cintha into town. That morning, Gretta Betts was the only one at the newspaper office, except for Hannah, who was asleep on a pallet in the corner until I walked in and disturbed her. I was caught so off guard at finding only Gretta, her hands black with ink, I blurted out, "Andy isn't here?" calling him by his given name when I should have said mister.

She didn't seem aware that I'd blundered. She held her arms cocked at the elbow as if to keep her hands from touching anything. She wore a gray dress that had been turned inside out and made over. I could see the old needle holes where the sleeves had been reset. And the apron around her waist I recognized plainly, by its deep hem, as the skirt to an old red, ripped-apart calico.

"No, but he'll be in later," she answered. "Once they're all through over at Brother Browning's place. It shouldn't be long now, though. Do you want to wait?"

"No, I . . ." I had forgotten all about the man with the broken leg. I saw her looking at the rolled-up paper in my hand. The essay. The silly essay. I had thought to show it to him. It was my excuse for coming in here today, and a lame one at that. I *did* want to wait. More than anything I wanted to see him. It felt like an eternity since last Thursday, and another until the next. And this time, I would have Nathan to see me home, so there would be no more lone buggy rides.

I made a move to hand over the essay, to leave it for him to read. She wiped her hands on her apron and reached for the paper, but at the last second, I changed my mind. I wadded the essay in both my hands and gave her as warm a smile as I could muster. I'm sure she thought me peculiar.

"I wanted to ask if I might bring my brother to the meeting with me next week," I said, thinking quick. "He expressed an interest in coming."

"Of course, you can bring him. You don't need to ask permission for that. Everybody's welcome. The meetings are open to the public."

I'd known that already, but I smiled and stood there awkwardly, holding the essay in my fist behind my back. Hannah got up from her pallet and stood beneath me, looking up. I leaned down and touched one finger under her chin. "Good morning, little one," I said, and she grabbed the bodice of my dress in both her hands. She drew me down to give me a kiss on my cheek, and it startled me so, I dropped the wadded paper. "My goodness," I said, and lifted her up. She flung her arms tight about my neck.

"Now, I can't hardly believe that. She's usually so shy with folks." Gretta bent for the wadded-up essay. She left black fingerprints on it. "Willie's got a cot set up in the back room yonder for the young'uns, but I can't get her to go back there and take her nap. She wants to be out front. You'd think the racket up here would keep her awake. Mr. Flaxman downstairs complains enough about it."

I pivoted toward the open door at the other end of the room. Hannah held on to my shoulder. "Is Quintus here, too?"

"No. Him and Jordan went with the men. It's just me and Hannah today." And she smiled with real affection at the child in my arms.

"You're such a big help to An—" I couldn't bring myself to say his name again. ". . . to her papa. I'm sure he's grateful."

"It's me who's the grateful one. Hannah's my little doll. I can't have any more children. Something messed up with Jordan." She reached with the back of her wrist to wipe Hannah's bangs out of her eyes. "I always did so want a little girl."

"I haven't been able to"—I looked at Hannah, then at Gretta, who was waiting for me to finish—"have any children at all." My voice caught on the last two words. I felt my eyes cloud up.

"I'm sorry," Gretta said.

I shook my head. I didn't know what had caused me to speak of such a personal thing with this woman I barely knew. It was something I didn't like to talk about. Mother had said that I would find it a trial to be a barren woman, and I had begun to understand what she meant.

I set Hannah back on her feet. "You learn to accept," I said, repeating another thing Mother had told me. I smoothed at my skirt, touched the cheek where Hannah had kissed. "Well, I guess I'll see you both on Thursday, then."

Hannah grabbed onto my hand. "I want to go with Miz O'Bert," she said, suddenly, surprising me again.

Gretta was surprised, too. "Oh no, now, Hannah honey, you stay here with me."

Hannah hugged in closer to me, practically wrapping herself in my skirts. "I want to go home with Miz O'Bert."

"It's all right if she wants to. I don't have anything else to do in town. I'm sure it would be all right with An—with her papa. You all know where I live."

"Well . . ." Gretta looked doubtfully at me, then back at Hannah. "If you're sure you don't mind. She gets so bored cooped up in here."

We gathered her few things from the little room in back: her ragdoll, a fresh pinafore, a small feather pillow. I was elated by this unexpected turn to my day, and also a little frightened. Tante Lena didn't work on Saturday unless it was a special occasion, so

I would have the care of this little girl all alone. I didn't have much experience with children. I had always been too busy with school, and then with becoming Daniel's wife. After our first few months, when I didn't conceive right away, I found I got in the habit of mostly ignoring the children of those at church and of our acquaintances. It was simpler, easier on my pride, and on Daniel's.

To my relief Hannah was taken with the house and didn't need much tending. She went from room to room picking up one thing and then the next, asking, "What's this? And what's this? What's this called?" and never waiting for me to answer. She was a lively child once she got past the initial shyness at being someplace new, once she realized it was just the two of us here.

In the downstairs water closet she found the flush-commode and pulled the chain three times before, fearful of flooding the cesspool outside, I made her stop. I'm sure she had never seen such a modern contraption in her young life. In the sitting room she found the piano. I was sorry I couldn't play a proper tune for her. I had always been all thumbs when it came to any musical instrument, but we sat on the stool together, and she banged away happily for most of an hour, pleased with the noise she made.

I remembered Tante Lena's kolaches and brought out a plateful. I sat Hannah up to the table, and she ate so many I worried she'd have the stomachache later. When we went upstairs, she crawled onto my bed, and began to jump up and down until I pulled her attention into a game of hide-and-go-seek. She did all the hiding in the game since it frightened her for me to disappear. And each time she gave herself away, pretending to cough or else jumping out with a "boo!" from behind the vase of peacock feathers and dried cattails. And sometimes for no apparent reason, when I discovered her in her hiding place, she would hug me tight like she had in the newspaper office. I fell in love with her and understood completely Gretta's attachment. I also began to daydream that she was mine.

I pulled out scraps of leftover fabric from the cedar chest, and held one or two up to her chin to see which colors would bring out her natural rosiness. I had three yards of blue muslin left from the frock I'd made for the Masonic Celebration, and while I envisioned the dress I could sew for her, she draped the fabric pieces over her head and made noises meant to scare me. She brought a gaiety and a lightness that had been missing from the house. And I knew that after that day of play and pretend, the walls and rooms, the floors and ceilings, would seem forever gloomy to me.

It was after five when Andy came to fetch her. She had worn down by then and fallen asleep on the sitting room sofa. I heard him out the front way, tying his saddle mule to the fence. Britches and Old Boy raised a ruckus. I went out to shoo the dogs to the back of the house, and for once, they minded me.

Andy finished tying his mule and looked up the footpath at me. It had been my hope all afternoon that he would be the one to come and not send Gretta or Willie or someone else. I tried not to show how fast my heart was beating as I stepped out around the climbing rose that spread itself horizontally along the gallery rails, drooping thick with clusters of bright pink blooms.

He had on work clothes, mud on his boots and the hems of his duckings. His eyelids seemed swollen as if from lack of sleep, or more probably, from labor and sweat. He took off his hat and his hair underneath was unruly and crimped. His gaze moved from me upwards to the upstairs gallery and farther to the high-peaked turret on the roof, the eaves fringed with elaborate gingerwork and lattice, the stained glass in the attic portholes, and I knew what he was seeing and thinking. I was suddenly embarrassed for the house and how I lived.

I stepped down into the pathway and started toward him. "I guess you've come to take Hannah from me." I made my voice light; the cheerfulness I didn't have to force. It had been the best day I'd had in quite a while.

"Gretta said this is where I'd find her." He pressed his hat against his chest, and acted apprehensive and timid, or maybe unnerved by coming here. And he sounded different, less sure of himself, awkward. I wanted to put him at his ease.

"We've had a lovely day. She's taking a little nap. Can you sit a minute? I could get you some tea, or"—I recalled the well water he'd offered me when I sat on his porch—"a glass of water, maybe? I thought you might bring Quintus with you."

"Is your husband at home?"

I shook my head and stepped aside for him to come up even with me on the pathway. "Did you have some business with him? He's still out of town."

He compressed his lips. "It probably wouldn't be a good idea for me to stay if you're here all alone."

I tried not to seem aware of the suggestion in his remark, though I knew as well as he did that if people saw us sitting alone without Daniel, they would talk. "But I'm not here all alone. I've got Hannah, and it would be such a shame to wake her when she's just gone down. You can sit for a minute, can't you?"

He looked at me, then glanced at the three wooden rockers on the porch, the wicker settle and table. His eyes moved back at me, hesitated. "Well . . . I reckon so. For a minute." He took the wicker and seemed to enjoy it, shifting and situating himself until he got comfortable. He leaned forward and laid his hat, crown down, on the table. Smiled.

As usual, his smile stopped me, made me forget my offer of refreshments. I sat down on the rocker nearest to him, unable, suddenly, to make the feeblest attempt at pleasant conversation. I stared at him, unmindful of his dirty boots, the sweat-stained neck of his shirt. He felt like a force drawing me to him, as strong as steel to the magnet. As if I ought to hold fast to my chair in case I should slip across to end up where he was. It was, all at once, powerful and frightening, but also wondrous that I could be moved so strongly.

He spoke finally, filling in for my silence, telling me some about the work out at the Browning place, chopping the cotton field, which had grown all up in sunflowers. Thomas Dillon had had to run a sulky down the middles before anyone could get in with a hoe. And it was, Andy said, just one more example of the narrow edge a farmer walked between a living and the almshouse.

"He was cleaning his own barn loft when he fell through the rafters." Andy shook his head. I knew he was thinking it could have been him just as easily as farmer Browning with a broken leg.

"Well, it's a good thing he didn't break his head," I said, meaning to sympathize, but Andy let out a piping laugh. When I looked up he was looking at me, his face all lit like he was starving and I'd just said let's eat.

"You're a card, Dellie." My name seemed to ring and slide on his tongue. For a moment, I sat there trying to think of something else to say that would make him laugh, but the moment passed. He said, "Gretta said you're bringing Nathan to the meeting next Thursday. I was pleased to hear it."

"I didn't know he was interested until yesterday. He reminded me, he's a voter this election."

The smile on Andy's face didn't leave, but it became less, just a small bending up of the corners of his mouth, as he nodded. He had the widest jaw I'd ever seen. Nice flat ears. His gaze traveled around him again, shifted up the walls of the gallery, at the blue buttermilk-paint on the ceiling, toward the open window beside us. A panel of English lace fluttered in the light breeze. The prisms on the table lamp inside tinkled.

"Don't hold it against me," I said.

"Hold what against you?"

"I saw you noticing the house."

He canted his head, then dabbed at a drop of perspiration that had rolled down by his ear. More had beaded up on his chin and in the lines of his forehead, too. It was hot for June. "Well, I wasn't. But now that you brought it to my attention, it is a fine place."

"I felt more at home sitting out on your porch the other day than I ever have living here."

"Well, it's that first place you live, it's always home, isn't it?"

"This house belongs to my mother-in-law," I said, wanting to make him understand. "Almost everything here is hers. Where she lives now, she doesn't have room for all her things. She says for me to treat them like they were my own, but it feels, I don't know, it feels"—I looked at him; he was still listening—"wrong for me to have so much."

"Well, I say be glad and thank your lucky star."

"But I'm *not* lucky. I don't feel lucky at all." My eyes welled up. The tears surprised me as much—maybe more—than they did Andy, but I couldn't seem to do anything to stop them. I tried a laugh but it didn't come out whole. I put both my palms flat against my cheeks. I knew I was as red as morning.

He shook a handkerchief out of his pocket and handed it to me. "It's clean."

His smile had disappeared. I hated that I had made it go away with my weeping. Why couldn't I be lighthearted, gay like other women, like Priscilla would be? What was wrong with me that I'd gotten so emotional, so morbid inside, and over nothing? I had never thought of myself as the sobbing sort, the whimpering, sniffling, weepy female sort, but that was how I knew I must seem to him.

"Oh, my word," I said, dabbing at my face, pretending again to laugh. The handkerchief was slightly damp from being inside his pocket. It smelled of lye soap and of airing on a clothesline. "This is just plain crazy. Just loony of me—" Then I remembered about his wife, and that he might be offended by those words, *crazy* and *loony*. "Oh, I beg your pardon," I said. "I truly do."

"No need to apologize. Not to me anyway. I don't think it ever does anybody any good to choke down on something that's bothering them."

"Oh, nothing's bothering me. Really. I just didn't mean to—I didn't intend to—" My tongue kept tangling, and in my exasperation with it, another tear slid out.

"Oh. So that's why you broke down crying. Because nothing's bothering you." He gave me a gentle smile. "You've been through something terrible with your daddy dying the way he did, and if you didn't cry about it, why"—he shrugged—"then I might really think something was wrong with—"

"That isn't it," I interrupted. What could I say to him? How could I tell him that nothing felt real to me anymore, and I couldn't even explain why? I looked at him, leaning forward with his forearms resting on his knees, honesty plain on him. I clutched tight to his handkerchief. "I was afraid I had insulted you by saying I was acting crazy, since your wife . . . Well, you know about your wife. Sometimes I say the most foolish, horrible things."

I waved the handkerchief in front of my face and looked out at the mimosa trees all in blossom along the road. I tried to get my breath back. The tears would not stop coming. It was almost as if once that first one broke free, the levee had split. I was sure my nose was red and my cheeks splotchy. I wasn't one of those girls who cried prettily, and I was beginning to sound nasal. I dabbed at my face with his handkerchief and tried another laugh. It came out sounding more like a hiccup. "I don't want you to think less of me because of where I live."

"I don't think less of you. I think it takes a lot of gumption to live here the way you do, and still come to our meetings to listen about how this country's suffering. I admire gumption in a person."

"I just wanted to tell you I didn't choose all this. It was chosen for me, and if I had it to do over again, I'd stand up for myself and say no. I truly believe I would."

"I believe you would, too."

"Everything changed after we moved in with Mother. I can't explain it, but it did some way. I missed living in that house, your house, and I miss being a child. You lose something once you've grown up. I don't know what exactly, I can't say, but I know I felt more myself as a child than I do now. That probably sounds crazy to you." I covered my mouth. I'd said that word again. I could not believe I was so insensitive that I'd made the same blunder twice. "Oh, my God. I'm so sorry."

He laughed and shook his head, then sat back, his cheeks puffed out a little. He exhaled some air, mulling me over, like I was too much to take in all at once. "Why do you always apologize for everything?"

"I don't."

"Yes. You do. Almost every time you open your mouth, you're apologizing for something you've said. It's aggravating. You have so much . . ." He tapped his forefinger to his head. "I hate to see somebody as smart as you so lost."

"Well, maybe I've been found." I said it with a light laugh, but still it sounded fresh. The words seemed to echo in my head, and I felt a little faint anticipating his response. He waited a long time before he spoke—an eternity.

"I'm just a common man, Dellie. The commonest. Whatever's on your mind, let's hear it. And for God's sake don't worry over words. *Crazy* is just a word. It won't shatter me to hear you say it."

I shook my head. "You're hardly a common man."

"Well, I didn't mean it as a thing to be ashamed of. I'm proud I'm common."

"But you're not. I don't think I've ever met anyone more uncommon than you are." I let myself smile and I didn't try to keep from blushing this time. I believe I may have even batted my lashes at him. I hate to think of it, but I'm fairly certain I did. And what I said next just came out on its own, right along with the wind inside me. I said, "And I know I've never seen any bluer eyes than yours are, Andy Ashland."

I guess I thought it would be funny, would lighten the mood between us, but of course, it didn't. It had the opposite effect completely. He stared at me with his mouth open, then closed it tight. He looked off for a befuddled moment, out at where his mule was slouching, tied to the fence. When he leaned forward and reached for his hat, I knew I'd gone too far with acting the coquette. I started to apologize, again, even though he'd just told me not to do that. And yet, here he was, about to go because of something I'd said.

Before he could rise, I jumped up. The rocker slapped the gallery boards, back and forth. The handkerchief in my lap fluttered to the floor. He stooped for it and so did I. We almost bumped our heads together, but he snatched it up first. I righted myself, smoothed at my skirt. "I wish you'd let me wash that."

"You barely used it." He tucked the handkerchief into his

pocket. His face had closed down, his voice gone formal and distant. "Thank you for watching Hannah for me."

"I'll go wake her up now." But I didn't move. I wanted to think of something to keep him from leaving. I didn't want his visit to end like this. But nothing, absolutely no excuse to stop him would come to me.

He stood there, holding his hat. "All right," he said finally, as if to jar me into motion.

I felt slightly off-balance. I raised my face and looked at his eyes, one and then the other, and they were the deepest of blue, just like I had said. But me staring so straight at him was bold and too much for me. We both of us looked away.

9

Between the train station and the house, Daniel heard that I had gone to the Populist meeting. He never said from whom he heard it, though by the time he got home on Tuesday, the gossip was all over town. More than anything he just seemed confused, not angry, and upset that I'd gone alone.

I was in the sitting parlor when he arrived home. He came straight there and found me reading poetry. Robert Burns. "A Red, Red Rose." That one poem, over and over. Memorizing it line by line. It was mostly all I'd gotten done since Saturday, the memorizing of poetry. First Elizabeth Barrett Browning. Now Burns. And when Daniel came into the room confronting me with the town gossip, I had the nearly uncontrollable urge to recite to him aloud.

"If you need something to do," he said, speaking slow and uncertain, "I'm sure Clifton Mauney would be delighted to have you help him get things under way for the Normal School."

"I'm *not* looking for something especially. They invited me to the meeting and I thought I would go see what it was like."

"Who is *they*, Dellie? William Betts? He's already asked me to come to his meetings a dozen times or more. He thinks by asking you he'll get me—"

"It wasn't Mr. Betts. Andy Ashland invited me." I set the open book spine down on the tea table between us, and tried to control the anger creeping over me.

He sat on the cushioned chair opposite mine. His traveling suit was musty and soot-stained from the long train ride. "Ashland?" Surprise came in his voice, and my neck burned just hearing Daniel speak the name. "Well, the same goes doubly for him. They need contributions. In the worst way is what I've heard. He naturally assumed I'd come along with you, I'm sure. He was probably counting on it."

I wanted to shout at him that he must think a lot of himself and not much of me if he supposed they were just using me as bait for him. I wanted to tell him that money didn't enter into everything in this world, that greed was a trait of Republicans like Louis Bassist and Democrats like himself. I wanted to tell him that I had beliefs, opinions, thoughts on things of consequence. And that just possibly Andy had asked me to attend the meeting because he thought I was clever and could be of service to their cause—that I could be invaluable. But I said none of this. I sat there and seethed.

"If you're bored," Daniel went on, "if you wanted to come along with me, you should have said something. You know you're always welcome, I just didn't think you cared to go. We could've made a holiday of it, if you'd said something. You might've gone shopping—"

"I'm not interested in shopping."

"Since when?"

"I have everything I could possibly want or need. More in fact." I heard the sass in my tone. "There happen to be other things I want to do."

He let out an edgy laugh, taken back by me. "Join with the Populists?"

"Why is that funny?"

"Well—" He spread his hands. They were long, slender hands, neat rounded nails. "I don't know what to say, Dellie. It's just"— he shrugged, groping, a look of dumb puzzlement on his face— "sudden. All of this. Isn't it?"

"Because you think of me as lightminded."

"No. That is not so. I absolutely do not." But then he looked away and I could see he was trying to keep his face straight. His laughter infuriated me. I had to restrain the urge to stand up and slap him. Never before in my life had I ever wanted to strike another human being. When he turned back to me he had control of his expression again. "Do you know what they stand for, Dellie? These Populists? What their causes are?"

"Yes, I most certainly do."

"Then tell me which one it is that has so stimulated you."

"Stop making fun of me." My voice had risen high and screeching.

"I don't mean to sound that way. I'm truly interested to know which issue has grabbed your attention."

"Women's suffrage for one."

"They don't stand for that."

"Yes, they do. It's been spoken of—"

"It isn't a plank in their platform." And I felt then he was trying to stump me. Platform? I didn't know what platform he was talking about, and I believe he knew that I didn't. "I've already listened to William Betts and half a dozen others like him. They have some good ideas, I'll allow them that. I agree the railroads have too much land and power. But I can't go along with a break from the gold standard. What would that do to this country in the overseas markets? And I don't want a graduated income tax either, so, therefore, I can't support the Populists."

None of what he said made much sense, but I didn't let on. I kept my face straight, my voice level. "Then you won't be interested in attending the meeting this week. Nathan's coming with me." I stood up. "Unless, of course, you have any objection."

He sat back, both his hands gripping the arms of the chair. His knuckles were white. He looked up at me, shook his head. It was clear he didn't know what to make of me over this. "No. You're free to do what you want. You've always been . . . free. You know that."

No, I didn't know that. I had never felt that. I felt caged. Chained. By Papa first, and then by everyone. I picked up the book, keeping my finger inside at my place:

> *O my Luve's like a red, red rose*
> *That's newly sprung in June . . .*

I remembered the girls at Miss Langburn's school reciting that poem, making dramatic faces as they did, and pretending to swoon. I hadn't understood then. I hadn't known.

I left Daniel there in the sitting parlor and went up to my room. I didn't go back down for supper. I didn't read anymore either. I sat in the slipper chair by the window looking out, the book of poetry limp in my hands, and I vowed that I would learn all there was to know about the People's Party, about the gold standard and graduated income tax, so that the next time I could argue intelligently and not be made to feel a simpering fool.

When Tante Lena came upstairs I told her I had a headache, so she brought me a bowl of soup and a cup of tea with lemon. I wasn't hungry, though it was already well past sundown. I took the tray from her and set it on my lap, but I didn't eat. I looked down at the gold-leaf china bowl and saucer, the silver-plated spoon, the tiny crystal salt shaker, and I couldn't help but remember the farmwife's bustle leaking cottonseed at the Populist meeting, the scuffed boots on Andy's feet, little Hannah's tattered hem.

"Books," Tante Lena said, taking Robert Burns from me. "It's no wonder you have a headache. You read too much, it make your eyes bad." She set the book on the night table, reached deep into her apron, and came out with a small, flat box tied with pink ribbon. "Mr. Danny said give this to you. I reckon he bring it back from his trip."

The box was light in my hand, and there was a note, scrawled hastily: *I know you have everything you want or need, but perhaps this small gift won't offend you too much.*

"Where is he?" I said, feeling guilt come hot to my throat.

"At his lodge. He said he'd be late." She stood beside my bed and waited for me to open the box. I could see her curiosity was high. She probably knew we'd had cross words. I'm sure she knew over what.

Inside the box was the daintiest lace handkerchief, scented with lilac and scalloped around the border with elegant Battenburg. She was craning her neck to see, so I gave her the whole box. She took the handkerchief out, holding it delicately between her fingers.

"Ain't this just the finest," she said, bringing the linen to her nose for a smell. "That Mr. Danny, he's the sweetest boy."

She folded the handkerchief back into the box. It was true. He almost never failed to bring me something home, some trinket, something like the handkerchief, to let me know I had been on his mind while he was gone. That he had remembered this time secretly pleased me, yet it annoyed me, too. I wasn't used to feeling hypocritical.

I lay awake that night listening for his horse, for the door and his footsteps, determined to wait up. We didn't quarrel often, and I thought I should ask him to forgive me. Maybe next time he had business out of town, I would go with him. It might do us good to get away together. The weather was ripe for it: *June newly sprung . . .*

> *O my luve's like the melodie*
> *That's sweetly played in tune!*

I fell asleep. I didn't wake until the next morning, and by the time I went down to breakfast, Daniel had long since gone out to work. But I had a new outlook. I would be a better wife. This rift between us was as much my fault as Daniel's. I had become obstinate and unforgiving. Traits I could never tolerate in others. Traits that had belonged to Papa, not me. I shoved the anger I had felt last night, the sting of his laughing tone, into the back corner of my mind. If I changed, maybe he would, and we could get back on an even keel. And maybe, I thought, I should send word to Nathan that I'd decided not to go to the meeting tomorrow night after all.

I threw myself into cleaning the house, starting first in the dining room. I dusted the walls, and the bird's-eye maple table Daniel's mother had left behind. Her silver needed shining. I took apart the chandelier and cleaned each crystal drop. I took the rug out to the backyard, hung it over the clothes-wire, and beat it until my shoulders ached. I pulled down drapes and shook them out, scrubbed window sills. It was as if something had come over me. I skipped nothing. I set the papers straight on Daniel's desk, took down every book, wiped off the spines, polished the globe on the stand in the corner. Upstairs, I pulled the mattresses off the beds and dragged them onto the upper gallery to air. As I finished each room a numbing satisfaction settled on me.

Tante Lena came behind me with the screaming carpet sweeper, but she kept giving me looks, like she thought I had gone berserk. At noon, she begged me to stop. "Come on, Miss Dellie. You need to take a bite of nourishment."

I gobbled down a quick meat sandwich and kept on with the work. All of it needed doing. We hadn't had a spring cleaning yet this year and it was already June . . . *newly sprung* . . .

At twilight, Daniel came in wearing his work clothes and saddle boots, leaving a trail of dust in his wake. He spoke to Tante Lena first, asking her if she could spend tomorrow baking bread and beans. "We're going to be out there awhile," I heard him say, and then he looked up and saw me skulking in the kitchen doorway. In my hand I held a needlepoint I'd neglected since Easter, a pillow cushion I'd been planning to give Mother on her birthday, but that had already passed.

A fence was down and cattle were scattered all the way to Blue Branch. He'd had fence trouble last year, too, when a herd ruined a Lee County farmer's cotton crop, and Daniel had nearly been sued over it. I saw he was worried. He'd left his men camped out across the Knobs. He said he wanted to get back there to them before daylight. He acted as though we hadn't had words last night, and I didn't mention his gift. I helped him gather provisions he would need. Tante Lena and Sinclair loaded the pack animals.

"Nathan's out with the other fellows," Daniel told me when we were saying goodbye. "He brought Linn and Coo with him." Two colored hands that Papa had hired regularly when needed.

I knew what Daniel was telling me: that Nathan wouldn't be available for tomorrow night's meeting. And even though I had nearly decided not to go, I felt betrayed. It was almost as if Daniel had planned everything—had broken down that fence himself. After all the fuss that had been made, he didn't believe I would think of going alone again to the meeting. He knew I didn't enjoy being the object of so much talk, but now I was determined to go, and by morning I had worked out the solution.

I sent Sinclair to tell the Bettses that I would need a ride. After meeting Gretta again at the newspaper office last Saturday, I felt comfortable enough asking for such a favor. They lived just up the road from us, less than a mile toward town, so I wouldn't be too far out of their way. And even though I could barely stand the thought of facing Andy again after the fool I'd made of myself on the front gallery, I also had hopes that he might go along with us.

He didn't. They were alone, the Bettses, the three of them, in a dilapidated phaeton that had evidently once been a showpiece, with ironwork and wooden curlicues. It had belonged to a rich planter down near Houston, where they had lived before they came to McDade and rented the old Kellermeir farm. Gretta tried to give me her place at the front of the buggy, but I preferred the backseat with Jordan. He was a nice-looking boy of nine-going-on-ten, with big front teeth and freckles, and so much energy he could hardly sit still for the ride.

Neither could I. It was the prospect of seeing Andy that had me in a tizzy. I hoped Willie and Gretta didn't notice my agitation. We talked of things: The drouth—it had been so dry cinders from trains had been setting fires all along the tracks. The snake under Rose Barbee's feet last week. We said the men would be required, from now on, to do a thorough inspection of the hall before the ladies would go inside. Willie laughed and said it was probably the Democrats who had planted that snake there to try and stop our meetings.

A cloud of blackbirds lifted from Tory Peeler's hay field as we passed. They flew off in rippling waves on the evening wind. Willie had to steer the team out of the way of a turtle crossing the road, a sign, Gretta said, that meant coming rain. "Let's just hope so," Willie said, and he reached across to pat her knee.

We were the first to arrive. The hall was hot inside, and I helped to throw open the windows while Willie and Jordan half-heartedly looked around for snakes. People began to gather outside. I watched for Andy's big wagon. Gretta had brought a large jug of lemonade and I helped her carry that in. Together we heaved the jug up onto the table at the front of the hall.

She said, "We try to do a little something extra when we have a visiting speaker."

"There's a visitor?"

"Mr. McClaugherty's come over from Smithville, and we've sent Andy there." She said it in a casual way, but almost too casual, as if she had seen me waiting for his wagon and thought she would spare me the anxiety. She didn't look up from her task, which was arranging the jug and a few tin cups on the table. "We're discussing the candidates tonight. And the St. Louis convention in July. We're sending a delegate from this region."

"Andy's in Smithville?" I said before I could stop myself. I couldn't help the disappointment that tinged my voice.

"We swap out like that sometimes. Last month he went over to Paige."

"He took his children with him?"

"He's got his sister down from Louisiana. She came in the day before yesterday. Brought her whole family down with her."

"I didn't know he had a sister."

Finally she looked at me and I felt the scolding from her eyes. "We all got family, don't we? I've got eleven brothers and sisters myself, all scattered to the four winds. And Willie's the baby of six." She smiled. "I'm sorry *your* brother couldn't make it tonight."

I didn't say anything else. I had already said enough, asked too many questions. And anyway, my mind was in a muddle. If Andy wasn't here why was I? There didn't seem to be much point to any of it. I completely forgot my resolve to become more informed on the issues. I sat through the whole meeting, through songs I couldn't sing, through speeches I didn't hear, and thought about Andy over in Smithville while I was stuck here at Fletcher's Hall. Mr. McClaugherty's voice was a monotone that nearly put everyone to sleep.

10

All morning Friday I spent with Tante Lena in the kitchen. While she boiled beans and baked bread, I put up twelve quarts of plum butter in Mason's fruit jars. Around one, Daniel rushed in after the food we'd packed, and to jot a note to Mr. Canaday in Chicago on when to expect delivery of the eight hundred steers. He wrote another to an R. J. Kinney in Corpus Christi about four hundred head, and asked would I see that both messages got wired today. He also asked would I wire Mr. Sitzler at the KATY office in Bastrop about ordering the cars for the cattle. He wrote that down for me, too.

He was sunburned, smelled of sweat and dust. "I'll be home Sunday in time for church."

"All right." I reached to wipe a smudge of something black off his cheek. Since I wasn't in the habit of fussing over him, his first inclination was to flinch from me. It came awkward to both of us.

"I'll take a bath then, too," he said, half joking. He leaned to give me a quick peck on the forehead and it surprised me. "I'll see you Sunday."

"Daniel," I called after him. He paused in the hallway, just outside the kitchen door, and looked back. "I don't think that I thanked you for the lovely handkerchief. It was thoughtful of you."

He smiled and didn't say anything, but at least when he was gone, my conscience felt clearer. I had thanked him. I had tried to show affection. I had always done all I could to be a good wife to him.

When I went to town that afternoon to send off all his wires, I got enough corduroy material to make him a vest. A good one he could work in this fall and winter, with strong buttons and double stitching. I also bought two new needles for my sewing machine in case one broke while I worked the heavy fabric.

Saturday morning, around eleven, while I was cutting out the vest, I had an unexpected visit. Daniel had taken the dogs when he left yesterday so they didn't raise a warning. No one hardly ever used the door chime, so it startled me when it sounded. I was even more startled to find Quintus Ashland and another boy about his same age standing on the front gallery. One tired mule was tied to the fence, the same gray mule I'd seen Andy ride before.

"My dad sent me with this to give to you." Quintus held out a folded and rumpled copy of the *Plaindealer,* the latest issue.

I took it from him. "Would you and your friend like to come in and sit for a spell?"

"He's not my friend. He's my cousin Philip Treadway." Quintus ran the words together as if they were one name. The boys trudged inside, one after the other. I noticed Philip was as blond as Andy and Hannah, and I thought about the sister Gretta had mentioned from Louisiana.

Both boys' eyes were popping out on stems as we went through the rooms toward the kitchen, so I let them dawdle, remembering the first time I ever came inside this house and saw the crystal-drop chandeliers, the burl-cypress wainscot, the wallpaper of fleur-de-lis. I led them to the kitchen and sat them and the newspaper down at the table.

"I bet you boys are hot after that long ride from town." I took two bowls down from the cupboard and went out to the ice box on the back porch. I left the door open, though, and I said, "Where do you live, Philip? You're from Louisiana, aren't you?"

"Cheneyville, ma'am," he said. "We come here on the train to visit Uncle Drew."

"Drew?" I said to myself but Quintus answered, "That's Dad's other name."

I used Tante Lena's paring knife to shave ice from the block inside the chest. The ice was melting fast in the heat. This would be the last block until the weather cooled again, yet I wanted to treat the boys to something nice. I scooped the shavings into the two bowls, dashed in some sweet cream.

The boys were restless when I went back inside. I smiled at them and set the bowls in front of them. "There you go." I gave them spoons and put the sugar bowl in the center of the table. "Try that."

"What is it?" Philip said. He looked uncertain.

"Put on some sugar." I did it for them, sprinkling in more than I intended.

Quintus dug in with his spoon, said, "Mmmm," when he tasted the ice and cream. His face lit, and his tongue came out to circle his lips. It caused me a chuckle. Then Philip started eating his, too.

I sat down with them and enjoyed watching them, although they both had horrible table manners, slurping and smacking their lips, wiping their chins on their shirtsleeves. I pulled the newspaper around and read the headline. It was a boilerplate item about Mr. Bryan who was the People's Party's choice as their presidential nominee. It was beginning to look, the paper said, as if Mr. Bryan would be seeking the Democratic nomination instead. The boys kept shoveling the iced cream into their mouths.

The next article was written locally, from the looks of the type, and was entitled "A Few Words About Common Sense." At first, just by skimming through, I couldn't tell if Andy had written it or Willie Betts. I unfolded the paper as I read. It was a general appeal for humankind to think freely for themselves. And of course, it was the party doctrine the writer wanted the thinker to contemplate. No name was signed at the bottom, but there was a bit of Scripture: "Lead me, O Lord, in thy righteousness because of mine enemies; make thy way straight before my face." I couldn't keep my smile from coming. *Andy*.

And then underneath that article was another, this one labeled "A Call to Populism." Reading that title, my stomach flipped over. My hands gripped the page. I raised the paper higher, shielding my face from the boys. It was my essay. My stupid, silly essay. I jumped up from the table so quick, I upset my chair and startled both boys. They stopped gobbling long enough to round their eyes up at me.

"Excuse me." I left the kitchen, holding the paper clutched in my hand. I raced up the stairs to my room and found my pocketbook. I had thought the wadded-up essay would be in there. I went to the chifforobe and pawed through the dresses till I recalled which one I'd been wearing that day with Gretta and Hannah at the newspaper office. A polished cotton, one without pockets in the skirt. I sat down on the chair and let the humiliation of it sweep over me.

The last I remembered was the wadded paper falling to the floor and Gretta picking it up. Then Hannah had distracted me so, I must have left the thing there. I wondered if it was Gretta or Andy who had read it first. And if he had, I wondered if it was before or after he came that day to fetch Hannah. That day I'd made such a fool of myself, weeping and then flirting miserably. I still could barely stand to think of my behavior, or of his reaction to it.

I forced myself to read the printed essay all the way through. Not one word had been changed, but it all still sounded like rote to me, hollow and affected. Someone had put *Sister Dellie* at the bottom, identifying me as the author. And there was some pencil writing in the margin that I hadn't noticed downstairs, Andy's handwriting. It said, "Can you do some more of this?"

More? I rubbed my thumb over the penciled words until they smeared. He wanted more of this drivel? He liked it? Or Willie Betts did. And they wanted me to contribute again. I couldn't believe it. I sat there for a good while, a silly smile taking hold of my face, before I went back downstairs to my little kitchen guests.

At church the next day my article was almost all anyone wanted to talk about. Daniel acted stupefied over all the attention. He had come in the house that morning in such a hurry, I hadn't even thought to show him the newspaper. Nathan, on the other hand, teased me about it. "I didn't know you were a writer, Sister . . ." he said, then added with a grin, "Dellie."

Mother was appalled. Over dinner at her house, she ignored me as though I were a cockroach come uninvited. Not until we were in the kitchen washing up the dishes did she speak to me, and then it was to tell me again, and with more force, that well-bred ladies didn't meddle in politics. "It's unbecoming, Dellie. You're not one of these so-called *new* women."

I quit pumping the sink full of water, but my hand stayed on the pump cock. I looked at her. Water trickled out of the spout. "How do you know I'm not, Mother? Maybe I am. Maybe that's exactly what I am."

She was gathering dishes to the drainboard. "You never showed signs of it before."

"Well, I'm showing them now. This isn't just a passing fancy with me. Mother? Don't you want your rights? The same ones as a man has?"

"No, I do not. I'm happy just how things are. I own this land, and this house you're standing in, and that's rights enough for me."

"Yes, and you have the right to pay taxes on this land, too, but you don't get a say in how your taxes get spent. Mother, don't you see? That's against the Constitution. It's against everything the country stands for."

"Don't go spouting that Constitution nonsense at me, Dellie. Your trouble is you've got too much leisure time on your hands. Daniel ought to let Lena go so's you'll have something better to do than sit around all day dreaming up this nonsense. He pampers you too much, that's what's the matter with you."

"It isn't nonsense, Mother. Stop calling it nonsense. They asked me to write more articles for their newspaper, and I intend to do it. Isn't that what you sent me off to school for? To get an education? To learn to use my brain?"

Mother tightened her lips. She laid down a hand-load of silverware. "Your papa sent you to school, he told me, to learn you how to behave like a lady. He thought if you were among strangers you might acquire some ladylike manners. I know just how much it would pain him to see—"

"Oh, Mother, don't start that again!"

"Well, it's the truth, Dellie. I can't believe Daniel will let you get by with this nonsense for long."

"Daniel? This isn't Daniel's decision to make!" I yelled it at her and she gaped at me in horror. We stood there, gaping, both of us, and staring at each other, and that's how we were when Nathan came to the kitchen to see what all the shouting was about. Daniel stayed away. He seemed determined not to involve himself, though he'd have had to be deaf not to hear his name yelled out so loud. But he wouldn't comment, not even on the way home when I told him, too, that I would be writing regularly for the *Plaindealer* now.

We rode past the old farmplace—the Ashland place—going home. Daylight was fading fast, but they were in the cornfields,

Andy and Quintus, a woman and a man, some other children, stripping the lower stalks. Quintus stood up and waved boisterously at our wagon, running a little so we could see him in the dusk. I recognized Philip. Andy just straightened, took off his hat, and ran his forearm across his brow.

Daniel glanced at me. It was nothing, just a small glance. I caught it in time and gave him a smile in return. I did not turn to look back at the Ashlands, though I wanted to. I was curious about the others in the field, but I kept my face turned forward the same as Daniel did. The quiet overtook us.

Later that night, the Craddocks came to call. J.T. still had Daniel working on some legal something for him. J.T. had gone into the insuring business at the end of last year, and his legal affairs had something to do with this new line of work.

Daphne gave me a hug, and she made no mention of my newfound notoriety. The lace handkerchief Daniel had given me was tucked inside the pocket of my linen suit, one delicate, scalloped corner showing, and she remarked about it, fingering it lightly.

"That is absolutely the loveliest thing," she said, once the men had shut the door to Daniel's study. It seemed to me she was positively aglow. She had news, she said in a whispered tone. "A baby." Her hand flittered down to her midriff, and she nodded, her face about to burst with joy. "Dr. Rutherford confirmed it Friday. I'm due in December." It would be her first, and finally. She and J.T. had been married four months longer than me and Daniel.

I took her hands in mine. "Congratulations," I said, and meant it sincerely. Two months ago I might not have. My own envy might have prevented it. But now, with my new purpose, the newspaper and the Populist Party, my childlessness no longer seemed so devastating. I could even sit there smiling, listening as she told me how she hoped it would be a boy, and that she knew just which room of her house she would make into a nursery. Her mother had already ordered a turned-wood cradle from a furniture maker in Bastrop. "And Jeremy is simply thrilled," she said; yet later, when J.T. came out of the study with Daniel, I couldn't see quite the same glow on his face.

The men walked out reeking of dead tobacco smoke. J.T. began talking loudly about women's suffrage, for my benefit I knew. J.T. had always thought me a trifle. He thought all women were, though coming out of Daniel's office that night, he professed that to give women the vote would debase them, that they should not have to muddle in the mess that was American politics. Yet in the next breath he said that someone would have to stand by the polls anyhow, just to show the females how to fold the ballot. Then he laughed heartily at himself, and to my amazement, so did Daphne.

But then Daphne had never been known for having good sense where J.T. Craddock was concerned. She had accepted his proposal of marriage less than three weeks after he'd been involved in a saloon fight over a loose woman. The fight had even spilled out into the street and gotten so nasty it made the next week's *Mentor*. Marshal Nash was there to break the whole thing up, since he was the proprietor of the saloon where it all happened. Both men, J.T. and the other one, who'd been a stranger, a traveler passing through on the Houston train, were assessed fines of twenty dollars apiece.

For a while, the incident was all anybody talked about. Some thought J.T. had only proposed to Daphne when he did to clear his name of scandal, being as Daphne's family was a good one. Her father owned the cotton-oil mill on the Elgin road and made a good living. After they were married, though, J.T.'s philandering didn't cease. Rumor was he had a regular woman at

Miss Lovie Brast's bordello outside town. And it was said he had already fathered a child or two by another woman he'd left in his wake, a woman who lived over close to String Prairie. Priscilla said Daphne was a little fool for ever saying yes to such a man as J.T. And now here she was carrying his baby and laughing with him as he made mockery of the whole female race.

Daniel sent a small smile my way, made a little shake of his head as if to say there wasn't need for me to take J.T. so seriously. I did not smile back. And later, after the Craddocks left, I got my next article out of it, sitting up at my writing desk till after midnight, scribbling down my indignation.

I wrote that while a woman might waste a little time in learning how to fold her ballot, the vote inside that ballot would be what she honestly thought it ought to be, and not what was suggested by the man that bought the last round of drinks for the crowd. And I vowed to myself that when the issue with this article came out, I'd see to it that J.T. Craddock himself got one delivered right to his door. That was the way I knew Andy would do it, and I promised myself that I could be just as brave. I would show anyone that cared to see that I did indeed have the gumption Andy had said I did.

11

For the next two weeks Daniel shipped his cattle, driving them into the feed pens at Bastrop, and eventually filling twenty-nine train cars, some headed north to Chicago, the rest south to Corpus Christi. Another two hundred head, all yearlings, were sold to Curtis Holman, who had a ranch over in Lee County near Lincoln. All this kept Daniel busy and away from home a good deal of the time. Nathan, too, was busy herding and shipping, selling off some of Papa's cattle along with Daniel's. But Nathan did find time to make it to the Populist meeting with me on June 11th.

Andy was there this time. It was the first I'd seen of him since the last Saturday in May, since I'd said that foolish thing about his eyes on the gallery, a long enough while I had begun to think of my feelings as about like a schoolgirl crush, which I'd never had myself but had seen the symptoms of at Miss Langburn's the week Mr. Montgomery from Baylor College had come to teach us astronomy.

As soon as Andy saw me and Nathan he came over to speak to us, and to introduce his sister and her husband who had come down from Cheneyville to help him get his crops laid by. "They'll be going back to their place tomorrow," he said, and he looked tired enough to fall asleep walking, but his voice was just as rich-textured as ever. I felt I should say something special to him, to let him know that I'd come to my senses in the two weeks since I'd seen him, but nothing witty or appropriate would come to me. I let Nathan do all our talking.

Lavinia Treadway was small and dark-haired, plain with a flat profile, as stiff and cool as Andy was warm and friendly. They seemed almost total opposites. She looked more like a sister to her dark husband than to Andy. Their children, too, seemed all mixed up and mismatched, with Hannah and Philip the blond ones, and Quintus and his two older girl cousins dark like his aunt and uncle. I couldn't help but stare across the room at where they all sat, Lavinia between her husband and Andy, the children on the floor in front.

During the meeting, Andy only got up to speak once and briefly to the crowd, just to say he was ready with his freighter to start hauling store-boughts from Austin if folks would bring him their list of needs next week. I had to explain to Nathan what Andy was talking about. I felt wise and well informed, and also well known since everybody had taken to calling me Sister Dellie. Since that first article appeared in the paper, I had been accepted into their flock.

Nathan didn't seem to care much for the singing part of the meeting, seemed, in fact, embarrassed by it. But he wanted to know more about Andy's plan to bring in goods from Austin, and about the dispute with Mr. Bassist. He asked questions of the Grossners, whom we sat beside, and also of Wes Peterson and Stan Tackaberry when the meeting was over. We knew most of these families from church and Nathan was never shy. It wasn't until we were back at the house that I found out why he was so curious.

We were at the kitchen table. Daniel was in Bastrop or on his way, camped someplace between here and there with the hands and the cattle. Lately, I couldn't keep up with his exact where-abouts. Nathan agreed to have a bite of leftover supper, Tante Lena's sausage pie and string beans, which I warmed up and served to him. He ate quickly and was wiping out his plate with a cold biscuit when he told me. "Papa left some debt." He said it simply, but with a trace of worry that made me sit up straight in my chair across the table.

"How much debt?"

"Not a lot. A few hundred dollars." He stuffed the biscuit into his mouth. It made a hump in his cheek like a quid of tobacco. "To Bassist's store just like everybody else at that meeting to-night."

"Why haven't I known about this?"

"It just didn't come up." He finished chewing the wad in his mouth; swallowed it down with a gulp of buttermilk, then wiped the white mustache off his upper lip. "But now that you understand public questions . . ."

"Don't make jokes."

"I'm not making jokes. Elias Franklow says there's a big market in Britain for Angora wool. I'm thinking of going into goats."

"Goats?" I blinked at him.

"I'm looking for a way to earn a fast dollar." I saw the fun on his face. I laughed despite myself.

"Daniel will loan you money if you need it. You know that."

He reached for the salt cellar in the middle of the table, spooned a dash into the palm of his hand. "He's already done enough by taking my cattle to market to sell—well, Papa's cattle."

"You mean, Mother's cattle."

"No, I mean Mr. Bassist's cattle. They sure as hell aren't mine."

"Nathan."

"Well, they're not." He looked at me and dabbed his tongue into the salt in his hand. As long as I could remember he had eaten salt like that. It curled my lip to watch him. He dusted the remains off on his pants. "I'm not interested in cattle. Not interested the way Daniel is. And I know I don't care to farm row-crops like Papa. I might like to do something completely different."

"Like what?"

"I don't know. Something else. And away from here where there's new money to be made. Not the same old dollar changing hands over and over again." He wagged his finger at me as if to stop me from speaking, though I had no intention. "And don't think I've become one of your dewy-eyed Populists. I still believe in free enterprise. And I don't think I could ever bring myself to sing their stupid songs anyway." He laughed. It sounded false, almost annoyed.

"I never knew you were discontent here," I said.

"Not really discontent. Just—" He shrugged. "I want to see something else. Don't you ever get the itch to see other places, Dellie?"

"I've been to Austin, and to Houston and Galveston—"

"I mean *other* places. Faraway places. Spain. Italy." His eyes got a gleam. "I'd like to go see Rome."

"Rome?" A laugh staggered out of me. I covered my mouth. "Write me a letter," I said.

He looked at me and grinned. He liked me teasing him back. He laughed, too.

"Does Mother know about all this?" I asked.

"About Rome?"

"No, the debt."

He grunted and shook his head. "All Mother does is moan around the house, fretting over Papa's soul burning in hell."

He sounded bored but I knew better. We looked away from each other. It got so silent for a minute that I could hear the flame guttering inside the kitchen lamp.

"Why do you think he did it?" My voice seemed piercing and loud. It was something we had not spoken of except in passing —Papa's suicide. We hadn't said what it meant to us. Or didn't mean.

Nathan shrugged. "He was dying anyway."

"Dane said something when he was here—"

"Said what?" Nathan's tone went harsh. Since Dane's visit, he had become an uneasy subject.

"That Papa took the coward's way out."

His mouth went thin. "Depends on if you believe in the mercy of God."

"Do you?"

"I don't think Papa's burning in hell." He said it with such sureness, so convinced. As for myself, I didn't even know if I believed in hell. Or heaven either.

"I've wondered if it was only because of the cancer. You said he'd spoken of Sister and Dane. And he was acting so peculiar at the Veterans' Reunion. Maybe he was having regrets for how he'd been—"

"Don't go dreaming up things, Dellie. Papa was still Papa right up to the minute he put that old thumb-buster in his mouth."

I winced at the image. I reached across the table and laid my hand on top of his. I squeezed. He turned his palm over and squeezed back, smiled at me, a dim smile that didn't hide the gloom he felt. Since Papa's death, Nathan had grown older overnight. It was there in his eyes, yet I hadn't really noticed before now.

"You look tired," he said to me, speaking aloud the exact same thoughts I was having of him. "I'm going home."

He stood up. He'd left his hat on the rack by the back door. He took it down, held on to it. It was a nice, tan, never-flop Stetson. Wearing it, and with his pants tucked down in his spike-toed saddle boots, he looked like a cattleman, a thing he didn't want to be.

"How'd we get on this subject anyway?" he said. "I'm supposed to be here cheering you up."

"Cheering me up? I don't need cheering up."

"Your husband thinks you do."

I felt my shoulders stiffen. "What did he say?"

"That something's grieving you. That you're as mixed up as a mad dog's guts." He grinned.

"Daniel didn't say that."

"No, but it's what he thinks."

"And he sent you here to cheer me up? Is that why you went with me tonight? Because Daniel asked you to?"

"You know it isn't. I told you I wanted to go before. And I'm glad I went. I just don't care for the singing." He grinned.

"Well, he can ask me about it himself." And I wouldn't say more. I didn't want to talk about Daniel with Nathan. And I didn't like it that they had discussed me between themselves either. Whatever was happening with Daniel and me, whatever was happening with me, was private, and Nathan had enough on his mind without my troubles to burden him further.

I walked out on the back porch with him to see him off, and rubbed on the dogs while he got his horse from the feed stall. Standing there, my mind went back to when we were little, right after Sister left us and Papa married Mother. That was when Nathan and I had gotten close. It wasn't something we planned, but so much was happening to us then, our lives changing. For Nathan, school became harder. For me, I suddenly got afraid of the dark.

We didn't share a room at Mother's house like we had at home, and after Dane left, too, I ended up trembling in my bed alone at night, scared of the shadows the low-post bed made on the wall when the moon was high. On those nights, I would creep into Nathan's room, and get under the covers with him, so he could keep me safe.

He came out of the horse stall on his big golden bay and waved a hand goodbye at me. The dogs were frisky and excited over having someone outside with them after dark. I couldn't hold them back from following Nathan out to the gate. I leaned against a post on the back gallery and felt the old emptiness, like a big, dark hole in the middle of me. A slow rain had started, and I stayed there listening to it fall on the ground and the garden stones to the springhouse, until the dogs came back and forced me, with their muddy paws and wet noses, to go inside to bed.

Nathan's remark about the songs had given me an idea for the *Plaindealer,* and that was to print the lyrics to one song each week in the paper. I felt sure that if Nathan could have just understood what everyone was singing, he wouldn't have thought the songs were silly. And I thought maybe others would benefit from having the words printed, too. I knew I would. I went into town on Saturday to tell the Bettses and Andy—mostly Andy—about my idea. I hadn't been able to speak to him at the meeting, and I wanted another chance.

There was a commotion in town, outside Van Burkleo's notion store. People had gathered. I thought at first it was an animal on the loose, since I recognized Clyde Deatheridge, who had been appointed catcher because he had all manner of ropes and snares and traps left over from the days when he'd been a pelt hunter. But then I saw Jack Nash, too, and I realized it was Willie Betts and Andy the marshal was talking to. Andy's face was knotted up and he kept raising his hand in slashing gestures that Willie tried each time to quiet.

Such a crowd had gathered, its being Saturday and trading time, that I had to tie Cintha clear across in front of Sapling's and walk over from there, bumping my way through the people. I heard Andy's voice first, loud and angry, saying, "I'm telling you, Jack, you hadn't got to look any further than that—"

"Watch your language, Andy. There's women and children." This was Willie Betts, and I thought it was an odd thing for him to say since I'd never heard Andy swear. I edged sideways through the crowd, and got up to the front in time to see Willie put his hand on Andy's shoulder. Andy's smile was so brittle it looked ready to break off his face.

"Just let me say what I want to say," he said to Willie in a voice overloaded with forced calm.

"We've already heard your accusations," Jack Nash said.

At that, Andy took a threatening step forward. The veins in his neck bulged like whipcords. "Accusations? Did you say accusations? This is no accusation."

Willie stepped between them, still playing the peacemaker. I was completely confused. My throat felt tight, and people around me were mumbling, some trying to get into the argument.

"No, it ain't right," Andy said, loud. "It ain't goddamn right."

Some of the ladies around me gasped and covered their ears. I held my breath, too. At that moment, Mr. Bassist stepped onto the gallery in front of his store across the street. I thought Andy was going to go barreling over there, but Willie caught an arm. I wanted to know what was happening. I'd never seen Andy act this way, or talk this way. He didn't notice me there. His hand shot out and he pointed across the distance toward Mr. Bassist, who stood on his gallery smirking like a birddog after the hunt.

"There's who you need to be questioning," Andy said to Marshal Nash, pointing at Louis Bassist. "There's the sonofa—"

"We can't prove anything." Willie pulled Andy back. As menacing as Jack Nash looked right then, I was afraid he might arrest Andy any second.

And then I felt a hand on my arm. Gretta Betts had me. I turned to her and grabbed her hand with mine. "What's happening? What's going on here?"

She guided me away from the crowd a few steps, watching with anxious eyes as Willie restrained Andy once again. "Come on," she said, leading me to the door of the newspaper office.

I saw that Sam Alexander and some of Mr. Bassist's store customers had come out on the gallery, and the street between here and there was filling up. "What is it, Gretta? What's this about?"

"Just come."

Right as we were about to go in the door, Mr. Bassist called out something I didn't hear well, and Andy yelled back, "Why don't you come over here and ask *me* that?"

Gretta was trying to force me in the door, but I hung back. "Come up," she said sternly, and then I saw that Willie was trying to get Andy off the street, too, so I let Gretta steer me up the stairwell. I kept looking back, though, watching Willie bring Andy in after us.

"Dammit, Willie, let me go," Andy said.

"Get up there," Willie said. "And stay up there. You're making things worse."

"How can I make them worse?"

Gretta squeezed around me and held out her hand. "Come on, Andy," she said, and he looked up the stairwell at her. I thought he saw me for the first time, too. He started to climb the stairs, and relief swept over Willie's face. He ducked back out the bottom door.

Andy's eyes kept straight on me so I waited for him on the landing. The stony expression on his face frightened me. "Have you seen it?" he said.

"Seen what?"

"No, she hasn't yet," Gretta answered for me. She took my elbow.

"Well, you're about to." Andy reached over my shoulder and

pushed open the upstairs door, which was already partly ajar. I stepped in and could not believe what was there in front of me.

The office had been destroyed: drawers pulled out from the desk and upturned on the floor. Papers had been thrown in a pile and set afire. Luckily the fire had gone out on its own or else someone had come soon enough to douse it, because the papers were only partly scorched, but they stank up the room. Ink jars had been thrown against the wall, and worst of all, the press had been dumped over onto its side. Screws and machine parts leaked out onto the floor in a maze.

I was so stunned I couldn't move. Then Andy went past me to the windows, which were already thrown wide. The door to the back room opened and Jordan Betts and Quintus peered out with cautious looks on their faces.

"I'm going to take the children," Gretta said, striding past me. Hannah had ventured out, too, and Gretta lifted her, gathering the three of them up to go. All were unusually quiet.

Andy didn't say anything or move from the windows. Gretta was occupied with getting off with the children. And I was busy trying to piece everything together, the ruckus outside on the street, Andy's rage, Mr. Bassist's smug smile. The devastation in the office around me was overwhelming, frightening in its viciousness. I heard the door at the bottom of the stairwell close before I realized I hadn't even spoken to the children, not even a hello or a goodbye.

Over at the windows, Andy's back was as stiff as if an iron rod had been run up his spine. He had on his white shirt, a vest I'd never seen, dark green with a paisley shell design. It seemed new and out of context, accented his ramrod back. He still had not moved or uttered another sound. The 10:55 whistled into the station. Voices still droned outside on the street.

The fountain pen from the desk lay at my feet. I bent to pick it up, set it on the one upright filing cabinet. "You think Mr. Bassist did this?"

"Or had it done. Who else?" He shifted from one foot to the other, but didn't turn away from the windows.

"The Democrats maybe?" I meant to lighten the tension, maybe get a laugh from him, but he wasn't in a laughing mood. I moved through the mess, stepped around the soggy wad of burned newspapers. I bent to scoop some trash back into the spilled-over bin.

"This is the work of that German son of a jackass." He glanced at me. "Don't touch anything," he snapped.

"Why not?"

"Just don't."

I stood up. "Somebody has to clean up this mess."

"Not you. I don't want you to do it." His tone was hard and I flinched from it. He turned from the window, I thought to say something else to me, but then I heard someone on the stairs and saw his expectant look. Gretta had left the upper door open and Willie appeared there.

"What?" Andy said, as if Willie were interrupting us from something important. I'd never known his voice could sound so harsh. Willie didn't seem to notice it.

"I've got to go over and give a report to Jack Nash. Tell me again what time you got here."

Andy took two quick strides forward. "I'm going with you."

"No. You stay here." Willie looked at me. "Keep him here."

"I'm going," Andy said.

Willie put out his hand. "No, you're not, Andy. I'm the editor of this newspaper, and I'm the one who'll go. I just want to know again what time you got here."

Andy folded his arms. "Half past nine. But be sure you say

who did this. Name names. Tell Nash that German jackass was standing out on his gallery with a cigar in his mouth."

"That doesn't prove anything, Andy. You heard what Jack said."

"Get it in the report. You know as well as I do whose work this is." Andy turned back toward the window. "And I'm going to prove it. I don't know how yet, but I will."

Willie shook his head, then gave me an exasperated look, silently begging me to keep Andy here, to somehow get him calm. Maybe I imagined all that in Willie's look, but it seemed to me he was asking something of me, and I didn't want to let him down.

When he had gone again, I moved toward the windows, craning to see what it was that so held Andy's interest out there. There was nothing. The crowd had broken up. Mr. Bassist wasn't in sight. It was just the usual Saturday afternoon congestion of wagons and horses. I could smell the dust. Thursday night's shower hadn't lasted long enough to even make mud.

Andy gave me a sidelong glance. "You don't have to stay and tend to me," he said, so I knew he had also seen Willie's look. "I'm not going to go down there. I've made things bad enough for Willie."

"I was going to . . ." My eyes moved around the office. "I came because I had some ideas—"

He made a noise, not a laugh, just a noise, like a pig's snort. "For the paper? There won't be a paper any time soon, thanks to that sonofabitch."

He leaned both hands on the window ledge, as if he'd lost his balance along with his temper. His eyes narrowed. His forehead furrowed deep between his brows. I wanted to some way comfort him.

"I feel so sorry for all this, Andy. I really do. I know how important the paper is to you."

"Feel sorry for Louis Bassist."

"I don't like to hear you talk that way. It makes me scared." I said it without thinking about how personal it sounded until the words were out there between us.

He turned fully from the window, and for the first time that day he seemed to really take me in. His face dissolved, though not to soothe me. Something inside him seemed to melt, and I realized that his rage of a moment ago had been mostly to escape the defeat I saw come on him now. His shoulders sloped. He sighed deeply. I couldn't bear for him to look so unhappy. It was even worse than the anger.

The desk chair was still in one piece, just shoved over into a corner. I reached for his arm. He looked at my hand, then back at me, watching my mouth as I spoke.

"Come sit down over here. There's nothing you can do about any of this right now. Just stick to your plan to bring goods in from Austin. It's the best way to get back at him. Right now, though, why don't you just sit down here. Relax yourself a minute."

As I said all of this, I was leading him to the chair. He let me, even sat down like I wanted him to. He seemed as pliant as sculpting clay, but then he caught hold of my arm with a firmness and a steadiness, and he looked at me with something new on his face. Before I grasped what was even happening, he drew me onto his lap. His arms went around me, pinning my elbows tight against my ribs, and without a word, he laid his head against my breast. I was immobilized by the shock of it, the awkwardness and the thrill. He held me that way for a few moments, as if to still and quiet me, almost as if he wanted to hear my heart and lungs working inside my chest. But I could hardly breathe, not with him so near. When he finally raised his head, his eyes held a softness, yet there was trouble in them, too.

"I wish I could be what you think I am. What I see when I look

in your face. That I'm noble and true. Or some kind of a hero."
His hands moved to my neck. One work-rough thumb rubbed
my throat. "I'm just a farmer, Dellie, with two kids I can barely
feed. That's all I am."

I swallowed and nearly choked myself. I let my fingers twine
around his wrists. I couldn't speak. I wouldn't have known what
to say anyway. His eyes searched mine.

"I'm no lover man." He was whispering now. "I don't have time
for it. Do you understand?"

I wet my lips, nodded. My mouth was so dry, and my skin
where he touched me so tingling. My pulse raced, but I didn't
move from his lap. I didn't get up and run in shame for having
been discovered. For one thing, he had not let go of me, and for
another, the tenderness in his hands and his eyes did not agree
with the words he spoke.

I had the feeling he had known all along how I felt about him,
knew better than me even when it had begun. He leaned to kiss
me and I was not surprised by that either. I didn't think it at all
odd that he would say one thing and do another. It made perfect
sense. We were not free for each other. And yet, in that moment,
with his hands on my face and his lips holding mine, I felt as free
and complete as I ever had.

The kiss grew and we both let it. His back came away from the
chair. I felt us roll a few inches forward. He circled me with his
arms, and I clung to him.

It was not one of the tight, chaste kisses I was used to, tenta-
tive and almost apologetic, from Daniel. This kiss had fire in it,
and life. It drew the breath right out of my soul, a soul I never
even knew before it vanished. And after we heard Willie downstairs and had scrambled apart, while we stood there white-faced
and huffing, I looked across at Andy and knew he still had me
inside him.

Willie came in and saw us. We must have looked strained and stiff to him, but all he said was, "Well, that's done with." He put his hands on his hips and glanced around at the mayhem. He could only see half of it but he didn't know that. "Are the two of you game to pitch in with this?"

I looked again at Andy and I don't think he had ever taken his eyes off of me. He nodded and I spoke for both of us. "Where do we start?"

PART TWO

12

The following days are a jumble in my memory: Daniel coming home, Sunday church services, and dinner at Mother's. Sometime during the week, Mrs. Slater and Priscilla came by to talk about the teachers for the Normal School and the party we were all going to give. They must have brought Mother with them, because she was there and Nathan wasn't. I can't recall the details. Andy's kiss had dazed me better than if he'd knocked me in the head with a hammer. I couldn't think of anything else but it, and him, the two together. The whole time anyone spoke to me I watched their lips, thinking of Andy's lips, moist and firm, and of what an odd thing it was to do, kiss, and wondering why it felt so magical, touching lips together. I had come almost completely unraveled. I was just living for Thursday when I could see him again.

I sent word to the Bettses that I would need another ride to the meeting. They came for me before sundown. I'm sure we talked about the newspaper. We must have. We had nothing else to say. Willie was going to Brenham at the end of the week after parts for the press. I tried to seem interested.

Andy was already at the hall when we arrived. He was outside with the children, leaned against a honey locust discussing something with Stan Tackaberry and Seamus Murphy. He didn't notice us, and I almost went straight to him before I held myself back. Instead, I helped Gretta haul in her water jug. It was all I could do to walk by Andy leaned there underneath that tree and not go to him. I ached for another kiss.

As I stepped back outside the hall, Hannah caught my skirts, and it was her singing out, "Miz O'Bert! Miz O'Bert! Come swing me!" that made Andy turn from his conversation to find me with his eyes.

"Swing you?" I said, watching her papa watch me.

She took my hand and started pulling me. "Over here. I'll show you."

Around in back of the hall someone had hung up two plank swings from an oak branch. Quintus was on one of the swings. Jordan Betts had the other. They were both soaring high, the ropes creaking around the limb. Hannah broke loose from me and ran to Quintus. She started trying to bully him out of the swing so she could take over.

"Quintus has it now, Hannah. You'll have to wait your turn." I glanced again at Andy and saw him start my way. Quickly, I turned back to face the children. I imagined I could feel his footsteps coming behind me.

"Make him get down now!" Hannah yelled.

Andy's voice came firmly. "Watch your temper, young lady. You get in line like the others." He stopped beside me. "I have to speak to you."

I took a couple of breaths before I realized the second part of what he said was meant for me. I turned fully toward him, and he looked away.

"Not now," he said. "Are you with Willie and Gretta?"

I nodded. His face shone with perspiration.

"All right then," he said. "We'll talk when the meeting's done."

He didn't sit with me, and I had hoped since I was with the Bettses, and since he didn't have a sister here or some other distraction, that he would. When he got up to speak about the newspaper offices being closed and about his supply run to Austin, he never once found me with his eyes. I knew it didn't mean anything except that he was trying to keep our secret. But in light of how friendly we'd been in the past, I thought if folks were watching us, him ignoring me would look more suspicious than speaking to me would, even sitting with me, acting as we always had.

The meeting that night seemed interminable. The state convention of the Populists was being held in Dallas the following week, and since Willie was representing our district there, he asked for a hand vote, women included, on each of the four candidates. But before he could get a count of the hands, people started in asking questions about things that had nothing to do with party politics, and asking them out in the open, so that pretty soon, the whole meeting dissolved into a discussion of everything in the world but the state convention. Things like Wayne Shirley's well running dry, and Virginia Dillon's seventh child coming due in two weeks. I wanted to shout out that none of these things was of concern to the party, and for everyone to shut up so Willie could get said what needed saying and wind down this meeting.

Finally, it was over. People began to leave the hall, but even then they moved slowly, as if they were reluctant to go home. Some of the older boys ran back and forth the length of the room, jumping with their arms up-stretched, trying to see who could touch the ceiling. I wanted to whack them with my broom as I swept the floor, to tell them to pipe down and go find their parents. I watched Andy out of the corner of my eye while he saw folks off into the night. He spoke at length with some of them, took orders on scraps of paper for goods from Austin. Come Saturday, he'd be leaving. I heard him say it, time and again. Come Saturday . . .

And then I felt the quick touch of his hand on my shoulder. It sent a quiver involuntarily over me, raised the hair on my arms. He still looked pale, still distracted. He motioned with one slight tilt of his head for me to follow him outside. I looked around.

No one was watching us. Across the room, Gretta set chairs to rights. I leaned the broom against the wall. Willie stepped back inside just then. He stopped to speak to Andy about something. I went on out the door.

The children were playing in back of the hall. The boys had Hannah, pushing her in one of the swings. I could hear their voices and their laughter, hers higher pitched than the boys'. I stood in the shadows and waited for Andy to come out. When he did, he took a few steps toward the rear of the hall, checking that the children were occupied, then he put his hand on the small of my back and turned me the opposite way.

The light from inside the hall didn't reach the front side of the building like it did the back side. I stumbled a little in the dark, and he caught my arm. "Watch your step." He sounded familiar yet stiff. He let go of me quickly, as if my skin gave off an electric shock.

When we got to a spot where the grass wasn't ankle thick, I stopped walking. When I did he did, but he seemed to want to continue farther on, away from the hall, to hide us completely from view. He paced a few steps, measuring what he wanted to say. I waited. I tried to be patient. I couldn't bear the suspense.

"What is it, Andy?"

He quit moving. I couldn't make him out well in the darkness, only his shadowy form there in front of me, but I knew he was looking at me. "I wanted to apologize to you for the other day. I wasn't myself. I acted in ways I shouldn't have, and I wanted to say . . ." He paused, cleared his throat. His voice was so quiet I had to lean forward to hear him plainly. ". . . I shouldn't have compromised you—"

"I'm not compromised." I wondered if he could see me better than I could him. I felt exposed.

"What I said to you was the truth. You remember what I said?"

He seemed reluctant to repeat our conversation, as if he were ashamed to even mention it again out loud.

"You said you were not a lover man."

"There's not enough of me, Dellie. I'm worn down."

"I don't believe that."

"It's the truth."

His arms moved upward to his face, to rub his eyes or to smooth his hair back from his forehead. He was close enough I could have touched him. I thought of his lips on mine.

"Take me to Austin with you when you go," I said.

He stayed still. The close, damp night air enveloped us. The laughter from the children came, the sound seeming farther than it really was. Insects filled the silence. Fireflies winked in and out of the cornstalks in a field nearby.

"How could I do that?" he said, asking as if it were a real question he wanted me to answer. I knew what he meant: the town had eyes. The countryside did. We could not be seen together leaving in his wagon.

"When will you get there?"

He hesitated, but then answered, "Sunday evening. If I get an early enough start Saturday morning, maybe that night or Sunday morning."

"And when will you leave to come back home?"

"Soon as I get the supplies. Monday noon. No later than that." He stood quiet, waiting for me to speak next. He would let me plan things, let this be my idea.

"Could you go up a day earlier?"

"You mean leave tomorrow?"

"I could catch the train there Saturday morning. I could wait for you at the depot."

He pivoted away from me a few steps, before he turned back. "I came out here to tell you I couldn't—that I'd made a mistake."

"I know."

An owl hooted somewhere close. I trembled almost uncontrollably, as if it were dead winter instead of the middle of June. His hand touched my arm, drew me close to him. He moved the hair at my temples, pressed his lips there. "God help me," he whispered.

Relief came to me. I wound my arms around his back, felt the curve of the long muscles there folding into his spine, and the dampness from under his shirt. He pulled a kiss from my lips, and when he broke loose, my mouth followed his. He nudged back from me, let me go.

"If I'm leaving tomorrow morning, I better get home," he said, and I nodded, fighting for my breath. He strode away from me, and when he got around the corner of the building, called out, "Quint! Hannah! Let's load up!" I thought he sounded almost angry.

I went straight back inside the hall, thinking I would finish my sweeping, pretend I'd only stepped away to the privy for a moment. Gretta already had the broom. She raised her eyes at me. I hoped my face wasn't flushed, and as soon as I had the thought, I felt the heat spread out to my earlobes.

"Is there something needs carrying out?" I said. She shook her head, but didn't speak.

Willie was at the row of windows. He leaned his head out of one. "Andy, wait a minute! Can you help me get this table moved back?"

There was a long table we moved every week to clear the front. And even though the Populists were about the only people who used the place anymore, Willie always insisted that we put the table back the way we found it.

When Andy came inside, he made a special effort not to look at me. I wondered if it was as hard for him to do that as it was for me. His face was damp, his mouth drawn up tight. He ignored me completely. Too completely. I tried not to pay attention to him either, even when I heard him ask Gretta if he could bring the children over in the morning. "I've decided to go on ahead to Austin tomorrow. Get an early start on things. I've got a long list to fill."

A thrill washed through me at his words, a thrill so strong it threatened to burst loose. The day after tomorrow we would be alone together. No more of this pretense in front of others. No more interruptions. We could speak freely, tell each other what was in our hearts. It would be like a dream, just the two of us.

I told Quintus and Hannah good night, kissed both their cheeks, but I didn't say one word to their papa.

13

The sky was dusted with high spiraling clouds when I went with my one small bag out to the carriage house Saturday morning. Sinclair was there, watering the animals, and I told him my brother from up in North Texas had wired that he would be in Austin this afternoon. "So I'll need Cintha hitched up." The mare raised her head when she heard her name.

Sinclair looked at me with confusion, scratched his woolly chin. "I didn't see Tater Nance come out here this morning."

Tater was Mr. Felty's runner at the telegraphing office. I shook my head. "I got the message last night. I'll be staying over until tomorrow. Tell Tante Lena for me, will you?"

As it turned out, he didn't have to tell her. She came out of her garden nearly running when I drove by. She held her apron, full of the yellow squash she'd just picked, while I gave her the same story. "But you should have Sinclair drive you," was all the comment she made.

And I said, "I'll leave Cintha at the livery."

Once in town, I had to tell my story to a few more—Mrs. Browder, whom I saw coming out of Bassist's store; Jennings Previne, who ran the livery for Clarence Bright; and Mr. Schuster, who sold me my two-way ticket to Austin. Mayor and Mrs. Seawell were on the train, heading for a day with their daughter in Webberville, so I had to expand on my story about Dane going to Austin, said he was on legal business there, clearing up title to some land he'd bought up in Parker County, something I knew Daniel had done once for Seamus Murphy when the time came for Mr. Murphy to prove-up on his 260 acres out along Goodwater Creek. I was relieved when the Seawells got off at the

Manor station. My capacity for lies was reaching its limit. I sat the rest of the way, through stops at Daffan and Currie, with my clutch sitting in my lap, and my thoughts stayed on Andy. I'd be with him soon. Alone with him.

It wasn't until I was at the station, waiting on the gallery outside with my grip, that a flurry of nerves and doubt set in. What caused it was listening to the hack drivers call for those seeking accommodations at various hotels in town. It made me wonder, quite suddenly, where we would stay the night. Times I had come to Austin with Daniel we had rooms at the Driskill, but a bell clerk might recognize me there, or some other of Daniel's acquaintances might. And it was then, while I contemplated lodging, that the impact of my coming here, of meeting Andy in this clandestine way, settled in.

Until that moment, I had barely considered the actual meaning of our meeting here, the physical part of it. The thought had been lurking in the corners of my mind but not in a wholly formed way. I had packed my best nightgown of white lawn and cotton lace, part of my honeymoon trousseau, but I'd been thinking more of looking pretty, not of actually staying together in the same room, or God forbid, the same bed. I didn't even do that with Daniel. It made me uncomfortably warm to think of it.

I fanned myself with my pocketbook and tried to calm down, reminding myself that Andy was a gentleman. And he always seemed to understand me so well, to practically read my thoughts before I even did so myself sometimes. Likely as not, he knew my true desire was only to share some time with him, not to have a consummated love affair. That would be too indecently sinful for either of us.

A woodpecker worked on the phone pole above me. I leaned my head back against the wall behind the bench and watched him bore his hole, and I got a kind of yawning feeling in my stomach as I imagined Andy stretched out full-length beside me, our hearts touching, our flesh. I remembered the feel of his arms around me, the strength in them, the urgency.

I straightened myself, smoothed at my skirt. A lady should not be having such thoughts. Such uncouth, animal thoughts. How embarrassing it would be for him to see me unclothed. He would know then how sharp my hip bones stuck out, that I had skinny legs and big knees, how small my breasts were. And worse, what if I were to see him. . . . I folded my arms, tucked my hands in next to my ribs. My corset felt stiff and suffocating. Perspiration damped me under my dress.

Another thought came to me—one even more despairing than the others. What if he didn't come for me at all? What if he had changed his mind? He'd been reluctant. It was me who had thrown myself at him at every turn, starting clear back to the day I'd chased him down with the bottle of medicine for his mule. He was probably thinking it would be a good lesson for me to sit here all day waiting for him to never show. And here I would have to stay, in this noisy, stifling, smelly depot, because I wouldn't begin to know where to look for him in this city.

I opened my watch. Two hours had already passed. My backside was sore from sitting so long on the hard bench, and I'd lost count of other trains that had come and gone, had tired of watching the people around me. I began seriously to feel deserted, hot and grimy, and to think I should inquire into getting my return ticket changed from tomorrow to this evening, when I saw him.

He came up on the east side, walking across an intersection of two streets, searching through the faces in the crowd standing on the platform. He wore the dark paisley vest, a shirt I'd never seen with a thin green stripe, darker green Windsor tie. His pants were down in his boots, straw hat shading his head. I thought he looked dapper, and my heart nearly lifted me off the bench.

"Andy!" I waved my pocketbook. "Right here!" I started toward him. He didn't see me until I was within ten paces of him. Then the frown around his mouth eased.

"No hat?" he said, taking my grip from me. "Don't you know you'll get sunstroke without a hat? I was looking for feathers and folderol." He made a gesture at his head with his fingers splayed like a cock's comb. I laughed.

He took my hand—his was dry and firm—and he hurried me across the street. Traffic was heavy. We had to wait for a wagon loaded down with bags of meal to pass us by, a group of bicyclists. The dust hovering over the road was almost overwhelming but I didn't take my hand out of his grasp to cover my mouth.

His wagon and four mules were standing in harness on a side street. He tossed my grip into the back and lifted me up to the seat. The leather seat covering had once been black but was faded to dull gray and cracked, with the hay stuffing coming out, showing the board plank underneath.

"It's no hansom cab," he said by way of apology.

"It'll be fine."

He took up the team anchors, hauled them over the sideboards, where they landed with a jolt and a thump in the wagon bed. Then he climbed up beside me. His driving gloves were on the seat between us. They were buckskin, worn dark and shiny, molded to the shape of his hands and fingers and the reins down inside. He tugged them on and smiled at me where I sat next to him, high above the street.

"I had a load to deliver for Mr. Williams. That's why I'm late. I just couldn't see making the trip up here empty-handed. We could have supper someplace if you're hungry."

I was a little, but I didn't want him to spend whatever money Mr. Williams had paid him for hauling over a load of pottery. I said I didn't need to eat yet.

"Well, what do you want to do? This thing ain't especially made for gadding about." He laughed, but he was trying too hard and it came out forced.

I scooted nearer to him, and thinking to relax him, I slipped my arm under his elbow. So far he had not moved the mules. He raised his eyes, and even in the shade of his hat brim, I could see the deep color and the mildness in them.

"I'm not at all sure about this, Dellie," he said.

"Sure about what?"

"That you ought to be here. That we should be here together. What did you tell your husband?"

"He wasn't home." I didn't want to think about Daniel.

"Well, you had to tell somebody something."

I clasped his arm a little closer. He felt hot underneath the sleeve of his shirt. The sun beat down on us. "I said I was meeting Dane."

"Your brother."

"Yes."

"Nobody thought that was odd?"

"They didn't say."

He looked out over the backs of his mules. They were standing, flicking their tails, but otherwise still and quiet. His jaw tightened. "I hate a lie."

"I don't much like it either," I said and he looked at me again. "But it was the only way I could think of to come. And I wanted to come."

He studied me for another second or two, then reached with his gloved hand and touched the back of his fist to my chin. He lifted my face a little, and I smelled soap and hair oil, the bay rum. And I realized he'd gone somewhere and cleaned up for me. A man who has just traveled thirty-five miles behind four mules does not smell of bay rum.

The place where he took me was nothing I could have dreamed up in my wildest imaginings back at the train station. For one thing it was not a hotel at all but a private house, or rather more like the root cellar to a private house. The foundation and walls seemed to have sunk into the ground about six feet. Built of fieldstone and enclosed by a fence covered with wild honeysuckle and dewberry vines, the place seemed almost eerie, like a rabbit's warren rather than a house for human beings. A thatched roof would not have been out of place, but the roof on this house was of shining new sheet metal, the only new thing I could see around me.

"Who lives here?" I said when it became clear we had reached our destination.

"You remember Ben? My sister Lavinia's husband? You met him at the meeting." Andy had brought the mule team to a halt and held them. "Well, it's Ben's brother's place. He's a line walker for the Great Northern, Christ help him. He lets me stay here whenever I'm in town. He isn't usually at home."

I gave the building another uncertain look. Then I gave one to Andy. "Is he home now?"

He shook his head, sort of lowered his chin before he let his eyes meet mine. He got down to tie off the mules and reached a hand up to me. It was a long step down, and I thought he held on to my waist just a heartbeat more than he needed. The flounce at my hem snagged and tore a little. He heard the rip and bent to see the damage.

"It doesn't matter," I said, pivoting away from him, self-conscious that he might get a glimpse of my calves. "It's on a seam. It'll be easy to fix." I smoothed down my skirt, gave him a smile. He looked at me for a second more, then led the way inside the fence.

Bees were busy at work on the vines and overgrowth inside the yard. Someone long ago had planted irises, oxalis, and spider lilies and they had flourished in the deep shade. Beside the door, he moved a loose stone and took out a black iron housekey, opened the lock, and we went inside.

The room we stepped into smelled a hundred years old. Two high windows, so dirt-encrusted they did little to lighten the gloom, faced south and east. There was a bed, an eating table and two benches, a cookstove, and a hole in the north wall that served as a fireplace. Everything was crude and seemed ancient, except for the single incandescent lightbulb that hung from the ceiling above the table. Andy pulled its cord and it sent out a glow, yellow and weak.

"He's got electric," he said, and we both admired the lightbulb for a few uncomfortable seconds. Then he said, "You get yourself situated. I'm going to go put up the mules," and he left me.

I didn't know what I was supposed to do to get situated. I ventured into the other room, which was nearly identical to the first: a bed, a table, the hole-in-the-wall fireplace. The bowl of water on the washstand had been used. A razor lay there, and a brush, a bar of shaving soap. I uncorked the bottle of toilet water and smelled bay rum.

Underneath the window stood a richly varnished chiffonier that looked out of place in its rude surroundings. On top of the chiffonier sat a photograph in a cabinet case, of a pretty woman in a patterned dress. Engraved on the outside of the frame was "Julia." I wondered who she was, and who he was, Ben's brother.

When Andy came back inside, I was sitting at the table on the long bench underneath the lightbulb. I'd found a book of Chaucer among a few on the window ledge and had it open. I'd been planning to look relaxed—*The Canterbury Tales* in this underground lair, this dungeon—but I jumped to my feet when Andy came inside the door.

"You have an unusual family," I said, forgetting what witty thing I'd intended to say regarding *The Canterbury Tales,* this place, his relatives. I held on to the gilt-bound book, lifting it out with my words, showing it to him in a feeble attempt to explain what all I meant.

He unknotted the tie at his neck; frowned, confused. "How's that?"

I looked at the book, then couldn't say really what was so unusual. It seemed an almost snobbish observance now that I'd said it out loud, that people who lived the way this relative of Andy's did could not read. I mumbled, "Chaucer."

He paused on me a second, and I wondered if he thought me snobbish, too. But then he went on with his tie, pulling it free from his collar. "Larry isn't really family. . . . Well, I reckon he is, at that."

"His name's Larry?"

"Lawrence. Treadway."

"Lawrence." I set the book down on the table, ran my hand over the outside binding. "Is he married?"

"She died. Of consumption."

Idle talk. It was nothing but idle talk to keep our mouths and our minds occupied. I didn't like how I was feeling, awkward, wicked, weak-headed, and terribly thirsty. I kept my hand on the book, tracing the bumps and the engraving on the leather cover.

"Did she live here in this house? Those flowers outside, they seemed like a woman's—"

"No. She died in New Orleans. Larry—the Treadways are Louisiana people. My father rode a circuit that took him into Louisiana. Lavinia is . . . well, she's my half sister."

He was giving me a look but I didn't attempt to read it. I had to keep my face turned away from his. I tried a smile, aimed it his general way. "You have a stepmother, too. I didn't know that. We truly do have so much in common."

"My father never married Lavy's mother." He said this so quietly, I thought at first I had misheard him. "He built her a house, and she bore him three kids, but she was his secret. Except his heart gave out on one of his trips across the Sabine. And Addie—that was her name, Lavy's mom—she brought him home to us in the bed of a wagon."

"And your mother was still alive?"

"She was. Raising four kids of her own."

I didn't know what to say. I stood there at a loss, wondering why he was telling me all of this. And telling me right now. Here. In this house. Not that I didn't want to know. I yearned to know everything about him, but this felt different someway, as if he had more in mind than just filling up silence, like there was a moral to this fable, or a message he intended for me to understand.

He lifted his chin toward the window. "I won't ever forget the look on her face when she realized about Addie, that other woman, that whole other family my father had in Louisiana. It takes a lot of forgiving to get over a thing like that."

He dropped his tie on the table, took off his hat and laid it there, too, done with his story. His hair had started to curl in the outside heat and had creases on the sides and in the back from his hat. Most of the pomade he had used had rubbed off so that in the blaring light overhead, I could see the flecks of gold in each lock. He smiled at me, a smile intended to put me at ease but it didn't work. He took a step nearer to me.

"We could snoop around for some food if you're hungry," he said.

I shook my head. "Don't you usually go visit Cova when you're here? You can go on ahead if you'd like. I won't keep you from it. I can read or"—I glanced at my drab surroundings—"or do something."

He didn't answer right away. He was so close, maybe two feet from me was all. The tension between us seemed suddenly loud enough to hear. "I oughtn't to've lured you here," he said. "It was a mistake. Gather your things. I'll take you somewhere else."

"You didn't lure me. I wanted to come. It was my idea—"

"Why? I wondered that the whole way here. Why did you want to come?"

"To be with you."

"What did you think would happen when you got here?"

I blinked at him, recalling my near panic back at the depot. It rushed over me again. I tried to swallow the dryness in my mouth. "I don't know," I stammered. "I just wanted to—"

My throat closed and I made a strangling sound. He stepped even closer, reached for me, but I put my hand out, trying to keep some distance between us. It was too quick, too frightening, and too frank, this nearness. My finger touched a button on his vest. Smooth, round button, a bump of thread in the center.

"I'm fine. Really, I am. Nerves. It's just, I'm—" *Nervous* was the word I wanted, but his hands closed around mine and I couldn't speak anymore. I felt the blood stop in my veins.

He brought my fingers to his lips, cupped my hand gently inside both of his, as if he held a crystal goblet he was about to sip from. Then he pressed my palm to the side of his face. I felt the sharp angle of his jaw, the cleanness of his skin, and suddenly, I wanted it done with and over, this thing we had come together for, this desire that neither of us could speak of but both of us felt. My arms went around his neck, and in an instant, it was as if I'd been swallowed.

He bore me backwards over the table. His hands moved clumsily down the row of buttons on my shirtwaist. One popped off and hit the floor somewhere. He worked through the hooks of my corset, pushed aside my undervest, bared my breasts to the air in the room and to the musty sunlight through the windows. He didn't seem to care or even notice that I was small, that my ribs showed. He lifted my skirts. His fingers found the string on my drawers.

A hunger came over me. It started at the base of my spine and spread down to my knees and my feet, causing me to become like something else, or someone else, as if I had caught the same fever he was in. I wound myself around him, drawing him close, and still it wasn't close enough. I wanted to crawl inside his skin. I slipped in the sweat between us, sweltered in the heat of his breath. His grip on me tightened, and a tremor burst from him. Then as quickly as he had grabbed me, he let me go.

He scrambled away, moved to the other side of the room near the high window, righting his clothes as he went, wiping his face in his hands. He left me there on the table, exposed for a moment, like a common trollop. Cold. Sodden inside and out. Panting like a dog in summer.

I pushed down my skirt, hurried to cover myself. My cheeks felt tight. I glanced again at him. He leaned with his shoulder against the wall, his back to me, head bent, studying his hands as if they'd been wounded. The light through the windows and the incandescent bulb overhead were ugly and harsh. I longed for the kindness of night to hide in.

My drawers were in a heap under the table. I stumbled down after them, feeling faint, cheaply used and discarded. I leaned against the table for a second, sick at my stomach, while the room got white and wobbly. I bumped my head on the underside of the table, coming back up, and a tear streamed instantly down my nose. From the shock and the humiliation, not from the pain. I sat down flat on the floor.

At the noise I made, he turned, looking to see what I'd done to myself. And there I sat, holding the back of my head in one hand, my flannel drawers and the front of my shirtwaist in the other, mortified to have his eyes on me. He looked so solemn, so lost in himself and in the shame and the sin of what we'd just done. Another tear slid down my face. I tried to get a grip on myself, but it was a struggle I lost.

He came to me, gathered me against him, and took me into the other room. He made me lie on the bed and he lay down with me, facing me, looking at me, wiping my tears, stroking my hair. In a slow, quiet voice he told me I was beautiful, and that it had surprised him how much he wanted me. It had been such a long time, three years, since he'd touched a woman. And he hadn't meant to scare me. He hadn't meant to make me cry. He kissed my eyes, then my cheeks. I felt like a small girl inside the warmth of his arms. No one had ever said I was beautiful, not even lying.

He took off his vest and his shirt and he raised the window above us wide open so the air would billow in and cool us. He was lean and hard, and the second time, as tender as he'd been rough before. A songbird chirped and called just outside the window. A thrush maybe, or a cardinal.

Night fell and we stayed in the bed. We didn't eat; we didn't think about food. I never put on the fancy nightgown I'd brought. And I thought of something Mother had said once, an odd something about how she'd never, since the day she was born, been completely without her clothes. Like she was proud of it, like it was a thing all well-bred ladies should aspire to. Andy even took off my stockings, one by one, and kissed the instep of my foot until I couldn't stand the tickling anymore.

In the darkness of that ugly room, with just the glow from the electric bulb coming through the doorway, we held each other, we laughed about nothing, and we talked. I told him about Sister running off with her outlaw husband, and about what Dane had done to Papa's grave. He told me that he'd been born in Jefferson County on the twelfth day of January 1861, which made him thirty-five, and he chuckled when I said I'd always preferred an older man. His name had come from that "cur Democrat," Andrew Jackson. And his favorite color was green.

"Like a brand new stand of cotton before the bloom, before the bugs set in and the sun gets too wilting. I'm a happy man when my ground's greening up."

"So you like farming. I never could tell for sure." I backed up against him, our knees cupped together. I felt I could have stayed that way forever, and been content the rest of my days.

"I take some pleasure in it," he said, against my neck, his breath moving my hair and sending chills over me. "But I ain't fond of starving."

"It isn't as bad as that, is it? I mean, you do exaggerate your terrible hardships, don't you?"

"Well . . . let's put it this way. If I don't make a good crop this year, I might as well write finish to it. I never did get last year's rent paid all the way to your daddy, and I owe that—"

"Who cares about that. I don't even think Nathan knows about that."

"He knows. And then there's Louis Bassist, the swine." The words came like phlegm from his throat. I felt him stiffen, and it took a second for him to relax again. "I've got forty acres under cultivation. That's all I can handle, one man. So I've almost got to get a bale to the acre to break even, and I don't think the land's got that in it. My corn's ruined with this drouth. Even if it came a soaking rain today, it's ruined. I'm going to go home and see if I can't chop it up for forage."

I raised myself on my hands to look at the shadowy outline of him beside me. "What are you saying?"

He rubbed the soft part of my arm, in little, drowsy circles. "I probably won't make it, that's what. Unless I get real, real lucky. But I'm already broke so that's nothing new. Want and suffering have been stalking me hand in hand for years." He said this last part lightly, as if to make a joke of it. He even laughed a little.

I felt a lump rise in my throat. "You won't leave? Move off somewhere else?"

He reached up and ran both his hands behind my neck. His fingers pressed in against the base of my skull, rubbing in deep. It started the gnawing-feeling in the pit of my stomach that was beginning to get familiar. "Now, where would I go? And what good would it do me? You know of someplace better?"

"No." I felt myself ease into his hands. I wanted to arch my back up like a cat. It surprised me at myself, the hunger I felt when he touched me, as if some other person had come down and taken me over. It was not the least bit ladylike. It wasn't even decent. I kept waiting for guilt and shame to take hold, but they never did.

We slept finally, a little, restlessly, arms and legs twining round each other, neither of us used to sharing a bed. I awoke with the dawn and left him sleeping in the soft, lavender light. Beautiful, tender sleep he had; peaceful. I wanted to kiss him awake, yet wanted to watch him sleep, too, as if he were a jewel to be studied under microscopic light: the tiny lines fanning out from the corners of his eyes. Lashes too long to belong to a man. Golden hair tousled about his forehead. The two tones of his skin where the sun had tanned him and where it hadn't. The birthmark below his left rib. I felt new and full, achy in the places where he'd been, with more happiness than I'd ever known.

As quietly as I could, I rose from the bed and pulled on my skirt and my undervest. The waist with the button missing lay in a heap with my other clothes and with his. I went to the backhouse and when I returned, he was awake, sitting at the kitchen table in just his pants, his suspenders drawn up over naked shoulders. He looked sleepy, his eyes like a Chinaman's. He noticed my bare feet, let out a tired smile. I smiled back and went to the cupboard to see what there was to eat. Bread on the brink of molding. A can of store-bought peaches. My stomach growled loud enough to fill the silence in the room.

In a drawer, I found a sharp knife to cut the bread and to pierce the can top, and while I was busy doing that, he lifted the hair off my neck and put his lips just under my ear. My hands stopped with their busywork, and he held me that way, standing behind me with his arms loose around my waist. We kind of swayed side to side, like we were dancing to music only the two of us could hear. Then he reached his arm in front of me and opened his hand. The button to my shirtwaist lay there. I pinched it out of his palm.

"When does your train leave?" he said, so close to me I could feel his voice inside me.

"One-fifteen." It made me sad just to think of it, let alone speak out loud.

"Then you've got time to ride with me after the staples I came for."

I had forgotten about the supply run, and it was the reason we were even here. "All right," I said, turning against him, happy again.

The mules had eaten hay all night long, so once harnessed

they commenced to break wind and drop manure piles all the way to the store where Andy had his business arrangements. *W. P. Walker's,* the sign said over the store awning. A disinterested store clerk helped us gather the things on Andy's list: a bolt of heavy muslin and one of white lining, forty pounds of coffee beans, one hundred pounds of flour, meal, salt, dried apples, coal oil, turpentine, bluing, and a can of yellow trim paint. Cotton sacking, baling twine, hay hooks, paraffin, and twenty pounds of roofing nails. It was a full load.

Once the supplies were packed in the wagon, Andy's mood shifted. The lines around his mouth loosened. When he helped me up to the wagon seat, he gave me a quick squeeze on the backside. It shocked me and I turned in time to see his silent, naughty grin, daring me to tell him he couldn't do that to me after our night together.

He untied the harness lines and handed them up for me to hold while he dug out a paper sack from the back of the wagon. Then he hiked himself up beside me, took the lines from my hands, and set the sack on my lap. "It's almost two hours till your train leaves. We've got time for a picnic by the river. Ever been there before?"

He looked so pleased with himself and his idea that I shook my head no. I didn't have the heart to tell him I'd been there many times. It was a favorite place of Daniel's, too.

The city had a trolley line out to Lake McDonald behind the Austin dam on the Colorado River. The dam was 1,150 feet long and 60 feet high, and was the largest in the world. It put out 16,500 horsepower of electricity. Daniel knew these things and had already told me. I let Andy tell me again. Once when the trolley cars came too close and clanged a warning, Andy had to stand up and hold on to his mules. He whistled through his front teeth, then sang out, "Whoa there, you louts! Get back into your collars!" as loud as any mule skinner I'd ever heard coming through town on a busy afternoon. After that, he drove us well away from the other traffic.

We stayed by the wagon at the edge of the park, and ate our sandwiches. We talked about his children first, habits Hannah had picked up, her tendency to sulk and her temper; Quint's devotion to her and to Andy. "He keeps the family shored up."

And then we talked about the *Plaindealer* and the last article I'd written, the one about women's suffrage. I told him about J.T. Craddock's remarks being the reason I'd written it in the first place, and Andy said that J.T.'s arrogant way of thinking was the more common one amongst men of his station, that it was usually the working man who saw the inequality in a woman's lot, since he had so much inequality in his own life. We talked about the meeting to elect the delegate to the national convention in St. Louis, how Willie Betts was the natural choice to go. And while we were talking, Andy finally explained to me so I could understand it, the significance of the free silver issue, how it would put more money into circulation—money that had been taken away by the government after the war—and bring back prosperity to the people on the land.

The whole question of free silver, he said, was a compromise to begin with, that hard-line Populists wanted greenbacks printed without regard to a metal base at all. "Money doesn't have to be just gold or just silver. Those rocks down there, they could be money if everybody agreed they were worth something." He pointed out toward the pebble bank along the river. "Instead of dimes and quarters, or dollars, we could be trading rocks. Or sticks, or . . . I don't know, mesquite beans. Or we could trade paper."

"But we do that already."

"Except the paper money we have now stands for so and so

much in gold. But what if it didn't? What if it just stood for itself? A melted-down twenty-dollar gold piece brings twenty dollars because the government says it does, and that's the only reason."

I liked that he made things simple but somehow kept me from feeling stupid. And I listened hard. I wanted him to know I cared and that I thought about these issues when he wasn't around, that I had discussions. I said, "Daniel thinks it would ruin us with foreign countries to go off the gold standard." But as soon as I saw the light go out in Andy's face, I wished I hadn't mentioned Daniel's name.

He stuffed the rest of his sandwich into his mouth, and while he chewed, he brooded out at the river. There was an old white-haired Negro man out there, sitting on an overturned washtub with a cane fishing pole. Beside him on the ground was a tin can that he reached down in, and drew out a long earthworm to thread onto his hook. Andy seemed to focus on the old man, and I let the silence between us get uncomfortable before I thought to say, "But I don't see what matter it makes about other countries. It's just this country I care about."

He gave me a close-mouthed look, and with my eyes I begged him not to think about Daniel or how wrong or unholy it was for us to be together, but I knew it had taken over his mind. When he finally spoke again, his voice was stiff.

"It's not foreign countries your husband's worried about. It's Britain. Most every other government already recognizes silver. But we've been letting Britain rule this country for a hundred years. Our forefathers might as well not have fought the Revolution for all the change it's brought to us." He stood up, squinting out over the lake, and dusted off his pants. He held out his hand for me to take. "I reckon we ought to get you to the station. You don't want to miss your train."

"I don't want to go back, Andy." I grabbed his hand and he looked down at me. He pulled me to my feet.

"Don't say things you'll come to regret."

"I won't regret them. I don't want to go back to how I was. I can't. I love you. And I love Hannah and Quintus, too. I'd be good for them, I know I would. And I'd be good for you, too."

He put one finger to my mouth and shook his head. "Stop it right there. Hear what you're saying. Listen to yourself."

I took his wrist. I thought I could feel his pulse, or else it was my own I felt. "I do know what I'm saying."

"No, you don't. You're a married woman. You knew that, and I knew it, before any of this—"

"I'll leave Daniel. He's a lawyer. He can do a bill of divorcement—"

"Dellie . . . Dellie, stop it." He took firm hold of my hand, drew it to his lips. He gave me a forlorn smile and a sigh, then rubbed my fingers together like he was stirring my circulation to life. I saw him looking at my wedding ring. I wanted to take it off and fling it from me. "Even if you did that," he said, gently, "even then . . . I've got Cova."

I felt my eyes burn. "But she's—"

"My wife. She's my wife."

He looked straight at me, unflinching, and I understood, in the depth of the silence in his eyes, what it was he was saying to me: that he would not make the same sacrifices I would. That our love was unequal. In that one sickening instant, I understood this clearly.

14

Daniel was at home when I got there. He came bounding out the front door when he heard me and Cintha pulling in the gate. He'd come home last night, thinking to surprise me, and had gotten my story about Dane from Tante Lena and again from Mr. Schuster at the depot. He had even checked with the telegraph office and Mr. Felty had no record of any wires coming to me from Austin.

"You don't believe I was there?" I said, making myself sound as indignant as he did.

He stood above me on the back gallery, looking down the four steps on me. He hadn't offered to take my grip and I couldn't remember an oversight like that from him. I also could not recall ever seeing such anger and hurt mixed upon his face before. Guilt almost swamped me for a second, but I didn't allow it to. I stood my ground, chin raised in defiance.

"I know you were somewhere," he said. "You surely weren't at home."

"I went to see Dane. If you don't believe me, write to him and ask."

"I'm not going to write him—"

"Then you'll have to believe me, won't you?" I went up the steps past him.

"Dellie." He grabbed my arm. The suddenness and the anger in his hands surprised me. Instinctively, I twisted free, moved out of his reach. "Where were you?"

"In Austin."

We stared at each other for a few more seconds, both of us

fuming. When I'd had my limit, I turned and went inside the house.

He followed after me. "Where did you stay? What hotel?"

"It wasn't a hotel." I didn't turn or stop, but continued through the kitchen. "It was a private home. Friends of his."

"What friends? What were their names?"

We were in the hallway when he caught my elbow again, and this time turned me all the way around to face him. I dropped my grip to the floor, and with both hands flat against his chest, shoved him away. He stood back a foot or two, looking dazed.

"How dare you put your hands on me." I turned my arm over to look at my elbow where he'd jerked me. There would be a bruise. He came forward an inch, contrite for a moment.

"I didn't mean to hurt you." Then his shoulders stiffened again. "Don't walk away from me, Dellie. I think you can grudge me a minute of your time. You are my wife."

"I don't need reminding of that." I bent to pick up my grip but he swooped down and got it first.

"I came home," he said, the edge in his voice beginning to die. "You weren't here. Everyone told me you'd gone to Austin but no one knew anything more than that. What was I supposed to think? I started to come after you, in case . . . in case something had happened to you. Or to Dane. But I didn't know where you were. I used Bassist's telephone. It took me an hour to get connected to the Driskill. I thought that's where you might've stayed."

"It was the home of some friends of his," I said, giving in. "Their name was Walker." I said the first name that came to mind, remembering the store, W. P. Walker's, where we'd gone for the supplies. It hurt me to lie to him, to have to do it, but I was sick at heart by then, and almost numb. He looked so pale, so fraught with worry. "They used to live up in Parker County, but now they don't. They had a spare room."

"And Dane stayed there, too?" He bent to look into my face; his eagerness to believe me troubled me. I couldn't meet his eyes.

"He's applied for a homestead. Something like that. I know you don't approve of him—"

"That isn't so. I have nothing but respect for Dane. For every member of your family."

"Except me, you mean."

"That's not true, Dellie. I was concerned for your safety."

"You treat me like a child. You do. Like a little child who doesn't have a lick of sense. You make light of things that interest me. You keep things from me—"

"What things have I kept from you?"

"Papa's debt, for instance. When were you going to tell me about that?"

I could see I had surprised him. He moved his eyes away, shook his head, wearied, off his guard. He set the grip down again. "Well . . . it isn't a big thing, Dellie. I—*we've,* Nathan and I have got it well in hand. I didn't see any need to—"

"Upset me with it? Do you see what I mean, Daniel?" He didn't. I could tell by his befuddled expression. He only had one way of looking at things—his way.

"Nathan's going to sell cattle until the debt is settled. It's that simple."

"Why is it Nathan's debt to settle? That's what I don't understand. He was my papa, too. If it's Nathan's debt why isn't it mine, too?"

"Actually, it's Ava's debt since she was Josh's legal wife. If you will let me finish a sentence I will explain it to you. It's Ava Nathan wanted to keep in the dark. So *she* wouldn't worry. He thinks she's had enough grief, and I agree with him. The debt's almost paid anyway, so—" He folded his arms and studied me a moment, then unfolded them again. "You know, if Nathan wasn't so stubborn, I offered to buy the old homeplace. That would've well covered Josh's debt."

"The homeplace? You mean, the Ashland farm?"

"I know you have a special fondness for the old place, and I thought if I could make sure it stayed in the family—"

"What would you've done with it? If you had bought it."

He shrugged his mouth. "Use it. Mostly, I was trying to help Nathan—"

"And what about the Ashlands? Would you have just set them out in the cold?" I could feel my anger rising again.

"No," he said, slowly, considering, keeping his eyes trained on me. "Or is it yes? What's the correct answer here, Dellie? Have I missed something? I didn't buy the land. Nathan said no." He reached for me. "It seems I've made you unhappy again, and I don't even know how."

I looked at his hand holding on to my arm and a fit of tears spilled from my eyes. I could not stand another second of his concern. Of my infidelity and lies, or the way his arms when he put them around me felt different than Andy's did. The difference in how I felt inside. I wanted to be happy—I was in love—but I couldn't be, not with the way things were so mixed up.

Daniel thought I was just exhausted from my trip, and that probably was part of it. He put me to bed and brought me tea that he'd made, weak tea, little more than brown water, but it moved me that he tried.

All the next day, I had these crying jags, and they would come upon me sudden and unbidden, at inappropriate times. I took to my bed during daylight hours, which had never been my habit. Tante Lena believed it was female trouble, but Daniel would not leave it at that. Over my protest, he sent for Mother, which meant Nathan had to carry her in the buggy, so then I had a crowd worrying over me.

I got out of bed, forced cheerfulness, confounded everyone more than if I'd gone ahead and let them call for Dr. Rutherford. I invited Mother and Nathan to stay to supper, then rushed to the kitchen to help Tante Lena pluck two chickens to fry. I didn't want to be questioned, just then, about my trip to Austin, about Dane. I didn't want to have to make up more stories to tell.

"You should stay in the bed if you've got the female miseries," Tante Lena said to me, but she let me take the chickens out to the back gallery. Mother insisted on helping, too, though she'd been down for days with the old rheumatic stiffness in her back. Her pains gave her something to talk about while we sat there working on the chickens and shooing away the dogs.

A songbird trilled up in the live oak by the buggy house, and it made memories swell within me of wind breezing in through high windows, the smell of wild honeysuckle mingling with the scent of time and damp stones. I could see again the glow of electric light falling golden across the floor, and feel the cool pillow against my neck. A current of desire passed through me and weakened my hold on the legs of the chicken. It nearly spilled to the ground, but I came back to myself in time. Mother was too involved in telling me of her ailments to notice my clumsiness.

Of course, they all did ask about Dane eventually. Nathan first, at the supper table. I said the same things that I had to Daniel yesterday, that Dane was declaring a homestead, that he had some friends from Parker County living in Austin now, that their names were Walker. I couldn't think of anything new to add, and thankfully, no one asked for more details. The subject of Dane still made everyone uncomfortable to talk about in the open, just as if Papa were still alive and sitting at the table with us.

That night at bedtime, when Daniel came to my room, he told

me he was glad I was feeling better. He didn't even understand me well enough to realize my good humor of the evening had all been an act.

I nearly confessed to him right then. I could even hear the words forming in my head: *Daniel, I'm in love with someone else.* But I could not feature what would happen after that, how he would react. Would he strike me, or would he dissolve into a shamble of self-pity? Would he throw me out into the night? And if he did, where would I go then? Hadn't Andy so much as said it was impossible for us to be together? And I would never go back to Mother's. Her house had never been a refuge for me. My possibilities seemed so limited, so dire. And at heart, I was still a coward.

Full of self-loathing, I lay against the bed pillows while Daniel told me about the letter he'd had from his mother. "She needs for me to come to Navasota. She has some financial matters she wants me to attend to for her. She's bought into a pig farm, of all the things." He laughed, trying to make me smile and so I did, lightly. His mother was a prim lady, tiny, always properly dressed. "I told her I couldn't make it before Thursday. I thought you might need me here for the party Wednesday night."

"Party?"

"For the teachers." He turned his head at me. "The Normal School starts this week."

"Of course."

He bent slightly to have a look in my eyes, examining me. "I should've gone for Doc Rutherford."

"No, you shouldn't have. I'm completely fine. I am."

He seemed unconvinced, but he straightened away from me. "This is the last trip for me for a while."

"Good. You need the rest." I felt as if I were acting out a role— the dutiful wife, concerned foremost for her husband's well-being—like the play parties Miss Langburn had given on weekends. The pretending made me angry at myself but I couldn't seem to quit it. A hellgrammite had come in the window to swirl around the chimney of my bed lamp.

"I'll ask Tante Lena to come use the room at the end of the hall while I'm gone," Daniel was saying. "So you won't be alone here with the teachers when they come. I don't know why you agreed to two of them."

"I don't know either. Because we have the extra rooms. Daphne talked me into it."

For one brief second he looked as if there were something particular he wanted to say, something of importance that would change the way the world turned, but then the look passed from him. "Well, I'm sure it'll be fine with Lena down the hall. Or . . . would you rather I asked Nathan to come over for the weekend?"

"But then that would leave Mother alone with her teacher, whoever he might be. No, Tante Lena down the hall should be enough to keep scandal away." I hardly realized how flippant I sounded until I saw the hurtful look come to him. I lowered my eyes. "Forgive me. I don't mean to be ungrateful. I know you mean well."

"I want you to feel safe while I'm gone."

"I know that."

"You think I'm treating you like a child again. Is that it?"

I raised my face and saw the frustration in his eyes. I felt a sudden melting rush of affection for him. I reached for his hand and coiled our fingers together. "Don't go, Daniel."

"It'll only be for two or three days. I promise. No longer than Sunday."

"No, I mean tonight don't go away. Stay here . . . in my room." My voice went to a whisper. I had never, in all our married life, made such a request, and I amazed myself with it as much as I did him. And yet at that moment, it was unexplainably what I wanted, and needed, and felt.

White-faced, he leaned toward me, hesitating once, before he brushed my lips with his. Softly. Too softly. I put my arms on his shoulders, drawing him closer. For a moment, we were awkward with each other. Our teeth clinked together. His breath spilled into my mouth. When he pulled quickly from me, before he put out the bedside lamp, I caught a glimpse of his ardor, an aspect of him I'd never seen in the light.

In the darkness I heard him rustling, his boots hitting the floor one at a time, and then more rustling, and more, until I half lost the urge. I could see only an outline of him, a blacker spot in the blackness of the room. No moonshine came through the windows. No singing of insects. Just pure darkness hugged me close.

The bed frame creaked. The mattress gave to his weight. It felt odd to have him come to me, almost like a betrayal to Andy after our time in Austin. Daniel was in a passion, and I was bewildered by it: that he could be that way, that I would respond to him. I kept my eyes closed and pretended it was Andy in my bed. Inside my soul it was him.

Afterwards, I fell asleep with Daniel's arms tight around me, until I got too hot and pushed him away. In the middle of the night, I woke to find him gone. Just the smell of him—the pipe tobacco and the faint tang of his shaving soap—lingered in the sheets. I pulled the empty pillow in to me, curled my body around it, and fell quickly back to sleep.

15

On Tuesday, our first teacher arrived unexpectedly, a day early, in a black two-seat surrey with red pneumatic wheels and red fringe hanging down, rippling in the June breeze. He wore an iron leg brace, a legacy from some childhood illness, but he could climb the stairs to his room just fine. His name was Bickham Laramore, and he'd come all the way from Gay Hill in Washington County.

Despite the leg brace, Bick Laramore was a fashionable dresser, in a tailor-made, round-cut sack suit of white alpaca. I sent Tante Lena up to help him unpack, and she came down saying he had black worsteds and French twills, and fancy undershirts of white India gauze.

"Not on teacher's pay," Daniel said, then scolded both of us for gossiping about our guest.

Bick Laramore claimed to love teaching. Over supper that evening, he compared the mind of a child to a fertile valley. "The teacher is the farmer. And books, knowledge, is the soil." I thought he sounded like a Populist, but I didn't say so out loud. Not just then, with Daniel at the table, and with how well we were getting on since last night.

Wednesday morning, after Daniel had gone out with his hands and his fence, Priscilla came to the house to get a look at Mr. Laramore. She said she had come to go uptown with me to shop for the party. She made out like it was something we had planned on, and that I had let slip my mind, but I knew what she was up to. While I got dressed she stayed downstairs and chatted with Mr. Laramore, and by the time I came down, they were well acquainted.

Mrs. Slater had sent a list with Priscilla of things to buy, and everything she needed was at Bassist's store. I refused to go inside with her. She pouted about it, but I would've felt like a traitor and a debtor stepping inside his doors, now that I knew Papa had owed a sum of money to Mr. Bassist just like every other farmer around for miles. I said I could do quite well buying my goods at Sapling's Fancy Staples and Grocery store. I had a list of my own from Tante Lena.

"Oh, Dellie, you'll pay two prices." Priscilla stamped her foot at my stubbornness. She carried a parasol, and her fan, which she kept on a satin sash tied about her waist. She flipped open the fan and waved it furiously at her face.

"I don't care if I spend every dime in my pocketbook."

She mashed her mouth together in exasperation. She had put on some garnet lip rouge, and her pouting caused the color to run into the creases outside the line of her mouth. I took my handkerchief from my purse and dabbed at the run. She held still until I had finished, then she grabbed my hand. She had worn gloves, little lace, fingerless ones.

"Well, at least wait for me," she said. "I'll go with you to Sapling's."

So I stayed out under the gallery awning, speaking to people that passed. It was hot. So hot already for just the twenty-fourth day of June. One hundred degrees according to the temperature meter on the wall outside the store. I paced the length of the gallery, feeling faint and dripping. I gazed across the street at the door to the office of the *Plaindealer,* nestled there between Van Burkleo's and Flaxman's.

It was Wednesday, yet the Bettses' carriage wasn't out on the street. Neither was Andy's gray saddle mule, nor his farm wagon nor his big four-in-hand freighter. The windows on the top floor were closed, but the sunlight against the glass made it appear as if a shadow of someone stood there.

Feeling reckless and a little out of myself, I stepped down into the street. The heat seemed to wrap around me as I moved through it. In front of Flaxman's store I spoke to Columbus Crager, to Ike Landers and Vernon Jack, who were all loafing there under the awning, sharing cigarettes. They had all worked for the O-Bar-J at one time or another. Vernon Jack still did on occasion, so he fumbled quickly for his hat, and he opened the door to the newspaper office once he saw where it was I meant to go.

"Thank you, Mr. Jack," I said. I ignored the curious looks I got from the other two.

Vernon Jack nodded, "Ma'am," and let me pass. I had a right, after all, to go in there. Everyone knew by now that I contributed article writing to the newspaper. I was Sister Dellie.

The second door at the top of the stairs was unlocked, but no one answered when I called out. I stepped into the office and let go of a breath I didn't know I'd been holding. Work was spread out on the long table. Most of it was covered by the dust cloths Willie kept thrown over everything when he was gone. The desk was cluttered with slips of paper, letters from readers. I picked one up and glanced at it without reading what the writer had to say. It felt eerie alone in the office. The press stood proud and silent, repaired, in its regular spot near the south wall.

In the back room, a pallet lay on the floor. It looked rumpled, as if it had been recently used. But what took my notice right away were the bolts of muslin and white lining, alongside a can of roofing nails and one of yellow trim house paint, all things I recognized from Walker's store in Austin. Standing there looking at it all caused the memory to bathe over me, along with the perspiration from the close heat in the little room. Andy had been here. I could feel him as if he were standing right there beside me. If I closed my eyes, I could even see him, his face gentle and easy as it had been alone with me in Lawrence Treadway's house. And his words—"You're a married woman. You knew that, and I knew it."—came to me, too, along with the sickening feeling they had caused when he said them.

The downstairs door slammed shut as if a sudden gust of wind caught it, then footsteps, and the upstairs door opened and closed. I jumped and caught my breath, moved closer into the goods stacked there. Long strides moved across the floor. A window rattled up, then another. I kept still, wondering what excuse I could give for being back here in the storage room.

The footsteps went back and forth, paused, moved again. I knew whose they were. I knew and yet I stayed where I was. It struck me that I could probably hide here and get away with it. In amongst the bolts of cloth and store goods. Maybe even for days without anyone finding me. It was a liberating thought. I even crouched down for a second, but the footsteps moved again, shaking the floor underneath me. I gathered my courage and went for the doorway connecting the two rooms.

As I expected, it was Andy, as clear as in my imagination, wearing his red-striped suspenders over an everyday shirt rolled to the elbow. The sight of him, so real and unassuming, gripped me with joy. He stood quietly beside the desk reading a yellow telegraph wire. When he looked up at me, I thought he flinched just the slightest to have me appear so suddenly, but then he calmly went on with his reading, as if we had just seen each other a few seconds before, or as if my coming out of the back room were a perfectly normal occurrence.

The scant breeze from the newly opened windows raised a chill on my arms. The clock on the wall above the press ticked.

It was the only sound in the room, and seemed louder even than the clink of trace chains and the clop of horses down on the street. I wondered why I hadn't seen his mule, or his wagon, outside.

A small laugh escaped from the back of his throat, at whatever it was he read. Then he raised his face at me once more. "It's from Willie," he said. "The vote was unanimous. Kearby's our candidate for governor."

Even in the agitated state I was in at that moment, I managed to remember the state Populist convention going on in Dallas this week, and that Willie Betts had gone there representing our district. Andy lifted his smile full onto me, but I could see clearly enough his mind was not on me, not on us, not on our night together or whatever it was that we meant to each other.

"He says to start the press."

I stood there, cast in stone, and watched him go toward the worktable. He yanked aside the dust cloths. His hands rummaged through the stacks of papers. He glanced in my direction. "Have you got something?"

"Something?" The question stupefied me.

"For the paper. A piece to put in?"

"Oh. . . . No."

He straightened, frowned. "No?"

I went for the window, appreciating the breeze. I felt as though I were melting, literally, like a cake of butter. "No. I, well, I didn't know we would be ready to put out an issue so soon. I didn't know the press was already fixed. I didn't realize anyone . . . that *you* . . . would be here. I didn't see your mule, or your wagon."

He frowned for a second more, as if he were wondering about his mule and wagon, too, though I knew that wasn't it. He was wondering about me, and why I had come empty-handed. I could hear well enough myself how wrought upon I sounded.

He pointed at the desk chair. "You can sit down there and write something."

"You mean now? Right here?"

"Why not?"

"I don't know." I pressed my hand to my chest. "I wouldn't know what to write."

I looked at him hopefully, wanting him to say something, do something, anything to acknowledge that what had happened in Austin was real, that we had become lovers, and that it meant something to him, that I meant something.

He let a smile pass his lips, a slow smile, a real one intended for me, like he had read my fears and uncertainties and understood them. I always felt he knew me better than I did myself. I smiled back, blushing. I couldn't help it. I felt like I had suddenly awakened, girlish and shy. "I reckon you'll think of something," he said, and then he turned back to the work at the table.

I unpinned my hat and sat down at the desk. Having him there, the two of us alone together in that room, inspired me. For a while I watched him move around the table, so busy, so contained and confident, then I began to scribble words. Nonsense at first. His name. My name. His and mine together. Like a schoolgirl drawing hearts and arrows.

"Gretta'll be here directly, with the kids and some sandwiches," he said, as if to prod me along. "We intend on getting this paper out today."

So I wrote about the store goods from Austin, the ones I had helped select, the ones that had filled Andy's wagon from W. P. Walker's in Austin, the ones sitting in the back room with the pallet. *And wasn't it wonderful,* I wrote, *and purely satisfying to know that humankind could work together on the simple things, that there wasn't any reason to go out and hang ourselves like Judas did, just because store goods couldn't be gotten at a fair price locally.* I read this aloud to him and joyed in the grin that crossed his mouth, a little wicked grin on those lips I wanted to touch again, to have touch me.

"That's it," he said, nodding his head. "Stir the stagnant pond and get the green scum off." And I wrote that down, too. Everything he said seemed to cry out to be recorded.

The door at the bottom of the stairs opened and closed, rattling the walls and the upper door-glass. I expected Gretta, with little Hannah and Quintus and Jordan in tow, and with sandwiches. I was hungry all of the sudden. I felt my stomach turn and growl. Instead, it was Priscilla who flounced in on us. She looked wilted, beet-red in the face, a little out of breath, a little angry. I had completely forgotten about her, about what we had come into town for, and I jumped to my feet, ready to apologize.

Before I could, she said, "I've been searching all over for you. I didn't think to look here until Mr. Crager said I should. He said he'd seen you come up, and of course"—she shot a look toward Andy—"I should have known."

"I only meant to come up for a minute, and then Andy needed my help, and so we've been—" I glanced at him, too. He seemed uneasy with me now, eager for me to go on with my explanation, to clarify myself, to say what it was we had been doing up here alone. My tongue stiffened inside my mouth. I turned back to Priscilla. "You have met Mr. Ashland, haven't you?"

"Not properly, no." She gave me another disapproving look before she went toward him, her hand in its white lace glove held out for him to take. "How do you do?"

He held up his hands to show her that they were both black from the type trays he'd been working in, but Priscilla, oblivious, uncomfortable, pressed her hand straight inside his. I heard him mumble, "Proud," under his breath.

When he took his hand away, she looked glumly at the black

smudge on her glove, sniffed, then turned back to me. "We really must get back, Dellie. I have a thousand things to do before this evening, and so do you." She gave another glance at Andy, with suspicion this time, I thought, but then I consoled myself that I imagined it. She couldn't know anything just by looking. No one could. I was just overreacting. "You do still have your list to fill," she said.

She waggled her fingers at me in exactly the same way she had at Nathan that day in our hallway, as if I were a disobedient child. I felt my heels almost dig in like a sullen cow. I said, "I'll be along a little later. You go on ahead. I'm not quite through here."

She shifted her stance, one fist on her hip. "But Dellie, what about . . . your list." She nearly whispered the last two words, glancing again at Andy, and I understood then what all the glances were about. She was far too well mannered to mention the purpose of the shopping list since someone not on the party's guest list was present.

"It's all right, Dellie," Andy said, keeping his tone polite, completely guileless. The only thing better would have been for him to call me Mrs. O'Barr. He should have. I'm sure Priscilla noticed that he didn't. "I can finish up here."

Priscilla made a move toward the door, but I didn't pretend to follow her. To Andy I said, "We're having a party and a supper for the incoming teachers tonight at our house. I wish you'd come. Bring the children. You could bring Gretta since Willie's out of town."

A glint came into Andy's eyes as I spoke, a glint that grew harder with each word. I don't think Priscilla saw it. She was too busy staring at me, as if she couldn't believe I would invite a poor dirt-farmer like Andy Ashland to my party. But she smiled weakly. "Yes," she said. "That would be lovely." Then she put her hand on my arm as she moved for the door. "I'll wait for you at

Sapling's." She sounded oddly becalmed, like a stranger, but my mind stayed on Andy and that glint I wanted to erase.

We stood perfectly still, frozen as in a photograph, staring at one another, neither of us smiling or pretending to do otherwise, until the door at the bottom of the stairs closed. He was the first to let down his guard. He wiped his hands on a rag, and threw it on the table. The glint was still there. "Do you want to ruin me in this town?"

"What?" I felt myself wither under his glare. "No. Of course not. Don't be angry."

"I don't move in your circles, Dellie, with your . . . crowd."

"Am I supposed to pretend I don't know you? Why shouldn't I invite you to my house?"

He didn't seem to hear me. He motioned at the table, then walked to the windows. "All my work. Everything I've tried to do . . ." He turned his back toward me. "Your friend, what'll she think now? I saw how she kept looking at me."

"She won't think anything. I'll tell her you declined my invitation. I'll say you had other obligations. She won't think anything. Please, Andy, don't be angry with me." I went up behind him, put my arms around him, and laid my face against his spine.

He wheeled around sharply and took me by my shoulders. He rustled me out of the line of the windows. "Do you want the whole town to see us?"

"You haven't thought of me at all these last days, have you? I haven't come into your mind not once."

"I hardly thought about another thing. But we can't stand here in front of the windows—"

I put my arms around him again, laid my head facedown on his shoulder. "I've been sick with wanting to see you." I waited for his arms to hold me, too. They did, finally, coming up slow, patting me between my shoulder blades.

"I wanted to see you, too," he said in a shushing tone.

I lifted my face and raised my lips for him to kiss me. His expression clouded for a moment. His fingers moved a lock of hair beside my ear, then his mouth came to mine, but only briefly—a peck, a smooch. I wanted more, but he broke away. He rubbed my arms, and gave me a little backward push.

"Go meet your friend," he said.

"I didn't finish this article."

"It's finished enough. Go on."

I went for my hat, pinned it on, feeling lighter inside. "I'll see you tomorrow night."

"You're coming to the meeting?"

"Of course. You'll be there, won't you?"

"I will be," he said, and with such a note of sadness in his voice, I was gladdened at the thought of him missing me till then. I raced back to kiss him again, quickly, holding both sides of his face. He didn't stop me this time.

Smiling and happy, I stepped out into the sunshine downstairs. Mr. Crager was still there, idling beside Van Burkleo's gallery post, gnawing on a raw carrot now. He nodded at me. I nodded back.

Priscilla waited inside Sapling's. I fished my shopping list out of my pocketbook. I felt so lighthearted, I wouldn't have even minded going to Bassist's now. I felt I could've faced him without cowering. I could have faced anything with Andy's kiss still on my lips.

"He isn't coming," I said, and Priscilla cocked her head at me, questioning. "Mr. Ashland. He isn't coming to the party. He has some other obligations."

She took my handkerchief out of her pocket, I thought to return it to me, but she took hold of my chin, and used it on my mouth this time. Her eyes stared directly into mine.

16

Tante Lena worked hard all day, even bringing her niece Nanalee in to help her with the cooking and the cleaning, getting ready for the supper party. I laid out the table with the sterling and with Mrs. O'Barr's best china. I cut flowers from the front garden—zinnias and lilies, cosmos, yesterday-today-and-tomorrows—setting them in vases around the house and in the center of the table. I brought out the tapers and the brass candelabra. Daniel said how lovely everything looked.

Our other teacher, Riggan Hockaday, arrived. He was much older than the rest of the teachers, and had a flatness to his voice that pegged him as an eastern Yankee. He told us he had taught school for many years, seemed even a bit snobbish about it, as if he thought he should be in Professor Mauney's shoes rather than attending the Normal School to learn new methods. He now taught at the school in Hutto, and his board there had required him to attend the academy. He complained about it, and about the summer sausage Nanalee brought out on a serving tray as snacks. He said he was easily made peptic, and then proceeded to eat more of them than anyone.

Mother brought a red satin cake decorated with frosting flowers and flourishes in green that spelled out "Wellcome," with two ls. We put it on the sideboard, and no one mentioned the misspelling until Mr. Hockaday noticed. It was practically the only thing he said to her, and I had never seen Mother so flustered. She went straight to the kitchen, and came back in a minute with a spoon to scoop out the extra letter.

"Mother, don't, you'll just ruin it. And it's a beautiful cake." I managed to get the spoon from her hand.

She looked at me, and her eyes seemed almost childlike to me. "I could just drop dead, Dellie," she whispered.

"It doesn't matter, Mother. It doesn't." I glanced through to the parlor where Daniel stood with Miss Idalou Sparks, the Slaters' teacher from Red Rock. She was about twenty-two, pretty in a bookish sort of way, kind of dainty and polite. Uninteresting, though Daniel seemed to have found something to say to her. "Now, come help me entertain everyone." Mother didn't seem consoled, but she came with me into the parlor to sit on the sofa with Mrs. Slater and Priscilla.

Nathan was in an unusually gay humor, over in the corner near the piano, laughing with Bick Laramore and Miss Karen Quick. Miss Quick was the teacher assigned to Mother's house. She was around thirty, tall and raw-boned, not the least shy, coming right up to shake a person's hand in an almost mannish sort of way. She wore her skirts straight, without a bustle or a petticoat, or even a corset so far as I could tell. She bobbed her hair short, and she smelled faintly of tobacco smoke and ash. Mother said she smoked cigarettes, aside from which she'd scandalized Mother by having her bicycle shipped with her from Jollyville, and shortly after she arrived, had put on her bicycle bloomers to go for a look around.

"And she rode into town thataway," Mother said to Mrs. Slater. I smiled, and wanted to laugh out loud, imagining the shock and dismay among the townsfolk as Miss Karen Quick pedaled by.

"Well, I do allow," Mrs. Slater mumbled as she leaned around Mother to look at where the shameful Miss Quick stood chattering. "Shades of decency." Priscilla didn't make a comment, but I noticed she couldn't seem to take her eyes off that corner either. She seemed awfully quiet, and I wondered about it.

"And to think," Mother said, under her breath, "Clifton

Mauney has saddled me with this lurid person for six whole weeks."

I went over to join the group in the corner, curious now about Miss Quick, but Nathan had the conversation hogged, telling about his last ballgame played on Saturday evening. "They had this one fella they all kept calling slugger. Loud, too, so we could hear it. And we knew they were just trying to get our goat, since this so-called slugger was a grandpa-looking fella, old as dirt. He stood up there by the plate, hunkered over like he could barely heft the bat. But the joke came when he swung. He suddenly stood up straight as an arrow and hit the stuffings out of the ball." Nathan let out a horse laugh. Miss Quick and Mr. Laramore laughed along with him.

Baseball stories tended to bore me, but Nathan could tell them until I went to sleep. Both the teachers seemed interested, though. And when Nathan was smiling so bright, and when he was in such high spirit, people just naturally gravitated to him.

"And he got a homerun?" Miss Quick said.

"That's what *they* said, but we didn't let them get away with that. There wasn't anything left of the ball to field." I could imagine what had happened next. I'd seen Nathan's ballgames end in fisticuffs before, and he had the telltale yellow bruise that I only just then noticed, high on his left cheekbone. When he got mad enough, he could fight like sin. "We demanded a rematch. For this weekend."

"I'd love to see it," Miss Quick said.

"Well, maybe you can come out to the park," Nathan said. And Mr. Laramore said he would like to go, too. And then Miss Sparks expressed an interest in baseball games, and for a moment, it looked like everyone in the room wanted to go to the game. Conversation seemed to take hold. Everyone relaxed.

But then the Craddocks arrived, late. Supper had been scheduled for seven, and it was already a quarter past. Daphne walked in the door first, looking flushed and anxious. Then J.T. stumbled in on the arm of their teacher, a young man named Mathias Chase, who was the new teacher at the Grassyville schoolhouse. He hardly looked old enough to shave. He seemed just as nervous as Daphne, and it didn't take but a moment to see why.

J.T. had been drinking. Strong liquor smelled plainly on him as he guided Mr. Chase around the parlor, introducing him as if they were old lodge fellows, or long-lost relations. J.T. kept one arm thrown round Mr. Chase's narrow shoulders, and he apologized loudly for their being late, explaining that one of Daphne's buggy horses had been afflicted with a sudden bad case of the sleepy staggers. They'd had to borrow Mr. Chase's rig to get here.

Daniel said, "Louis sells Pain Killer for that," but J.T. didn't care to listen to Daniel's advice. J.T. was too busy making the rounds of the guests, making a fool of himself as he did.

He stared at Bick Laramore with glassy eyes, and slurring horribly, said, "I don't believe I know you, sir?"

Mr. Laramore took a step forward, put out his hand. "No, I don't believe you do. Bickham Laramore."

J.T. moved back as if he'd dropped something on the floor, and he didn't shake Mr. Laramore's outstretched hand. "Is that a club foot you have there?"

"Jeremy," Daphne said. She gave me a horrified glance.

"Good eye, old man," Bick Laramore answered, and clapped J.T.'s upper arm. I was grateful for Mr. Laramore's good humor. "But it isn't club. It's the leavings of a fever from when I was small."

"Is that so?" J.T. said.

"Well, now that everyone's here," I said quickly, interrupting before the conversation worsened, "we can all move to the dining room."

J.T. straightened, as if he had just taken notice of me. He still had Mr. Chase by the left shoulder. He hadn't let go since they'd walked in the door, and poor Mr. Chase was already favoring that side, leaning into J.T.'s grasp.

"Ah yes. Meet out dearest Dellie," J.T. said, his too-bright eyes reminding me of Papa's the day of the reunion. He took my hand, put it into Mr. Chase's hand. "Our handsome hostess, *and* our leading member of the shrieking sisterhood."

I had grasped hold of Mr. Chase's hand before I heard the insult in what J.T. said. Mr. Chase heard it, too, and he didn't know what to say to me, or how to act. He mumbled how pleased he was to make my acquaintance. We shook hands, and J.T. smirked. Daniel wasn't standing but four feet away from us. He kept silent, didn't come to my defense, and I was too stunned by J.T.'s rudeness to defend myself.

Miss Quick stepped out from around the piano seat where she'd been standing all this time. She took a firm hold on my arm, smiled at me, much kinder than she needed. "Am I standing in the presence of an enlightened woman? Is that what Mr. Craddock, here, meant by his unfortunate remark?"

"Unfortunate?" J.T. said in protest. Daphne reached to restrain him, but he brushed her hand away.

Finally, Daniel seemed to realize the situation. He wasn't normally slow, just blind when it came to J.T.'s ill manners, or anyone else's either. He had a tendency to think the best of people, even when they didn't deserve it. He pulled J.T. away from Mat Chase and they headed off toward the study, away from me and Karen Quick and everyone else in the room.

"Come along and meet the Slaters," Daphne said, taking Mr. Chase by the hand.

Nathan said, as explanation perhaps, to Miss Quick, "Dellie writes for a local newspaper."

"Is that so?" Karen sounded genuinely interested. Then she noticed me glancing after Daniel and J.T. She whispered, "You have to stand up to a bully like that one. If you let them get away with it one time, they'll think they can run over you all the way into the Hereafter."

"He's a friend of my husband's," I said, venturing a laugh. "They've known each other since they were boys."

"He's still a bully," she said.

Daphne came up, after leaving Mr. Chase at the sofa with Mother and Mrs. Slater and Priscilla. "I really must apologize, Mr. Laramore, for my husband's behavior."

Karen Quick reached for Daphne's arm. "Why, love? Why must you? *You* haven't done a thing wrong."

Except marry a disgusting man, I had to keep myself from saying. But I could see Daphne's face had dissolved in embarrassment. I took her hand. "Come with me to the kitchen to check on the food," and I pulled her away from the others.

"I'm so sorry, Dellie," she said once we reached the hallway. "I hope he didn't ruin your party."

"Of course, he didn't. Are you all right?" I meant the baby.

She knew. She nodded her head. "Perfectly. The baby's fine. It's just that sometimes Jeremy, well, sometimes it seems he has demons inside him. I don't ever know what to do about it."

There was nothing she could do. She had made a bad choice, and it was almost pathetic how she went about always trying to please. She was a good person, but I could feel no sympathy for her husband. There wasn't much I could say.

Tante Lena leaned out the kitchen doorway. "We'll serve now, Miss Dellie," she said, and I could have kissed her for interrupting us.

Only after Tante Lena and Nanalee were bringing out the food did Daniel and J.T. reappear. They took their places at the table. J.T.'s face was drawn tight, but everyone had forgotten his display. At least, they pretended to.

The food had come off delicious: a roast of beef in spicy gravy, sweet potatoes, one of Tante Lena's Bohemian dishes into which, it seemed, she had thrown all the vegetables from her garden. There was an egg custard with berry sauce, Mother's red satin cake. Daniel poured wine, a claret. He even put a drop in Mother's glass, though she giggled and put her hand out to stop him. He wanted to raise a toast to our teachers, to education, and to the growth of young minds. And for that, Mother gave in and took a sip, though she made a wretched face afterward. The stuff did taste sour, but I drank my glass dry. It made me feel daring, and a little glimmery inside. The flesh around my mouth numbed.

"I'll have some more," I said, and I passed my glass to Karen beside me.

"Dellie," Mother said, but the glass made its way to Daniel.

He gave me a look, a taut smile, but he poured more wine. Then Karen asked for more, and so did Priscilla, making a big show out of it, a joke. Everyone laughed then, and Daniel held up the empty bottle. "The ladies have drained us," he said.

Karen leaned toward me and whispered, "What an attractive man your husband is." She was smiling. "You make a nice pair."

I sipped my wine and looked at her over the rim of my glass, trying not to seem jarred by her comment. No one had ever made one quite like it before. Then I looked at Daniel where he sat at the head of the table, Mother and Mrs. Slater at either side, and I tried to see him as a stranger would. I thought back to my first impression of him, after he'd come back from all those years in Austin, when we met again at Lottie Matson's party.

"I think it's you he's come to see," Lottie had said when he first arrived, her voice a frizzle of excitement. I had no idea why she said that, or thought it, though after a while, it seemed what she said was true. I had just turned seventeen, had only been home from Miss Langburn's school a few weeks. Daniel was a full-grown man to me, with his hair already silvering and his suntanned face. I felt lucky and flattered and undeserving of the attention he paid to me that night.

Now I didn't know what I felt as I watched him chat with the two old ladies beside him, and to Miss Sparks who sat across from Mrs. Slater. How confused feelings could become. I still admired him—his social graces, his intelligence, the simple elegance he had about him, even when he was dusty from work, and smelled of his horse. Tonight he looked sleek in his brown suit that fit him well. He caught me watching him and gave me a private smile, as if he wanted to know what I was thinking. I pretended not to notice his glance. I let my gaze travel back to our guests.

Mr. Slater sat next to Riggan Hockaday, and they had found something to mumble about between themselves. At our end, we listened as Karen told us about her home in Jollyville, where she lived alone, and of her cat named Cootee that she'd left in her sister's care. Karen Quick was a modern woman and proud of it. A suffragist, and not afraid to say so right out loud to the whole table. "It's perfectly ridiculous for women not to be treated as human citizens." She looked around the table for an argument and got none, not from Mother or Mrs. Slater. Not even from J.T., who had by then sunk deep into his chair.

The talk came round to Populism, inevitably, and it turned out Miss Quick had Populist leanings, too. I invited her to tomorrow night's meeting. I didn't notice Priscilla's glances, but she surprised me later, at the end of the evening, when everyone had eaten and moved back into the parlor to sing songs, by saying she'd be interested in going along with us tomorrow. Then Bick Laramore was asking to come, and Nathan was saying we would all go together, and I felt a little odd about it, as if it had all been taken out of my hands. I wondered how it would seem tomorrow night when I rode up with my *crowd* in tow.

Priscilla played the piano. She had come out of her quiet from earlier, but it seemed forced somehow, as if she was desperate for the attention. We all sang, "Daisy Bell" and then "Barbara Allen," when Mother complained that she didn't know the words to any of these newfangled songs.

I tried to imagine Andy here mingling with these people in my parlor, with my crowd, as he would say, and I couldn't. They all seemed much too frivolous, too leisured. I wondered what he was doing at this moment. I thought about things he'd said to me in Austin, about his corn crop being ruined, about his debts and how he and his family did without. I pulled back the curtain and gazed into the night for a moment, off across the three miles toward his house, before the laughter and singing of my guests, and Daniel's hand on my shoulder, turned my attention from the window.

"Daydreaming?" he said. I nodded, smiled in a way I was sure he would see as false. "Turned out to be a nice party."

"No thanks to J.T."

Daniel kept the smile on his face, too, and I sensed it might be just as false as mine. "He drank a little bit more than he should have."

"A little bit? He was soosed."

"Soused."

"You know what I mean. Why do you always make excuses for him?"

"I'm not making excuses. He knows his behavior was bad. He apologized for it."

"Not to me."

"Well, he did offer to apologize to everyone, but I said it wasn't necessary. I thought it would just make things more uncomfortable for everyone, and I didn't see any reason to humiliate him any more."

"Humiliate *him*? What about Mr. Laramore? What about me?" I looked across the room where J.T. was nearly asleep in the corner chair, while everyone else moved around him as if he didn't exist. Mr. Slater was off to the side with Mr. Hockaday, who smoked a foul-smelling Mexican cheroot. The two older women had gathered with the younger ones around the piano. The room seemed filled with music and singing, airy laughter. It *was* a nice party. No one appeared to even remember that J.T. had come in drunk. "I guess it doesn't matter."

Daniel stood beside me for a moment longer without speaking, though he kept his eyes on me. Then slowly, almost tentatively, he said, "I could beg off on my visit with Mom for another day or two, if you'd like for me to go along tomorrow night."

I turned fully to him then and tried to read his expression, to see how earnest this offer was. I didn't understand why he was making it now, after everything. Did he think he would be missing out on some fun with the others? Was he jealous of my time? Or was he worried about appearances again, how it would look to these visiting teachers, me without my husband? I didn't want him to go. It could be disastrous if Andy, with his guilty conscience, saw us together as a married couple, more than it was going to be already with everyone else along.

"I wouldn't dream of asking you to compromise your moral views," I said.

"It isn't a question of morals."

"What is it, then? You think I need an escort? For heaven's sake, Daniel, I'll have Nathan and Priscilla, and Mr. Laramore, and Karen Quick. I will hardly be alone this time." I tried a more genuine smile. His face had turned ashen. "No, your mother would be too upset with you—*and* with me—if you don't visit her as planned."

And then to soften my refusal, I reached to cup his cheek. It startled me when he pressed his hand to mine and made me linger there longer than I intended. I didn't expect such a show of affection. It was plaguesome of him, and I moved away quickly. For the rest of the evening, I stayed as far away from him as I could.

17

Daniel left as scheduled on the 10:05 to Brenham. I was relieved to see him go. He made things too complicated, and I wanted them simple. He made me think about the future and the past, made memories and doubts come to my mind, and I didn't want to doubt. I had enough to worry over wondering what Andy would think of me when I showed up with my friends at the meeting. I was afraid it would seem as if we were all out for an excursion to visit the lower class, to see how the poor, destitute farmers lived. I felt as if they were intruding upon this new side of me, this other life I had now, and I resented the intrusion.

Bick Laramore insisted he drive. It almost seemed like a point he wanted to make, to prove he could do anything, and more, than any normal man could. So the two of us started out together, made the detour over to the cemetery road to pick up Priscilla, who had overdressed just as I knew she would, and then we went to Mother's for Nathan and Miss Quick. We passed Andy's farm on the way. I saw the brown stalks of withered corn in his fields. I didn't see him anywhere. We were running later than when I rode with the Bettses, so I was certain he had already gotten there.

Sure enough, Quintus was out in front of Fletcher's Hall, keeping watch on the road, and it was to his credit he recognized me even in the unfamiliar buggy. He raced to the door of the hall, then turned and ran out to where we had stopped.

"Howdy-do, ma'am," he said, and I saw Andy coming out of the hall and toward us. "My daddy says he needs to speak to you, and he says I ain't to let you get by me."

"This is Quint Ashland. He's a tough old fella." Nathan was helping Bick tie his horses to the hitching rail.

Bick said, "So I see."

Karen leaned down to look in Quintus's face. She touched the cleft in his chin. "I bet you go to school, don't you?"

"Yes'm." Quint nodded. "You want to hear my ABCs?" And he didn't wait for her to answer before he started in singing.

By then Andy was almost upon us. He looked from me around at the others. He let Quintus finish with his song and waited while Karen praised him. Then I introduced Andy around.

"Glad y'all could make it," he said. He shook hands with the men.

"You have a smart boy there," Karen said.

Andy thanked her and shook her hand, too, and I couldn't help it; I felt proud of him, the easy way he had with people. I wondered if I could awake with him in every one of my days, if he were my husband, would I still have this overpowering feeling each time I saw him. Or was it just in the nature of marriage that couples should weary of each other?

To Nathan, Andy said, "You know the way inside. Find a seat up front and make yourselves at home. I need to speak with your sister." He smiled as the others trooped off toward the hall. Only Priscilla hung back for a second, and he gave her a friendly smile and a nod, too. She went on with the group. He turned to me. "You brought yourself a gang this time."

"I couldn't keep them from coming."

"Why would you want to?"

"For your sake. I didn't want you feeling uncomfortable around my crowd."

His eyes met mine. "When they get here they're my crowd."

"Is that so? Well then, you might've enjoyed the supper party, too. We talked politics and women's suffrage. You might've felt right at home."

"Dellie." He crossed his arms; frowned, not at all amused by me. "I'm not going to argue with you tonight. I need your help. Are you willing to give it?"

"Help? Doing what?"

"Willie stopped off in Elgin on his way back from the convention in Dallas. He'll be speaking over there tonight, and Gretta's gone to be with him, so I've got it here alone." He glanced toward the hall where people were filing in. He lifted a hand to wave at Lucky Speck and his wife, Martha. "Well, save for the Barbees I've got it alone. But I need you." It pleased me hearing him say that, even if he didn't mean it the way I wanted him to. "I want you to talk. Right after the singing's done. For five or ten minutes."

"Talk?" My throat caught in a knot. "You mean, get up in front of everyone? What would I say?"

"Whatever you want to. Anything that's on your mind."

"Oh, I don't know." I laughed, but I could feel my heart start to jump. I had never gotten up in front of people before. In school when we'd have oral examinations, I was always sick for a whole week. "I don't know, Andy."

He moved around so he was between me and the lane, like he thought I might run. He wasn't far wrong. "It won't be hard. There's not that many folks here, and you know them all anyway. They've heard me a couple of hundred times, Dellie. Look, all I've been doing all week is chopping up my corn. I'm just not up to this tonight."

A desperation had slid into his voice, and I reached for him, laid my hand in the crook of his arm. He clamped my fingers for a quick second, then unfolded his arms so my hand dropped away. He stepped back a foot. His face cleared again.

"Will you help me? We need to give them something new. Especially the ladies. It's important that we keep the ladies involved. I know you can do it."

Fright nearly overtook me, but I nodded my head. Only for Andy. It was only for him I agreed. Because he seemed to think he needed me so much. Because I could not then or ever resist him.

As we walked together to the hall, he told me what to do. We would sing as always, three or four songs. He'd tell the Reverend Barbee to say some words, and then I would come up to the front. It would be a good night for me to cut my teeth, he said. I didn't say so right then, but if I made it through this, I never intended to do anything like it again as long as I lived. We walked slowly to the door of the hall. It wasn't nearly slow enough for me. I felt like Marie Antoinette marching to the guillotine.

At the steps, Hannah spotted me with her daddy and came running from where she'd been playing with the other children. She had on her same little pinafore, grown more ragged than the last time I'd seen it. I thought of the dress I'd planned to make for her out of the leftover muslin in my trunk at home. She grabbed me around my legs, nearly tippling me over. I bent to pick her up. "Ooh, you're heavy," I said. Somehow, having her in my arms comforted my nerves.

At the door, Alex Hirschfield waylaid Andy. I took Hannah on inside with me and she sat in my lap after I found the others. They'd taken up the whole second row of chairs. Nathan was at one end, Priscilla the other, looking sulky because she hadn't managed to grab the chair next to him. She glanced now and then down to where he sat bent in conversation with the teachers, and with the younger Tackaberrys in the row behind us. The whole Tackaberry family was passing out plums to everyone, saying they had fruit falling from their trees at home.

Priscilla made a distracted comment, aimed in my general direction, about how adorable Hannah was. I took one of the plums Jewel Tackaberry handed up and gave it to Hannah to eat.

I knew Priscilla had only come tonight because of Nathan. Of course, he knew it, too, and that was why he ignored her. She cared nothing about the meeting, but I couldn't find fault in her for that. Not when I had been guilty of the same sin. Tonight, though, felt different to me already. Talk about what's on your mind, Andy said, but the only thing truly on my mind was him. I had to think, and think fast about what I would say to these people who had come to hear words of encouragement, words to make their days seem brighter, a little less hopeless, words to make them feel they'd come, even if for just one evening, out from under the galling yoke of their lives.

Rose Barbee sat down to the piano, pumped the foot pedals, and began chording the beginning strains of "When the Roll Is Called Up Yonder," Populist-style. A clear contralto came up from my left, and when I glanced down the row, I saw it was Karen, giving the song both her lungs, and getting the words nearly perfect, too. I felt a little better about them all coming along. Even Nathan wasn't laughing at the "silly songs" this time, but giving them a try himself, though I have to say, for all his other talents, his singing voice was lacking.

Andy came and moved a chair in next to mine. Priscilla leaned forward to give him a look. He kept on singing. I sang, too. He smiled at me like he knew how nervous I felt. Hannah crawled from my lap over to his and got herself settled. She left a stain of plum juice on my skirt.

When the time came for me to get up and speak, I was so scared my voice shook. Even though the hall was only half-full it still seemed like an ocean of faces to me, standing alone up at the front. Merle Grossner had her crochet basket with her, and she was working on that. Otherwise, though, everyone's attention was aimed at me. I tried to concentrate on Andy, on the encouragement I found in his face.

I don't know exactly what all I said. As soon as it was over I didn't want to remember it. Some things about being a child, growing up on a farm, doing without certain luxuries, being as poor as church mice. I told about the Christmas we had only a tow-sack of pecans to share among us, and thought we were rich. But I didn't mention my life now, living easy in the big house on the hill above the Yegua. And I didn't tell about Papa marrying a widow woman with eight times as much land as he had owned, though everyone knew about that anyway. I certainly wasn't as slick-tongued as Willie Betts or as agile of mind as Andy when he got up, which he did just as soon as he saw me running out of things to say.

He came out of his chair smiling, pounding his hands together, and everyone else followed his lead. I felt my face perspire as I sat back down. Priscilla leaned to me and said into my ear, "You didn't tell me you were going to speak, Dellie," and I could hear she was impressed with me suddenly.

Karen leaned down the row and made a gesture with her hand that was supposed to mean I'd done well. Nathan made his fingers into an OK sign, something he'd picked up at his baseball games. Bick Laramore just smiled and nodded my way.

Andy took the front of the room and started talking. I wanted to pay attention to him, but I was still shaking. Though, now that it was finished, it didn't seem it had really been so bad. I thought I might even could do it again sometime, if I had more warning, if I could have some time to plan out what I might speak about. Maybe I could think of something to say that got the crowd joining in, like Andy did when he started railing about the weather, about the money sharks, about the galvanized goldbug Democrats.

He walked around up there, casting his spell, making the whole front of the hall his. After being up there myself, I realized it was sort of like acting in a theater, what he did, and I felt a little bit different about it this time, watching him. Everything seemed plotted out, even the seeking of someone's eyes to look into. And I noticed he used words and phrases he had used in private on me, as if he'd been practicing his speeches on me when I didn't know it.

He said, "Want and suffering have been stalking the common man far too long, my friends. When they tell you that this country has got more money than it ever had before, they lie." He paused, looked out at everyone as if he were seeing something none of the rest of us could see, as if he'd had a vision. Then he stepped over to the table, and scratching at his head like he was confused, he said, "Now, supposing there's a plate of biscuits sitting right here on this table. And suppose there's two plates of butter the same size sitting here next to them. Except one plate of butter's white and the other one's yellow. Now, suppose the housewife, she picks up the plate of white butter, smells of it, says it's not sound, and throws it out the window, plate and all." While he talked he moved over to the row of windows and pretended to sail a plate out into the night. Then he looked at us all again and grinned just a little the way he could, like he knew a secret he was going to let us in on. "Now, is there anybody in this room that'll tell me there'd be just as much butter to spread on those biscuits if both plates had been left on the table?"

Someone in the back laughed, but Andy let them alone for a minute. He said, "The object of the gold men in demonetizing silver was to get more of your sweat for the same money." And now he pointed to the back of the room, where the laughter had been. "What sort of fix are you in, brother?"

"Same fix," came the answer.

"Amen to that," came another.

Andy nodded. "What I thought. Your corn has sunk, your cotton has sunk, and your liberty has sunk."

Someone else yelled out, "Our mules have sunk, too."

Andy let go a laugh himself, and even that seemed rehearsed. He strolled a couple of steps across the front; nodded. He raised his face. "They tell you to lay still while they finish skinning you. They tell you to tighten your belts and push away from the dinner table. Brothers and sisters, ordinary people are being sacrificed to the rich and powerful. And what can we do about it?" He pointed, looking for an answer. None came. "We can vote, my friends. That's the ticket out of this predicament we're in. We can vote."

"Not all of us," Karen said, and I looked down the row at her.

Andy pointed at her this time. "We're going to change that, too, sister. We've got to take this country by the neck, and wring it around to our way of thinking."

Again, I felt myself well with pride in him. I wanted to stand and shout something, too, but not the same kind of things the rest were saying. I wanted to tell them all that I was changed by this man, that whenever he touched me I was fearless, and that just hearing his voice made me forget everything bad that had ever happened to me: Sister running away and leaving me. Dane going from me, too. Papa blowing out his brains in the barn, and his cancer. And Daniel . . . At that moment, looking up at Andy, I didn't see how I could go back to a life I had already left in my heart.

I was so caught up in my own emotions, in admiring Andy, in loving him, that I didn't pay attention when someone sang out the word "Fire!" Not until the cry came louder, more plainly, did I listen. "Out yonder! Something burning!"

All at once, the whole room surged. People poured for the door. Some even leapt through the windows. I held tight to Hannah's hand and went with the crowd. Once outside, men raced to their wagons looking for canvas sheets or feed bags or shovels, whatever they had handy to beat out the fire. But it was too late for that. The flames were roaring.

It was Andy's wagon on fire. His big freighter. The one we'd sat in together by the lake in Austin. The one he'd carried all the store goods in back to McDade. I saw him go running toward it, pushing his way in close to the flames, then falling back from the heat. His mules had been unhitched and moved off a ways, still in their traces. And then I realized the whole wagon had been moved away from the other wagons out in front of the hall. Animals shied and bellowed. A pair of horses down in the line of wagons on the lane bolted loose from their tie-downs, trying to run. Men hurried in that direction, too, to prevent a second disaster from happening.

Fletcher's Hall had no water well, no creek close enough to haul from. A few people flung their drinking water at the fire, but that didn't help. Nothing helped. The wagon burned mighty and hot. Tongues of flame licked thirty feet in the air. The best any of us could do was to try to keep the sparks from spreading to the grass, dried from such a long stretch without rain. Men stomped at the firebrands that landed. Women beat at them with shovels.

The wagon went up faster than anything I'd ever seen. Like it was made of paper instead of oak and metal. And after a while, people quit trying to fight the blaze. No one spoke much, except a few mothers urging their children to stand back. I kept Hannah's hand clutched tight in my own. I spotted Quintus with a group of children his age, gathered near the locust tree in front of the hall, their faces flickering red with the reflection. It was as if a hypnotic trance had been thrown over everyone, by the power of the fire, the hellish beauty of the flames. I heard no conversation until the fire began to burn itself out, then the sounds were mostly hushed murmurings of disbelief, of speculation. Two cans of coal oil and a box of fire matches were found by Lurana Dillon and her little brother, Ara, just over in the tree line.

Once the wagon lay in a heap of red ember, completely lost, folks began to wander over to Andy, to give him words of condolence. I knew what he must feel. I felt it, too. I ventured forward with Hannah squirming to let go of my hand as soon as she saw her papa. His face turned my way for one second. I said, "Oh Andy—" But it was all I got out before Seamus Murphy stepped in front of me.

"We'll come out here tomorrow," Mr. Murphy said to Andy, "and we'll scavenge through this ash for your hardware." And then others filled the gap between us. Hannah pulled free of me, and Nathan came up at the same instant. His face was smudged with soot from fighting the grass fires.

"We may as well go home," Nathan said. "There isn't anything else we can do here." I raised on tiptoe, strained to see Andy, but he had moved off a little way with the group around him. I saw Hannah hanging on to his hand. Nathan said, "He wanted me to take his mules."

"His mules?"

"Three of them. As part of his rent. He said he didn't have need of them anymore, and he didn't see how he could square with me any other way."

I glanced again, spotted him standing with the Peelers now, head bent. His shoulders seemed to sag. I wanted to run to him. "He's had a hard time of it. Such a terrible time."

"I told him I don't need any mules."

I quit walking and turned to Nathan. "You said no? After what he's been through here tonight? You told him no? How could you be so cruel?"

"He can sell them as well as me. Better. He'd get more than I could." He looked at me firmly, then latched on to my arm. "They're waiting for us."

I didn't move. "You couldn't help him that much? Not that much, Nathan? Where's your heart?"

"I'm not in the mule business." He tried to jerk me into motion then, but I stayed still so that he had to turn back to me. Even in the night I could see him plainly. Our faces were less than two feet apart. He lowered his voice. "You're too attached, Dellie."

I pulled my arm out of his grasp. "What do you mean by that?"

"You know what I mean. There's been—" He looked around us. People passed us on either side. He stepped an inch closer. "There's been talk."

"What talk?"

He bent his head down toward the ground. "That the two of you . . . that you and Andy . . ."

I let out a laugh. I don't know why I wanted to deny everything. Not to Nathan. I couldn't recall a time I had ever lied to him so boldly, so specifically, about something that mattered to me so much. "Small minds," I said. "Small people thinking small thoughts. It isn't allowed in this town for a lady to have a man friend unless he's her husband or her brother, or some other close relation. And I'm tired of it. I'm sick of it. We have interests in common. We have"—I looked out toward where Andy had been standing with Hannah and he was no longer there— "things in common."

Nathan laughed a little, too, but he had raised his face again, and I saw no humor there. "I didn't say I believed it. But you *are* attached. I can see that much myself. I figure it's his children." He paused. I didn't say anything. "I just thought you should know there's been talk, that's all."

"Talk from whom?"

At first he seemed surprised, like he didn't expect that I would ask. He glanced toward the road, and I glanced, too. The three of them, Priscilla and our teachers, stood lined up beside Bick Laramore's fringe-top buggy. Priscilla was turned our way, watching us. I felt the air go out of me suddenly.

"I swear, Dellie, she'll do almost anything to get my attention. You know she will."

"Priscilla?"

"I don't say it to flatter myself. It's a joke with all the fellas. She's desperate for a husband."

"You mean she's starting gossip about me?"

"Small minds, remember. You said it yourself." He took my arm again. "Now, come on. They're waiting for us."

I let him lead me along, and I felt like a hypocrite climbing into that fancy rig, leaving the scene of destruction and despair like casual observers, sitting with my oldest friend in the world, who would talk behind my back. I almost balked. I almost ran back to find Andy and what was real. All the way home, I wished I had. And I wished I had told Nathan the truth, too. He had been so honest with me. I felt like a coward. I don't think I said three words to anyone.

Tante Lena was waiting up for us, her eyes drooping with fatigue. I left Mr. Laramore to tell her about the fire. I didn't have the energy. I trudged up to my room and dropped on the bed. I didn't even take off my dress. I could smell the smoke in my hair and on my skin, and I lay there in the dark and listened to the house get quiet until I could stand it no longer.

18

When I pulled Cintha through the gate, Patch came running, barking up from his place by the front door.

"Hush. You'll wake everybody in the house," I said, as I got down to tie Cintha to the fence. She didn't like the dog jumping around at our feet. She whinnied and tried to rear so I jerked her cheek strap to make her settle down. Lamplight glowed faintly in the window.

Patch kept yipping but quieter, almost like he was excited to see me, though I couldn't imagine why. I couldn't recall us making friends. I bent to pat him, then lifted the lid on the buggy lantern and blew out the wick. I started to go to the front door, then decided against it. The light inside seemed nearer to the back of the house.

The moon came in and out of black clouds, a half-moon. Patch led the way down the side of the house. I could hear his sharp dog breaths. As we turned the back corner, the kitchen door opened.

"Who's there?" Andy said gruffly, alarmed, ready for a row if one came.

I moved forward into the light that fell through the open door. "Just me."

Patch hopped up the three steps to the porch as if he intended on going inside, but Andy kicked him back. The dog landed with a yelp on his belly, got up, and scrambled off somewhere behind me. I turned to see if he was hurt, but he looked all right.

Andy said, "What're you doing here?"

"I came to see about you." I went up one step.

"See what about me?"

"How you are."

"I'm drinking." His voice sounded flat, toneless.

"Liquor?"

"I've been known to take a drop." He leaned out the door, looking into the night. "Where's your buggy?"

"Up in front."

"On the road?"

"Around in the yard. Should I move it somewhere else?" I felt uncertain now. He acted strange, so aloof, almost as if I were to blame for his troubles.

"What the hell," he said finally, and moved aside, stretching the door open for me to enter. I passed under his arm. He put his hand on my elbow to guide me inside, and his touch reassured me.

When I stepped into the kitchen, it nearly took my breath to see the room, the sameness, the familiarity. I remembered bathing in a washtub in front of the cast-iron stove, huddling by the fireplace in winter, lying on a pallet at Sister's feet while she read to us, staring up at the crevices where the spiders lived amongst the lamp black. Home. It felt like home in this room.

The power of it made me forget why I had come. I wandered forward a couple of steps, ran my hand along the pie safe. I could almost hear Papa coming in the door, asking was supper ready, or sending me out to pick something ripe he had spotted in the garden on his way in. I turned to Andy, to see if he understood all I was feeling, but he had just taken a swig from a crock jar, and was lowering it from his lips. A single lamp burned over the stove, hung by its bale from a hook on a chain. The flame flickered and cast deep, trembling shadows on his face.

"Who do you think gave me this?" He raised the jar to show me what he was talking about. I judged it would hold about a quart. "The Reverend Barbee. Claimed he had it for medicinal purposes, hid under his wagon seat. Right there in easy reach. Same place my father kept his. Somebody's home brew. Somebody else's, not his own." He snorted. "Another damned preacher whose religion is more habit than devotion." He took a long drink, and from how far back he had to tip the crock, I guessed the jar to be nearly empty. He coughed and drew in his breath, so I knew he wasn't in the habit of strong liquor, despite what he'd said.

"The children are asleep?" I asked.

He wiped his mouth on his forearm and nodded. Then in silence, he went to the other end of the room where three chairs sat around the fireplace. I followed him.

The front room seemed smaller than I remembered it, older, the walls and floor out of true, so much so I could feel the floor slope under my feet. He took the cane-bottom chair and motioned me into a slat-back rocker. I sat but didn't rock. I kept myself out to the edge and tried to remember if this chair had been here before. I didn't think it had. The arms were rough and Papa would have never stood for that. He'd have sanded and sanded until we all choked on the dust, but he would have smoothed down these wooden arms till they were as slick as glass.

In the shallow light from the kitchen, Andy's eyes were huge and luminous. He propped his feet on the fenders and stared across the hearth as if a fire burned there. Millers and mayflies made the only sound, as they flickered against the kitchen lamp behind us. After several more hushed seconds, he glanced my way.

"Well? Now you see how I am." He tipped the jar again.

"I didn't get a chance to talk to you after the meeting. I wanted to—" I flattened my hands on my knees and collected my words. What was it I wanted to say? How sorry I was that his wagon had burned and how angry? Somehow that didn't seem good enough. How much I cared for him, loved him? I thought of Priscilla spreading rumors about us. "What will you do?"

He leaned forward and set the crock on the hearth. "I don't know yet."

"You could file criminal charges."

"Against who?" His tone sharpened. "Ghosts? Everybody knows who did it and nobody saw a thing."

"Well, maybe someone did. What if they're just scared to say? If you filed charges, there'd be an investigation—"

"By a Democrat sheriff? There's people that don't want me around here, Dellie. Haven't you figured that out yet? Even your own daddy called me a Socialist."

"We could hire one of those detective men. They have them in Austin. I've read about them. I don't know, we can do something. If we could prove it was Mr. Bassist, or someone he hired—" Andy laughed, a hateful, ugly laugh. I felt so alone I could barely think straight. "I just want to help you. Can't you even see that?"

"How can you help me? What can you do? Tell me what." The bitterness in his voice chilled me.

"I don't know. Give you ideas. Something."

"Ideas like hiring a detective?" The bristling laugh came from him again. "Go home to your rich husband. Don't bother me with your foolish ideas. I'm tired, and I'm drunk. And I want you to leave me alone."

If he had struck a knife into my heart it could not have hurt as much. I felt my voice leave my body, my breath went with it. My head pounded. If he'd have looked up just then he'd have seen that for a moment I was dead.

I stood up, smoothing my dress, holding my stomach for fear of vomiting all over the floor. I turned and walked away from him. I got almost to the jelly cupboard before I was certain he wouldn't call me back, wouldn't say he didn't mean what he'd said. I didn't make it to the door before I broke down into a fit of tears. He looked up at me from his chair. I started to run on out into the night, tuck my tail and go as far away from the bitterness on his face as my feet would take me. Instead, I turned back toward him.

"Why are you treating me this way?" I said, my voice wet. "What have I done? All I want is to take away your pain, but you treat me like a piece of trash you'd throw out the door. I'm sorry your wagon burned, Andy, and I'm sorry there's people who want to run you off. I'm sorry your wife's a madwoman and that you're alone. I wish your children were my children, so much I wish they were." He got up and started toward me. I saw his face change, but I couldn't stop raving. I took a step back from him and said I was sorry for his childhood, and that his papa was no good, that his life hadn't turned out like he wanted. I said I was sorry I loved him, but that I couldn't help it. My eyes ran rivers. I choked when he grabbed me up.

"That's enough of that," he said, through gritted teeth.

I felt myself wilt, as if I was hollow inside, like there weren't enough bones in me to hold me upright. "Dellie." He shook me to get me to look in his face, but I wouldn't. My knees sagged and only his hands held me on my feet. "Dellie, don't fall to pieces on me. I won't have it, do you hear me?"

There was something almost fearful in his voice, and I thought of how he'd already had one woman go crazy on him. But I couldn't help my tears, or my choking. He let me down on the kitchen floor, and he came onto his knees beside me. He gripped hold of my jaw and forced me to look him in the eye.

"You think you know what's inside me, but you don't. I'm a bastard. I don't want you to love me. I don't deserve it, and I don't want it." He pushed my face back, moved the hair stuck to my forehead, and kissed me there between my eyebrows. Then he drew me close and rocked me in his arms. "I don't want to hurt you."

I laid my face against his shoulder and held tight to him, getting back my breath. "I'm all right now. I am."

"You ought to go away from me. You know you ought to. It isn't right for you to be here."

"I don't care about right. I only care about you. I have to be where you are."

There was something in him that needed me, too. It was clear no matter what he said. I could feel it in his arms around me. I reached for his lips and he kissed me, but I don't think he meant for the fire and passion to come. It carried him away, carried me, too, just like in Austin. One kiss turned into more kisses. Just when I felt myself sinking, drowning in him, he stood up.

He jerked me to my feet and took me through the doorway between the kitchen and the side room, his room, the room that had been Papa's long ago. He closed the door behind us. It was steamy hot in there. Our clothes stuck to us as we peeled them off, layer by layer, down to nothing. The bed was an oven, the mattress lumpy and old. The rope slats creaked and gave beneath us, until it seemed we had fallen into a hole together. We struggled there for a moment, and then he was pushing himself up, holding his hand out to me.

"Come on," he whispered.

Dim light came from the kitchen under the door. I groped for my underclothes, but he pulled them from my hands, dropped them on the floor. He stepped out the open window and drew me out, too. I'd never been outside raw naked before, never skinny-dipped in the cistern like Nathan and his friends when they were boys. It felt shocking and I couldn't keep from giggling a little, crouching to hide every time the moon popped out from the clouds. Patch heard me and came out from wherever he'd been. He didn't bark, just followed along with us.

Andy led me down to the creek, and then he dragged me in after him. The pebbles on the bottom hurt my feet, and the water was laughing cold. He cupped it in his hands and poured it over me, then covered my mouth with his to keep me from shrieking. "Isn't this better?" he said, next to my lips. I could taste the whiskey.

The dog stayed at the bank, whining a little, pacing, confused by our splashing about. Lightning bugs flickered so close, I felt I could almost reach out and catch them in my hand.

We were in a deep hole to our waists before Andy drew my legs around him. It felt joyous in the water, and reckless. Free. I floated backward until my breasts were laid bare. The moon shone down and it seemed I could feel the beam of light touching me, whispering against my skin. The creek riffled in my ears, and then Andy's murmurings came to me. I raised my head to hear him.

"'He hath made all things beautiful in his time. He hath set the world in their heart, so that no man can find out the work that he maketh from beginning to end.'"

It was Scripture. While our bodies were locked in lovemaking, he was quoting Ecclesiastes. Was he trying to say in this way that he loved me? Was he only telling me he thought me beautiful? Or was he saying our sin was so deep, even God couldn't forgive us? I was afraid to ask so I never knew. I never did understand him; he was right about that one thing. Wrong about so many others, but right about me. What foolish things desire will make people do.

I didn't go home. Nothing was said, no firm decision made,

but when we returned to the house, he left me on the back porch steps while he went around to bring Cintha and my gig to the barn. I watched him turn the mare into the lot with his sleeping mules. And then he came to me, across the chicken yard in the moonlight, as bare as the day he was born.

19

I awoke dazed, lost, until I remembered I was in Andy's bed. His smell was in the pillows. My hand reached out to the place where he'd slept. We had kept each other awake most the night. The sheets were cool. The house was as quiet as church, except for birds rustling under the window eaves. Daylight poured in through the cheesecloth curtain.

When I raised my head, the first thing I saw was his green paisley vest on the old wall-peg where Papa used to hang his hat. The same five-drawer chest stood against the south wall, and like it was only yesterday, I remembered watching Papa bend pieces of cable wire to make pull handles for those drawers, and I remembered the squeal they made opening, no matter how much Sister soaped the runners. Sometimes when Papa was out in the fields, Nathan would get into those drawers and take out the photograph of our mama that Papa kept hidden in there beneath his britches and his socks. And looking at Mama's face, Sister would whisper us stories about how pretty Mama could sing, and how she always went barefoot even though Papa fussed about it, saying, "Emma, you'll step on a nail if you ain't careful." I wondered what happened to that old, creased-up picture of her. I couldn't remember having seen it again once we moved away to Mother's house.

The wallpaper in the room was the same pattern of tiny blue roses it had always been, faded now, and soot-stained, torn above the doorway, crinkling loose along the corners. I thought it must have been Mama who had put up this paper, since I couldn't feature Papa's taste running to blue roses. Thinking of her, a young woman not much older than me right now, it felt right and proper to me that I should be lying here in her house, grand and in love.

And quick on that thought came another that struck me so hard I had to sit straight up to contemplate it. Had Mama, I wondered—this woman who liked blue wallpaper—was it possible she had been just as in love as I was? Only with Papa? My papa? A young Papa. Could she have felt just as overcome in her heart as I did in mine? She had borne him four children, so they had surely shared a bed. This bed. It was a strange new thought for me. One I had never lingered on before now. I could hardly imagine Papa in that way—lovable, young, certainly not possessed of passion. Yet, he couldn't bear to have her picture out and in full view. He'd had to hide it away from his own eyes, underneath his socks and his pants. Was that why he never spoke of her? Because her memory pained him too much? But then Papa had never talked of much of anything that I could recall, past the weather, the cattle, the crops, and what was best for us.

He must have changed. He couldn't have always been so stern, so overbearing, like I remembered him. Or else would Mama have married him? Would any of them? He'd had another wife before her, one that he brought with him from Mississippi just after the war. She had died, too, of yellow fever, and so had their child. And then, finally, there was Mother, long-suffering Mother, who had been the Widow Kennedy until she married Papa. And if that marriage had been one of convenience for him, for more land and a woman to raise his children, what had it been for her? What did she stand to gain? A husband was all, so far as I knew. Three wives Papa had. Three who had been willing enough to take his hand. Sitting there in that bed—his bed—I realized there must have been something about Papa I had missed.

Thinking of him in this new way, and sitting in his bed, raw naked, I felt suddenly wicked and full of sin. My clothes were in a pile in the straight chair beneath the window. I hurried into them. The dress was a rumpled mess and I tried to smooth out the wrinkles. I stepped into my shoes. There was a slop jar under the bed and I used it. Then I just sat in the straight chair, my hands in my lap, too ashamed to leave the room. I ventured a glance through the curtain but all I saw was a brown hen pecking in the yard.

Here I was in this house where I'd always felt I belonged. I had stayed through the night and whatever came next, I would have to face. The thought of that sat like a heavy lump in my stomach. It was Daniel I thought of most. I tried to convince myself that he would be relieved, that I had become a burden to him, but in my heart I knew that was not so. I remembered the pressing of my hand to his cheek, the hurt in his eyes, and I knew he would feel betrayed. I thought of the life we had led, comforts he had given me that I would have to learn to do without. But also, I thought of the sameness of the days.

The light scuff of bare feet came, and the door to the room slowly opened, with Hannah on tiptoes to reach the knob. She was in her nightdress, which she had long ago outgrown. The draggled dust ruffle barely covered her knees. The sleeves just reached to her elbows. She gave me a shy grin. Her hair was all a-tangle from her pillow.

"Good morning," I said, unsure if I should give her an excuse for why I was sitting here in her papa's bedroom. She didn't seem surprised to see me. She let go of the doorknob and came toward me.

"Daddy said I could stay home, but that I couldn't come get in the covers with you." So he had told her something. I wondered what. I recalled him saying once that they kept no secrets in this family.

"Your daddy's gone?"

She nodded. "With Quint." She climbed on my lap, fingered a strand of my hair. She had a faintly sweet smell about her, and her feet were cold. "Your hair is very long. Daddy won't let me grow mine long. He says he can't brush it so he cuts it all off."

"Not all of it." I petted my hand over her hair. It was as fine as down, and I thought that if she were mine, I would let her grow it out until I could plait it into braids, or brush it back into a pretty china clip. Suddenly, I felt all right again, and I gave her a hug. "Where did your daddy and Quint go?"

"To Fletcher's Hall." She kept winding my hair around her finger and all the way up her little arm. Then she laughed, and put her hands on both sides of my face. "Can you sing? I know a song I'll sing you. Can you make biscuits? I'll sing it for you if you'll make biscuits."

"Biscuits?" I sat up a little straighter. She took her hands away from me, and they left two warm spots on my cheeks.

"Gretta makes me biscuits when I stay at her house."

"She does? Well, all right then. We'll make biscuits, too." I stood and set her on the floor. She took my hand and we went together to the kitchen.

There was white flour in the cupboard, some lard, two pails of fresh milk, with cream gathered thick to the top like skim on a can of paint. I could have nearly lifted it from the pail all of a piece. A pot of coffee sat on the stove, still warm to the touch. He hadn't been gone long. I poured myself a cup and drank it with a spoon of the cream.

Hannah sang "Little Annie Rooney" while I stoked up the fire in the stove. She knew the words pretty well, but it sounded funny, this love song coming in a three-year-old voice. I couldn't help but laugh. She didn't seem to mind my laughter. She grinned and went from that song to another, "Daisy Bell," which I sang along with her.

I didn't have an easy time with the biscuits. I had never been too clever in the kitchen. At home, Mother had been the cook, and Sister before her. And then I had Tante Lena. What little I knew, I'd mostly been taught at Miss Langburn's, and there I had learned how to make fancy dainties, truffles and tortes, not wholesome foods like biscuits. I got flour all over me, the kitchen, and the stove. Hannah went on singing without me.

The biscuits came out hard and as flat as washers. She didn't complain. She showed me where the molasses was and I dipped some on her plate. That didn't help soften them any, so I added some cream and made a mush. But that was worse and she wouldn't eat it, didn't even want it in front of her, it looked so nasty and slopped together, fit for pigs and nothing else. Finally, I had the idea that we could see if the hens had laid eggs overnight. An egg I was sure I could cook. And it was while we were out in the chicken yard that Andy and Quintus came home.

I jumped at the rattling sound of the farm wagon, and almost dropped all the eggs—eleven of them—out of my skirt where we'd been gathering them. I managed to get them to stay in a pile on the back porch. The dog came running at Hannah and she laughed and dodged his licking tongue. The chickens scattered, squawking. When I saw the wagon, and Andy and Quintus up on the seat, I nearly rushed back inside the house, thinking maybe he hadn't expected me to still be here. But then I remembered he had left Hannah for me to watch.

Quintus jumped down and came on the run, until Andy called him back to tell him something. When Quintus came again, he wasn't running. He had a handful of buckeye seed he'd found somewhere, and he showed them to me as if I were always there standing in his yard when he came home. Hannah wanted to hold one of the hard, round seeds, and he showed her how to roll it in her palm so it would bring good luck.

I eased toward where Andy was busy unhitching his mules, feeling timid, like we had only just met. He looked up at me coming and smiled. I felt my step lighten.

"Need some help?"

"No." He kept on unhooking harness straps. "But there is something I wanted to tell you."

A dread came to me. "All right." I knew I sounded uncertain.

He pulled the mules out of their collars, and popped them each on their hind-ends. They hurried on through the barn and toward the lot behind. Then he turned his attention back to me. "You gave a good speaking last night. I should've said so before now. It's about all they were talking about up there this morning."

I let out my breath and felt my smile come. "It was?"

He picked up the wagon by the tongue and dragged it forward. I heard the rattle of metal in the wagon bed. "Reclaimed most of my nails. Got all the tires. I think the axle's still good." He let the wagon drop, dusted his hands. "Are you staying?"

"Staying?" I took a few steps closer. "You mean, here?"

"It won't be easy. Either way."

"You said before you'd be ruined."

"Well, I reckon I already am." He looked out at the day. "And so are you. By now I expect they're looking for you. Somebody is."

"And you have regrets."

"No." He leaned back against the wagon, crossed his arms and his feet. "I'm sober. That's what I am. Last night I wasn't thinking clear. I don't think either one of us was. But this morning, waking up with you . . ." He paused and I wanted him to finish what he'd been about to say, but he just looked at me, then off again into the sunlight outside the barn. "I expect we'll be seeing your husband."

"He's out of town."

"But he'll be back. And he's liable to come over here with a gun loaded." He laughed a little, trying to sound unconcerned.

"No, he won't. Daniel wouldn't do a thing like that."

"Are you sure? I can't say as I'd blame him. It's probably what I'd do in his place." His face went serious. "I can't offer you nothing, Dellie. Not even my name. But whether you go or whether you stay, as soon as my crop's out of the ground I've decided to leave here. I can't stay in the same town with a man like Louis Bassist, but if you had a mind to go with me—"

"I do. You know I do." I went to him. We put our arms around each other and stayed still for a moment. I could smell the soot on him, from foraging in the ash for his hardware, and I drew strength from it, and from knowing he wanted me with him from now on, just as I did, though it frightened me to think of leaving McDade. I'd been here all of my life. "Where would we go?" I said against his neck.

"To Cheneyville, I reckon. Ben and Lavy, they asked me to come last spring but I wouldn't. They've got good dirt over there. Better rainfall." I could barely breathe. He was talking my dream out loud. I watched his mouth move as he went on with it. I wanted to put my fingers against his lips, touch them, kiss them. I wanted to lie down with him right here in the barn. "They've got a People's Party over there that needs building up. Don't have a newspaper like we do here, but we could start one ourselves if we had the time, and can find a press to use."

"We'll make the time."

He squeezed my arms and rubbed me, stood me back a foot or so from him. He kept his hands on my shoulders, and he looked me in the face. I thought I knew what he saw. The love I felt for him had to show all over me. "It'll be hard work," he said. "I'd expect a lot out of you. So think it through. I ain't an easy man to live with. You ought to know that by now. Be sure you're clear about everything."

"I want to go with you. I'd go today."

He smiled, rubbed some more. "Well, we can't do that. I got a crop to get out of the ground yet."

Around the corner came Hannah's voice, calling him. And both of them, her and Quintus, appeared at the front of the barn. They stood there a moment looking at us, at their daddy holding on to me and me to him. I wondered what they thought of it. I couldn't tell by their faces. I wanted to say something, tell them I would be a good mother to them, and love them like they were my own. I felt I already did love them in that way.

Quintus said, "Come and look at what Patch has done," and Andy went with him.

The eggs I'd left on the back porch were, every one, cracked to pieces. The dog had his nose in the middle of them, licking up yolks. He lifted his head at us for a second, and eggwhite trailed from his jaw. Hannah laughed, and I started to, but Andy didn't think it was funny. He waved his arms and ran at the dog, and Patch darted down the steps to hide under the house, where he lay to lick his chops. He peered at us, just eyes and pointed ears.

"Look at this mess. Go get some water and clean this up," Andy said to Quintus; then to me, "Who left these eggs here?"

"I did. I didn't think about the dog."

"That's a couple of meals he just ate. Our meals, Dellie. At the least, we could take them and sell them. Sometimes those eggs are all we've got."

"I didn't know. I'm sorry."

"Well. Now, you learned," he said, looking away from me, softening his tone. I could see it took an effort. I thought of what he had just said about not being an easy man. He had a temper, but that I already knew. It was part of what I loved about him, yet I felt small and stupid, the same child I'd been when I lived here with Papa.

When Quintus came with the bucket of water, I took it from him and scrubbed the porch myself. I used the can of soft lye soap I'd seen in the kitchen, and an old worn-out grooming brush. Cleaning was something I did know how to do, something I was good at. So when I finished with the porch, I moved inside the house.

The children's room didn't look like it had been touched in months. Andy stayed outside in the barn, sorting through his burned wagon parts. I didn't bother him. After the eggs, I thought he was probably already having second thoughts about me, now that he knew how inept I was at farm life. And it seemed we needed time apart, to think through the decision we had just made. It was all that was in my mind. I knew it was bound to be on his, too.

I couldn't imagine how we would tell Daniel, if I would go alone to do it, or if we would face it together, or if we would wait for him to come here and find us together. And then there were the others: Mother and Nathan and Sinclair and Tante Lena, all the people in town, the Bettses, and the folks at the meetings. The Craddocks. The Slaters. What a scandal we would cause. How we would be shunned. I knew Papa would have disowned me like he had Sister and Dane, and for far less sins.

The apprehension was almost more than I could bear, the nerves. I wished that I could get it over with, that Daniel would come home. I wished the cotton was already in and we could go away right now. I busied myself cleaning the children's room. I gave Hannah a rag to dust off the bedsteads, the chifforobe. She did a poor job of it, but she chattered happily all the while, telling me of a butterfly Quintus had caught by the wings, about a rainstorm that had scared her once in the night. While she chattered, I went at the cobwebs on the ceiling with a broom, made the beds, and swept the floor.

After a while, Quintus came inside. He said, "Dad says we're about done out yonder. And he wants to know, can you make coffee?"

Andy hadn't seen my attempt at biscuits, but the question made me cross just the same. "Yes," I snapped. "Of course, I can."

I stopped what I was doing and went to grind coffee. I rinsed out the pot, opened the stove to stab at the embers. Before I got up a good fire, though, Andy came in. He looked about as solemn as I'd ever seen him, and I could tell right away that he'd been thinking as hard as I had been.

"Should we go after some of your clothes?" he said.

I straightened from the stove. "You've changed your mind."

"No." He took a deep breath, like it would be easy for him to lose his patience. "I was only just wondering about your clothes."

"What I have on will do."

"One dress?"

"It'll do."

"That's not sensible, Dellie."

"None of this is sensible. That's what you're thinking, isn't it?"

"Are you?"

I shook my head and poked again in the firebox on the stove. He leaned his hand on the wall, propped himself there, and watched me. I tried to stay busy and ignore his eyes on me, but the coffee was ground, the pot had water. All that was left was to wait for the fire. I let my gaze meet his, and he looked down at his feet.

"I keep on wondering, how did this all happen?" He raised his head, shifted from the wall. "One minute I'm just a farmer with two kids to feed and a sorry stand of cotton in the ground. And the next, my wagon's burnt and I've got another man's wife in my house . . ." He noticed Hannah in the room with us. "Go outside with your brother," he said sternly.

We both stayed silent until she was gone, and she took her time, dawdling, throwing back looks at us. He thundered at her to get on outside, and this time she scurried for the back door. He was on edge, addled by my being here.

"You don't love me, do you?" I said.

"I don't think it's right for me to."

"Then why did you say all those things about us leaving here and making a new life? Was it just because you knew I wanted to hear it?"

"No." He squeezed his eyes shut like he had a splinter in there, and he took another deep breath. He looked at me. It was a grave look. "This morning when I woke up, I knew it was what I had to do. Because I've done this thing . . . we've done it. And now I've got to take the responsibility for it."

"I don't want to be your obligation, Andy."

"That's not what I'm meaning to say."

"I think it is what you mean."

"Dellie." He held up his hand to quiet me. "You got to be able to see that I want you. You've got the gentlest ways about you. You make a man want to love you, even when he knows he shouldn't."

He reached out to smooth back my hair, and even with his children playing right outside the door, he leaned to kiss me. But then he heard something that took his attention away from me, a horse out toward the front. A voice called "Hallo," and I recognized the voice. We looked at each other, and the call came again.

"It's Nathan." My heart had started to pound. He nodded and headed toward the front door. I went after him. "No, Andy! Don't go out there."

He turned. "What do you want me to do? I've got to answer him." He went out onto the porch. I heard Nathan's voice say, "Morning," and Andy said, "Morning," back.

Hannah and Quintus bounded in the kitchen door. Quintus said, "Here's your brother," and it surprised me, him knowing who was here, and saying it like it was a warning, too. Children always understand so much more than we think they do. Seeing their little honest faces looking up at me mobilized my courage.

Outside, Nathan said, "My sister. I believe that's her buggy horse in your lot," and that's when I walked through the door. He quit speaking when he saw me. Andy glanced back at me and smiled, but it was a smile so distant, so empty, I nearly shied from it.

The air was heavy, hot and sticky. Birds had already quit their songs. Patch came around to see who was there, and even he didn't have much energy. He barked once or twice, halfheartedly, at where Nathan stood, with pressed lips, on the pathway at the bottom of the porch stairs. He glanced from me to Andy, and back again, lingering on my face a brief instant.

"You're looking for me?" I said. "This is where I am." I stepped closer to Andy, but I didn't touch him, nor him me. It seemed I could hear all of us breathing: Andy and myself, Nathan, even the children behind us and the dog on the ground.

Then without another word, Nathan turned and headed back down the yardway path to where his horse was tied. And walking away from me that way, in silence, was far worse than any scolding or words aimed at shaming me. I had to stop myself from running after him, from begging him to go on and say what was on his mind, to tell me what a coward I was for lying to him last night when I'd had the chance to confess the truth. I forced myself to stand still, though, head high, and watch him swing himself onto his bay. He heeled the horse to a trot out through the gate and to the road. Never once did he look back at me. It was as if I had been erased. As surely as if Papa had risen from the dead and stolen me back from myself again.

"You've got to go home," Andy said, without emotion.

"I wonder why he didn't speak."

"I shouldn't have let you stay here last night. I don't know what the hell I was thinking of." He moved from beside me, and I turned to look at him. His face had gone to stone. Both children stood in the doorway, watching everything we said. "You've got to go home till your husband gets back, Dellie. It's the only right way."

"And then what?"

"I don't know. We'll have to see."

He steered the children inside the house, and then he came to catch Cintha, hitched her up for me. He worked quietly, quickly, and he walked with me as far as the road, but we didn't kiss or embrace. He told me goodbye. That was all.

20

Sinclair wasn't out in the stable, but Tante Lena came running to help me unhitch Cintha. "We was all so worried," she said. "You shouldn't head out so early without telling somebody something." I know I must have looked confused. I didn't know what she knew or didn't know. I decided to keep quiet, and she went on scolding. "You could have fallen in a hole somewheres and we would still be looking for you. Come inside. We'll get you some soup."

"I'm not hungry. And I don't feel well." It was a plea I had evidently used too often lately, for she offered no words of sympathy.

When we were inside, she said, "Sit down there and eat something."

"No, I'm going up to my room."

"Well, I'll bring you fresh water?"

I didn't pause to reply. My feet felt like lead as I trudged up the stairs. In a minute or so, she came with a pitcher and poured my basin full, laid out a fresh cloth.

"Will you be to supper?" she said. "We have the teachers, you know."

I didn't want to be bothered. I wanted to bolt my door and keep everyone out. I didn't want to pretend nothing had happened, or that I was the same old Dellie everyone thought they knew.

"Yes. Set me a place," I said, and she seemed pleased. She went out smiling. I couldn't imagine where she thought I'd been all morning and night, and she didn't say. Maybe she didn't feel it was her place to ask questions. Whatever the reason, I was grateful for her silence.

I bathed off in the basin and changed out of my rumpled dress. I brushed my hair and pulled it back from my face. I studied myself in the mirror. Adulteress. I didn't feel like such a thing, or look like I imagined one should look. In the olden days I might have been stoned for such a transgression, or called a witch and burned at the stake. It happened in books I read. A man could be castrated for it, put in stocks, or hung by the neck until he was dead. It was a serious crime we had committed.

The room, this house, felt like a prison to me. The air in the room seemed tight, sultry. I opened the windows and the gallery door. I went out to stare at the blank of blue sky, and out over the pastureland rolling down to the creek. I watched Cintha move off down there to water. Somewhere the cattle lowed but I couldn't see them. I paced. I checked the clock over my writing table. I had been back for just twenty minutes.

Daniel had said he'd be home on Sunday. Day after tomorrow. I didn't see how I could stand this being pinned up in here that long. I sat down to my writing desk, cupped my face in my hands, and tried to concentrate on Andy, on being with him every day the way we'd planned, living as a wife to him and a mother to his children. The photograph of Sister's family hung on the wall above me, and I looked at it, thinking again how brave she'd been, just up and leaving with the man she loved, never minding the consequences. *We'll see,* Andy had said, and I wondered what he meant by it. That he had doubts? That our plans to go might change once Daniel came home? I didn't see how I could wait until Sunday to know my future.

As we were finishing supper, Nathan came. I had gone down to have a bite with our teachers, had managed to put on a face long enough for that, and then Nathan walked in looking tired, wearing the same blue shirt he'd had on this morning. It seemed odd to me that he should still be wearing it. So much had passed between then and now, yet so little actual time.

He said his greetings to Bickham Laramore and to Mr. Hockaday, but he kept throwing looks my way, and I gathered he was surprised to see me here. Bick asked about tomorrow's rematch ballgame against Smithville, and Nathan chatted briefly about that. Then he leaned over my shoulder, said he'd like to speak to me if I had a minute. I looked back at him.

"Now you want to speak," I mumbled.

"If you don't mind." He smiled at Mr. Hockaday.

Tante Lena came out with a plate for Nathan that he tried to refuse. She said, "No, you sit yourself down there."

He held up his hands to show her how dirty they were. "I've been out salting cows all day, Lena."

"So you wash," she said.

I scooted back my chair and stood. "I've got a basin you can use in my room," and before Tante Lena could argue, I took him upstairs.

We went in silence, out through my room to the gallery where we would not be overheard. A glorious sunset reddened the sky, but I hardly noticed. He sat on the gallery rail, leaned his back against a post, one foot up off the ground. I thought how easily he could fall. I took the old Boston rocker that had belonged to Daniel's father. The runners were smooth from years of wear, and a little rotten besides. They rumbled over the gallery boards as I rocked back and forth.

Nathan stared out at the sky. "You did the right thing coming home."

"I'm only here till Daniel gets back," I said. My voice sounded wooden. "I decided—or rather, after you left, Andy decided . . . I can't just leave Daniel without telling him. It wouldn't be fair to him. He's been good to me. Mostly he's been good. I know what you must be thinking of me, but I can't help it. It's what I want to do. I've made up my mind. I know you can't understand—" I kept waiting for him to interrupt me. He had said he wanted to speak to me, but now he kept his face turned toward the sky and let me fumble on a little longer about my love, my feelings, until I ran out of words. We sat silent after that.

He stepped down from his perch on the railing. "He's gone."

It took a moment for what he said to soak in. "What do you mean, gone?"

"Andy. He's gone. Lock, stock, and barrel. I was just by there before I came here. I thought you knew, but I see you don't."

"Gone? He can't be gone."

"I went back over there to talk to you. You caught me off guard this morning, and I had some things I wanted to say. When I saw the place was empty, I wasn't sure whether I'd find you here or what."

"That can't be. We're leaving once harvest is over. He said we were. We're leaving together. He must've just gone off some-where—"

"No, Dellie. He's gone for good." He reached into his money pocket.

"You did it, didn't you?" I almost ran at him. "You made him leave. You threatened him, didn't you?"

"No, I didn't." He pulled an envelope from his pocket. "He was gone when I got there. He left this." He held the envelope out toward me. "It's addressed to me, but you can read it."

"To you? Why to you?"

He came and dropped the letter in my lap. "Take it inside under the lamp. I'll stay out here and smoke."

I took the envelope, balanced it on my fingertips. It had smudges around the edge. The words in the center were smeared

—*Mr. Nathan DeLony*—in Andy's handwriting. I smelled the tobacco burning in Nathan's cigarette.

He said again, "Why don't you take it inside, Dellie. Read it in private."

I looked at him. He had a cigarette between his fingers, pity in his eyes. I hated the pity. I got up. I felt I was sleeping. I wished that I were. I went inside my room and sat down at the writing desk.

Dear Nathan DeLony,

I wanted to thank you and your family for the chance you all gave me here. I know I owe you rent from last year yet, and all of this year, but the cotton's been laid by and ought to bring in something at the gin. It's poor, but the best the land could yield this season because of no rain. There is six good layers amongst the hens, all the Rhode Islands. The cow, Pet is her name, will need freshening this fall. I know what you said about the mules, but they are all fair workers. Maybe somebody will give you a price for them. Try Early Horner. He bought that place out at Pleasant Grove, and he might have need of them. There's two hogs running somewhere with my notch, triple-fork. Hope this squares us. I never had a key to the house.

Yours sincerely,
Andrew J. Ashland

I raised my face. Nathan stood in the doorway, holding his cigarette cupped in his hand. He took a draw, and it struck me that I never even knew that he smoked. Never had seen him do it before. It looked odd on him somehow. Unnatural. He picked a piece of tobacco off his tongue.

"The cow was full when I got there. Moaning. Tame as can be. I led her over to the Grossners. Told them to pass her milk out around their family. Christ knows I don't need another cow to wring out every morning and night."

I put the letter down on the writing table, then picked it up again, slid it back into its envelope. "This doesn't mean he's gone."

"What else does it mean, Dellie? The house is bone empty."

I shook my head. I pushed the letter to the edge of the table, finished with it. I never wanted to see it again. I stood up, smoothed at my hair. I smiled at him. "I'll go have a look for myself."

"You don't believe me?" he said, but I had already headed for the door. And I didn't look back, though I heard him follow me.

I didn't say anything to Tante Lena, to Bick or Mr. Hockaday either, though I passed right by them in the parlor when I came down the stairs. "Ain't you gonna eat?" Tante Lena said to Nathan and I didn't hear his answer. He came after me. There was still enough sunlight to hitch Cintha by. I refused Sinclair's offer of help, told him please to let me do it. I refused Nathan's hands, too. I heard him behind me on his horse as I went off down the road.

It was fully dark by the time I got to Andy's house, though the moon was rising fast and bright. It threw down shadows on the ground, made it easy to see the door to the house hanging open, the blackness within, the rows of cotton in the fields, the three mules hugging the board fence. Nothing moved about the place, except for one hen who didn't mind the night. The rest were in the roosting coop. Andy had built a sturdy one.

Nathan was wrong about the house. It wasn't *bone* empty. In fact, most everything was as it had been last night and this morning: the crock jar on the hearth in front of the chairs, the lamp hanging dark in the kitchen, my pitiful biscuits piled on a plate. Except for the clothes and the bed linens gone, it still looked as if people lived here. On the floor in the children's room, like it had been dropped by accident, I found Hannah's ragdoll, one button eye missing, a hole in its neck with the cotton thatch coming out. I clutched it to me and caught a scent of sweet little girl. I felt dried up inside.

Behind me, Nathan walked into the room holding the lamp from the kitchen by its base. He took it over to the chifforobe in the corner and set it down. The wick needed trimming. A tail of black smoke curled from the chimney.

"Do you remember sleeping in here?" I said, still hugging the doll close.

"I sure do. In that bed over there with Dane. Hated every minute of it. Always fighting for the window. Sometimes I'd go to bed when it was still daylight just to get the side by the window." He walked across to the bed and punched with his fingers at the mattress. "I can't believe two people slept here."

"Two small people."

"Not that small, Dellie. Dane was almost fifteen when Mother married Papa. And I was ten. We were crowded. You always have remembered those times as better than they were." He sat on the bed. The mattress tried to cave in at the center, forced him to the edge. He held to the foot post. "Nobody knows you were here this morning except me. I told Mother you broke down on the road coming to see her, and that Andy helped you. I told Tante Lena the same thing when I stopped by there after I found you. Mother's hip's been acting up. I said you had gone over to nurse her—"

"Why did you lie?"

"For all I know it wasn't a lie."

"I went to him after the meeting. I stayed through the night."

"Don't tell me anything, Dellie. I don't want to know."

"You already know."

"What I'm saying is, Daniel's my friend. You know we're close. But you're my sister. And I can keep a secret." He came to put his arm around me. He tried to take the doll from my clutches, but I wouldn't give it up. "Come on, let's go now. Why don't you come home with me for tonight. It would make Mother happy."

"No. Thank you. I know you want to look after me. But I want to stay here."

"He isn't coming back, Dellie."

"Maybe not. Probably not. But this is home. It's always been home." I glanced around the room, satisfied with the decision. "This is where I'm staying."

He tried to talk me out of it. When he saw he couldn't do that, he said he would stay, too, but I insisted he go. I did let him bring me some things, bedsheets and a pillow, a change of clothes, a pan of Tante Lena's cornbread. He told her another lie, said that I had decided to stay with him and Mother tonight. He used Mother's hip for an excuse again. He asked me once more if I was sure I would be all right, and I had a time convincing him I would be. He was hardheaded. He left me the six-shooter from his saddlebag.

After he was gone, loneliness closed around me. I pulled it to me like a wrap, wallowing in it, wandering from room to room, my mind wandering, too. Back to my childhood, then to Andy and to all the days since the Confederate Reunion, things I should've done differently, what might've happened if I had taken charge of myself and not just washed along in his wake.

But who can follow the wanderings of a mind? Especially one as distressed as mine was that night. I went from crying, feeling sorry for myself, through hopelessness to anger and wanting revenge. Not quickly, but over the course of several hours. I couldn't sleep. I didn't even try. I checked the crock jar on the hearth and it was empty. I opened the gun Nathan left and it held four bullets. And I thought how altogether wrong Dane had been to call Papa a coward. That he had found the nerve to squeeze that trigger seemed suddenly to me to be an act of supreme courage.

The oil in the lamp ran low, and it was the only light Andy had left me. I took it with me out to the barn to find more fuel. The moon had gone down, and the light from the lamp barely cut into the black darkness of the barn. Nathan had fed the mules before he left, but they seemed to want something more from me, hovering near the barn, and coming when I approached the door.

Just as I went inside, a bat flapped loose from the rafters and passed so close on its flight to the door that I let go a scream. And it was something to do with that bat and my scream, and with that barn and the low light from the lamp, that settled my mind. It was time to quit relying on other people.

I found the lamp oil, and I took it outside the barn and set it on the ground. Nathan had unhitched my gig and moved it around near the smokehouse, and he had put Cintha out in the lot. She wanted to play games with me, or else maybe the mules had made her restless. She wasn't used to being around mules. Whatever the reason, she was hard to catch that night, and she never had been before. I led her by her halter, got her hitched in the darkness. The lamp was fast losing its flame. With a stick I lit the headlamp on the gig, and I set the can of fuel in between my feet on the floorboards. I was half-delirious from lack of sleep. It was as if a kind of lunacy had taken hold of me. Somehow I got to town. I remember feeling grateful to my smart horse for seeing me there.

It must have been nearly four o'clock in the morning by then. The town was asleep. Not a light burning anywhere. Even the saloons were dark and silent. Cintha's hoofbeats echoed against the buildings and the night.

I tied her to the rail in front of Van Burkleo's, gave the door to the *Plaindealer* one rueful glance, then I took the can of oil from the floorboards and carried it across the street. I had never set a fire that wasn't inside a stove. I wasn't even sure I was doing it right, but I dribbled lamp oil all up and down the gallery outside Bassist's store, and as I did I thought of Andy saying he could never stay in the same town with a man like Louis Bassist. And I thought of the big teamster wagon lost in a heap of red coals. I recalled the day of the Masonic Celebration and Mr. Bassist's red face as he blustered out in bitter clipped-off words that Andy would never win this war.

There was enough coal oil in the can to go nearly the length of the store gallery, even with my having to walk round the cultivator sitting out on the sideway for sale. Papa had had a cultivator almost like it, probably bought on time and paid for with his sweat and labor like every other farmer around. I shook some oil on the cultivator, shook the oil can empty, and threw it on the gallery. It landed up close to the front doors.

I hadn't thought to bring matches, wouldn't have known where any would be anyway. Matches were something I felt sure Andy would have taken with him, along with his children and his dog, and his dreams and ideals. Not one stick lay on the street around the gig, not even a tiny one. I tore a strip of cedar bark from the hitch-rack, and used the flame from the buggy lamp. My makeshift match burned out before I could get halfway back to Bassist's. It took me three tries to get a good enough flare going. I dropped the splinter of burning wood into the trail of lamp oil, and the fire took hold all at once, and with a loud *whump* that surprised me. I jumped away, watching the gallery benches go up, and the cedar posts, the facing around the double doors. Paint on the wooden walls sizzled, then fried to nothing. It scared me, and the brightness of it, the noise, seemed to bring me out of the trance I was in.

All at once I changed my mind, realized what it was I had done here. I stomped at the floorboards nearest to me, then raced across to Cintha for the carriage blanket I kept in the box. Halfway back across the road I stopped, getting my breath, hearing my own heart pound. The flames had already reached to the awning. They licked up and caught the roofing shingles.

I ran back to Cintha. She was dancing around, wilting her ears flat. By the time I got her untied, the whole front of the building was engulfed. Dark smoke rolled like a fog into the sky. I half stood in the buggy, beating the lines down on her back. She went on the fly, and she nearly passed the fire station, even with me pulling back with all my might. Just as I jumped down, she pranced forward, and I lost my balance. I fell hard, scraping my ankle, tearing the hem of my dress. I didn't stop to inspect the damage. I crawled to my feet. My ankle pained but I threw myself on the firebell. The gong it made stayed in my ears long after I rounded the bend in the road out of town. When I looked back, I could still see the fire and the smoke, jumping high above the treetops.

PART THREE

21

By the time the sun came up, I was to Elgin. The man at the livery was a better horse-trader than me; he got Cintha and the gig for thirty dollars. I was almost certain Daniel had paid much more than that. I caught the first train into the station, the 7:24 to Austin. The ticketmaster swore there was no direct line east to Louisiana, so I bought a one-way to San Marcos, where I could pick up the KATY Flyer and take it all the way to Houston.

Once I got to Austin, an exhilaration suddenly sprang over me, a lightness and an eagerness that brought to mind a time when I was little, a time we had planned a visit to our mama's people in Columbus. We had an aunt there, some cousins we'd never met. Hutchinson was their name, and just the fact that they were kinfolk, especially Mama's kin, gave the trip an added importance to me. The night before we left, I couldn't sleep. I couldn't eat my breakfast in the morning. It seemed to take all week to get there, even traveling with good horses Papa had borrowed. With each mile my anticipation grew until, by the time we got there, I felt ready to pop. I was shy then, could barely bring myself to speak two words once we arrived, and they were all strangers to me. They had a big house that rambled in odd directions, but other than that I don't recall much about the visit, besides the waiting for it, the planning, the excitement of going somewhere away from home. The same feeling I had now, pacing the Austin station.

I came to the bench where I'd sat a week ago, and my eyes wandered out to the street. Another time of waiting, watching, wondering. Was it only a week? For a second I could almost see Andy come across for me with his long-reaching stride, his paisley vest and straw hat, looking dapper in the sunshine. He had gone to Louisiana; I felt in my bones that he had. And I would go there, too. We could still be together just as we'd planned, now that the decision had been made, by both of us, although not in the way we expected, to leave McDade. It was what we should have done in the first place. Just pack up and go, once we realized this love we had could not be helped.

And he did love me. I knew he did, though he might not wish to, or want to say it aloud. And I knew I could make him happy. I would surround him with my own love, given freely. I would pamper him, comfort him when he was low, warm his bed at night, make him want and need me so much, he would shout out his love for me to anyone who would listen.

I sat down on the bench. The fire still smelled on my clothes, my dear Cintha on my hands. Down on the street a bus filled with people as they headed for the capitol building, the state's congress being in session. The people looked so finely turned out in their cassimere and their fancy walking skirts, in their hats trimmed with Valenciennes lace, in their lisle hose and opera-top shoes. All I had were the clothes on my back, yet I didn't care about that. I felt freed from it suddenly. I bent to finger the rip in my hem, and I could hardly stop the smile that kept breaking on my face. I'm sure the people passing thought I was a craven loon, so disheveled, so maddeningly content with myself and with the decisions I had made.

By the time I reached the KATY station in San Marcos, it was well past noon and I was hungry. No other ladies traveled alone or sat alone in the dining hall, but I took a place at an empty table and ordered a stew, the least expensive item on the menu board. It was thin and tasteless, but I gave it my full attention, and I drank lots of coffee to wash the train grit out of my throat.

I paid extra for a sleeping berth. It was a frivolous spending of money, but I needed the rest. Mine was an upper berth, and I was happy with that so I could look up at the high ceiling, the way the wood molding curved downward to meet the walls, and at the thin chains that held my curtain and swayed with the motion of the car. I stared at the ceiling until I couldn't keep my eyes open, and then I slept all the way through to Houston.

The next day I awoke sick from the weak stew and from the motion of the train, the fumes and dust pouring in the open windows, and from the heat. At the Houston station I changed trains. I sat in the ladies' car, beside a young woman named Miranda Tow who came from Friendship Creek. She was on her way to New Orleans to see her husband, a merchant marine on a six-day shore stopover in that city. Though I was in no mood or condition to talk, she had a soft, pretty voice that lulled me, and she let me borrow a needle and some thread to fix my hem.

She wanted to tell someone about her Edward. He had been all over the world—Persia and Amsterdam. And he'd sent her letters from these places, letters he hadn't actually written himself, but there had been a man on board his ship who had a pretty hand. She had had to take them to the preacher's wife to get them read, and it touched me hearing her honesty, and her devotion. From the lilt in her voice when she spoke of her Edward, I knew that she thought him fine, despite he couldn't read or write. And it struck me odd how much less it took to please some people than others.

I told her I was on my way to Cheneyville to meet my husband-to-be. I still wore the gold ring that Daniel had put on my finger two years ago, but Miranda didn't seem to notice it. I said my betrothed had land in Cheneyville, and that we were going to farm and raise children, and it sounded good to say it even if it wasn't all true. She didn't doubt me. I could make up any story and she wouldn't know the difference. For a little while I could be someone else.

We talked and laughed together like two schoolgirls, compared our men one to the other. We said what strange creatures they were with their high-minded sense of obligation and wanting to always protect us.

"Edward just about pitched a walleyed fit over me coming on this train by myself." Miranda had bright brown eyes and round cheeks. "He says it ain't seemly, a woman traveling alone."

I nodded. "I know. My husband's the same way. He doesn't like for me to go anywhere alone, either." She didn't catch that I'd slipped and said the word *husband,* but I caught it. I was getting the men in my life mixed up in this story I was telling.

Up until then, I had tried not to think about Daniel, but he came into my mind now. It was Sunday, and he would probably be home from Navasota, would know I was gone. I hoped he would understand that I had left him. I hoped Nathan would explain about Andy. I wanted Daniel to know it was useless to try to find me, and I wished for him to look back on all that had happened between us these last months and realize this had been coming, that the gap between us, always wide, had become a gulf. I prayed he would not be too hurt. I would rather he got angry. A little anger might do him some good. He had always expected far too much of me. They all of them had.

At the stop in Lafayette, Miranda and I said goodbye. We hugged and kissed each other's cheeks. And it didn't seem the least bit odd to me that I should connect so easily with a complete stranger, with someone I would never see again, when all the people I'd known since I was born had become distant and confusing.

Louisiana wasn't having a drouth like in Texas. When the train rolled into Cheneyville, the sky was pouring. The station platform was unprotected from weather, with just a shallow awning to crouch beneath. The main road in the town—Front Street I learned later—ran like gravy. Board sidewalks had lifted up and floated away from their anchors, some downroad, others into the middle. Barrels of drinking water standing on the corners sloshed full to the brim and overflowed. The downpour didn't show signs of letting up, so there was nothing for me to do but lift my skirts and head across the quagmire to the livery, where a man leaned in the doorway watching as I swamped toward him.

"Excuse me," I called when I was near enough he could hear me, but he just stood there like he was deaf. He had a chaw of tobacco in his cheek and he leaned out—though not far enough—to spit. A blob hit his boot top and a dribble clung to his checkered shirt. I dragged myself into the barn, drenched to the root, my skirts as heavy as canvas cloth. The man eyed me up and down. I tried to shake myself dry, but it was hopeless.

"Would you happen to know where I might find the farm of Ben and Lavinia Treadway?" I said.

He leaned and spat again, this time with more success. The glob hit in front of my shoes. I took a step back, out of range. "You a relation of tharn?"

He had a musical sound to his speech, and combined with the rain pounding on his stable roof and a cheekful of tobacco, I had trouble making sense of his words. When they finally registered, I said, "No," then changed my mind. "Yes, I am. A distant cousin from Texas."

"Lavy's cousin?"

"They're not expecting me," I added. If he called her Lavy, I figured he must know her well.

He didn't move but kept studying me. I wanted to meet his gaze but I could barely stand to look at the brown tobacco stains on his shirt and chin. My stomach was still queasy from the bad food and the train ride, and now my throat was beginning to feel sore as well.

"T'aint never saw no blond-headed Babineauxs," he said finally.

"I'm not a . . . My name's DeLony," I told him. "I have money. If you could take me to their farm. It's been such a long while since I was here, I can't remember the way." I sounded shrill and false. My lying skills seemed to vanish under his dark stare. I felt uneasy and began to wish I had thought to bring Nathan's saddle pistol. It might have served me well in this place where I was a stranger.

The liveryman looked me over a final time. "Soon's this weather lets up."

So I stood dripping inside his smelly barn for twenty minutes. It was the usual length of the rains here, though I didn't know that just yet. Gnats and stinging horseflies deviled me. Finally, he motioned me to a buckboard wagon of a type I hadn't seen since I was a child.

The ride was hard and over a miserable road but, thankfully, short. I tried to act as though I recognized the Treadways' place once we were outside their gate, but it was just a farm, like any other. The house was L-shaped, with a shallow gallery and a flock of chickens in the yard. A well, a barn, several other sheds and outhouses stood between the road and the cultivated field. A backhouse looked to have been recently moved and painted a bright red. Instead of a half-moon, there were two stars cut into the door.

A dog came yelping, a black-and-white feist with a pirate's spot over one eye and a bobbed tail, and for a moment, I stopped breathing. I recognized the dog as Patch. I paid the man for the ride and jumped down on my own. I landed in a mud hole, but I was aware only of my heart beating in my ears, of the hair on my neck bristling in the rain-cooled evening breeze. It almost felt as if I could reach out my nose the way Patch was doing to me, and smell Andy in the air.

"Evening, ma'am," a voice said from my left. I turned and there stood Philip Treadway, looking the same as he had in my kitchen that day with Quintus, eating sugared iced cream. Except now he had a yoke of pails slung across his shoulders. He had evidently been on his way to get water when he saw me jump down from the wagon.

"Good evening to you, too, Philip." I straightened away from the dog, who continued to jump around my feet, and then around Philip's. "Have I interrupted your chores?"

"No, ma'am. We're just done with supper, and I was fetching up dishwater." My back was to the waning sun. He cocked his head, squinted one eye and half his mouth, trying to see me clearly. "Did you come all the way from Texas?"

"Is Quintus here with you?" I said. Philip shook his head. His feet were bare and dusty. I bent down to rub Patch behind the ears again. "This is his dog, isn't it?"

Lavinia came out on the porch and shouted, "Who is it out there, Philip?" He turned quickly, and head down, marched off toward the water well. The dog went close at his heels. "That's right, boy, you'd better get. Your sisters is waiting for that water." She started down the steps, her attention on me. "Is there something I can help you with?"

I tried to smooth off the mud flung up from the wagon wheels onto my skirt. I fingered my hair. I could feel it was a tatty mess. "You don't remember me?"

"Should I?"

"I'm Dellie DeLony—Dellie O'Barr. Your brother—Andy— he introduced us when you were in McDade." She didn't say anything, just kept on staring. "At the Populist meeting."

"So?"

I blinked, taken back by her disregard, and by her unfriendly manner. "So," I said, "well, so I gather you don't remember me."

Her expression was almost mean. "Was lots of folks there. What is it that you want?"

"Is Andy here?" I looked around her toward the house. One of her daughters had stepped out on the porch and stood watching us with interest. "We were to meet here. I've come a long way."

"Here? You and Drew?" She let her eyes travel slowly down to my feet, taking me in. I couldn't tell what she thought.

"I saw his dog." I glanced toward where Philip and the feist had disappeared into the line of trees surrounding the fields. "I thought he must've made it already."

"That ain't his dog. Out of the same litter, but that un's a bitch."

"Well, he's on his way here," I said. "He left . . ." I tried to think when it would have been, and felt confused suddenly. I hadn't expected her to be rude, and I had thought Andy would be here. The land around was so flat, it seemed to go on and on. I recalled him saying how good the dirt was here, good bottom-land dirt, but it all looked like sour land to me. I rubbed my neck where I was perspiring behind my collar. "It might take him a day or two longer since I rode the train. But we agreed this was where we'd come."

Lavinia tilted her head an inch to the side and squinted almost the same way Philip had. "He lose his place?"

"He . . . in a way, yes, he . . . there was a fire." I thought about touching the firebrand into the stream of lamp oil, feeling the heat and the vicious rush of flames. I put my hand to my forehead. "His wagon," I mumbled, but I don't think she understood me.

She said, still gruffly, "You come in on the train? All the way from Texas?" She didn't wait for me to answer her. Maybe I nodded my head. She hollered at the girl on the porch, "Mary, get down a bowl and dipper this woman some supper." She didn't take her eyes off me while she was yelling. "And hurry up with it. Can't have her fainting dead away in the yard." Her eyes were black and penetrating. They stayed on me the whole time I was in her house.

The two girls—Mary and Martha were their names—spooned food left over from their meal just finished. It was hearty fare, a soup of beans and jowl, with some kind of garden greens and cornbread on the side. I had no appetite but waste didn't seem like something the Treadways tolerated. I cleaned up every bite, and felt stronger for it.

Ben Treadway stayed at the table for a minute or two, watched me while I ate, and listened to Lavinia tell him that Andy and the children were on their way to meet me here. Then, with a nod, he got up and went over to his chair to smoke his pipe, his back kept to us. Philip sat across the table with his sisters, quiet and big-eyed. I winked at him and he grinned, ducked his head. He had huge dimples in his cheeks.

"After Uncle Drew gets here," Martha, the oldest girl, said, "what'll y'all plan on doing then?" Lavinia reached over and pinched Martha on her arm. "Ouch, Ma. I was just asking."

"Mind yourself."

"It's all right." I smiled at the girl. Looking at her made me feel as young as she was. The exhilaration of the train station in Austin Saturday came back to me. "We're going to farm," I said. "We're going to find a place around here somewhere. Raise crops. I don't know what. Cotton, I suppose. Corn, perhaps."

"Of course, he'll grow corn." Lavinia gave me an impatient look. "Got to feed the animals. Be smart to put in sugarcane, too. Grows good and we got a press out yonder on the Bayou Boeuf now."

"I wouldn't be a farmer's wife. You couldn't pay me," Martha said, and Mary laughed. They both fell into a fit of giggles.

"Hush with that," Lavinia said. "Get to them dishes. Both of you."

I turned my smile to her now. She smiled, too, but didn't mean it. She waited till the girls got up to the sink before she said, "Did Cova Lee finally die?"

"Lavy." Ben's voice came booming from where he sat with his pipe.

"Well, Ben, I got some things to know. She come in here saying Drew's headed to meet her here. We got some things to know."

"You've talked enough." He stood up. He wasn't a tall man, but his standing shut down the room. Martha and Mary got busier with the dishes. Philip vanished out the back door. Lavinia looked at her hands, and I felt the relief of not having her eyes on me. Ben said, "If you're done with your supper now, I'll carry you back into town. They got rooms to let over at Tanner's. We'd ask you to stay here but you can see we ain't got an inch to spare."

"No, I didn't expect you to put me up . . ." I stood, too, and Lavinia snatched my bowls off the table. She kept her eyes away from me, and she didn't say goodbye or another word at all. I told her, "Thank you for the food," and I followed Ben out to the wagon. He helped me to the seat.

"You ain't got a bag?" he said, and when I shook my head no, he didn't press me for the reason. He didn't appear to even think it out of the ordinary. He handed me a lap sheet made from fabric remnants pieced together like a quilt top. "We've had some rain. Roads are muddy 'twixt here and town."

"Yes, I know." I spread the sheet over my skirt, though it wouldn't matter much. The underside of my hem was already coated heavy with crusty red clay, and with other things I didn't even want to think about, picked up on my earlier walk across to the livery. I felt dirty, shameful.

Ben Treadway wasn't a man to chitchat. He was dark complected, dark haired, with a strong profile and a black unwaxed mustache beneath his nose. He kept his eyes to the road and his team firmly in hand. When we got to town he went straight to the Hotel Tanner and pulled to a stop in front of the two-story building. He made no move to get down from the wagon, but simply leaned across the seat to give me a hand. It was a long step to the ground, but I made it. I thanked him and he nodded, took up the reins again.

Before he got away, I said, "When Andy comes—"

"I'll see he finds you," Ben answered abruptly.

I nodded and moved away from the wagon. I had never before been dropped in front of a hotel this way. It was after dark. Men had gathered at a saloon down the street, and some were outside on the gallery. I kept my face turned away from them and went inside the hotel.

The desk clerk said the hotel didn't rent to single ladies. "It's against policy." When I told him I was a married woman just visiting the area, he demanded to know who it was I had come to see, what my husband's name was, and where I'd come from. I gave my name as Ashland. I said I'd just traveled from Austin, Texas, and that I didn't think I would need the room for more than a day. Two at most. Just until my husband got here with our children. The clerk was reluctant, but he gave me a key.

The hotel room was plain, four square walls and a window, but furnished well with a four-poster carved from mahogany, a highboy, a washstand and clean basin, a straight chair in the corner, and a gas lamp with crystal teardrop spangles. On the night table sat a pewter pitcher of clear water, and a drinking glass. Pictures of a New England maple forest in switching seasons hung on one wall. On the floor was a Brussels carpet.

I went to the basin to wash with the new bar of Clairette soap laid there. I scared myself in the mirror. My face was smudged with dust. My hair hung lank, dark with dirt. I washed, scrubbed my cheeks till they glowed, and with water dripping, I stared at myself again. I felt lonely, strangely homesick, anxious for Andy to come, yet also as if I were looking at someone else in the glass.

Andy didn't arrive the next day, or even in three. In the meantime, I came down with a fever, so the hotel clerk didn't evict me. A doctor was sent for. He dosed me with quinine, though it didn't improve me much. Lavinia came. Somehow she'd heard of my plight. Like in McDade, I guess, news traveled. She brought some soup and her daughter, Mary, and they sat stiff and watched me eat. After they left I vomited every bite I'd swallowed. I couldn't keep anything down.

The following day, Lavinia came again, alone this time. "You still ain't pert," she said when she saw me. She hurried to shut the window, though the room was already stuffy and hot. "There's miasma out there, coming up from the bayou. Does it ever year this time. Makes folks sick as dogs."

She put her hand against my cheek. My fever had gone down, I knew, since the chills weren't so shuddering anymore, but I still felt miserable, weak in the stomach. I wondered what was taking Andy so long. I knew I would feel better if he were here. My face must've shown what I was thinking.

She said, "He ain't come yet," and I nodded. I wished she would go away. She made me self-conscious and even more uncomfortable the way she watched me every second she was around me, like she was trying to see through my skin. "We just ain't got room for you," she said, as if she felt guilty about turning me out, with me ill.

"I'm fine here."

She paced around the foot of my bed. "Eat that soup I brung. It's got lots of marrow in it. It'll heal you up right fast."

"Thank you," I said, but I couldn't bring myself to touch food yet.

"I brung you a garment, too. Ben said he didn't think you had nothing."

"My trunk was lost on the train," I said. "The porter said it might take some time to retrieve it."

She listened to me, then unfolded a dress out of the carrybag she'd brought. "It probably ain't long enough, but you can let the hem if you need to. It's old but it'll wear." She held the dress up to herself. It was a simple line, faded calico print in pinks. She draped the dress over the highboy. "Eat up, now. Here, you want me to spoon it to you?"

"Thank you, no. I couldn't swallow anything."

She sucked in her cheeks, studied me. She put one fist on her hip and the other on the bedpost, and shook her head like with pity. "Cova Lee was frail like you."

I raised up on my elbows. Moving made my head swim. "I'm hardly frail. This is the first time I've been ill in—"

"Talked prissy like you do, too. Like you're reading something from a book. Drew always did like a fancy woman. One with a passel of fourteen-dollar words."

"I'm not a fancy woman."

"You a widow? I seen you was wearing a ring on your finger. And I know Drew didn't give it to you. He ain't got money for such trinkets."

"I'm not a widow."

She stared at me even harder. So hard, one of her eyes, the left one, seemed to pinch down at the corner. "Surely is a lot of things you ain't. Ain't a widow woman. Ain't hungry. Ain't frail, so you say. Are you a whore? That's the only thing left we ain't decided."

I settled back against the pillow. "My God, you are a horrible woman."

"I reckon Drew'd of said if he was coming here, if he was bringing you, or if his Cova Lee had passed on. I reckon he'd of wrote me and told me some of that, but I ain't heard nothing from him. Ain't heard nothing except what you say."

"Go away." I reached for the soup on the bedside table. "Take this and go." I wanted to fling it at her, but I didn't have the strength in my arms, and anyway, she came across the room to peel my fingers off the bowl.

"Ungrateful," she said. "Serve you right if you starve to death. Trying to put asunder what God hath joined together." She yanked the bowl away from my hands, and some of the soup splattered out on her apron. She looked down at the stain, then back at me. She shook droplets of soup from her fingers onto the rug. "You ain't even that pretty."

I tried to rise from the bed, to show her, or maybe shove her, out the door, but I was too woozy and she sauntered quickly enough from the room. Once she was gone, I held on to the side of the bed and let the sickness in my stomach curl over me.

22

For five days I was so ill that I mostly stayed in bed. At times I thought I might even die alone in this room. On Thursday, the doctor came again, to give me another dose of quinine and to collect his bill of ten dollars. The hotel clerk had been sending a houseboy up every day with a plate of food for supper, and on Friday the boy also had a polite note inquiring about my husband's arrival. Attached to the note was the tab I had run up so far at the hotel—eighteen dollars, which I did not have. I'd been keeping my money, what was left of the thirty dollars from the sale of Cintha, inside my undervest. Once the houseboy left, I took out my small roll. After paying the doctor his ten dollars, I was left with only thirteen, five dollars shy of what I owed the hotel.

I had a nightmare, caused probably by the fever leaving my body. In the dream, I was back in McDade, ringing the firebell but it wouldn't make a noise. And all around me an inferno raged, almost like a windstorm with lightning and hail. I woke in a sweat. Even the sheets were soaked. I got out of bed, and haunted the darkness until morning.

Saturday was the Fourth of July, though I didn't realize it until I heard the trumpets and trombones, and looked out my window at the parade passing by on Front Street. Our family had never celebrated the Fourth, owing to the fact that it was, in Papa's words, "a damned Yankee holiday." There had always been a ball-game Nathan had to miss, footraces through town, a marching band like the one outside my window. Gay floats rocked by, pulled by prancing teams of horses or plodding mules, and I stood there watching to the last, till the dung boys came with their wheelbarrows and their shovels to scoop up the mess left in the street.

The day had turned off bright blue and I wanted to get out in it, but I had nothing, not even a comb for my hair or a change of underwear. Regardless of my bill at the hotel, I decided I had to buy some necessary items. I washed my face in the basin, raked my fingers through my hair as best I could. I put on the dress Lavinia had left, though I hated to after how she had treated me. The dress was a dreadful fit, but my other clothes were filthy. Bad enough I had to wear dirty underwear. I gathered myself together, pinched some color into my cheeks, and I went out the door and down the stairs with my thirteen dollars tucked inside the dress pocket.

I tried to slip by the desk clerk. Mr. Seaberry, I had learned from the houseboy, was his name. I didn't make it by him. "Going out, Mrs. Ashland?" he said as I passed. "I'm glad to see you're well."

"Yes, I'm much better, thank you." I turned, couldn't meet his eyes head-on. I didn't even get any pleasure out of him calling me by Andy's name. I looked down at the pitiful dress I wore. The entire uppers of my shoes showed, and an inch or two of stocking besides. And in my illness I'd lost weight. The bodice hung on me like a cotton sack. "I thought I'd take a stroll."

"Lovely day for it," he said and that was all, though I felt like he was watching me, judging me, all the way out the door.

Hardly anyone was left in town. Folks had all followed after the parade. I went down half a block to the general store, also called Tanner's, and as I went inside, I overheard the young counter clerk grumbling to a girl of about fifteen that he couldn't go with her down to the bayou. "I got to stay here all afternoon tending this place." He didn't ask if he could help me find anything and I was glad enough of it. I had to mind my money, and felt I could do that easier on my own account.

At the bargain counter, I found a little Quaker purse that would tuck into the pocket of a skirt, a five-cent comb and seven-cent hairbrush, a box of stockings for a quarter. I gathered all these things into a pile. The least expensive corset waist the store had in stock cost eighty-five cents, so I decided I could go without. An undervest I could get for twenty-one cents and it would do almost as well. I looked at shoes. Too much. Underskirts, also too much. I found a cambric chemise that I could use for sleeping and for day wear underneath my dress. Lace-trimmed drawers were fifteen cents higher than the plain ribbed, but I just couldn't bear the thought of a pair of untrimmed flannels next to my skin, and besides, the lace would also help lift my skirt.

Next, I rummaged through the dresses, selected the lowest priced one I found, an ugly thing of striped gingham in blue, pink, and gray, but with a nice sailor collar and a big bow I could pull off and use in my hair. I picked up a small pair of scissors, a card of needles, and a spool of white thread.

When I took my armload of things to the counter, the young clerk eyed me with impatience. Clearly, he didn't want to leave the attentions of his girl. They seemed to be in the midst of an argument about something.

I said, "Would you please add up what I have so far?" I hated to ask, but I needed to stretch my money as thin as it would go, and I had never been much good at figuring in my head.

He acted put out about the trouble, but he totaled everything up. "Seven dollars and forty-seven cents," he said.

So I hurried back to the bargain counter for a package of handkerchiefs. Men's, but they were only thirty-five cents for a dozen, as compared to the women's, which were fifty cents. I snatched up a ten-cent hairlock, since I didn't have enough money left for a proper hat. The clerk counted my change into my hand, exactly five dollars and eight cents. I couldn't help but think about my pocketbook back in McDade with all of June's household money still unspent. Stupid of me not to have thought to bring it with me.

"You wouldn't happen to know," I said on impulse, "where a person might find a job in this town?" The thought had come to me as I watched him write up my ticket. I was going to need some way to raise money.

He lifted his head to look at me and then at his girl leaning on the end of the counter. She put her hand to her mouth and giggled. "You can have mine for the day if you want it," he said, and I felt a jolt of eagerness until I saw he was only moaning aloud his misfortune at having to work on the Fourth of July. The girl started to nod and he frowned at her. "Pop would skin me."

"Isn't nobody going to come in here anyway," the girl said. "Not on July Fourth. And how's your pop to know, him gone up to Alexandria?"

The boy got busy wrapping up my package. "I can't, Dorine."

The girl crossed her arms, tapped with one finger against her elbow. "Well, I can't believe you're going to sit in here while they fire off the cannon."

"I can't go, and that's that." His fingers moved quickly with the binding string.

"Thank you," I mumbled, and reached to take the package, but he didn't let it loose.

"She probably can't read anyway," he said to Dorine.

"Oh, you know she can, Archie," the girl said. "You're just making excuses. Well, I'm going. And I bet Hoop Abercrombie'll be there just waiting for me." She started from the place where she'd been leaned. A panic came over his face.

"Wait." He reached out, then looked at me. He sounded half-desperate. "*Can* you read, lady?"

"Beg pardon?" I said, only just then understanding they'd been talking about me. I slid the package off the counter and into my arms. It was burdensome, but not heavy.

"She can," the girl said. "You know she can. Illegible people don't say *I beg your pardon,* Arch." She took another step for the door, threatening. "I'm on my way."

At that, he got so agitated I thought he might bound over the counter. He stood back there, shifting from foot to foot. "I'll give you three dollars if you'll stay with the store till four o'clock." He said this to me, but he couldn't take his eyes off Dorine. "That's twice the money I make here in a day. You don't even have to sell anything. Just stand back and make sure nobody steals nothing."

"What if they want to buy something?" What I really wanted to ask was how old he was, and if he had the authority to give me this job. Three dollars would go a long way toward resupplying the money I'd just spent.

"Tell them it's a holiday and you can't sell to them," he answered. He was warming up to the idea of getting out of the store for a few hours.

"Then why would you even be open?" I asked.

"Oh, Archie," Dorine said, exasperated. "She can fill out a receipt. If I can do it . . ." She reached behind the counter near Archie's cash box, picked up a pad of lined forms, and flopped them down on the counter in front of me. "See? Just fill these out. Put down what they buy and how much it is, then add it up. It's easy as pie."

"What's your name, lady?" Archie started untying his apron.

"Dellie O'Barr," I answered automatically, and I didn't even think till later that I'd given him a different name than I had to the hotel clerk. "You'll have to let me go change clothes. I couldn't work anywhere looking like this."

"You look just swell," Dorine said. She gave Archie a bright smile. "Don't you think so, Arch?"

"Yeah, swell." But he barely even glanced my way. He tossed his apron down and came from around the counter. "Be back around four," he said, and he went to take Dorine on his arm. As they went out to the street, I heard him say, "Pop's going to skin me."

"Well, she said she needed a job," Dorine answered. "Quit worrying, would you? We're going to miss the cannon."

Once they were out of sight, I stood there with my package of clothing still clutched to my chest, and I looked doubtfully around at the store. The girl was right, though: how hard could it be? And the street outside wasn't exactly teeming with folks shopping. I saw one wagon tied over in front of the hardware store and that was the extent of it.

I went around behind the counter, set my package on the floor, taking care to tuck the receipt up under the twine. I tied on the apron Archie had taken off just moments before. It still felt a little damp and warm. I looked over the things in front of me, bills of sale, a ledger sheet, price tags with short lengths of string glued to them. The cash box was locked. I hadn't noticed when he did that. How would I give change? Though as Dorine had said, most likely no one would even come in. I'd never seen a town more dead. Not even McDade on the day of the Veterans' Reunion.

A feather duster hung by a hook behind the counter. I took it loose and flicked it around the work area. Dust fluttered up from the receipts and the ledger like small clouds of smoke. I thought that maybe, if I did a good enough job here today, this could turn into permanent employment for me. I thought Andy might like that I was earning my own wages when he got here. Lord knows, we would surely be able to use the help getting started.

My head felt a little woozy for a minute, the leavings from my sickness of the past days. But then I recognized what I was feeling as hunger. I hadn't had any breakfast and it was almost time for dinner. I went over to the fruit bin and picked out a banana. I figured Archie could deduct it when he paid me. The banana was fully ripe and tasted sweet and smooth.

No one came into the store, and after a while I got down a book from the shelves behind the counter. It was on palmistry, and after reading awhile I found out I had a long life line, and a good, deep health line. I was right in the middle of reading about my love line when my first customer walked in, a little old woman with six dozen eggs to sell.

She asked for Mr. Tanner, and said, "I told him I'd be bringing them in today. He said Archibald would be here." I could see she was disappointed. I didn't know she would throw a fit, though, which she did after I told her I didn't have a key to the cash box. She started telling me, in a loud voice, that for twenty-four years Mr. Tanner had been buying her eggs on Saturday, and that she would see to it that he gave me a right smart dressing down for treating her so rude. She carried on so, I finally paid for her eggs with my own money, six cents a dozen. I wrote it down on a pad of unlined paper, and breathed easier when the woman was gone. Then I decided I had better write down the banana I'd eaten, too, just to keep everything straight and square.

The next customer came in almost as soon as the old lady left. A man this time, who went straightaway to the tobacco jars and the little cloth drawsacks stacked beside them. He was pleasant enough, had the exact change, though I wasn't sure of the exact amount he took out of the jar. He seemed to be, though, and he didn't seem to mind that he didn't know me, either. On his way out the door, he wished me a happy Fourth of July.

I began to feel a little easier, even went with the feather duster to the jewelry cabinets and the case of pocketknives. Everything in the store was dusty. While I worked, I hummed a song that had been on my mind—"Little Annie Rooney"—and remembered Hannah singing it that morning I ruined the biscuits. I thought about her ragdoll left somewhere behind in that old farmhouse. I wished I had thought to bring it along with me. I could've sewn up the hole in its neck and found another button for its missing eye. I was going to be so glad to see her again. I missed her, missed them all. I couldn't imagine what was taking Andy so long to get here. I hoped he hadn't run into some kind of trouble with his wagon or his team, or God forbid, that the children hadn't taken sick.

My own illness was still fresh in my mind. So fresh, I decided I could use another piece of fruit, an apple this time for strength. I wrote it down on my list to settle up with Archie at four o'clock. Just another hour. The time had gone by fast.

All evening I'd heard firecrackers. Now cannon shot came. It was next to impossible to ignore, and so I went out on the gallery to listen. I could even hear the crowd celebrating, their revelry. I wondered if I would ever feel at home here, like I belonged. I couldn't imagine never going back to McDade.

I wandered back into the store. I stared at the apple in my hand, a hole bit into its side, and it brought an image of the fire leaping the walls at Bassist's store. A tremor shook through me. I took another crunching bite. I was down to the core when the next person came in.

A man in a town suit, with a bow tie at his neck, and wearing a white straw planter's hat at a cocky angle, came three steps inside and stopped. He looked at me, then out at the rest of the store. "What, young lady, are you doing eating my apples?" he said. "And where is that scalawag son of mine?"

I realized who he was, and I straightened from where I was leaning on one elbow behind the counter. I tried to explain the situation, but he had surprised me and had used such a gruff tone that I stammered in my telling. Meantime, he came around and swooped up the cash box.

"Stole me blind, I suppose?" He thumbed a lever and the box opened, without the need of a key.

"No, sir. I didn't know how to—"

"I should call the police. We do have a policeman in Cheneyville. Don't think we're a backwards town, that we don't enforce our laws." He scowled at me. "What is your name?"

"Dellie O'Barr."

"You aren't from around here."

"No, sir. I'm to meet my husband here."

His eyes went long. He snapped his fingers and pointed at me. "The vagrant from Texas at the hotel. That's not the name Seaberry used. What is your real name?"

My heart was jumping. He knew who I was. I hadn't counted on that. I sputtered, "DeLony. No. No, sir. It's Ashland. Dellie Ashland." It sounded awkward now, like the two names didn't fit together. I thought he must know I was lying.

He folded his arms, arched backwards from the hip, and looked me square in the face. "Are you trying to hurrah me?"

"No, sir." I tried to sound more indignant.

"Where's my son?"

"With Dorine. They went to the bayou to celebrate—"

"Damn his hide." He brought his fist down on the counter and I nearly jumped out of my skull. Papa—it was Papa's hand hitting that counter.

"He said he'd be back around four. He said he'd pay me three dollars for minding the store."

"Three dollars?" His eyes got big; eyebrows went up. "That's half a week's pay. The scoundrel. The good-for-nothing. Well, I'll deduct it from your hotel bill." He gave me another smoldering look. "I have no way of knowing what you took from the cash box."

"Nothing. I didn't take a cent. I didn't even know how to open it. A lady came in selling these eggs." I gestured at the six dozen in the basket on the floor. "I paid her with my own money. Right here. I kept track of it." I riffled through the things on the counter until I found my paper. He yanked it from me; read it.

"You took a banana, too?"

"And I wrote it down."

He dropped the pad on the counter. "I'll call us even. When is your husband arriving?"

I tried to think calmer, to look the storekeeper straight in the eyes. "I expect him any time."

"Seaberry said you were kin to the Treadways."

"My husband is."

"Then I suggest you find accommodations with them." He was evicting me. I hardly believed it. I'd had such hopes. It didn't seem fair, but he squared his shoulders. "I don't run a charity house, Mrs. Ashland. I'm in business to make money."

There was nothing I could do. I couldn't pay him and I wasn't about to beg, and I could see he had dismissed me. I held my head as high as I could get it, bent down to retrieve my package from behind the counter.

"Where do you think you're going with that?" He tugged the bundle from me, holding it by the twine, but I didn't let go, and we tugged our own directions for a second.

"I paid for this."

"I'm warning you, Mrs. Ashland. I will call for the police."

"It's mine! I paid for it!" I jerked the receipt out from under the string that held it, and let go of the package. I held it face out in front of his nose.

He snatched the ticket out of my hand and looked at it, apparently recognized his son's handwriting. He shoved the bundle against me, almost knocking me off balance.

"I'll tell Mr. Seaberry," he said, "that you'll be checking out tomorrow morning."

23

My last night at the hotel, I washed my dirties and hung them on the back of the chair beside the open window. Not enough wind blew, though, so they were still damp in the morning. I used the paper and twine from my new clothes to bundle the old. At least when I left the hotel I was clean, hair combed. I could walk out with that much dignity. The gingham dress was stiff and scratchy, and smelled so strong of dye my eyes burned.

Sunday was not a good day to find either work or lodging. Even Tanner's store was shut tight. Back home Mr. Bassist never closed, not even for Christmas, though I supposed he must be closed now. I wondered if someone had heard the firebell in time, or if the building had been completely engulfed like in my dream. I hoped no one was harmed.

I felt I was still in a dream, an endless one, as I started off walking through the town. I hardly knew what to do, or where to go. Nothing in my life so far had prepared me for this kind of existence. I'd never had to fret over money or where I would sleep at night. There had always been Papa and Nathan to take care of me, and then Daniel. I'd never been quite this alone, physically by myself. I even missed Papa. It seemed treacherous, even traitorous to myself to miss him, but I did.

The first public building I came to was the Methodist church. It was a two-story building of white with gingerwork and a cupola. The Freemasonry insignia shared space with the belfry and cross. Wagons and horses crowded the lot. A few quality carriages, with matching pair, stood out from the rest. There were people with wealth in Cheneyville.

From inside the building, piano music and singing started up as I passed. The hymn was a familiar one, and I hummed along, but the words that came to me weren't from a hymnal. They were the words we had sung at the Populist meetings, and they nearly choked me when I recognized them. Yet, for a moment, they made me happy, too, and I lingered in the churchyard, singing to myself. A cat came from somewhere, a little fluffy calico who rubbed its face against my skirt, but then scratched me when I bent to pet it.

I stamped my foot and the cat bounded away, causing me to remember Andy kicking Patch down the porch steps. Then came dark memories of cruel things he'd said to me that night. I had to turn my mind from such black thoughts. With the heels of my hands, I pressed against my eyes, as if I could shove the tears, now so near the surface, back into my skull where they belonged.

People started coming out of the church, children running, shrieking to have their freedom. Mr. Tanner came out with his son, Archie, and with a lady I assumed was Mrs. Tanner. I stepped behind some shrubbery, watching with curiosity, as they got into one of the finer black carriages and rode away. For one wistful moment, I thought of my Cintha and my gig, and of my feather bed with the lace counterpane, my walnut wardrobe full of beautiful clothes. I felt aimless and misplaced, in the way here, as I watched all the unfamiliar people leave the church.

The Treadways came out of the church building, all five of them, and stood on the front steps shaking hands with the preacher. I was surprised at the sight of them, but too prideful to step out and greet them. I crouched deeper behind the bushes, holding my bundle—the bundle with Lavinia's dress folded inside—close against my breast.

Ben started down the walk first. Philip followed. He stooped to pluck two yellow flowers from alongside the path. He tried to give them to his mother, but she was too busy hurrying his sisters along to notice him. He let his gift to her fall to the ground. Later, when the people had gone and the side lot was empty, I stepped out to pick up the flowers. They had been crushed underfoot.

Back home, if you needed help, you could find it at the churches. And since the Treadways came to this one, and since Andy had been raised Methodist, I figured that once he got here and we were settled, this would be our church, too. So I went up the steps and opened the big double doors.

When I entered, the preacher was using a long window hook to close up the church house. He wasn't as friendly with me as he had seemed with his congregation out on the steps. He stood off several feet from me without smiling, the hook resting on the floor like a tall shepherd's staff, and he showed no sympathy for my woeful tale. He told me he knew of no employment for a woman, but he did direct me to a boardinghouse over near the Bayou Boeuf.

The bayou meandered through the town. In several places water hyacinth grew delicate and of the palest lavender. In other places a red scum had taken over, wallowing in and around the knees of cypress that lined the banks. I recalled Lavinia speaking of a miasma, so I walked with a handkerchief over my nose and mouth. I wondered what miasma looked like, if you could even see it, or if it had an odor. The air around the bayou smelled sort of rotten and fishy.

It took me half an hour to find the address the preacher had given me, but once I was there, I felt a fate at work. The sign, hanging by a rusted chain at each corner, said *EMMA'S ROOMING HOUSE* in faded, but fancy, cursive letters. Since Emma had been Mama's name, I felt my luck was about to change. My spirits lifted at once. No matter that the proprietress was a Maudie, the grandniece of the Emma from the sign. Emma herself had passed on three years ago from a disease of the lungs. Maudie had just never gotten around to getting her sign repainted. She was near to my age, and had a simpleton brother whom I caught peeping through my keyhole my first night there. After that, I stuffed a piece of the brown binding paper into the hole to block his view.

The boardinghouse was old, and my room small with a sagging narrow bed, a dressing table just large enough to hold a basin and pitcher on top. There was one chair, one lamp table, one lamp without a chimney. The window was covered with a roller shade curling at the edges, and the blanket on the bed was filled with holes. But it was summer and so hot I didn't need covering at night. I lay in bed sweating, unable to sleep, listening to the mice running inside the walls.

The rent was a dollar fifty a week plus fifty cents board, and "board" meant breakfast in the kitchen at six o'clock. At breakfast, I gorged so I wouldn't need to eat again for the rest of the day. There were seven other boarders, one an untidy woman of questionable character who came down of a morning reeking with heavy perfume that didn't quite cover another mustier, embarrassingly female smell lying underneath. She had a racy laugh and blondeened hair, and all the male boarders, even the old bald one, paid her much too close attention.

Within a week I had exhausted job possibilities. I thought about walking the four miles to the Treadways and throwing myself on their mercy. I worried that Andy would come and not know where to find me. And in any case, I still had Lavinia's dress, which I would not wear again. Pride is a hard thing to swallow, and I had little enough of it left by now. I wrote a letter to them on paper Maudie gave me, telling them where I was staying so they would know when Andy arrived, but no reply ever came back.

Farmers around were cultivating their cotton, getting the crop laid by. I had chopped cotton in my life, though it had been a while, but I thought I could remember well enough how it was done. I asked around at some of the larger plantations, but soon learned that field work went to colored labor.

And then one evening, my third week in Cheneyville, I stepped outside to get some cool air, and coming out the back door, I almost ran into Fannie Duval, the woman who did laundry for the boardinghouse. She had a rag tied about her head like the field hands, and a plain cotton dress with no underskirts. Her skin was the color of Tante Lena's rye bread. She had four baskets of towels and bedsheets to load into the back of her wagon, and I stepped over to help her with them. She was surprised by my doing that, and she thanked me at least ten times before we were done.

"It's nothing," I told her.

She said, "I'm running so far behind I don't expect I'll catch up any time before Christmas. A girl I had up and left me, so now I has to do the gathering, the carrying back to my place, *and* all the scrubbing and starching and ironing. The days just ain't long enough. Nights is shorter." She smiled, and then hoisted herself up onto the seat. She took up the reins to her mule, who looked too old to even move. "I'm obliged to you, ma'am."

"*I'm* looking for work."

"Don't know of nothing," she said right off, then kind of tilted her head at me, as she understood I was asking for the job. "You is a white girl."

"But I can wash clothes, and I can iron and do mending. People have said I'm fairly good with a needle."

"Washing is nigger work around here."

"Everything is," I said, and she laughed.

"Well, that's mostly the truth. The white ladies don't like to sweat."

"I don't mind it." Though I knew that, before, I had been just like the ones she was talking about.

She shook her head. "Folks would talk if you was to come to work at my place. And Lord knows I don't need no white folks talking about me." Then she raised her chin at me, like something had just crossed her mind. "How come you's to be looking? Got man troubles?"

I hated to think it was that obvious on me. I clasped my hands together and turned them inside out to crack my knuckles, a habit I'd had when I was little and that Mother had broken me of, or thought she had, until now. I nodded my head.

"Mm hmm." She nodded, too. "I know all about that. Believe me, I do. Ain't never anything but trouble when there's a man around."

"My husband is supposed to meet me . . ." It was beginning to sound unlikely, even to me.

"Husband?"

"To be." I looked up and saw Fannie had noticed my wedding ring.

"Could sell that and get more'n I could pay you."

I twisted the ring on my finger. It had belonged to Daniel's grandmother, and was solid gold, inlaid with silver. It had never occurred to me to sell it. I should have left it behind, with the tatters of my old life. I lifted my face at her. "I can't. It's not really mine to sell."

She gave me one more doubtful look, then said, "You go down the Boeuf, half a mile past the bridge. You go down there tomorrow after sunrise, and you'll see me working there. I reckon I don't care what the people has to say about it if you don't."

"Thank you," I said, following a few steps as she drove her old mule off into the dusk. I don't know if she heard me, though. She never did turn back again to look at me.

The next morning I went before sunrise. Fannie set me right to work, underneath a hickory tree with a three-legged ironing board, a sadiron, and a fire. If it rained, which by then I knew it did every day around four o'clock, she said I would have to lug the board and iron and the basket of clothes I was working on inside her house.

Her place was a shack with walls made of scraps, an old slave house, she told me. Wind blew in through the chinks, which made it bearable in summer, but I hated to think of her winters. A clattery bead curtain with a scene of nymphs painted on it divided the room into halves. She lit the house with old grease lamps stuffed with cotton flannel wicks that smoked black and choking. She paid me forty cents a day and my dinner, which we ate on a board table with two overturned apple boxes for stools. She mostly fixed soup since she could leave that cooking untended.

I found out she had two children who lived with her mother in Punkie just down the Lafayette road, and whom she only got to see on Sundays, the one day of the week she didn't work. She told me the story over soup and cornbread one noon. The children's father, a man she'd never married, had run off with her baby sister, and neither had been heard from again.

"But way I look at it, he's the one going to pay. Them children is fine things, and he ain't ever going to know them. The Lord acts in mysterious ways, like the Good Book say. My mama's always telling me, say 'Fannie, we got to let the Lord tend to that.' And I guess we do. But there's sometimes I wisht I could help Him just a little bit, when He gets to throwing down them lightning swords."

She had an easy laugh that was catching. It made me feel better to talk to her about my troubles. I didn't tell her everything, but I didn't make up stories either, like I had to Miranda Tow that day on the train. Fannie never gave me advice. The difference in our skin color was always hanging like a curtain between us, but she listened, and nodded, and made little agreeing sounds in her throat.

Despite what she said against men, she had a new one coming around, a tall man with saffron-colored skin named Pip Murrah, who wore a white straw hat and liked to tease her out by the clothesline of an evening—in her words, "give her a hard time." Sometimes he brought her sweet treats, a stalk of sugarcane to peel and eat, a honeycomb he'd gotten out of a bee tree where he lived. Watching Mr. Murrah court Fannie, and seeing how she'd start in acting girlish and sassy whenever he came around, just made me all the more aware of how out of place I was here. And it made me envious that she had someone and I didn't. I tried to ignore their laughter, and their frolicking down along the bayou, though I couldn't help but remember, sometimes in those weak moments, me and Andy in the Yegua Creek with the big half-moon hanging in the sky above our heads. I prayed he would come soon.

Time passed. July turned into August, hot and sulky, seemed heavier even than back in Texas. I got to be an expert at pressing collars and cuffs, shirts and dresses, tablecloths and curtains. Fannie started me doing some of the needlework. She bragged about my stitches and paid me twenty cents a dozen extra for the work, which I did in my room each night by lamplight. It took hours to do by hand what at home with my machine I could have rattled off in minutes. If folks in town ever did talk about me working for Fannie, I never heard and she never mentioned it. But then I rarely went anywhere but to work and back to my room. Just back and forth like a red ant. I wore a path beside the bayou, and a hole in my shoe.

I had never had a paying job before, never earned my own keep, and there was a satisfaction about it, even if the wages were less than Daniel had given me for household money, even if with the money I earned I could never pay my debt at the Hotel Tanner. I just barely made enough to pay my rent and eat, but Fannie was good to me. She had a whole trunkful of clothes left by customers and never retrieved that she let me hunt through for something I could wear. She helped me let down hems and take in tucks at the waists. She had a bit of lace she gave me to make a collar for one dress, a blue percale a little bit nicer than the others. I wore it the evening I finally walked the four miles out to the Treadway place to return Lavinia's dress to her.

Before I left, I had written out a note telling them where I was working and thanking Lavinia for the use of the dress. In case they weren't home, I had thought I could leave the note and the dress folded up on their front gallery, but they were there, the whole family, out in the cornfield pulling ears. Their corn had grown to six feet high. Little Philip held the work team, and the wagon behind him was half full. The dog that looked like Patch came out on the road to bark at me, and the five of them all looked my way.

I waved, but no one waved back except Philip, just barely, one little hand raised against the backdrop of sky. It made my heart lighten just a little. The girls both looked at their mother, who pitched the ears she'd just picked into the wagon bed and started coming toward me. I kept walking, too. She had on a skirted slat bonnet with a brim so wide I couldn't see her features at all, until she got within twenty feet of me.

She said, "What d'you want?"

"I just brought your dress back to you. I'll leave it here on the porch if you like." I tried to forget that we'd insulted each other the last time we met. But as she came closer I saw she wasn't going to make any such pretensions. I stopped at the foot of the gallery steps.

She snapped at the dog to shut its barking, and when it didn't mind, picked up a stick to wield his way. She didn't throw down the stick either as she came straight to me. And I had no doubt that if I said something she didn't like, she might use it on me, too.

"I brought your dress—" I began again.

"I heard you. I didn't want it back."

She saw the note and snatched it from my hands, ignored the dress. While she read, I bent to lay the folded dress on the top gallery step. I would have just as soon headed back right then, despite my aching feet and legs, than to have to exchange another word with her. Her lips moved as she read slowly. It took her two full minutes to read a note of maybe eight lines. Then she crumpled the paper in her fist.

"So you still think he's coming?"

I forced myself to look her in the eyes. I wanted her to see that I wished for a fresh start with her. "I don't know. But if he does . . ."

"He ain't, and if you still believe he might, then you ought to be locked away with Cova Lee." She frowned at me. "Don't send us no more letters."

She turned and started back toward the field. I followed after her. "All right, I won't, but . . . I wondered if you knew where else he could have gone. I know he has other brothers and sisters. I know you have some yourself."

She stopped short, stood still for a second, then turned to me. "Drew told you we was only half kin?"

"And your mother's name is Addie."

"Was Addie. She passed away last Christmas."

"I'm sorry. I didn't know that."

She frowned at me, pushed at her ragged gloves. Her hands were too small for them and they wadded at the fingertips. When she spoke again, her voice had changed, grown more reflective and quiet. "What else did he tell you?"

"Nothing. Just about your father."

"He tell you how his ma took us all in? Did he tell you that, too? His ma was a saint."

"She's still alive?"

Lavinia shook her head. "Gone six years now. You listen here. You want some advice? Quit waiting on him. He ain't going to leave his wife for you."

"I never said he was."

"You never said it but you think it." She sounded hard, yet there was a hint of pity on her face. Pity for my foolishness. "He won't. I've known Drew most all his life. He's got his faults, but he ain't a wicked man. Now, maybe he done wrong by you, I don't know, and he ain't here to tell me. But if I was you, I'd go on back where you come from and forget him."

"I don't think I can," I said, and something in my tone must have reached her. She put her hand on my elbow, and her touch took away the last ounce of my pride. I felt tears slide down my cheeks.

"Yes, you can. You know I'm speaking the truth to you. You've been here two months with not a word. You know yourself as plain as I do he ain't coming. Pick yourself up, now. Get on back home. There ain't no sense in what you're doing to yourself. You're as skinny as a ghost. And them hands . . ." She grabbed my wrist and raised my palm for me to look at. "Girl, ain't you never heard of gloves?"

"But I love him," I sputtered.

"Well . . . that don't matter much either." She had a hard edge to her voice, though I didn't feel anymore that it was directed against me.

She sat me down on the gallery step, right beside where I'd left her folded-up dress. She sat down with me, but she didn't say anything else, or touch me again. She just allowed me to weep undisturbed until I was dry. It took a good while. And once, when Ben came around the corner asking what was taking her so long, she chunked a rock at him to keep him away.

24

Fannie loaned me the money for a train ticket since I was a few dollars short. I had at first considered calling on the Masons, saying my husband was in the Brotherhood, but I knew somehow that Mr. Tanner would be amongst them, too, and I felt guilty enough leaving Cheneyville owing Fannie, let alone my debt at the Hotel Tanner. I promised to pay her back as soon as I could.

A train ride can give you a lot of time to sort through your mind. I sat in the ladies' car, and didn't talk much to the others around me. I settled myself by the windows and watched the land change from the flat marshes of Louisiana and eastern Texas, to coastal prairie, and finally, to the pine hills of Bastrop County.

The cotton harvest was on. All along the roads, whitening both sides like blots of snow, lay the blow-off from farm wagons loaded to the hilt with their cotton. When I stepped off the train at the McDade station, the first thing I saw were all the bales fresh from Mr. Seawell's gin, stacked around the platform, waiting to be loaded into cars. Harvest was on. It was Tuesday, the first of September. I had been gone for two months and four days.

Fannie had given me a cloth drawstring sack for carrying my clothes, and I clutched the bag in my hands. My hair was loose down my back like a schoolgirl, no ribbon, no hairlock, and in some odd way, I felt like myself again. Maybe even more myself than ever before. Clearheaded. Dauntless. With a peace inside me, and a resolve that was propelling me along, and had been ever since I emptied my eyes out on Lavinia Treadway's front porch. I had come to realize how unfair I'd been to those left behind by disappearing, by not giving them a chance for their say, or for a real goodbye. It was time for me to face the mess I'd made, and straighten it up however best I could.

Town was quiet, except for the masonry men across at Bassist's store. Mr. Bassist was rebuilding, in brick this time, and the mixing of the mortar in the wheelbarrow, the scraping of trowels, made a steady, almost comforting, sound. Seamus Murphy and Stan Tackaberry were among the workers, and for one jolting moment, it seemed a betrayal that these two men would work for Louis Bassist, until I remembered one of the lessons I had learned through all this: that you can never predict how a man will behave, what drives him on, or what small temptation, be it money or earthly pleasure, it will take to turn him from his high-flown sense of honor. Mr. Bassist was most likely paying good wages, or else reducing the debts of the men who labored for him. Men like Mr. Murphy and Mr. Tackaberry, hard-pressed farmers who had more than likely made a poor showing on their crops this year. One could hardly blame them for eating their crow with such relish.

I didn't see Mr. Bassist anywhere about, although Sam Alexander was visible inside the finished part of the store, sorting goods on a three-tiered trinket shelf near the door. The building was going to be two stories this time. I looked at the framed upper floor, and I could almost feel absolved of my crime by the improvement of the new building over the old one. And it relieved me to see everything else around unharmed. Only the tall pine in Weede Millage's backyard appeared to have taken some damage. One side, the side facing Bassist's, was charred to a crisp brown, and shriveled so that the tree looked grotesque and lopsided, as if some hungry giant had bitten a hole in its center.

"Well, well, well. Who have we here?" a familiar voice said. I turned to see J.T. Craddock pulling up the reins on his roan gelding. The horse didn't seem to want to come to a stop. He bobbed his head, tried to throw his bit, and nearly reared until J.T. gave him a hard tug. I dodged out of their way. J.T. grinned at me, as if pleased with himself and his rough handling of his mount. "Is it . . . ? Could it be? Dellie O'Barr? In the flesh?"

I nodded in acknowledgment, but I didn't smile or pause to chat. I continued across the street. Someone's milch cow stood in front of Jack Nash's saloon, nipping at three sprouts of grass beside the gallery post. She ran when I approached, her bell clanging loud and discordant in the quiet town. I skirted around a large pile of horse dung.

"Are you just now arriving? Or have you already been back and I just missed it?" J.T. said behind me.

"What?" I glanced around and saw that he was following me. He'd come down off his horse and was tugging him by the bridle. When he stopped, the roan snorted, and stepped sideways toward the same clump of grass the cow had browsed.

"You. Am I the lucky one to welcome you back?" J.T. kept grinning, and I had forgotten how leering his grin could seem. "Let me buy you a drink. Or no, how stupid of me. A lady like yourself wouldn't drink harsh spirits, would she? What about a phosphate? I hear Leon Harvey at the drug fountain has learned to make one scrumptiously."

I tipped my head at him, confused by his offer. Something, an almost theatrical tone in his voice, made me cautious. "Thank you, but I don't really have the time."

"Too busy for old friends?"

Friends? It seemed an odd thing for him to say considering our past history with each other. "How's Daphne?" I said, and at once I sighed, exasperated with myself for not just walking on, as if it were required of me to stand here and small-talk in the middle of Main Street, and with someone I could hardly abide. As if Mother, Papa, too, the whole town were all standing behind me, chiding me to *be polite, Dellie. Be ladylike, now.* Or was I really only stalling, my courage failing me when I needed it most? I glanced toward the saloon, which was where J.T. had likely been headed before I happened along.

"She's not well, I'm afraid," he said in answer to my question, and he frowned deeply. "She's been trying for two weeks to lose the baby."

"Oh no. I'm sorry."

"Yes, Doc Rutherford's got her in bed." His face seemed to wilt. He put his fist to his nose and sniffed, and I felt a stab of pity for him until I realized he wasn't weeping at all, but was stifling a laugh. "And I say more's the power to him, since I can't seem to get her there myself lately. I hope he's getting himself plenty."

He had pulled me in, tricked me. I knew he had said such a nasty thing only to diminish and cheapen me. He stood there smug, his seedy grin aimed right at me, enjoying my indignation.

"You are the most disgusting—the most horrible . . ." I didn't finish. I couldn't think of words harsh enough for what I wanted to say. I turned my back on him, lifted my skirts to step up on the gallery. I just wanted to get away from him, but he jerked me backwards, nearly toppling me into the hitch-rail. It startled me and scared me.

"What do you think you're doing?" I shoved at him and managed to yank free from his grasp. But then he dropped his horse's reins and grabbed me tighter, and with both hands. I started to yell for help but he covered my mouth and, at the same time, manhandled me around to the side of saloon. We spooked some horses there. They bolted at their tie-rings, then crowded together, snorting. J.T. backed me against the wall. He held me so tight I couldn't move. His hand over my mouth smelled like cigars. I couldn't breathe, and I tugged at his fingers.

"It's time you learned a lesson long overdue." He pressed harder against me. I could feel him stiffen inside his clothes, like a rake handle against my stomach. I fought to push him away, to get his hand off my mouth. "You want to scream, do you? Well, go ahead. No one here'll listen to you anymore. They all know what you've been up to, what you are." His hand moved down my hip, bunched at my skirts. Between his teeth, he said, nearly hissing, "I ought to fuck you right here."

I bucked against him, hard, and managed to throw him off me. "How dare you say that word—" I swung for his face but he caught my wrist. He laughed and bent my arm behind my back, twisting me into the wall, mashing my face against the stone and mortar. "Let me go!"

"Louder. I want to hear you. Scream, damn you."

He snaked his hand between the wall and my ribs, covered my left breast, squeezed roughly. His mouth opened on my neck and bit down, breath hot. His tongue touched my ear. I felt his hold on me lessen, and I broke free. I picked up my skirts and ran. His laughter followed me.

When I turned the corner in front of the saloon, I nearly flew right into Jack Nash. He had J.T.'s horse by the reins, and he almost let go when he saw me. He clasped my shoulder to steady me. "Hold up, there! Great heavenly days! Is it Dellie O'Barr?"

"Marshal Nash." I was panting. I plucked at a strand of my hair that had flown into my face, wiped J.T.'s mouth from my neck. I glanced behind me.

"I didn't know you were back home."

"Just now I am, and you're the person I wanted to see."

"I believe that's my horse you're holding." J.T.'s voice came, and I whirled at the sound of it. He stepped up on the gallery. His boots made a thud. I moved an inch closer to the marshal.

"I know it is," Jack Nash said, annoyance in his voice. "You left him standing out in the middle of the road."

J.T.'s eyes slid to mine, mocking me. "I knew I wouldn't be long."

"Well, tie him up from now on." The marshal tossed J.T. his horse's reins, then turned to me. "You want to see me?"

"In your office," I said. "Can we go in there?"

He held out his hand for me to go first into the door right next to the saloon. But before I went in, I glanced once more at J.T. He was standing with his horse, an uneasy look on his face as he watched me step inside the marshal's office. It was me who wanted to laugh then. My turn to. It would have served him right to report him as a masher, but I didn't. I had a feeling J.T. was correct about public opinion. I figured I'd given folks plenty to gossip about.

"Marshal Nash," I said, as soon as the door closed. "I came to tell you . . ." I had to stop to take a deep breath, weak all of the sudden. He nodded, waited for me to continue. "I came to tell you it was me who set the fire at Bassist's store. I was the one who did it." And it felt good to finally say it out loud, to have it plain and in the open. And I realized what a burden it had been for me all these weeks, to keep shoving away the terrible deed I'd done, hiding the truth of it from myself, pretending it never really happened. Now I could be free of all that, and I felt so good, so light inside, I nearly confessed all over again, just to hear the sound of the words one more time.

The marshal didn't look at me. He kept his head bent, writing something with a pencil on a piece of paper at his desk. When I thought back on it later, he didn't seem much surprised.

The jail cell, or lock-up as folks called the closed-in corner of Marshal Nash's office, was built eight years ago, just about the same time the town appointed Jack Nash as our city marshal. In the cell was a sleeping shelf attached to one wall, a chair, a basin and pitcher on a rickety table, and a chamber pot next to that. No privacy. None at all unless the marshal's office was empty.

The last person to occupy the cell had been James Bridgewater, the clerk at Sapling's Fancy Staples. Friday two weeks before, James had drunk up all the extract of vanilla on the shelves, about twenty-five dollars worth, and in the delirium that followed, had become convinced that every customer who walked in the store was out to rob him. He held the counter gun on Mrs. Williams and Mrs. Franklow for ten minutes before Columbus Crager looked in the window and saw what was happening. Marshal Nash came and put James in the lock-up to sleep it off.

From the looks of the grimy towel beside the wash basin, it didn't appear the linens had been changed since Mr. Bridgewater's overnight stay. The air inside the cell still smelled suspiciously like vomit. In fact, everything in the lock-up needed cleaning, though mostly from disuse. Cobwebs clung to the corners and under the chair and bed.

I was sitting still, my hands folded in my lap, contemplating my new surroundings, when Daniel and Ike Landers, Marshal Nash's sometimes-deputy, stepped inside the office. When Daniel saw me, he said, "What is she doing in there, Jack?"

Marshal Nash rose to his feet. "Good. I'm glad you got here."

"Take her out of there." Daniel glanced once more at me, and I couldn't deny my own gladness at seeing him again. He'd been working. He wore his saddle britches and a heavy twill shirt. Something came to his face that I couldn't identify. His whiskers threw a dark shadow on his cheeks, but that wasn't what was different. His whiskers had always plagued him.

The marshal said, "She can't leave here, Dan. You understand that, don't you? I wired the sheriff and he's coming to fetch her in the next day or two."

Daniel hung his hat on the rack by the door. "But you can let her out of there so we can talk."

Marshal Nash seemed reluctant, but he came and opened the cell door. I walked out into the office, and Daniel pulled up the chair in front of the desk for me to sit. The marshal went back to his seat behind the desk. Ike Landers slouched over against the wall. Neither of them showed any sign of moving.

Daniel frowned at them both. "Good Lord, Jack. You act like you think she's dangerous. Can we have a minute, please?"

Marshal Nash gave us a hesitant look. "Come on, Ike." They left the office together. For a while, Daniel stared after them, hands on his hips. The room got so quiet I could hear the wind outside the window.

Then he turned to me. He rolled the marshal's chair out from behind the desk and moved it right in front of me so that when he sat down, his knees touched mine and he had to readjust a little. He smelled like sweat and wind, and faintly of his cow pastures. He leaned forward until our faces were level. I could see then the worry lines around his eyes, the hollowness of his cheeks. His hair had grown over his ears and his collar needed a press. With a stab of conscience, I realized how much grief I had caused him. It was the pain that was new to his face.

"Good God, Dellie." He reached for my hand and pulled it into both of his, kneading it like I'd been out in the cold and he had to warm me. I suddenly felt cold, inside my own skin. A shiver came. "Are you all right?"

I nodded.

"Did you sign anything?" he said.

"Sign any . . . oh, you mean— No. But I did confess."

"Are you protecting someone?"

"What? No." I knew the someone he meant. We both of us knew. "Nobody else did this," I said, pulling my hand from inside his. "It was just me."

"And you weren't influenced by some Populist notion that you'd been spooned—"

"No! Daniel, please. Let's don't start—"

"I'm trying to determine what we're up against, Dellie. That's all I'm doing."

"Speaking as my lawyer?"

"I can't be your lawyer. But I'll get someone for you. I know a man in Austin, Crawford Park." He slumped back in the chair with such emotion that I knew his mind had gone elsewhere. It seemed to take him a moment to bring himself back. "I'm not a criminal lawyer."

The word *criminal* shook me. I didn't feel like a criminal. I smoothed at a patch of dead skin on my fingers. The nails were ragged and short, showing the weeks of hard work at Fannie's. He was watching me. I let our eyes touch.

"It's been like I was acting out a bad dream," I said. "I don't mean that as an excuse. I have no excuse."

He let this settle on him for a moment. He rested his arm against the top of the desk, picked up the lead pencil, worried with it for a second before he laid it back down, lining it up against the nameplate on the desk that said *John D. Nash*. "Where did you go?"

"To Louisiana."

"Louisi—" He seemed almost to bite down on his lip. He winced his eyes, then looked away, as if my presence was too much for him. "I wired Dane. He wired back and said he hadn't seen you. I didn't believe him so I went up there. Louisiana would not have entered my mind."

"Why didn't you believe him?"

"I don't know, I just didn't. I thought he might be protecting you. From something or someone. From me." He grunted, trying to laugh, but of course it was not a laughing matter. "He thought maybe you'd gone to find Lily. We went up there next."

"To Sister's? You went all the way to Sister's?"

He nodded. "Why Louisiana?"

"And you found her? Tell me what's she like now. How are her children? I can hardly believe you went all the way up there."

"What did you think I would do? Sit here not knowing?"

I turned my attention back to my fingers, twisted at my ring, then tried to stop fidgeting and keep my hands calmly folded. "I didn't intend . . ." I raised my face. It was so hard to look him in the eye. "I knew Lavinia Treadway and her husband lived in Louisiana. I met her at a Populist meeting once. She's Andrew Ashland's sister. His half sister, actually." Icy shame rose in me, just speaking his name.

The care and concern on Daniel's face melted, transformed into the wry look of knowing finally, for sure and from me, what he had undoubtedly already heard regarding me and Andy Ashland.

He got up and went over by the gunsafe where the marshal kept two rifles and a box of cartridges locked up. With his thumbnail, he scratched at something on one corner of the safe, a rent in the wood, a speck of paint, nothing at all. My back was wet. My dress stuck to me. When he turned to me again, his face was back to familiar straight lines.

"Once Sheriff Davis comes, he'll take you to Bastrop where charges will be read. Then a judge will set your bail. After that I can get you out. A few more days. Two or three. It shouldn't be long."

He spoke in his tone for business—so remote—and as he did, I slipped the ring off my finger, remembering the day he had put it there, standing at the front of the Baptist church, so stiff and formal, dressed in his black suit like it was a funeral not his wedding. I tried to grasp hold of what my own feelings on that day had been, and it was all a blur in my mind. I pressed the ring into my palm. It made a circle in my skin. When I held it out to him, he stopped speaking.

"Here," I said. "I want you to take this. It belongs to your family."

He didn't acknowledge that he had heard. In fact, he barely glanced at me. He paced to the other side of the room and stopped near the front door, put his hand on the knob like he was going out, but just stood there, still and tall, facing away from me. Silent.

"I don't plan to squabble over your property, Daniel. I want you to know that. I don't consider that anything of yours belongs to me."

"I don't think now is the time to discuss this."

"Why not now? I'm sick and tired of us not talking about things. It's where we went wrong in the first place."

His shoulders rose and fell. He didn't turn around. "He was there, too? In Louisiana, wasn't he?"

"No." I shook my head even though he wasn't watching me. "No, I was alone."

"Sheriff Davis went after him. To bring him back to face a judge for the fire. They didn't find him." He turned to look at me, to gauge my reaction to what he said. "I guess you didn't know any of this."

"No . . . I didn't." But I wasn't surprised by it. In fact, it seemed logical, even natural, to me now, that Andy would be suspected. But they hadn't found him because he was hiding—from me, not the law. It was like watching mud in a river after a rain. When the water clears, you can see straight through to the bottom.

Daniel looked at me for another long second, measuring me, and then he came to my chair. He took the ring from my hand, turned it over and over with his thumb like it was a coin he was inspecting for defects. "Dane didn't buy any land. He said he'd been considering it, but hadn't been able to get up the money." His eyes flicked on me, head stayed bent. "You must think I'm a damned fool."

"No, Daniel. I don't."

"Well, I feel like one." He laid the ring on top of the marshal's desk in front of me, and left it there. Then he paced again, to the other side of the room. "The grand jury won't meet again until November. I'll get Crawford Park before then. He's a good attorney. The best, so there's no reason to be nervous." He continued on, pacing, telling me about the grand jury hearing, about all the legal proceedings I could expect, about my life for the next several months, explaining things to me before I could even think clear enough to ask them. But I understood it was the way he felt solid and in control of himself. Explaining to me the legalities of my situation was conversation he could predict. And Daniel valued predictability, solidity, and self-control.

When the marshal came back in and broke the tension, it was almost a relief. He'd left Ike Landers behind someplace. "I'm going to have to lock her up now." The marshal speaking seemed to startle Daniel back to the present. I tried not to notice the stricken look that came to him. Marshal Nash turned to me and said, "I'm going to have to put you back in, Dellie."

I nodded and stood up. I went into the cell. The door closed with a clank.

"What is it, Jack?" Daniel said. "Do you think she might try to escape?"

I turned to him. "It's all right, Daniel."

Marshal Nash said, "I've got the law to uphold, Dan. You know I do."

Daniel stepped to the cell door. He clutched one of the bars. I could see his jaw clench. He said, "Well, see that you do something about cleaning it up in here, Jack. It's a filth-hole. A pig's sty. It isn't fit for a lady in there. It isn't fit for an animal—"

"Daniel." I wrapped my hand around his where it rested along the bars. "It's all right."

He looked at my hand touching his. His eyes filled and swam. He swallowed, and his Adam's apple seemed like it might choke him, before he turned and strode out of the marshal's office. I strained to see him pass by the window, but he must have gone the other direction.

"Did you want this back?" The marshal had found my wedding ring lying on his desk. He brought it to me, and handed it through the bars. "Maybe once you get ready to go to Bastrop you'll want somebody to safekeep it for you, but here, you're all right to just keep wearing it."

"Thank you," I said, and put the ring back on my finger.

25

Mother came within an hour after Daniel left. She wept and clicked her tongue. She invoked the name of God, and blamed my downfall on Papa, shaking her fist at the ceiling, scolding him just as if he were present right there in the middle of Marshal Nash's office. She said, "Look at what a mess you've left for us, Joshua. I hope you're happy with yourself and what you've done. I hope you're seeing us. I hope you're watching us down here." Even in her anger, and in light of Papa's suicide, she still believed him to to be in heaven. It touched me a little.

Nathan told me later, after Mother had let him take her back home, and after he returned alone, that she was beginning to be laughed at around town because she wouldn't leave Papa's ghost to rest. She had even started talking to him in the middle of Sunday church services, and so loudly she interrupted Dr. Vermillion's sermons.

Nathan had other things he wanted to tell me about, too. Or rather, one other thing—Miss Karen Quick. For reasons only two people who have found each other can comprehend, he had fallen hard for the schoolteacher, even though she was six years his elder, and as some said, horse-faced to boot. Yet, as if to make up for all his years of persnickety waiting, he had apparently gone at his courting with the same exuberance he gave to his baseball games, an exuberance that caused Mother to have to ask Professor Mauney if Karen Quick could be moved into the Slaters' house for the duration of the Normal School, a decision I knew must have caused Priscilla considerable heartbreak. Especially when the Normal School ended on the sixth of August, and Nathan started making weekly jaunts to Jollyville to visit Karen there.

"I've been thinking," he said, his face going sober despite the sparkle in his eyes, "of asking her to be my wife."

The marshal had let Nathan come into the cell with me, had even left the door open, and Nathan had pulled the chair from the outer office in beside mine. I reached out and took hold of his hand. "You deserve to be happy."

He clutched on to me, too, for a second, blinding me with his smile, before his face went sober again. "Except she'd have to give up her teaching. And it's important to her. She really likes those children."

"Why would she have to give it up?"

"A married woman?" He shook his head. "You know the answer to that. There isn't a school in Texas would hire her married."

"Well, that isn't fair. A man doesn't have to give up his occupation when he gets married." Though I knew it was a fact: no school would allow her to go on once her virginity was lost, for fear her scholars would somehow be corrupted. Another stupid rule against women. It made me angry, even a little angry at Nathan for a second, simply because he was male. I started to pull my hand out of his, but he held on to me, even caused me to have to lean closer to him.

"Exactly the point I was making." He lowered his voice a notch. "You don't think I should ask her? She's already said she's resigned herself to being a spinster."

"A spinster? My God, what a word."

"Isn't it? I somehow can't think of Karen as a spinster. She's funny, Dellie. She makes me laugh all the time. I know you'll like her."

"I already do, Nathan. If you remember—"

Just then the marshal stood up. He glanced into the cell at the two of us sitting there, side by side. "I need to look in next door," he said, preoccupied, absently tapping his finger against a paper on top of his desk.

Nathan swiveled toward him. "I'll keep an eye on things."

Since they had their ballgames in common, Jack Nash trusted Nathan above most people, and the marshal was beginning to relax about having a prisoner in his cell. He paused to relight his cigar, then went out the front door. He still had a saloon to run. This was already the third or fourth quick trip he had made next door to check on business.

After he'd gone, Nathan turned back to me. "You want to run for it?" He was grinning. "Now's your chance."

I smiled, too. It was the first mention either of us had made of my predicament. "I wouldn't make it to the street," I said, and in fact, folks had been stopping to peer in through the office window all evening. I'd seen Mrs. Meyers do it. The Strong boys had also peeped in, and so had Columbus Crager, of course. Mr. Crager was a bigger busybody even than Mother. He had even ducked his head in the door to tell me hello and to get a look at me locked up.

"Why in God's name, Dellie, did you come back here?" Nathan said. "You were safe and away. Nobody would've suspected for an instant you were the firebug."

"Nobody? Not even you?"

"I couldn't imagine it." He bent his head downward. "But I knew you were . . ."

"Overwrought?"

When he raised his head again, any remnant of his earlier smile had vanished. "I never told a soul anything about you and . . . and that other business."

"Andy you mean."

He nodded. "I said I wouldn't, and I swear to you— It got all over town, but it did not come from me."

"It doesn't matter, Nathan. Why should I care now? I'm their enemy." I gestured toward the window. "I could've killed them all. I could've burned down the whole town." He reached to put his arm around me, to comfort me, but I held myself back. "I'm not going to cry." I squeezed his hand to try and take the startled look of rejection from his face.

He meant well. I knew he did. And manlike, he thought he could protect me, even now. He hadn't yet seen that I was the only one who could do that for myself. I figured there was no use in trying to explain that self-protection was one reason I had come back. Or that I felt a certain freedom sitting here in this jail, reclaiming a part of me I had nearly lost, or perhaps never really even had before now. I didn't think he would understand it, since he had never lived his life someone else's way.

And I was only just now coming to realize myself what had happened to me. That I had tired of always having my best foot out for the world, of being told I was bright and well mannered, of living my life half-adult, half-child, without permission to misbehave. And yes, I hurt. A lump of pain like a heavy tumor had lodged between my breastbone and my throat—the cost of my misbehavior.

But there was no way to tell Nathan this. I felt separated from him in a way I never had before, separated by our sexes, and by the differences inside our hearts. He would have me run from the consequences of this deed I had done, while I could see no other way forward but to face whatever came next. All the days and nights from here to the end of my life seemed to stretch out long and uncertain.

Marshal Nash returned, and then Daniel came back again,

with Tante Lena in tow this time. She had an armful of her cleaning rags, soap and ammonia, to scrub my cell. I protested against it, but they overruled me. Daniel had brought my supper in a basket, so I sat at the marshal's desk and ate while Tante Lena cleaned and the men talked. They gabbed about nothing, the cotton coming in, the poor condition of the roads outside town, about the convicts Nathan had seen camped on the Wilbarger Creek. "They were building a bridge there," he said, and they all got quiet, reminded of convicts and my likely fate.

I wolfed down the food. I felt almost ravenous, and I had missed Tante Lena's good cooking. She'd even packed in two apricot kolaches, my favorites. When I finished eating, I went to help her mop the floor. She looked up from her hands and knees, smiled. She had her hair tied back in a kerchief, but a sprig or two had escaped at her forehead. It was blond going silver. Wide cheekbones. It struck me she had once been pretty. An old maid now. A spinster. I realized, for the first time, that she was probably smarter than me.

"Mr. Danny say we get you out of here real quick. So you don't worry, you hear?" She put vs in place of her ws. I had forgotten the soothing sound of it.

I smiled and nodded, dipped a rag into her pail of soapy water. I knew Daniel's eyes were on me, but I didn't check to see.

He wouldn't leave. He asked Nathan to carry Tante Lena back home, but not before he brought in a pillow from my bed, and a feather mattress that hung over the edge of the sleeping shelf. He fixed a blanket across the cell door that I could move back and forth when I needed privacy. Marshal Nash said he guessed it would be all right to leave it up there. I don't think he'd ever had a female prisoner before. If Daniel slept a wink that first night, I never saw him. Every time I looked he was either pacing the room or jotting a note to himself on a piece of paper. Or else staring back at me. He'd brought a book to read but he never opened it. In the morning, it still lay in the same place on the corner of the marshal's desk. I started to ask for it myself, just for something to fill time, until I saw it was a book on the law, one of *Blackstone's Commentaries.*

The marshal or Ike Landers was always there, too, one or the other. And early my second morning as a jailbird, Garland Wilson, the editor at the *Mentor,* came. He was in his thirties, wearing a well-waxed handlebar above his lip, and a fob watch stretched across his breast. I had never known Mr. Wilson too well, but he stayed for more than an hour behind my curtain, over Daniel's objections, inside the lock-up with me. We talked of other things besides just the fire. Political things, because he knew I had written for the *Plaindealer.* He explained to me what fusion meant by telling me about the Democrats' adoption of some of the ideals of Populism into their new platform, ideals such as the issuance of bank notes by the Treasury Department, the coinage of silver at sixteen to one, term limitations for civil servants, and antitrust regulations. Most importantly, they had nominated the Populist candidate for president. I thought that a lot had happened while I was in Louisiana, though we said nothing, Mr. Wilson nor I, about the rights of women. I could go to jail and stand as a criminal before the court, but I could not cast a ballot in an election. That much was still the same.

It was odd the people who came to see me. Odder still, the ones who didn't. Daphne came, and I was relieved to see that she was in perfect health, round and rosy with the child inside her. But Priscilla, my best friend since childhood, never appeared. Neither did the Bettses, and that seemed an especially unusual oversight, until Daniel mentioned that they might want to separate themselves from any bad publicity, since they were having a hard enough time just keeping the party alive. Some of the people from the meetings at Fletcher's Hall did stop by—Merle Grossner and Rose Barbee, the Dillons, and the entire Peterson family—though mostly to satisfy their own curiosity, I believe, rather than to wish me well.

I had my share of sightseers, too, from other towns around, come over to have a look at the "lady incendiary," as Mr. Wilson called me in his article in Thursday's *Mentor,* a special issue devoted almost entirely to me, and to the fire, and to the Populists, who were, he wrote, "preachers without pulpits, farmers without farms, lawyers without clients, and patriots without patriotism. The party of the disgruntled, the extremists, and the shiftless, whose purposes are vague and whose existence is founded on negative principles, positive in nothing but the desire for pie and power."

"I tried to tell you not to talk to him," Daniel said, after I had read the article.

I felt foolish, and naive, two things I had thought I would never feel again. "All right, then. You keep them all away from me, if you think you can." He nodded, and it seemed to please him, my asking for his help.

He armed back the makeshift curtain, which was serving as my cell door all the time now, and he went out into the office. I heard him tell Marshal Nash I would not accept any more visitors, and that it was time to contact Sheriff Davis again, to find out what was taking him so long to fetch me.

"You can tell George Davis that if he doesn't come get her within twenty-four hours, I'm going to file a writ of habeas corpus. See if that will get him moving." I didn't know what that meant exactly, but Jack Nash seemed to. He went right away to send the wire.

While he was gone, Mr. Bassist himself tried to pay me a visit. Daniel prevented it. Mr. Bassist said he only wanted to ask me why I had done it, but that was as much as I heard before Daniel stepped outside and shut the office door.

I crept out of the cell and went to crouch beneath the window out of sight so I could listen. Mr. Bassist said, "Don't you think because you're her husband and a lawyer you can get her off for this."

"The judge will decide." Daniel sounded calm. Mr. Bassist was the excitable one. The German was rolling in his voice.

"I never have no quarrel with you, Daniel O'Barr. You know I never fight your family, but I will sue you if she don't stay in jail."

"She is in jail."

"Oh yeah, with parties all day long. I see the people come and go. Some jail. I tell you, I have my lawyer, too. And I know somebody's got to pay for this crime."

And then I heard Marshal Nash come back and ask what was going on. Somebody else answered him, so I realized a crowd had gathered. When I heard the doorknob turn, I rushed back to my cell, but I hooked the blanket through the bars so I could see if something more happened. Nothing did, but when Daniel stepped inside, the look he gave me caught me in my throat.

Then the marshal came in and went to stand at his desk. "I don't know," he said in answer to nothing. He plucked off the end of a cigar and stuck it into his mouth. "I don't reckon you can blame the man for being angry. He's mostly all blow."

I thought about the ransacked office of the *Plaindealer,* and about the big teamster wagon on fire outside Fletcher's Hall. I didn't consider Mr. Bassist harmless. "Maybe I should have talked to him."

The marshal struck a match to the end of his cigar and puffed, his cheeks flaring out like a toadfrog. He waved out the flame. A drift of smoke wreathed his head. "Would you have apologized?"

Before I could answer, Daniel came toward me and took me by the arm. He pulled the blanket down behind us, and steered me to the farthest corner of the cell, which wasn't all that far, maybe five feet. "I want you to be careful what you say, Dellie," he said, whispering and up close. "Jack has been a good friend, but he'll likely have to testify against you. Don't tell him anything."

"He already knows I did it. If I say I did it, why would he have to testify?"

"Dellie. Please. Listen to me this time. Don't say another word until Crawford Park gets here."

I looked at him, at the light that shone from his eyes. I didn't think he understood yet that I was guilty. That I had done this crime. I just nodded.

He let go of my arm, rubbed once where he'd held me like he thought he might have had me too tight. I put my hand there and watched him walk into the office, flipping the blanket back out of his way.

It was that night Daniel finally told me about his trip to North Texas to see Dane and Sister. He took the train to Fort Worth and then to Weatherford, where he caught a coach and four to a little spot in the road called Brock. He got directions to the farm of Dane's employer, Haywood Beatty by name, Sister's brother-in-law. They had a lot of Mexicans working, plowing up new land. With Dane's help, Haywood Beatty had made his farm a success. Mr. Beatty wasn't much like the man that Daniel remembered— a bully, a slob, untrustworthy. He was, in fact, the opposite of that. He treated his Mexicans well, spoke their language to them, and gave them their own houses to live in.

"He asked me if I had mistreated you," Daniel said, a self-conscious grin on his face. "He thought you might not want to be found."

"Haywood Beatty said that? He doesn't even know me."

Daniel nodded. "He was the one who finally took me up to Lily's."

"Not Dane?"

"Apparently he can't get along with her husband."

So Daniel let Haywood Beatty take him to the Panhandle and to Sister's. It was tame country. Daniel was surprised by that. The land had been put to the plow, though there wasn't much surface water around. Their house was near a river, and that was lucky for them, though their farm was still miserable and dusty, a few sprigs of cotton blooming in the field. Sister's husband was in the business of breaking oxen to the yoke, and was busy with that. She was expecting a child and showing the wear from it. She recognized Daniel right off.

"Is she still pretty?" I asked.

He was sitting in my cell, on the narrow cot with his back to the wall. He gazed toward the open window. It was hot and we weren't getting any breeze. Over at the marshal's desk, Ike Landers snored. "Like a rose that's gone one step past its brightest bloom."

It was the most poetic thing I had ever heard Daniel say. As a young girl, Sister had hurt his feelings. I had always felt like a consolation prize, though I only just then realized it well enough to put it in a clear thought.

"I wonder how things would have turned out if she hadn't run off with Marion Beatty," I said, letting the idea sink on him, with all its possibilities. "Papa probably wouldn't have married Mother, for one thing."

"I believe he would have."

"You think he loved her?"

"It was hard to tell with Josh. He didn't show much, but I know her heart was set on him long before. She used to talk about him to my mother when they didn't think I was listening."

I shook my head, and had to smile, thinking of Mother pining for Papa. "I can't see it."

"Josh wasn't the devil, Dellie. He always treated me with respect, even when I was too young to deserve his respect."

I nodded, felt something well up from deep inside, and bring an image of Papa's rosy cheeks, marching in with his old cavalry hat, singing "Dixie." "Is that why you married me? Because of Papa's respect? Did you feel pressured by him, or was it because of Sister? That I reminded you of her in some way. I never did know what you had to gain from it."

"Gain from what? Marrying you?" He shook his head at me. "You always think the least of me."

"That isn't true." But it occurred to me that he was right. I had, over time, come to regard him in a sour light, full of resentment and mistrust.

"What I gained was you." He said it quietly, simply.

The wall lamp fluttered. Its reflector sent light toward us. Not enough to read by, but I could see Daniel's face plainly, the facets of his cheekbones and chin, the paleness of his forehead, the shimmer of his eyes. He seemed fragile somehow, leaning there against the wall of the cell, and I longed, suddenly, to go to him, and sit down inside his arms.

"I wish," I said, "we could start again. I wish the Matsons were having another party and we could meet there, and you would come up to me and ask to swing me round the room."

"Maybe I wouldn't do that this time."

"Maybe not. But if you did—I wouldn't be afraid of you this time."

"Why were you afraid of me, Dellie?"

"Because you were—" I wanted him to understand, and I wanted to myself. The words came hard. "You always seemed too fine a man for me, too smart, too grown-up. I could barely speak to you for fear you'd see what a child I was, and how silly."

"You were never silly."

"I couldn't understand why, out of all the girls you could've had, you chose me."

"No matter what you imagined, I was never such a prize." He breathed a short laugh; paused. "I'd been gone a long time. And Lily might've had something to do with it, but not because she had stayed constantly in my mind. I had met other people in Austin. And I knew she was married. But I remembered her, of course, and when I got home, I asked about her. I don't recall exactly. Someone at the lodge. Clarence Bright, I think it was, just if he'd heard anything of her. And you were mentioned. Had I seen you. That you'd grown up, turned out, things men say. Enough to get my curiosity. You were a little girl when I left. I couldn't think of you any differently, until I saw you at Sapling's. You were buying soap."

"For my face, I remember. Mother's lye had given me a rash."

"I knew it was you. Blond hair. Still the same wide eyes. I thought you looked like a swan."

"Oh, Daniel." I smiled. "A swan?"

"An angel, then. You looked like something lovely to me."

"Don't make me blush."

His face turned serious. "I don't know why I could never say these things before. It isn't easy for me. I just don't have . . . it's something lacking in me. I thought if you knew how much I . . . you're right. We probably did get off to a bad start. Never talking honestly to one another. It's my fault. I was afraid, too. I'm still afraid. That if you know how much I care for you, how important you are to me, you'll just keep doing these things, because you know I'll tolerate it—"

"Doing what things?"

"Running away from me, for instance. Turning to another man." It felt like a slap, and I recoiled from him. He saw the change come over me, and he leaned forward, both hands on his knees. "I shouldn't have said that."

"Of course, you should have, if it's the way you feel."

"I shouldn't have made it sound so coarse. I apologize."

"No need."

"I love you, you know." He didn't look as offhand as he sounded, bracing himself forward on his knees. "I just thought you should hear it from me clearly."

In the natural course of things, I should've said the words back just then, but I couldn't make myself. Not with Andy so fresh, and with everything else that was happening to me. At that moment, I did feel love for Daniel, but I still felt love for Andy, too, that aching in my breast. And it didn't seem possible to me, at the time, that both feelings could exist together.

I stood up. I'd been sitting so long I ached. He straightened and I ran my fingers in his hair. It was fine and dark, softer than it looked, except for the gray, which I could barely see in the poor light. "You have been good to me." I whispered low, so only the two of us could hear. "Better than I deserve."

He stood up, too. He was taller than me by six inches, so he had to look down. He pulled me in close to kiss me, but then held back. He seemed suddenly to become aware of our surroundings again, and I was sorry. I wanted to feel a kiss from him. It had been a long while, and I thought how our kiss might also seem new, the way this talking from the heart did, saying things we never had before. But instead, he tucked my head underneath his chin, and hugged me tight. "All I want is to take you home," he said.

It was three o'clock in the morning when the men came—six men wearing lampblack around their eyes and sackcloth masks. They woke me from a fitful sleep filled with unsettling dreams of finding the flesh on my calves creviced and crusted like the gaping cracks in a parched field of turned earth; of feet with soles too sore and blistered to walk on even the softest of rugs. The men in their masks made a rumpus, yelling for me to come out in the night. They had a bucket of tar and another of chicken feathers, and one of them hollered, "We're gonna ride you out of town on a rail, we are!"

"Get away from the window, Dellie," Daniel said, coming out of the chair where he had dozed.

Ike Landers got to me first, and dragged me away from where I'd been peeping out at the men. He put me back in the cell, and he closed the door on me. I heard the lock clink.

Daniel fumbled through the ring of keys on the marshal's desk till he found the one that opened the gunsafe. He took out a Winchester rifle. He handed another one to Ike. Daniel was the one to open the front door, and I nearly screamed for him to get back. I expected a dozen bullets to rain into him, but only a voice came.

"Out of our way, O'Barr." It was Morris Bassist, Mr. Bassist's oldest son. I recognized his tired way of speaking.

"You'll have to get by me." Daniel held the rifle to his shoulder, cocked and aimed. Ike joined him, both of them barring the door.

"This is no way, boys," Ike said. "You've all been drinking."

"Sam Alexander?" Daniel said. "Is that you under that feed sack? And what about you, Gus Klemm? What are you doing out here in the middle of the night? Does your family know you're not at home in bed?"

There was a bump against the wall, a scrabbling noise, and Daniel jumped back, slamming the door into the wall. Then he and Ike both leapt forward, out of my line of sight.

"What's happening?" I said, holding tight to the bars across the cell door.

I heard a lot of stomping, then Daniel came in, his face powdery white, almost gray. "They're gone," he told me.

Ike Landers came by the open door with a torch flaming in his hand. He stuffed it down into the rain barrel outside. I smelled the kerosene smoke. Ike came in and closed the door. "They'd had too much liquor," he said, looking at Daniel.

"She can't stay here any longer." Daniel leaned the rifle in a corner.

"The sheriff says he don't have any place to put a female prisoner."

"Well, I don't care what he says, she can't stay here. It isn't safe." He pointed his finger at Ike. "Go get Jack. Wake him up. And go after Nathan, too. Tell him to bring horses. We're taking her to Bastrop ourselves."

26

Before daylight we left, the five of us. The marshal and Ike, Nathan on his golden bay, Daniel on his white-socked Brandywine, and me on another O-Bar-J horse, a gentle cow pony called Castaway. Nathan had brought me a sidesaddle, an old one from Mother's attic. I had never been fond of horseback, couldn't move smoothly with the animal the way you were supposed to do, but Castaway tolerated me. The men were all edgy and didn't speak much, each with a gun in his saddle boot. We got to Bastrop in the forenoon. By then, my backside was so bruised I could hardly walk.

The county jail was a new building, a stately three stories of tan and red brick, a mansard roof; a pretty place, except for the iron bars crossing every window. The jailer, Mr. Forehand, was not happy to see me. He knew who I was before Marshal Nash said. Mr. Forehand was the one, it turned out, who had been telling Sheriff Davis there was no place for a female prisoner. He said as much to us, too. But Marshal Nash and Nathan went off to find the sheriff, which they did fairly soon, down at the Gilt Edge Saloon, admiring the cream-colored squirrels the proprietor had just put into cages there. Everyone in town apparently was talking about these two albino curiosities, caught on a farm nearby. It was a relief to me not to be the center of conversation for a change. Sheriff Davis told Mr. Forehand to put me on the first floor, in an unused room that was part of the jailer's quarters.

Bars were over the windows even in there, but curtains hung in front of the bars, lace-edged curtains tied back with a cord. And there was a spring bed, a writing table, a rug on the floor, and a view out onto a garden planted in potatoes, sweet cabbage, peas, and turnips. Every day I could watch the jailhouse cook, a Negro woman whose name I never knew, gather in the vegetables for that day's soup. She reminded me of Fannie Duval, the way she moved so deliberately at everything and with a sureness. It seemed an eternity, not just a week, since I had left Cheneyville.

My stay in the Bastrop jail lasted two days, long days, with nothing to do but stare out the window and think. My future looked bleak and I didn't want to dwell on it. I longed for a book or some sewing, anything to occupy the time. I prayed—something I'd gotten out of the habit of—for the strength to face whatever lay ahead of me. Somehow, even in my comfortable surroundings, the severity of my situation had finally come clear in a way it had not while I was still in McDade.

Crawford Park arrived from Austin. He was a pleasant man, not even as tall as me. In looks he reminded me of a painting of Thomas Jefferson on the wall at Miss Langburn's school. A splatter of freckles like nutmeg dusted his nose and cheeks; carrot-red hair. I guessed him to be near sixty, though he had aged well and seemed somewhat younger because of his small stature.

Daniel brought Mr. Park in to meet me. The first few minutes were filled with their affectionate talk, one for the other. Daniel had attended classes Mr. Park had taught at the university, and a fondness had developed between them. It was odd to see Daniel as the admiring younger man, like a doting puppy at Mr. Park's heel. But once all this first talk was behind us, Mr. Park wanted to visit with me alone. He said it in such a way, so polite, so genteel, I hardly realized he'd asked Daniel to leave the room until it was done.

"The court's attorney will want to see you held without bond," Mr. Park said, once Daniel was gone. "He has called you a menace to society. Daniel has, of course, told me something of your case. But I'd like to hear you tell me."

"I'm guilty. That's how I wish to plead. I don't see a need for a trial. I apologize to you for your trouble in coming all this way. I didn't have the heart to tell Daniel."

"Dellie." He sat completely still in the ladder-back writing chair, looking me straight in the eyes. "I hope you don't mind if I call you that."

"Of course not."

"I wonder how clearly you have thought this through."

"There's nothing to think about. I started the fire. I have to pay for it."

"Do you want to go to the state penitentiary?"

"I want to get on with my life."

He nodded, paced, glanced at me. "Don't think they'll go easy on you just because you are a woman. If you plead guilty you could get as much as twenty-five years."

"Twenty-five years?" I lost my breath.

"It's possible. I would say, probable."

I sat down on the bed. I was too stunned to speak. Or to listen, either, for that matter. He was saying something about the various degrees of felony, explaining, but all I could think of was those twenty-five years. Five more years than I had even been alive so far. I felt like a fog had closed down around me.

After a while, he seemed to see that I wasn't listening. He stopped speaking and got my attention with his silence. "Why don't you tell me exactly what happened," he said.

So I did, hesitating at first, trying to get back my wits, and then warming to the telling once I saw how attentively he listened, his forehead pinched in solemn compassion. I saw no reason to hold back. He wanted to help me. I told him how I'd become involved with the People's Party, that I had even written for the *Plaindealer.* I said how everyone around me seemed to owe Mr. Bassist, including my own papa when he died, and that Mr. Bassist lorded it over the people. I detailed the ransacking of the newspaper office. I explained about Andy's wagon, how he'd been bringing in goods from Austin. And I told about Andy himself, calling him simply someone I had greatly admired. I couldn't tell by Mr. Park's face if he gleaned anything more from that, or if Daniel had told him anything more. I explained that after Andy left, I set the fire, then rang the bell as I fled, hoping someone would hear and come to put the fire out. Finally, I told him that I had stayed gone from Texas until I realized I couldn't live with the terrible reality of what I had done hanging over me, and so I came back to confess.

"And just before you set the fire, how were you feeling?" he said.

"Feeling?"

"Yes, were you so burdened with grief you hardly knew what you were doing?"

"I knew what I was doing, Mr. Park."

"But was there an irresistible impulse? Were you in a fit of passion?"

"Well, I . . ." He made it sound so simple, even logical. I hadn't been able to think of those moments, that night, with any clarity, let alone logic. "I suppose so. In a way."

"We mustn't be dodgy about this, Dellie."

"I wasn't thinking straight about anything, Mr. Park."

He nodded, pleased with this answer. "Have you been examined by a physician?"

"No."

He stood up from the chair he had taken, and put his hand on my shoulder. "I want a doctor to see you. We'll talk more later."

My arraignment was set for the next day. The doctor Mr. Park sent to examine me was a stranger to me. A Dr. Berckenhoff. I was frankly unhappy with his German surname, but he was friendly enough, and didn't sound foreign.

The purpose of Dr. Berckenhoff coming, I soon realized, was to establish that I was in a state of nervous collapse, a collapse due to the recent death of my father and to other unfortunate events in my life. The physical examination the doctor gave me was to support this belief, since it was a well-accepted, scientific fact that the womb controlled excitability in the female body and that the ovaries influenced all the commotions of a woman's system.

I stood with my back against the wall while Dr. Berckenhoff knelt before me and probed beneath my orange poplin dress, which Daniel had brought for me to wear to the arraignment. All during the examination, I kept my arms tightly crossed and tried to pretend nothing unusual was happening to me, though I could feel my cheeks burning. I felt as soiled as I had with J.T.'s hands on me in the street outside the marshal's saloon.

"How long since your last monthly return?" the doctor asked me, right in the middle of his examination.

I would have rather not had to talk at such a time. I heard my voice flinch a little when I answered that I didn't know. I had never been regular. It had been my curse. When he came out from under my dress, I felt such pure relief. I filled my lungs with a deep breath, and watched him wash his hands in the basin across the room. He was meticulous about it, soaping and soaping, round and round, scrubbing between each finger.

"You are pregnant, Mrs. O'Barr. Two months I'd say. Perhaps a shade more."

I laughed at that idea, shook my head. The word *pregnant* had shocked me. "That can't be right. Wouldn't I know it if anyone did?"

"You haven't had any unusual sickness?"

"No. I've felt perfectly well." I remembered the train ride to Louisiana, the bad food, the week of fever at the hotel. My hand wandered down to my stomach. Was it possible? No, my imagination. If anything I had lost weight. And you didn't lose weight when you were . . . I watched him dry his hands on the thin towel.

"By my calculations," he said, "you should be due in April. Spring babies are the best kind."

"Are you absolutely certain?"

He smiled. "I've never been wrong before." He folded the towel neatly and laid it on the sink stand. "I'll give my report to Mr. Park. And congratulations to you."

I could do no more than nod. When he left, I didn't even reach to put my drawers back on before I flopped down on the bed. It was that word I couldn't get my mind past; that word he had used: *pregnant*. A word we were never allowed to say as children, not even in speaking of our milch cows or of our sows out in the woods. I said it out loud. "Pregnant." Tested it. It seemed to fill up my mouth.

I had always wondered what it would feel like. Now I knew. Nothing. It felt like nothing. No different. Not even a swelling. I pulled my dress taut across my middle, felt and felt with my hand. "Pregnant," I said again, and lay back flat on the bed. I smiled up at the soot spots on the ceiling.

At the arraignment, I pleaded not guilty. I felt hypocritical doing it, but everything had changed now. I had a child inside me. A wonderment, a miracle. I didn't even care or consider which man might be the father, only that it was there, deep within me, to grow and become true.

Daniel was there, of course, when Mr. Park told the judge I

was a woman with child and should not be kept incarcerated, but Daniel's expression never changed from its same deeply angled intensity. He posted my bail of fifteen hundred dollars. How that sum was arrived at, I never understood, and how Daniel came up with so much so quickly, I didn't ask. Though I found out later, years later, that in the end, my legal expenses cost him over a thousand acres of his land.

He saw Mr. Park to the train station, and then he fetched me home in the carriage with Scamp and Hasty pulling. Nathan rode back with us. We were bristling with weapons: Papa's old double-barrel wedged between Nathan's feet, Daniel's rifle behind our seat, even a six-shooter I'd only seen him wear out on the range with his cattle. He wore it today, though, strapped around his hip with a cartridge belt. It was plain he feared some kind of trouble from Mr. Bassist's cronies, but I couldn't worry about that, or even think much of it. Too many things were happening, too much going on in my mind. And we arrived at the house without incident.

It felt strange, yet oddly comforting, to be back in my room, with everything just as I'd left it: the sham pillows on the bed, Sister's family on the wall, my pocketbook with the twenty dollars I had so needed in Louisiana, the wardrobe hung indecently full of my clothes.

I pulled out a cotton wrapper. It was nearly dark out and I was tired, glad to be left alone for a few minutes. My feet ached from my button shoes, and when I pulled them and my stockings off, my flesh had swollen and turned pink. *Pregnant.*

I stepped out of my dress and stood before the wardrobe mirror in just my underdrawers, but still I couldn't see any change. I unbuttoned my waist, tossed it toward the bed, unlatched my corset; tossed it, too. I opened my undervest. Maybe my breasts were a little fuller, tender to the touch. I rubbed my thumb over my nipple, tried to imagine a tiny mouth suckling there. But it seemed more like a dream still, than reality.

And why now? Why when things were so tangled, when my future was so uncertain—why give me this gift, this treasure, now? I remembered Papa saying at the reunion that it was time I gave him grandbabies, and I wondered if he could see me and knew. I remembered Dr. Rutherford saying to me, all those long months ago, that he believed I might be barren, and I was glad he was wrong. I thought about Daphne with her swollen stomach under her skirts, and of poor, childless Mother, and of Sister up in the Panhandle with her oxen and her sorry farm and all her children swarming around her. I thought about Hannah and Quintus, missed them wherever they were. I had so wanted to be a mother to them. I thought of Daniel and my regrets, and of Andy with anger and with shame, with longing still. And all these thoughts came quickly, one after the other, and with such force the tears I believed I had left behind me welled in my eyes until I could barely see through them.

Four light taps came at my door, and then Daniel walked in, just as he had always done, as if things were still the same between us. I blinked to clear my eyes, held my unbuttoned vest together, and let him come in on me standing there in my knee-length drawers, barefoot, my midriff showing. I didn't rush for my wrapper to cover up, as I used to would do. Three steps into the room he hesitated. I thought I saw him flinch ever so slightly at my immodesty. "I'll come back." He started to turn around.

"There's no reason to leave." I began to button my vest.

Slowly he came up closer. He couldn't seem to help the glances he gave my body, and I didn't hurry with the buttons. Whatever he had come in to say seemed to leave his mind. His face got still and flaccid. His hands went into his pockets.

"I'm pregnant," I said, using the word, and it made his eyes meet mine. He came another step forward into the room.

"I know." He faced out toward the gallery, as if something in the dusk held his attention. "I'll go down and wait till you're dressed."

"No, Daniel. Stay here and talk to me now."

He turned to me, came a few more steps forward. "I thought we could call Doc Rutherford. Let him look at you, too." His voice wavered, seemed sluggish. "It isn't my child, is it?" He reached out for the foot post of the bed, as if to steady himself, and then shook his head. "Never mind. You don't have to answer that. I shouldn't ask."

"It's all right—"

"No, it isn't all right! It isn't what I came to say!" He heaved a deep sigh and closed his eyes, as if to get control of himself, as if this outburst had surprised even him. I ventured toward him, reached out. He stepped back from my touch. His eyes glittered. "I cannot bear the thought of his hands on you. I can't bear it. If I see him again—if he shows his face to me one more time, I swear to *God* I'll kill him."

His face bunched in, like a cake that's fallen in the center. I stood still, amazed by the violence in his words. He strode across to the gallery doors and threw them open so the outside air would hit him. I saw his shirt was damp and clinging to him. With the air came the smell of summer grasses dying in the heat, the coo of doves settling down for the night, the low of cattle in the distance.

"I'm not used to these feelings," he said, calmer now, though his shoulders still rose and fell with each breath. I knew how hard this was for him: to show me his anger and his fear, to say what was in his soul. Something broke inside me, something unnameable for him and for me, and for the reckless damage I'd done.

"It's your child, Daniel."

He looked at me, both eyes red-rimmed, full. "Don't say that to me now. You would lie. And I might believe you."

"It's not a lie. It is your child I'm carrying."

He made a huffing sound. "How can you possibly know that?"

"Because I do. It was that night. Remember the night I asked you to stay with me."

"No, Dellie." He shook his head. "No. I won't let you persuade me that easily. I'm not that big of a fool."

"Daniel. Daniel, listen to me." I went over to him. I put my hands on his chest. His heart was beating hard. "Don't you think I would know something like that? It's your baby. *Our* baby. Don't you think I would know?"

He turned his face to the side, giving me his profile, as if by not looking me in the eye he could ward me off. But I saw the hope quiver around his mouth. "It doesn't matter, Dellie."

"Yes, it does." I leaned against him, laid my cheek to his breastbone. "I want you to know it's true. I want you to be as happy as I am. Daniel"—I looked up into his eyes—"I want you to believe me."

But his hands—ever so carefully, his hands braced my elbows. I felt the tension in him change into a new kind of tension, maybe caused by remembering the night I had mentioned, or maybe by me, in my underclothes, pressed against him. I saw the change come into his eyes. His arms went around me, and he drew me close.

I lifted on my toes to reach for a kiss. He gave it. I touched my tongue to his lips and his mouth opened. His arms around me tightened, and then he broke away and looked at me, deep into my eyes, while his fingers unbuttoned my vest. It seemed natural enough in light of all we'd been through for us to come together. A reclaiming. A healing. Forgiveness.

And I made a startling discovery, that day and in the days that followed: that it was me—I had been the squeamish one. Daniel was as warm-blooded as any other male animal. He wanted me in the morning first thing. Last thing at night. During supper. He wanted to sleep with me, to share my bed as well as my body.

Later, I liked to pretend that it was in those days before the grand jury hearing, those days when we blocked out everything else around us—the town, the Bassists, our families, the trial; those days when our appetites included more than the meals Tante Lena served; days when I could hardly look at Daniel without a rush of emotion almost overtaking me—I liked to think it was in those days that our child was really conceived.

27

The grand jury convened the first week in November, the day after the Republican, William McKinley, was elected president. By then, my condition was showing—a small rounding below my waistline. I had even begun to feel the baby quicken, and it so happened he chose to kick and cavort all through the hearing.

Mr. Park thought I would be No-billed. He said the only evidence against me was my own confession, and that it was merely hearsay since nothing had ever been written down and signed. As the witnesses took the stand, I sat placid, at peace, while the butterfly that was the child inside me bobbled a foot or a knee or a tiny elbow up my abdomen to my ribs. I'm sure I smiled a lot. Daniel said I looked regal.

One at a time witnesses were called to the front and their statements made. Several townsmen testified that I had been seen acting suspicious outside Bassist's store just two days prior to the fire. And shortly afterward, I had gone across to the office of the *Plaindealer*. This was attested to by several people. Allegations of a conspiracy were speculated upon. Marshal Nash went up to repeat my words of confession. And J.T. Craddock, since he held the insurance on Mr. Bassist's store, gave the loss at $29,000. Enough for the twenty-five years, I feared.

The grand jury, sixteen men in black suits and scowling faces, chose to indict. Daniel called it a temporary setback. It was something about him I had never paid attention to before, his dogged optimism, the way he refused to see for long the bleak side of anything. He had a steadiness that was comforting, a reassuring loyalty. It was tempting to think he was changed from the man he used to be, but I knew these were qualities he had always possessed. It was me seeing differently, noticing the goodness within him, a quiet thing so easy to overlook.

The trial date was set for December 7th. But on Thanksgiving while Daniel's mother and his aunt were there on a visit, with Nathan and Karen, and with Mother and everyone all there around the table eating dinner, I felt myself begin to bleed. Only a little at first, but then enough so I stood to excuse myself. I must have risen too quickly, or else my face really did go to wax the way Daniel later said it did. Something made him jump up to help me. He got me as far as the stairs, then carried me up.

"Go find Doc Rutherford!" he called, struggling with both me and his voice. I think it was Nathan who raced for the doctor.

The women bustled around me, plumping pillows, fixing rags for me to wear. All except for Mom O'Barr. She stayed downstairs to scrub at the stain I'd left on her upholstered chair in the dining room.

"Bed rest," the doctor ordered. "Complete bed rest. Daniel, you move into another room." And the way he said the last part, with a note of accusation, caused Daniel such terrible guilt.

"It's my fault this happened," he said to me later, when we were alone. "I think I've been too rowdy with you."

I laughed at the word he used, but not at the situation. We were back to separate beds again. Mr. Park got the trial postponed until the end of February.

I heard from Mother when Daphne had her baby, a little girl she named Carrie. I wanted to send a note of congratulations, but I found it next to impossible to write a letter flat on my back. Either the ink blotted or else it backed up inside the pen, and Daniel never seemed to get around to doing it for me. He knew already, I think, that J.T. would be a witness against me. I noticed Daniel had stopped going to his lodge meetings, had stopped mentioning J.T.'s name in conversation, or taking on any new lawyer work. He had stopped most everything, in fact, except tending to me, bringing me my meals, reading books to me, first *Anne,* a novel about an orphan girl, and then *Looking Backward,* because he thought I would like the author's political ideals. Once a day, for a couple of hours in the morning, Daniel rode out with Brandywine, and that was the extent of his absences from me.

Yet I felt fine, never had one moment of pain with the bleeding. And after a few days, the bleeding stopped, too, but he wouldn't let me up from the bed. Neither would Tante Lena. "We got to get you all well for this baby," she kept saying as she juned around my room, switching her feather duster over everything, hooking back the drapes to let in the sunshine.

By the third week in December, I was stir-crazy and fighting mad to get up. I tried to one evening while Daniel was in the room but he stopped me. He said, with such patience, stroking my arm, "You can't until Doc Rutherford says it's all right."

"I cannot stay flat on my back, Daniel. I can't do it another day." I already knew every crack in the ceiling, every blemish in the paint up there, every tuck and uneven line in the wallpaper. "Please, please, don't make me. I feel wonderful. I feel perfect."

He put his hand on my stomach, patted me there. "Dellie . . . darling. It isn't me making you. It's for our little one." And the baby picked that instant to give a hard kick, the first one Daniel had really felt. He jerked his hand away, but then laughed. "He's in there all right, isn't he?"

"Or she is."

"Well, I meant that, too, of course."

He put his hand back on my stomach and I held it there,

watching the wonder play on his face. I was happy to see it there, and to hear him call the baby *ours*. I worried—I couldn't help it—that the child would be born the spitting image of Andy Ashland.

I spent Christmas in bed. And New Year's. I couldn't go to Jollyville on the fifteenth of January to see Nathan and Karen married. I cried buckets over that. It seemed so unfair, so ridiculously cautious. I was fine now. I knew I was, and so was the baby. And just lying there day in and out, I was turning as fat as a hog penned up for the winter slaughter. My stomach grew into a huge ball, and the baby seemed to turn somersaults while I rested.

In February, right before my birthday, Dr. Rutherford finally blessed me and put an end to my confinement. Slowly, carefully, I got out of bed. I was weak from lack of exercise, and unsteady on my feet with all the new weight I carried. I went out to sit in the old Boston rocker on the gallery. It was wonderful to be outside in the nippy air. All the trees were wintry bare, but to me, it was a beautiful sight.

Daniel sat with me, smoking his pipe, though it was harder for him to enjoy the view, the pastureland rolling off down the valley to the creek and beyond, to the cattle dotting the hill on the other side.

"The winter grasses are poor this year." He rose to peer out over the railing, gazing moodily off in the distance. He spotted Sinclair coming out of the stable, and yelled out, "Go find Vernon for me! Tell him to come up here and see me!" He said to me, "We're going to have to start feeding hay." Then he gestured again at poor, confused Sinclair down on the ground. "Mr. Vernon! Go find Mr. Vernon!"

"You don't have to sit here with me," I said, and he turned. "It's time you got back to your work."

"I will. I will." He drew on his pipe and watched Sinclair start off across the pasture. "He's going on foot." He sighed and laid his hand on my shoulder, squeezed. He adjusted my old fascinator up closer around me. "Aren't you cold?"

I looked up at him and shook my head, let my fingertips rest against the back of his hand. I could almost imagine us fifty years from now, old folks on this same gallery. It was no longer an unpleasant thought.

The second motion for postponement came from the district court's attorney. Mr. Park tried to object to the delay, saying, "The prosecution is worried about the sympathy that might be shown my client by a jury, Your Honor," but the judge took one look at my monstrous stomach and said, "I think we had best wait until the May session to try this case." He hit the desk with his gavel so we would all know we had been dismissed.

I was disappointed. I had made a special dress, with lots of help from Tante Lena, to accommodate my new girth; and Daniel had put extra padding for me on the seat in the buggy, just for us to turn around and head back home with nothing settled. I was ready to be done with it—the apprehension, the aggravation and anxiety. The being unable to plan ahead for anything. I hated living with the uncertainty.

"This case will never come to trial," Mr. Park said as we left the courthouse. "I don't believe there's one thing for us to worry about."

Daniel reached to shake Mr. Park's hand, said, "Thank you," but Daniel didn't look any more consoled than I felt.

There'd been a recent spate of letters in the newspaper, bemoaning the injustice of these delays, all from Mr. Bassist and his cronies in the Sons of Hermann. Open threats of violence had ceased, at least for now, although I knew, as I felt Daniel did also, that if I did not face a trial and a conviction fairly soon, those threats would most certainly return. Louis Bassist was a man who would have his reckoning.

On the twenty-second day of March my labor began. It started out as a stomachache, but uneven and hard to locate beneath all the space the baby occupied. I spent the morning in the front parlor with my needlework, hemming sacques I'd made over the weekend at the machine, wondering what I'd eaten to cause such biliousness. Daniel was out with his hands gathering winter-born calves, and I didn't want to make an unnecessary fuss since he was back at his work. But when the ache moved in bands down my thighs and into my lower back, coming and going every half hour or so, I got up to tell Tante Lena.

She was in the kitchen at the stove with soup bones boiling in a kettle. She dropped her stirring spoon. The color drained from her face. "You go lay yourself down," she said. "I'll call in Sinclair. Mr. Danny said be sure to fetch him when the time comes—"

"I think there's lots of time yet," I said, but I went up to my room. Not to bed, though. I couldn't bear to get into the bed again when it wasn't needed. I went onto the gallery, pulled my wool fascinator over my head to block off the wind, which still felt cool for so late in the season. Usually by now we were having sunshine and warm weather. A storm seemed to brew off to the west. The wind blew strong from that direction, and I turned my face toward it, glad, relieved that at least this day was finally here.

For weeks I had worried that I wouldn't know or recognize labor when it came, or that the pain would become so unbearable I couldn't hold my dignity through it. But this tightening, these bands down my thighs and back, this was bearable, hardly worse than the onset of my monthly aches.

Tante Lena put out the word to everyone, and before Daniel

was even found, Mother had come, with Karen in tow, still sparkling like the new bride she was. She and Nathan had moved in with Mother, and the arrangement seemed to be working. At least, no one was complaining. Nathan was out helping Daniel with the calves.

"Lena said the stork is landing." Mother pulled the fascinator from around me and led me back inside the room. "I sent her to get Mattie Peterson. Now, you get into bed."

I let them help me. The baby had dropped low and made moving around awkward. I'd already shown some blood. Mother went off downstairs for rags, and Karen stayed to arrange the bed around me. She seemed unsure of what to do. "Are you hoping for a girl?" she said, smiling. "A girl's nice for firstborn."

I scooted back against the pillows she'd stacked. "Daniel wants a boy."

"Don't they always? It swells their manhood to father sons." She laughed. "But believe me, boys can be trying and wearisome. I know from my class. Full of mischief." I looked for some regret at having to leave her teaching, but couldn't see any behind her smile.

"I'll take whatever I get," I said, and I reached for her hand. I couldn't get used to having a sister again. It felt nice. Thunder rumbled outside. "If it's a girl, I would name her Karen if you don't mind."

"Mind? I'd be honored, and proud." She bent to give me a quick hug, and the first driving pain came at the same instant. I nearly gasped, but Karen didn't notice. "Ava might be hurt, though. Are you sure you want to?"

I nodded, my breath returning. "Mother never made Nathan as happy as you do."

She went back to tucking at the bed, but she was glowing. "Isn't it shameful? An old maid like me. You're brother is truly . . .

he is—" She straightened and looked off, listening to the first few pelts of rain, or trying to find the right words. Or perhaps just lost, for a moment, in the love that was as clear on her as it was on him.

"Remarkable?" I offered.

"Yes. Remarkable," she said, just as Mother came in with an armload of linens.

"What's remarkable?" Mother laid the stack on the trunk at the foot of the bed, and she straightened to look at us. Karen and I laughed at the same time. I was thinking about what Daniel had said about Mother having her cap set for Papa, wondering if she had ever considered Papa remarkable, or ever worn that lost look of love on her face. Outside the rain came harder.

Mattie Peterson arrived, and took things over, since she was the only one of the women present who had ever given birth. And she was an expert, having done it herself fourteen times. She told me there was nothing to it, though by then, great racking waves were sweeping over me. Tante Lena put one of her carving knives underneath the mattress. "For cutting the pain in half," she whispered to me with seriousness. If it worked, if one half the pain was all I felt, God help the women who feel it whole.

I thought I was dying. It felt like death. At times I seemed to leave myself. My own cries came like from another person, but I didn't care. I had stopped worrying about dignity. Someone put a rag in my mouth for me to bite. It didn't help, didn't keep me from wanting to moan and thrash about. I gripped Karen's hands and wrestled with the sweat and hurting.

By the time Daniel came, blood was everywhere. Oceans of it, soaking the bed, the sheets, my nightdress. Through a fog of defeat and terror, I heard Mattie Peterson say to him, "You'd best go find Doc. This one ain't coming easy."

An eternity passed, of suffering, of screaming out of control, before Dr. Rutherford arrived with his warm voice and his sweet-and-bitter smelling cloth that he laid over my face. "Breath in deep, Dellie. Slowly. That's it. That's fine." I sank into blackness. . . .

A sound from far off—as far as the lane outside the house—came creeping in through the dreaminess. Cats about to fight? Pictures swam up in my eyes. Gentle pictures. Cupid and the fairies dancing in the forest. Dark green birds. A cool wind. The earth beneath me rumbling.

From somewhere, "You have a son, Dellie. Open your eyes and see him."

"Let her rest."

It was like the words existed on their own, little colorful things dancing in my head. Then came dark, hard sleep. Barely moving. No dreams. Soulless dark. . . .

I became aware. A tiny notion way off, a cat purring. A pressure on my breast. Voices:

"She may not have her milk yet."

"She ain't got enough bosom for him to get a hold of."

A wet tingling on my nipple.

"Wake up, Dellie. Your boy's hungry."

"What?" I said from the distance, pulling myself closer. Awake. Groggy. I tried to rise.

Mother's face hovered over me. "It's your baby boy."

"You got to try and feed him a little something." Mrs. Peterson spoke. I blinked at her. She pressed a white bundle to my bare breast. With one finger, she guided my nipple. I felt the pull, warm, whining. I looked down. Little pink mouth, slanted eyes, round cheeks working. A dimple there.

"Oh." My arms folded around the bundle, the baby. My baby.

Mother reached to feel of my forehead. "Daniel!"

"There, now," Mattie Peterson said. She gave my wrist a pat. "That's just fine."

My hand was unsteady. I stroked the fuzz on the baby's head. He was solid, alive, heavy. I felt something in me move, a flood of emotion and the milk coming down into my breast. The rhythm of his mouth changed, grew stronger, slower.

"He looks just like his mother," Karen said, and I found her with my eyes, smiled deeply. I reached for her and she took my hand, squeezed hold. "Glad you're back with us," she said.

"Me, too."

Daniel bounded into the room, stopped at the door, his face a cloud of worry that went soft when he saw me sitting up. He came to my bedside, reached to touch the baby, my arm, my hair. He went to one knee. "Good God, Dellie," he said.

Mrs. Peterson patted his shoulder. "She's going to be just fine."

The three women crept from the room, glancing back, wanting to give us privacy but wanting to hear, too. I felt my milk flowing good now. My head was clearing. "Isn't he perfect," I said.

"I almost lost you," Daniel whispered.

I smiled at him. "No, you didn't."

"Doc Rutherford says no more. He says you won't make it through another."

"Nonsense." I'd never felt such downy hair. The baby opened his eyes. They were deep blue. The color of forged steel. Daniel's color?

"It isn't nonsense, Dellie. You should've seen . . ."

I reached out to blot the tear that had dripped onto his face. "Well then, we'll have to take good care of this one, won't we?" Nothing could beat back my happiness.

We called him Gabriel because he was our own angel, and

DeLony for his middle name, after my side of the family. He was strong and hungry all the time, kept my nipples so sore I had to bathe them in mineral spirits and cottonseed oil. And when he wasn't in my arms, he was in his papa's, walking the rooms, seeing the sights from the galleries, baby Gabriel snug inside Daniel's lanky arms. He rarely cried. He didn't need to. Before he could even decide he wanted a thing, he had it. A prince. Lord and master of the house. Tante Lena doted on him, though I had a time convincing her not to swaddle him head to toe. She still believed the old way, that a baby's bones were weak and would break without the swaddling. Sinclair came up to the house every morning to say, "Howdy-do, Mr. Gabe."

He was fair-haired, eyes bluer than any blue. And smart. He could smile at three weeks of age. "Gas," Mother said, but I didn't think so. I believed he was happy to be here and knew already that he was loved.

Mom O'Barr came to help spoil her grandson. She brought gifts for me, a crepe shawl, a lace nightgown with pink butterflies embroidered at the yoke, but she was distant with me, as she had been at Thanksgiving. I could feel her disapproval, her passing of judgment on me. And I couldn't blame her for it, not since she had lost a home and a child and, ultimately, her husband to fire. The true wonder was that she could bear to lay her eyes upon me at all.

"It's this business coming up," Daniel said that night. I knew he meant the trial. He had moved back into my room. We kept Gabriel in there with us, bedside in his cradle. "She doesn't understand everything. That's all it is. She means nothing against you."

"If you were my son, I wouldn't want me for you, either."

"Don't say that." He planted a kiss on my forehead, held me close against him. "Everything will work out, you'll see."

He persisted in looking on the bright side, but of course, some things were not within his control. A crime had been committed. A felony crime. One that could not go unpunished. By then, by the time Gabriel had arrived, I would have pleaded total insanity if it would've kept me at home with my family.

28

The trial began on the tenth of May. There was so much promise, beautiful weather, flowers blooming everywhere. From the beginning, I was nervous but Mr. Park assured me, over and over, that everything was in our favor. He didn't know yet that so much would come out during the trial. Things I had hoped no one would need ever know—especially not Daniel, who had been hurt enough, and had somehow found a way inside himself for forgiveness. Daniel knew—Mr. Park had told both of us—that something of my involvement with Andy would have to be revealed in order for a temporary insanity defense to work. "A minimum of details," Mr. Park had promised during our many discussions.

The state's attorney, Mr. Highsmith, had something else in mind entirely. He intended and set out to prove to the jury, all of whom were men from the community, some I had known all my life, that the burning down of Bassist's store in the early morning hours of June 27th, 1896, had been an act calculated as revenge for my lover, who had recently fled town in debt to Mr. Louis Bassist. Mr. Highsmith found witnesses whose testimony made what had been between Andy and me into something lurid and tawdry. Like the store clerk at W. P. Walker's in Austin, who remembered me and Andy coming in, and who remembered, in the clerk's crude words, "the gentleman giving the young lady over there a friendly pinch on the ass right outside the store."

Mr. Park objected to the clerk's language. The judge overruled the objection.

Several townsmen, including J.T. Craddock, testified that they had seen my horse in Andy's lot on the morning of June 26th, the day after the Populist meeting where Andy Ashland's wagon was burned by persons unknown. Fire for fire, Mr. Highsmith seemed to be saying to the jury. Gretta Betts took the stand and said she had believed from the start there was something more than friendship between me and Mr. Ashland. She called him mister, as if he had been little more to her than a passing acquaintance, and I wondered how she could have changed so in her attitudes. Mr. Park ruined her testimony, calling it speculation, and had it struck from the records, but of course, not from the minds of the jurors.

The most damaging testimony, though, came from Clyde Deatheridge, the appointed animal catcher, who in the wee hours of June 26th had been out all night hunting for coons in the woods along the West Yegua—trespassing, though nobody brought up that fact. He said he heard a strange noise, went to investigate, and found me, the defendant, and the aforementioned Andrew Ashland without our clothes on in the creek, locked in carnal embrace. As there was a bright moon he could see us plainly, and as he heard us speak to each other, he recognized our voices.

Mr. Park, in cross-examination and with contempt, said to Mr. Deatheridge, "Do you consider yourself an expert on human voices, sir?"

Mr. Deatheridge answered, "Yes, I do. And on critter voices, too," which got a laugh from the spectators. The courthouse was full, and I felt every eye on me, like splinters in my back.

Daniel tried to act unaffected. He gave it a brave effort, but I could see the change in his expression when he looked at me. I could see it in the way he carried himself so much less erect. And I could see it in the way he watched me nurse baby Gabriel that night in our hotel room. But all he said was, "Crawford Park will turn things around when he gets his chance." And even though he meant for his words to reassure, I heard the pessimism creep into his voice.

Mr. Park seemed also to have lost heart with the case. He said he thought it best I not take the stand. He didn't explain, but I imagined he feared I would appear too normal, too right in the mind, for the stone-faced jurymen. Instead, he brought in Dr. Berckenhoff to explain to the jury about female hysteria, and then Dr. Rutherford to tell them about Papa's illness and suicide, though they every one knew about that long ago. Tante Lena came to testify about the crying jags I'd been prone to all last spring and summer following Papa's death. Even Mother took the stand to verify the shock to the family. But not one person in the courtroom could forget the picture Mr. Deatheridge had painted of me and Andy naked, tainting the Yegua Creek. My crime no longer was arson but adultery, and for that, the jury found me guilty. They *called* it second-degree arson, but those were just words they used for the record. And they sentenced me to one year at the women's prison encampment on the Goree Ranch south of Huntsville.

Daniel bolted to his feet. "My God! My God! She's a nursing mother!"

The judge hammered his gavel. "There will be order!"

A sheriff's deputy made a move in Daniel's direction. I turned toward where he stood in the first row just behind me. He looked at me, his mouth an open grimace, forehead wrecked together. He sat down as if someone had kicked his knees out from under him.

A year. Twelve months. It doesn't sound like much time until you spend it. The place was nothing like I imagined prison would be. The women were kept in farm shacks, isolated from the main ranch, and conditions were so crowded, canvas tents were pitched here and there, hot in summer, freezing cold in winter, especially that winter when we had an unusual snow. They cut my hair off to just below my ears, dowsed me with Paris Green, and sent me into a shower bath. I was weighed and measured and given a number. My clothes were taken and new ones given me, plain skirts of dull gray cotton. They bound my breasts to stop my milk. That easily, they could tear my child from me, but not the memory of his tender mouth on me, the soft warm heaviness of him in my arms.

They put me in one of the tents with seven other women prisoners. My bunkmate, a prostitute named Iris, had killed her husband with a pickax. She didn't talk about him, except to say it had been self-defense, but I found out from some of the others her husband was what they call a pimp, which meant he set Iris up with other men, then took the money that they paid her. I was shocked to find out such a situation could exist. I learned a lot of things I'd never known before. Prison will do that—teach you things.

I learned to eat fast, and I learned to like rice. I learned to live with vermin in my bed, and with noises at night. And I learned to submit to the prison guard Miller McClay, who for some reason singled me out. For not to submit to him meant force and bruises in places that didn't show. Far easier to lie still and let him have his way. And he soon tired of me, anyway, and went on to a new inmate from Houston, just arrived, a pretty girl with soft eyes named Nola that we never got to know. She died in the infirmary of causes unknown, so the official record stated. But we all knew the girl bled to death after she used a stick to end a pregnancy she didn't want. I was lucky the same thing didn't happen to me, but all Miller McClay left me with was a dose of the clap, which they fixed at the infirmary, too. The doctor didn't even act suspicious about how I came by my affliction. The custom was to just turn their heads at our misery. It was prison. The time wasn't supposed to be easy.

There was a bird that sang at night those first weeks. A mockingbird that kept me awake. He was loud. His voice bounced around the treetops, as clear as a music box, and somehow he added to the unreality of it all. It was like war, being there. I felt the way I thought Papa must have, bivouacked in the wilderness, underneath the pine trees, scared and alone. In winter, when the cold set in like a sickness, wrapping around us inside our tent, I wished for that mockingbird again, and the hot nights when he sang. I had to work hard not to lose myself. I had to hold on to me every second.

Some of the girls couldn't do it. Some like Nola, and like the little Negro girl who drowned herself in the horse pond one evening, just after the supper bell. We were always under guard, but that girl was quick and she was small, and once she'd gone under, no one missed her. I wondered how a person could do that to herself. How she resisted the urge to come up and breathe. I had to keep going. For Gabriel, I had to.

They found out I could sew, and put me to work as a seamstress. We made military uniforms, shirts and trousers and tunics. And we made prison clothes, our own dull frocks and the striped ones the men wore at the Walls up the road inside the city limits of Huntsville. Sundays were our only day of rest. Mrs. Goree, whose husband owned the land where the encampment lay, insisted on worship services, and sent a chaplain to preach to us. Mrs. Goree was reform-minded and felt prison time could be used for rehabilitation. She sent speakers to talk to us, to teach us things like the canning of the vegetables in the prison gardens, and how to make cloth flowers from the bits of fabric that littered the sewing center. One time we had a puppet show, a rendition of *Romeo and Juliet* without the suicides. They didn't want to give us any ideas we didn't get on our own.

Strangely enough, it was in prison I first heard about the National American Women's Suffrage Association—or NAWSA it was called for short—and from a lady named Lucy Baxter. Baxter was her maiden name, but she had kept it after her marriage. She posed as a seamstress to get into the prison, come to teach us the art of appliqué. She even brought her own sewing machine, which a guard—not Miller McClay—carried into the assembly hall. Once we were gathered, though, she never touched the sewing machine. Instead, she spoke fervently to us on the rights of women, or rather the rights women did not have. And not just the right to vote either, but the right to serve on juries, the right to equal education, so that we could be judges if we wanted to be, or lawyers or doctors, so that the doors of opportunity would be open for women just the same as for men. She talked for at least an hour before the warden—another man, of course—got wind of her true purpose, and came to break up the meeting. She left calling cards. I took one and I kept it. And I believe I may yet have it. Her speech that day was one I never forgot.

Sundays, too, were visiting days. Twice Daniel came with news of Gabriel and of home, but it was a long journey and hard to make more often, just for the few minutes allowed us. There wasn't time enough for reflection, for looking inward, for examining our lives. And something had changed, for both of us. Something indescribable that we both tried to ignore. An emptiness. Disappointment hung between us like a thing you could almost touch.

He wanted to give me hope. He tried to make our old life seem real for me again, as he described for me how Gabriel had grown, how he was crawling and loved a mud puddle, how he ran Tante Lena ragged. "I show him your picture," Daniel told me. "We keep it on the dining table, and he points to it. I think he understands." The visits were hard for both of us. For days they left a knot in my throat that I could not swallow.

Surprisingly, Dane came once. All the way from Parker County. I wasn't sure why he came. Out of duty, perhaps. He was so serious, so gruff when he spoke. But for the spectacles he wore, reflecting my own face, it was like I'd gotten a visit from Papa himself.

Nathan was my last visitor. He came on his way to Galveston to ship off to Tampa, Florida, to learn to fight for General Shafter in Cuba. My dear, handsome, foolish brother would have his foreign adventure. He had left Karen at home, about to deliver him a daughter, but he had to go, he said. "They sunk our ship right there in their harbor," as if that made perfect sense, as if it justified his rushing off in a fog of patriotism. After he'd gone, after I knew he was probably over there fighting the Spaniards, I liked to think of him wearing a uniform I had sewn with my own hands. Maybe just that much love right there on his back would keep him safe.

At the end of my sentence—my year—Daniel came to fetch me home. We spent the night on the train and shared a sleeping berth, but our lovemaking was lifeless and polite, more like a requirement than heartfelt. I kept reliving the guard McClay's hands on me. And I think Daniel had in mind me with Andy Ashland in the Yegua Creek. Some things go beyond forgiveness.

Gabriel had grown a mile. I had missed his first tooth, his first Christmas, his first word, "Dada," his first steps on his own little feet. He was chubby, and so blond his hair was white. And I was a stranger. He peeped at me around doorways, and wouldn't come to me at all, not even when Daniel held his hand and led him right up to me. The picture on the dining room table was his mama, not the woman of flesh and blood who had suddenly appeared in his house.

"It's all right," I said. "He'll get used to me." But I often thought later that he never really did. He and Daniel had struck such a bond, one that never diminished through the years, a bond that made me feel left out and jealous. When they'd go off together on their horses, or when they'd sit in the study and talk cattle, I would always think of the year I had missed and wonder how my life might have been different. I could never seem to catch up to them.

The land seemed naturally to run deep in Gabriel's blood, and that probably would not have changed. He always resembled me in his looks, but he was never like me in any other way. He was fond of me, took his licks in school on account of my past and reputation, but we never had much of consequence to say to each other. We were always groping. It was Daniel he turned to for advice, and mostly just favored me with the occasional kiss on the cheek or rub of the head, about like he would do his special horse. In time, he became a better ranchman than either his papa or his grandpa O'Barr had ever been. And he never seemed spoiled by having so much, or by being an only child. I was proud of him. Always. But I never felt I knew him in his soul.

At the end of my first summer back home, Nathan returned from Mr. Roosevelt's "splendid little war" missing his left leg below the knee. It was sorrowful to see him so fragile, so thin, hopping around on his cane. The army promised him a peg he could fit right over his stump, but by the time it arrived, he had developed a poison to the blood. He wasn't counted as a casualty of war. He had made it to these shores and back to his home, but he died before six months had passed, leaving Karen a widow with one daughter and another on the way.

Sister came for the funeral, along with Dane and her brood of children. Five she had in all. One girl and the rest boys. Gabriel didn't know what to make of all these cousins. They clattered through the house and took over the yard outside and the barn, pestered Sinclair into a game of baseball in the horse lot.

Sister had changed so much I hardly knew her. She looked older than her thirty years. Her skin was leathery from working in the sun, and the pregnancies had taken their toll on her figure and on her teeth. When she smiled I saw she had a couple missing. But she was still pretty, with her features all lined up nice and neat, like a cameo. And whenever she spoke of her husband, it was clear as day she still loved him with every drop of blood in her heart.

She said, when I asked about her life, "Well, we ain't got things as good as you do, Dellie, but we make our way."

She never mentioned my prison time, or even acted like she knew about it, but of course she did. It was the first thing people knew about me, and I was always aware of how if affected them. Except with Sister. She hugged me just as hard as she had when I was a little girl, though I was taller now than she was, by several inches. I laughed, and said, "I remember when I never thought I'd be as big as you."

Dane stayed out with Daniel most of the first days they were there, and after the visit had lasted a week, they seemed easy with each other. I think he reminded Daniel of Papa as much as he did me.

One evening around the supper table, Dane told us he'd been considering the idea of staying around McDade. "Unless somebody has a reason why they think I shouldn't." From the way he looked at me, it was clear that I was the somebody he meant.

"He thinks he might want to take over Josh's old place," Daniel said, so I knew he had already given the idea his blessing.

Everyone seemed to be waiting for me to say something, even the children, who couldn't have possibly known the emotion I had attached to that old place. I looked at Sister, but she was wiping the hands of her youngest boy, Jonah. I looked across at young Emmaline, the oldest one, the girl, all red hair and blue eyes, and then at Dane, who looked soberly back at me.

"Wonderful," I said, and all at once, everyone started talking again.

Well, you can never tell how things will turn out. Dane made a success of the farm by growing yams, something no one else in the county had ever thought to do. He didn't have anything against cotton, he said, just thought its time had passed. Dane never sugarcoated anything, for anybody. I came to love him, but he never replaced Nathan in my heart. Too many years had passed between us, though I did find comfort sometimes, as I went by the old place, knowing Dane was there, puttering around, just like Papa.

And finally, he took a wife, one of the girls who worked for Mr. Williams at his pottery factory. Her name was Theresa, and she was as meek as Dane was stern, so I never could envision how they met up with one another. They didn't do much courting. She is a good cook. He is a big eater. For them, it seems enough.

I wish I could say we all of us lived happily ever after. But, of course, real life doesn't work out that way. And I don't believe in such a thing as "happily ever after." There's only happily every now and then. I find the hardest trick is to recognize the now-and-thens, and to bask in them when they come. Happiness is a choice we make, like how to wear our hair, or having coffee with breakfast and tea at night. It's a free country after all, just as Papa said that day so long ago at the Veterans' Reunion. We're all of us free to make our messes or to live uncluttered, to go by the rules or to break them. Most of the time we don't even know which one we're doing. And sometimes we fall flat as a busted bale of hay.

I became a hero to the suffragettes. I had burned down the male establishment and gone to prison for it, and so even when we finally got the vote, because of my record I was never able to exercise the right. That didn't matter to me. I went all over the country speaking out, writing articles for newspapers and magazines, picketing the voting booths, and marching in the streets. I became their martyr, their Sister Dellie. I made Mother sick with despair over my indecency. Everyone else back home just ignored me, something most of them had been doing by then, anyway, for quite a long while.

There was one other thing Papa got right: Andy Ashland *did* turn out to be a Socialist. He came to Bastrop in 1908 campaigning for Eugene Debs, their candidate for the presidency. I read about the rally in the *Advertiser,* where it said Andy was an alderman from the town of Avery up in Red River County, so far north it was practically to Oklahoma. I took Karen with me to hear him speak. I did not let Daniel know where we were going. He thought we were off on more NAWSA business.

In Bastrop, a platform was set up in the street, one block over from the county courthouse where I'd spent so much time. The platform wasn't but about six by six, not much space for pacing and pleading for votes. He still had magic, and a voice that could carry over the wind. His hair was gray, almost completely so, and the lines in his face had deepened. He had a woman with him, a younger woman named Jessica Buchanan who was a member of the Wobblies. And there was something in the way they looked at each other when he introduced her. I wondered about Cova, if she was still in the lunatic asylum in Austin. I wondered about his children. I looked around for Hannah, a girl of fifteen somewhere in the crowd, or for Quintus, a young man of nineteen. I saw no one with features I recognized.

In the end I was unmoved by the whole rally, by what the woman, Jessica Buchanan, had to say about the Industrial Workers of the World. And I was unmoved by Andy, still speaking of his new day to come. Only for one brief moment, when a man passing by threw a stone that hit Andy in the leg, did I feel anything for him at all.

"Let's go," I said to Karen, and she put her hand on my arm.

"Don't you want to say hello?"

I looked up at him again, at his outstretched hands, making those eye-to-eye contacts he was so good at, and I shook my head. "I think I've learned all he can teach me."

We laced our arms around each other's waists and walked away from the crowd that had gathered. When we got down about half a block, she said, "You'll probably run into him again somewhere, out on the stump circuit."

I laughed. Karen had a way of saying things, of taking out the sting. She had become my closest and dearest friend, my cherished sister, with her beautiful daughters whom she shared so generously with me. I gave her a squeeze. "I expect you're right. So I'll cross that bridge when I get there."

"Well, maybe you should've gone ahead and spoken to him here. Gotten it over with and behind you."

"Whatever in the world would I have had to say?"

She smiled at me, then shrugged one shoulder. We walked on together, hand in hand, bound for the wagon yard where Karen had left her buggy.

The End

Author's Note

One hundred years ago, the town of McDade, Bastrop County, Texas, boasted some two thousand in population. There was a town square, several saloons and business establishments, drugstores, clothiers, general merchandise stores, a bank, schools both public and private, a post office, and at least one hotel. The Texas and Houston Central railroad came right through the center of town several times per day. There were two newspapers being published there in 1896: the *McDade Mentor*, edited by Garland Wilson, and the *Plaindealer*, a Populist paper, edited by W. C. M. Betts.

At the time I have set my story, the United States was in the midst of an economic depression caused in part by the Panic of 1893, which closed thousands of banks and sent many railroad companies and industrial firms into receivership. Labor unions had begun to form and strike. Farmers were feeling the pinch.

Most farmers of late-nineteenth-century America lived under the crop lien system, which meant that in exchange for his crop (cotton, in Texas and most of the South), the farmer could "purchase" from his furnishing merchant the goods he and his family would need to get through the coming season. No money changed hands. The merchant made a notation in a ledger, and in the fall, after the harvest was over, the merchant and the farmer would meet and "settle up." Often, because of inflated interest rates charged by the merchant for carrying the farmer's debt, the farmer failed to "pay out." If this happened, the debt unpaid from one year was attached to the next year's debt, and so on, until either a bumper crop came in to get the farmer free or, as happened all too often, the farmer lost his land to his furnishing merchant.

The Populist movement, which evolved out of the Grange and the Farmer's Alliance, gained great popularity in Texas, a mostly agrarian state during the 1890s. Populism called for reform on a grander scale than either of the established political parties espoused. Women were coming out of their parlors to ask for the vote and demand equal rights. The Populists listened and, in effect, political and social unrest was the American order of the day in 1896. McDade, though a small city by today's standards, was not immune to these national goings-on. The Populists were meeting regularly at Fletcher's Hall just outside of town.

Louis Bassist was perhaps the largest merchant in the area. He had four frame buildings on the main town square, which comprised nearly all of one city block. At four o'clock one morning in 1896, the firebell rang, but by the time the citizens of the town had been aroused, the entire mercantile establishment of Louis Bassist was ablaze. For a while it looked like the whole south end of town might go up in flames, but a heavy rain and a change of wind direction saved the buildings north and west. The losses were estimated at between $25,000 and $30,000, a huge sum in those days when an average farmer earned around $300 or less in a year. The origin of the fire was said to be that of an "incendiary." All of this was recorded in the pages of the Bastrop *Advertiser,* the leading newspaper of the area. Also in the article about the fire at Bassist's store was a statement that Mr. Bassist was furnishing about three hundred families in the area, who would be left with no source from which to secure their supplies while making that season's crops. From this article came the idea for my novel. It didn't take a great leap of the imagination, knowing the dire circumstances many farmers were living in at the time, for me to make a connection between the Populists and the fire at Bassist's store.

Many of the townspeople in my story were real people. Whenever I knew a name, I used it. Jack Nash was the town marshal; G. W. Davis, the county sheriff. There was a Dr. Rutherford, physician, and a Brother Barbee who established the first Methodist church in McDade. Professor Mauney ran the McDade Academy and did indeed have his Summer Normal School in 1896. And on May 16th of that year, the McDade "Dudes," with umpire Nash officiating, beat the Smithville "Lions" 13 to 9.